MW01243121

# A Flutter in the Window

## brandon spacey

# a Flutter in the Window

by brandon spacey

spacebrew
publishing

First Edition

Cover art by brandon spacey.

Also by brandon spacey:

## Callie & Walter Novels

*Midnight's Park*
*Resurrecting Mars*
*Into the Darkness*
*Red Bell*

## Standalone Novels

*Shedding Sadness*
*Chasing Comets*

For Linda, my mother, who always
made me feel confident.

Flutter flutter, little necromancer!

And here we see flutter
as if waking from the dead!
My monarch with some necromancy,
like pinballs in her head!

Alight upon the headstone,
she whispers to the bones:
"Wake up now, sleepy angel,
I've come to take you home!"

Within the pages, yet unwrit,
a new song comes to life
And waking ghosts from pleasures past
join in to rile the strife

We take these voices at their word
and place them in a line
The stories told now have new tone,
no longer only mine

We build an effigy to those
we cannot waken strong
And mourn their voices, silenced now
and gone forever long.

So flutter flutter, little necromancer,
your wings are safe with me
No frost shall ground you in its wake,
your soul forever free

# One

Shawn Stedwin had only lived in Texas for six months. Having arrived in early November, she was excited by the cold. And there actually been a snow. Wasn't this proof that Texas had four seasons? Well, she had been disabused of that logic after her first week in her new apartment. With arms wrapped round a large potted plant and coming up the stairs for one of her last few trips, she had met the man who lived across the breezeway from her. His name was Cory Klein, and he was fucking amazing. Cory was the one who had ruined her hopes that Texas was a normal state that would offer snows *every* winter. Well, maybe he hadn't ruined it. Just set her expectations. Like someone else should have done.

    Technically, Cory lived in a different building. But since they took the same stairs up, and their front doors were twelve feet apart, it was hard not to say they lived in the same one. And how she knew he was awesome, was that he had taken the pot from her two steps from the top of the staircase. As she had climbed the remaining stairs brushing potting soil from her white sweater, he had shaken her hand. She was smiling a big, goofy smile, trying to thank him and introduce herself at the same time. The other thing was that they almost had the same birthday. He was born four days before her. That had to mean something. They stood there talking for almost thirty minutes before either of them realized he was still holding the plant, the veins on his forearm bulging and muscles flexing with the tiny adjustments he was making just in conversation. These small details had not escaped Shawn's perception. She was not actively looking for her next boyfriend. But she was never *not looking*, either.

It didn't hurt that Cory was cute. Like, really cute. He had brown shaggy hair that looked like it might be curly if he let it grow much longer. Like Matthew McConaughey. He had bright blue eyes, and he seemed never to stop smiling. No, that didn't hurt at all. Not that she was pinning him as the next boyfriend, but, well, you know. It was good to keep tabs on these things.

Another thing that didn't hurt was that he drove the same car as she did. She drove a root beer-brown Jeep Wrangler with a cute little lift on it. Just enough not to be too stock-looking. Shawn had bought her two-door model back before all the soccer moms saturated the highways with them, making them lose their cool status. And Cory drove a bright orange one, though his was significantly more modified. She had learned this when – during that first conversation – he had pointed at the key ring hanging from her wrist, where she wore it on a stretchy coiled bracelet.

"Jeep driver?" he had simply said.

"Yeah, that's mine right there!" Shawn had replied, pointing at her vehicle, just on the edge of visibility in the parking lot.

Plant potter still in one arm, Cory had guided her by the shoulder to the other end of the landing, and pointed down into the rear parking lot. Her eyes had popped open wide and she had looked up at him, putting a hand on his chest – a bold move that might have been a little telling – and said, "Oh my God! You drive one too? Holy fuck?!"

He had pulled his head back a little, frowning at that. He recovered quickly though and said, "Yeah. You ever heard of Jeep parking?" His motion had given her cause to think she might need consider cleaning up her language a tad. This was not quite the impression she was wanting to make. As it turned out, it had been okay. Things had settled into a regular routine.

The weeks between then and now had been standard fare. Getting to know each other happened more as neighbors than it did as friends. She saw him coming or going a couple of times a week, but nothing much more than that. They certainly didn't make plans to meet for a drink or anything. Cory was busy with whatever it was he did, she was busy acclimating to a new job and a new home in a new state. But it was fine. She didn't need to be getting her hopes up over a boy anyway. What if he had a girlfriend already? What if he was gay? No sense in getting her feelings dashed over false pretense or misinformation.

But now, it was the middle of May, and she was wearing a sweater again. When she took the job with BlueBird, she had been full of wonder and excitement. Some of the excitement she felt for getting a new job had bled over into the move itself, when in reality, relocation was a separate entity altogether. In and of itself, moving to a new state should have taken as much time and consideration as getting the new job. Since one was dependent on the other, she was without options, of course. But the subconscious connection between the two left her a little disillusioned. Texas was not Arkansas.

Shawn turned the key and opened the door to her apartment. Tonight would be a TV dinner night. She would pop something in the microwave and flip on the telly. She was re-watching Dexter. Tonight was season 4, episode 5. She was standing at the counter waiting for her food to heat, thumbing through her OuterCircle updates on her phone. She did not allow herself more than a few minutes a day on social media, because she knew the science behind the little shots of dopamine these apps would deliver. And it was just a time suck. But occasionally, someone did post something worth looking at. A friend went on a ski trip to Colorado. A cousin posted pictures of his baby boy. Those made it worth the minimal time investment she spent on it.

Just as the microwave beeped its message at her, her phone rang in her hand. "Woop!" she said, sliding the answer button across the screen. "Hello?"

"Hello, Miss Marcy," said the man on the other end. She rolled her eyes at this. She had to list her legal name on the job forms, so that's what her boss insisted on calling her. No matter how many times she had hinted around to him that she preferred *Shawn*, he wouldn't budge. He either forgot or just didn't care. Or maybe he didn't like using masculine names on females. Whatever.

"Hi, Sameer. What's up?" she said, turning to pull the plastic plate out of the microwave. She dipped her finger in the enchilada sauce then tasted it.

"I was wondering if you had some time to talk," said Sameer.

"Sure," she said, frowning and shrugging at the same time. She glanced at the clock. It was after seven o'clock. He never called this late. Was her job in danger already? Oh, good God, it better not be. She had moved her entire fucking life down here for this job. It wasn't the move that had made her take it, but she had been courting a couple of other companies, trying to decide which would be the best. And the real kicker was that the other two had work-from-home allowances. As a web developer, she could work anywhere. But Sameer insisted on people working in the office. Intellectual property or some such crap. He was also old-fashioned, and wanted to see his team's faces every day. The pay and benefits had been good enough for her to choose BlueBird over the others, moving to another state notwithstanding. Plus, she really liked Sameer. He was just a really good guy, and seemed like he would be fun to work for. So far, so good.

"Good, good. Can you come downstairs? I can take you to dinner," he said.

Shawn frowned and pulled the phone away from her face to look at it. As if that might reveal some trickery at play here. "What, you're here, at my apartment?"

"Yes, I'm downstairs in the car," he replied. She sighed, looking up at the ceiling and shaking her head. *Could have called four minutes ago and saved me a TV dinner.* These things sucked if you didn't eat them after their initial nuking.

"Wow, Sameer. You could have given me a little notice. I'm not even dressed."

"It's okay, take your time. I was debating whether to call you or to do in person, but I am thinking it is a conversation for the face to face," he said.

"Okay, can you give me five minutes?" Shawn asked. When they disconnected, she pitched the TV dinner in the trash and went to the bedroom to put some pants on. She still had her sweater on, but had a habit of shedding the pants when she got home from work. Most women ditched the bra. The bras she wore didn't make themselves memorable. For her it was the pants.

She slipped some sandals on while she gargled some mouthwash, then shut off lights on the way to the front door. As she was turning her key, she heard the door behind her open up. Shawn turned to see Cory stepping out of his apartment, hair a mess and looking like he had just woken from a hard nap. "Hey, Shawn," he said, squinting in the sunlight. At this time of evening, the sun shot right through the breezeway and they had a perfect view of the horizon.

"Hey!" she said, turning for the stairs. "Off to dinner with the boss. You okay?"

"Yeah. Just popping out to check the weather. Wanna knock when you get back?" he said, putting a thumb over his shoulder.

"Sure!" she said, and started down the stairs in a jog. "Later!"

The inside of Sameer's car was cool, in spite of the cool evening outside. Then she remembered how cold he kept his office. Consistent if nothing else. She pulled the door closed and looked at him before buckling in. "Sameer, is everything okay?" she asked, holding her hands up in front of her. She wanted to get this out of the way.

Sameer didn't smile, but he closed his eyes and nodded. "Yes, it is okay. Nothing is wrong, Miss Marcy."

"Okay, good," she said, turning back to the front and pulling her seat belt across her chest. "So where are we going to eat?"

"Well, I am supposing you are not liking the Indian food," Sameer said, turning to look at her.

Shawn frowned and smiled at the same time. "Actually, I've never tried it."

"I am kidding. We shall go to a Mexican place, if you are okay with this?"

"Yes, I am okay with this," she said, nodding.

"I am supposing you like the Mexicans better than the Indians, since you have never tried our food, no?"

Shawn rolled her eyes and laughed at that. She knew him well enough now to know when he was joking. That same joke would not have worked when she had first met him, though. Still getting to know her boss, *everything* was serious. Since he never smiled or laughed at his own jokes, it had been hard to tell. And navigating the language minefield was sometimes challenging. But after six months of spending five days a week with him, she had adapted well. And he certainly spoke better English than she spoke Hindi. In fact, learning Hindi was his native tongue had been a lesson in and of itself. Before she worked for Sameer, she had thought Indians spoke Indian. Now she knew there were over twenty distinct languages in India. She had almost embarrassed herself with that conversation. Talk about a minefield.

The Queso Grande was almost empty. For a Monday night, this was not abnormal. Sometimes, Shawn had come here on Monday nights just because she knew it would be empty. She wondered how they could afford to open the doors when there were only twenty customers on a given night. They sat at a booth near the kitchen and were almost instantly greeted by their waiter, a short but extremely muscular little guy with tattoos all up his arms. At five-foot-seven, Shawn reckoned she would be looking down on him if she were to stand up. He was cute though, she had to give him that. And the tattoos helped.

She propped her elbows on the table and tickled her thumb tips with her fingernails, both hands performing the habit like a mirrored image. She was furling her mouth in what she thought of as a readiness face, staring at Sameer as he looked at the menu. Did people really still look at menus in Mexican restaurants? They all serve the same things. And all twenty things were made of the same ingredients. It seemed to Shawn that everyone basically came to Mexican restaurants already knowing what she wanted.

The question she had was a moral one: should she order her usual strawberry margarita? Or would it be indiscreet to order alcohol on the boss's dime? Or with the boss sitting there, for that matter? But when the waiter returned and asked if he could take their drink orders, she gave an internal shrug and a *fuck it*, then ordered her usual. If he was going to show up unannounced at her apartment on a Monday night and guilt her into going out to eat, he was buying her a fuckin' cocktail. Perhaps it wasn't fair to say he guilted her into it though. Maybe it was more an obligation based on mystery. He had *mysteried* her into it. She laughed out loud then shook her head as he looked at her questioningly.

"Nothing, sorry," she said, wiggling her fingers in the air like jazz hands, elbows still on the table. But the smile didn't leave her face for several minutes. Sameer ordered a cherry Coke but he had not even raised an eyebrow at her drink order.

When the waiter disappeared, Sameer looked her in the eyes, his hands hiding beneath the table, presumably in his lap. "So. Miss Marcy," he said.

Shawn nodded, raising her eyebrows. She was still performing her little finger habit. She called it her hand ritual. She would scratch the pad of her thumb with her pinky fingernail a few times, then move to the ring finger on the thumb. Then the second, and then the index finger. She did this with both hands simultaneously, always. And she had been doing it for so many years now that her actions looked like she was preparing for a magic trick. People had commented on how gracefully she performed the movements. It was enticing to watch.

"I have been monitoring your progress in the company. You have been here now for half of a year. And I think you are doing well, and fitting in nicely, no?" he said, showing a hand over the table, palm up in question.

"Well, I have to agree, Sameer. I am loving it. Are you about to offer me a raise?"

He frowned at her. "Why would I be doing this?"

She shook her head quickly. "Kidding. Sorry." They sat staring at each other for a moment, then she said, "It's just you said in the car that nothing was wrong." She shrugged a quick, tiny gesture. "I took that to mean I wasn't getting fired. So maybe it's a raise."

"No, it is not a raise," he said. He took a sip of his ice water. "Do you need a raise, Miss Marcy?"

"No. Seriously, it was a joke. Sorry. Go on," she said.

He nodded slowly. "Well, I have become to trust you, Miss Marcy."

She now took her turn at a slow nod, looking out the sides of her eyes. "Oooookaaaaay. I would hope you had trusted me from the beginning. But okay."

"Trust is something I take very seriously. And it takes time to establish," said Sameer.

"Yes. I agree with that, Sameer." She decided to drop the front for a while. She knew well that a harmless joke told at the wrong time could mean something completely different than intended, and she didn't want to come across as being crass when he was trying to open up to her. "Look. Hey, I want to tell you something," she said, grabbing his wrist on the table. "Sorry. Can I tell you something real quick?"

She waited for him to nod. She pulled her hair back and tucked it behind her ears with both hands, once again in perfect mirror fashion. Symmetry was a subconscious manifestation in her movements. "I like you, Sameer. One of the reasons I took this job was because I liked you. I thought you would be easy and fun to work with. That's why I was okay with moving my whole life down here to Texas. I just think you should know that. So please, if you're comfortable, you have permission to speak freely with me." Then she spread her hands, palms facing toward him and added, "No judgment here."

After a long pause in which Sameer blinked many times and tightened his lips, he finally picked up his napkin and dabbed at his eyes. "Thank you, Miss Marcy. This is meaning a lot to me."

"Sure," she said, squeezing his wrist again.

"Well, I have tested you and I have come to believe that I can be trusting you," Sameer said.

Shawn laughed at this. "Tested me? What? What are you talking about?" she said. She was smiling and frowning at the same time.

"I cannot go into it. It might ruin a secret, no?"

Shawn rolled her eyes, not in an unfriendly way. "Sameer, I don't know where you're going with this, but you're killing me with the suspense."

"Okay. I see. I have been watching you and I have come to believe I can be trusting you, Miss Marcy."

"Yesssss," she said, stretching the word out and nodding slowly. "I think we established that already. What are you trusting me with?"

Suddenly, Sameer sat up straight returning his hands to his lap as the waiter appeared with the drinks. "Thank you," he said, nodding to the short man. They placed their food orders and turned in their menus. Shawn watched as he walked away, staring with perhaps a little too much interest. When she looked back at Sameer, he was looking at her with a different kind of interest. His was more of a *what the fuck are you looking at* kind of interest. Shawn licked sugar off the rim of the glass then took a sip of the 'rita.

"Okay," she said, "where were we?"

Sameer looked at her for a moment, chin elevated. Assessing. Judging? Nah. He wasn't like that. "My reason for asking you to dinner was to ask if you were interested in working on a project with me." He took a sip of his cola. "It is of most top secret importance, Miss Marcy."

She giggled at this. "Okay. Well, consider my interest piqued, Sameer. So do I have to NDA up before you can tell me what it is, or does your trust extend that far?"

"I'm sorry, Miss Marcy. I am not understan-"

"Do I need to sign privacy agreements before you tell me? Or can you tell me tonight?" She sipped from her margarita again. The sugar had a slightly bitter taste to it that called her tongue back for more. Probably much like Sameer's cherry Coke was doing to his own tongue. She took a thoughtful sip of the drink.

"No, I can tell you. That is why I am bringing you here tonight, so to tell you of my intention with the new project."

Shawn was amused at the formality of a dinner, though she understood that Sameer had been struggling internally with whether or not to talk to her about it at all. Dinner would certainly make things easier. Especially if they got a drink or two. Well, he had dropped the ball on that account. But he was loosening her up just fine. She was ready to hear whatever it was he was selling. But somehow, she thought that wasn't his concern. His concern was his own ability to vocalize whatever this big mysterious project was all about. It must be pretty serious to warrant a private dinner on a Monday night.

The company she had hired on with – Sameer's company, to be precise – was called BlueBird Innovation. It was a small company in the most literal definition of the word. There were only two other employees besides the two at the table here tonight. Shawn could see the potential for growth, as he was offering good services at good prices. But when it came down to defining exactly what the company did, she might have had a stutter. Shawn knew, of course, what her job was. She was a coder. But what did *the company* do? Well, it sold those types of services. Right? Or was that putting the cart before the horse? Was she assuming too many things? *This is a new company. I am a new employee. Everything I know about the company is all there is to know. Yeah, and Socrates is a lion.*

She had to admit that she had not done much research beyond what her requirements would be, because it seemed so innocuous. There was nothing to worry about here. She would be getting paid a handsome sum of money to code some web programs. Sameer had offered her a great salary, plus phone allowance, medical benefits, and commission. Lots of things she had never had before in her current career field. It was all very attractive. Why the hell should she care what the rest of the company did? They only had a few clients, but she also understood that to be a product of being a new company. And with that in mind, she felt like she was entering on the ground floor. She would get to help steer the company as it grew, being one of the first few employees.

Now, she waited for him to continue. Whatever this new project was, it was obviously important enough for him to have made the trip to her apartment. And the fact that he had not spoken of it at work earlier in the day only spoke to the point about it being heavy on his mind, when the opposite should have seemed true. If he had been struggling internally with this conversation all day – perhaps all weekend – then it made sense that he had just started driving. Wondering what to say, how to say it, would it be okay on the phone? Should it be in person? Over dinner? The more Shawn considered these things, the more she came to realize that it must actually be something huge. *Holy fuck. Is he going to ask me to sleep with him?* God, she hoped not. That would be a quick end to a great job.

"I would like you to work on a project with me. But you must understand that we cannot discuss this with anyone."

Shawn leaned her head forward to meet her hands. She ran her hair back behind her ears and massaged the back of her head with her fingertips. Her patience was still okay. But her anxiety was starting to elevate slightly. What the hell was this about? She looked up at him through the tops of her eyes. "Sameer. Spit it out, dude."

"Okay, Miss Marcy. I am looking for someone to help me-" he said, and was interrupted again. This time, by the waiter delivering their food.

*Oh my God! He is going to kill me with this suspense!*

They ate mostly in silence. She had pointed her fork at his plate at one point, asking with a mouthful of rice if his carne asada was good. But aside from that and a few grunts of approval, they ate in silence. Halfway through the meal, the waiter had come to check on them. He asked if Shawn wanted another margarita. She had glanced at the glass and realized that it was almost empty. Sucking it down through the thin straw, she handed him the glass and closed her eyes, lifting her eyebrows high. "In fact, I think I *would* like another one, my good man." One thing she had learned in life was that if the first one was hard to order, then not to worry, as the second one was always easier.

She had looked at Sameer after this and said, "I'll pay for my alcohol if it's a thing."

He shook his head and said, "No, it is not being a thing," and Shawn had laughed out loud.

When she finished her plate, she pushed it aside then wiped her mouth with the napkin and dropped it on the plate from a foot above the table. "Good word, I am stuffed, Sameer," she said. "I always eat too much at Mexican restaurants."

Sameer nodded, still poking small bites with the long tines of the once-shiny fork. Shawn pulled her drink closer and took a long sip, then licked more sugar off the rim. She was feeling relaxed and calm now that the drink was entering her bloodstream. Now all she had to do was wait patiently for him to finish his own meal so he could get to the damn point about what this was all for.

That time finally came, and he stacked his plate on top of hers, then took a long drink from his soda. "That was very good, yes, Miss Marcy?"

"Yes, it was, Sameer. Thank you for bringing me here tonight.

"I am thinking I might be Mexican rather than Indian. I am liking their rice better than my own."

Shawn giggled, sipping from her straw. "So are you going to keep me on the hook all night? Or are you going to tell me why you brought me here?" Her smile was genuine, though perhaps fluffed a little by the alcohol. She was happy to be here, and happy to be in the presence of her boss. The word boss, mixed with dinner, equaled free.

Sameer wiped his area with the napkin, then carefully set the napkin on the stack of plates. It looked as though he were stalling. But then he finally looked up at her and tilted his head. "I am wanting to bring someone back from the dead."

Shawn's smile slowly faded from her face. The longer she stared, and the longer his face remained stoic, unchanging, the more the smile felt cold in its memory. And after a long enough time had passed that she even lost the ability to pull liquor through the straw – all her concentration was focused on deciphering what he had just said – she finally cleared her throat and sat up straight, a perfect line of goose flesh running up her spine. She swallowed, then put her hands in her lap, afraid her hands might tremble. "I'm sorry. Did I hear you correctly?"

Sameer simply nodded. And the graven look in his eyes told her all she needed to know about his level of seriousness.

Shawn found she didn't have much to say on the way back to her apartment. Sameer had asked her what she thought, what she was thinking and if she had any questions. Several times. She could tell he was getting antsy about having spilled his secret to her. Early on, she had assured him that no matter what she thought, she would keep confidence about what he had said. But she was going to need some time to process this.

She watched out the window, staring at the scenery, the passing streetlights illuminating her face in slow rhythm. There were so many things on her mind that she couldn't even get them all lined up enough to figure out which one she should work on first. Having never heard of anything so stark mad in her life, she wasn't sure she would ever short it out. Shawn had her own thoughts about death and spirituality. And without even breaking the surface of the spirituality argument, she was pretty set in her belief that death itself was final. And she wasn't sure she was ready to tinker with that, playing Dr. Frankenstein and trying to undo it. Just thinking about the concept of it gave her the creeps. She had not yet dug in with Sameer and asked him any details. Like who, and when and – well, even *why*. Would he be visiting the local mortuary for fresh bodies or would their be graveyard exhumations? She got chills every time she thought about it. The whole thing gave her the creeps.

So she was not her typical self on the way home – responsive and inquisitive, playful and fun-loving. She was morose and nauseated, and just really didn't want to talk to Sameer at all right then. She was thankful when he pulled to a stop adjacent to the stairwell that led up to her apartment. She thanked him for dinner and said she would see him tomorrow, then closed the door. Shawn could tell he was a little worried about her. The look on his face said he was aware that maybe she had not been the right one to ask about this project after all.

Shawn trotted up the stairs, straight-backed and prickling all over. Her nerves were on edge and she felt like she was being followed by a ghost. Having that second margarita had either been a terrible idea, or the best idea of the night. If it were the latter, then she would need another drink as soon as she stepped through her door. She needed something to wash this down with.

As she reached the top of the stairs, she turned right instead of left, then pulled her hair back behind her ears as she knocked on Cory's door. After a long moment, he pulled it open and smiled at her. "Hey, what's up?"

"Hey. Sorry so late. You told me to knock?"

"Oh. Yeah. Wanna come in?" he asked.

Shawn twisted her mouth up and made a sour face, holding her shoulders up. She realized she was cringing at his offer and quickly shook her head. "Sorry," she said, reaching in and putting her palm against his chest. "I'm not trying to be cringey about coming in. I just got spooked by my boss."

"Ah," Cory said, pulling the door open and leaning against the jamb. He crossed his arms. "Wanna talk about it? I mean, shit, I guess we can stand out on the deck if you're not comfortable coming in."

"No, that's not it. I was just thinking that I don't want to do anything until I pour myself a big glass of vodka cranberry. Would you like to come to my place?" she asked, sweeping both hands dramatically toward her door. She shivered again. Those images of digging up a hundred-year-old coffin and cracking it open kept haunting her thoughts.

"Are you okay?" he said, half smiling and half concerned.

"Yeah. I really need a drink. I keep thinking about what he said, and it's tripping me the fuck out."

Cory nodded and pulled the door closed behind him, holding out his own hand. *Lead the way.* He followed her across the breezeway in his socked feet and waited behind her while she unlocked the door. As the door swung open, Shawn suddenly realized she had not planned for a visitor, and quickly glanced around the visible area of the den making sure there was nothing out that shouldn't be. Then she dashed to the liquor cabinet and grabbed a couple of plastic long-stemmed cups that looked like square wine glasses.

She filled them quickly, not taking the time to worry about the sloshing that was going on. And as she handed Cory his cup, she already had her mouth on her own. Cory stood, mouth agape, just watching her imbibe. "Holy shit, bro," he said as she gulped down the whole glass.

"Sorry," she said, wiping her mouth. "I really needed that."

"I can see that. You don't like a little cranberry in your vodka cranberry though?"

"Oh, I do. I just needed to wedge one in real quick. You wouldn't believe the effed up stuff I just heard."

Cory sipped his vodka as she turned around and refilled her own cup again. She went to the kitchen and grabbed the cranberry juice from the fridge. She poured a dash in her glass, then held it out for him. He stepped forward and raised his glass, allowing her to pour it in. Then he leaned on the bar with his elbows and said, "So you wanna tell me what's got you so spooked? You look like you've seen a ghost!"

Shawn blew a mouthful of vodka out in a spray. She was able to block most of it with her hand, but couldn't stop the rest from running out onto the floor as she doubled over laughing from her belly, eyes closed and fully engaged. Cory just watched. He had a smile on his face when she looked up again, apologizing and shaking her head.

"God, you don't know how apt that is. Shit. I made a mess. I'm sorry."

"Really, it's fine. But you are on a whole nother level tonight."

"I know," she said, raising her hands in front of her shoulders. "I know. I'm being retarded." She grabbed a towel from the fridge handle and ran it under the tap, then dropped to her knees to wipe the floor.

"Might want to take care of that," Cory said, pointing at her sweater.

Shawn looked down and saw the cranberry-colored droplets on her white sweater. "Oh, fuck!" she said, then whipped her sweater off without thinking. She was running to her room as she did it, though, so if Cory saw anything it wasn't much, and it wasn't for long. She still had a bra on, after all.

When she reappeared, she had on a Dead Can Dance t-shirt and was wringing her hands. "Sorry. I'm completely beside myself tonight. I hope I haven't freaked you out."

"Nah, you're good. But now you've got me seriously curious about what's going on. What the hell did your boss say to you?"

Shawn grabbed her glass and took a good-sized swig while she held up a slender finger telling Cory to wait. Then she licked her lips and rounded the counter, holding out her hand. He frowned, but took her hand. She led him over to the couch and sat down. He took the couch at an angle to her own, so they sat facing each other. Shawn let go of his hand and set her glass on the coffee table, then pulled her hair back behind her ears again. She took a deep breath, then relaxed, putting her hands on her knees.

"Cory, you're the only friend I have in town so far. I hope you know that as I tell you what I'm about to tell you. I'm so happy you're here because I really need to talk to someone. And I really don't want to be alone. Because I'm so freaked out."

"Okay," he said, nodding slowly. He raised his glass to his lips. "I'm all ears, Shawn."

She took a deep breath then rolled her head around on her neck. "Now here's the shitty part: I can't tell you what he told me."

Cory scoffed. His mouth was parted with a wide smile. But it slowly slid off his face. "You're serious. Like proprietary company information or some shit?" he asked.

Shawn nodded, pursing her lips. "Yeah. Something like that. I promised him I wouldn't talk about it to anyone. But I don't want to be alone right now."

She could see the disappointment in his eyes and felt bad for him. She was torn, too, between her integrity and reality, where people really did speak about things they weren't supposed to with those in whom they knew they could trust.

"I'm so sorry. I'm not trying to be a twat about this. I just don't like to break my word."

"No, I totally get that," said Cory, taking another sip.

"My daddy always told me growing up that if people lost faith in my word, I wouldn't have anything else." She took her own sip, looking over the top of the cup at him.

"That's perfectly respectable. So what *do* you want to talk about?"

"I don't know. I was hoping we could watch a movie or something. I mean, I know it's late, but – God! I'm just so freaked out."

"I usually don't crash until midnight or later anyway," Cory said amiably.

"You have anything good over there? I could come crash your couch with you. Now that I've got a drink in me," Shawn said.

"Yeah, sure. I have some stuff. We can always see what's on Netflix, too."

Shawn reached across the cornered couches and put her hand on his knee. "Thank you for being here for me, Cory. I know we don't really know each other very well. But this is exactly what I need tonight."

"Sure thing, Shawn. I'm happy to help. And I'm also happy we're getting to know each other a little better," he said. He took a thoughtful sip of his drink, looking her in the eyes. She was watching him with eyes that looked comforted by his presence. "Anything in particular you want to watch?"

She took a deep breath, and then blew it out with puffed cheeks. "Nah. Just no horror."

Shawn had let Cory go home and get the place ready – whatever that entailed in his case – while she showered and changed into her pajamas, brushed her teeth. She put on a boater hat and grabbed her drink and the vodka bottle, wrapping them in her arms with her phone and keys. She was excited to be doing movie night with her new friend. Excited to get her mind off of the subject of her conversation with her boss.

When she stepped out into the night air to shut and lock her door, trying not to drop anything, she realized she was putting herself in a vulnerable position with Cory, whom she didn't really know that well, come to think of it. She trusted him enough to know he wasn't a serial killer, but what did that really mean? People who knew actual serial killers never even knew they were serial killers. So perhaps that was a dumb horse to hitch her cart to. He seemed like a nice guy though, and you had to trust *someone*. Right? She stood between the apartments under the moonlight, her arms wrapped round the vodka bottle and her plastic cup, thumbs on her phone. She sent a quick text to her mom letting her know where she was going – just in case anything stupid did happen. At least they would know where to look for the body.

She took the few steps closing the final distance to Cory's door, and knocked. While she waited for him to answer, she went ahead and texted her boss, telling him that she needed to take tomorrow off work, and hoped it wouldn't be a problem. She would be back in on Wednesday. She thanked him for dinner again, for good measure. And as she heard Cory's hand on the knob on the other side of the door, she got a response. *Absolutely understandable.* Well. That was nice. He must have been sitting there on his phone.

"Hey, lady," Cory said, pulling the door open wide. Shawn noticed he had changed into his own version of pajamas. Some soft cotton pants and a t-shirt. "Nice hat."

"Ooh, thank you. I love my hats. I'm a hat girl."

"Love a good hat on a pretty girl," said Cory. Shawn frowned and pursed her lips, thinking about what he had just said. He was behind her, so he couldn't see the face she was making as she concentrated on what it might mean. She knew gay guys had no trouble complimenting a woman, but so did straight ones. God. Maybe she should just ask him.

Shawn looked around the place, that weird uncanny valley-type thing going on in her head, seeing a perfect mirror image of her own place right here in front of her. She set the vodka bottle on the bar and unloaded her arms of all her stuff before turning and pulling up on her pajama pants and asking him what was on the playbill for tonight.

"Okay," said Cory, clapping his hands together. "I have Kodi. Have you heard of Kodi?"

"Nooooo!" Shawn said, drawing out the O with mysterious excitement. "Is that the new Julia Garner thriller?"

Cory pulled his head back and frowned at her. "Huh? Who the hell is that?"

"You don't know who Julia Garner is?"

He raised his chin in the air and nodded. "Oh, yeah, okay, now that you said her name twice, I do."

Shawn made a straight face and slapped his shoulder. "Stop it. What is Kodi?"

"It's a media center interface." He stepped around the couch and picked up the remote and clicked a button. The screensaver departed and the television now showed a list of titles. He started clicking down the list and at each title, a synopsis and cover picture would pop up on the other side of the screen.

"Oh, neat!" she said, coming around the couch behind him, her vodka glass in both hands. This was intriguing. Shawn loved a good new gadget, and she had never heard of this one. She was already fascinated.

"So I have all my movies ripped. They're all stored on a RAID-five storage device in my closet. Kodi just installs on the TV and it creates a database of all my titles. Then you select one, and it streams the movie from my server," Cory said. He was looking at her with a sober expression that said he was waiting to see if she understood what he was saying.

Shawn looked away from the screen, meeting his eyes, and nodded. "Okay. Got it. How many do you have?"

He smiled widely. "About five hundred. I used to have thousands. But then I finally dumped all the DVD rips and started replacing all the good ones with Blu-Ray. So I have fewer now, but they're all in high-def."

"Bad ass," Shawn said. She rounded the edge of the couch and did that thing only women have the ability to do, which is to fold their legs behind them and drop gracefully into a sitting position. Her vodka didn't even wave in her glass. She was so dialed into what he was showing her that she had temporarily forgotten the Frankenstein conversation had even happened. Mission accomplished.

"So I've picked out a few that I think will lighten the mood and make you feel good for tonight," Cory said.

She looked up at him, brown eyes meeting blue, with true wonder behind them. He had parsed through over five hundred films and picked out a few that he thought she might enjoy for the night. To get her mind off the shit that had threatened to ruin the evening for her. That was pretty special. If nothing else ever happened, she thought maybe Cory could be counted on to end up being a good friend. Her heart warmed.

She deliberately didn't say 'Awww, how sweet!' and cover her heart. She was playing poker now. "Okay. Which ones did you pick, my guy?"

He nodded and looked back at the screen. "Well, you said no horror. So I picked some lighter-weight ones. So first, we've got *Big Fish*. Make sure you tell me if you've ever seen any of these," he said, holding up a hand. He paged down to that title and selected it to give her the benefit of the synopsis.

Shawn reached up and put her hand on his forearm as he stood beside where she sat on the couch. Her lips were moving as she read the text on the screen. When she finished, she nodded and patted his arm, telling him he could go on. "Okay. Next?"

"Okay. The next one is one of my all-time favorites. Going in alphabetical order, of course. *Fight Club*."

"Seen it," she said, squeezing his forearm.

"Okay. Okay, that's okay. I have a contingency plan in place!" Cory said, and began clicking down the titles until he came to rest on one she had not heard of. The text read *Passengers* and the picture showed Jennifer Lawrence and Chris Pratt standing in front of a window on a space ship of some sort. This looked interesting. She patted his arm to let him know she was reading the synopsis.

*A malfunction in a sleeping pod on a spacecraft traveling to a distant colony planet wakes one passenger 90 years early.*

She twisted her head toward him but kept looking at the screen. "Sleeping pod?" she said.

"Yeah. They're in like a stasis while they make this 120-year journey. It's pretty good. Maybe a little creepy though. Maybe not that one. Sorry," he said.

Shawn closed her eyes and took a sip of her vodka. She tried to shake off the chills before they came. Coincidence. Weird, but normal.

"Okay. How about this one," Cory said, turning toward her with the remote. "Third choice. A classic comedy. If you don't laugh out loud at this one at least fifty times, then you have *no* sense of humor."

"Okay, that sounds great," Shawn said, clapping her hands together. She leaned back and forth, pulling her ankles in closer. "What you got?"

Cory paged down until he got into the Ys, then started single-clicking until he stopped on one whose cover picture she actually recognized. It was a cartoon-style image of Gene Wilder, mouth open in yelling, opposite a blue-faced man tipping a top hat. It was *Young Frankenstein*. Her blood went cold. *You've got to be fucking kidding me.*

Shawn had not experienced much death in her life. Her mother called her a 'young twenty-nine'. Whatever that meant. Just because she hadn't lost a lot of loved ones didn't mean she didn't have life experiences. She was not in the large percentage of the population who thought a novel could be written about her life experiences. Nothing so crazy as that. But she had experienced things a near-thirty-year-old would have seen throughout the course of normal day-to-day living. The closest she had been to experiencing death had been when her Aunt Lily had died. The funeral might have been a normal funeral experience for a normal seven-year-old girl. But it wasn't. And it was all because the funeral had been the second time she had seen her aunt dead.

Having two working parents growing up, Shawn, who at this time in her life was still going by Marcy, had to stay with her aunt after school until her mom or dad could pick her up. Aunt Lily had lived only a few blocks away from the school, so little Marcy would just walk there after school and wait for mom to come get her. She would work on homework at the kitchen table, a little metal fan blowing on her with its nice comforting mechanical hum, and her aunt would give her snacks. Grapes and soda and chips. Those days existed in nothing but pleasant memories for Shawn. It was almost idyllic – from the smell of the house to the love and hugs her aunt and uncle would both give her. She would watch cartoons when she finished with her homework, lying on the rough velvety couch with her feet up in the air behind her. They had no air conditioner in the house, and thus always had the front door open. There was a storm door with a screen on it that would remain closed keeping the bugs out, but every memory of that house in Shawn's head was filled with that bright sunlight coming in the door and the way it stretched across the carpet. Being in the house for almost the same exact hours every day gave her the same pattern of sunlight.

Her uncle worked at the local grocery store, so she usually didn't see him, except for the days when her mom would get there a little later, giving him a chance to get home first. On the last day she ever stayed with her aunt, Marcy walked the two blocks just like every other school day, talking to herself, hands animated in front of her. She would often have these conversations with her imaginary friend, Paige. But sometimes she just talked to herself, solving all the secrets of the universe in a second-grader's mind. When she pulled open the screen door on this day, everything was different.

On a normal day, her Aunt Lily would welcome her and say hello from her recliner in front of the television where she was watching Family Feud. But on this day, she was sprawled across the couch in an awkward, almost inhuman looking position, convulsing and snapping her head back and forth on her neck. Fascinated at first by the movement, Marcy stood staring, not knowing what to think – what to say. Was it a joke? Was Aunt Lily playing a practical joke on her? Just being fun and silly like she was sometimes wont to do? But the longer Marcy stared, the more details she took in, and the more the fun-loving spirit evaporated from the scene. The sunshine coming in from behind her caught her aunt across half of her body, and Marcy finally noticed she had one arm caught down behind the cushions and there were tear marks in her flesh and she was bleeding profusely. Marcy knew the couch folded out into a bed, and it looked like maybe Aunt Lily was trying to reach in there and pull something out. Marcy also knew that those metal bars were full of twisted silver wires that would snag and cut your skin if you were too rough in your playing on it.

After an indeterminable amount of time had passed, Marcy's curiosity finally turned to horror. She realized this was not a joke – nothing funny at all about this scene – and her aunt was not acting normal. The convulsing was growing less intense, but still very uncomfortable. The scariest part of it was that her aunt was making no sound at all. The flapping of her free hand and the jerking of her legs, the snapping of her head – it was all silent but for the sounds her body made against the creaking of the steel structure hidden beneath the couch cushions. In retrospect, as an adult, Shawn would say it was the eeriest experience of her entire life.

"Aunt Lily?" she finally said, slowly, quietly, with the voice of a mouse. As she spoke the two words, little Marcy felt chills go up her spine, all down her arms. The top of her head suddenly felt like it was burning – hot. Uncomfortable. But she didn't want to step closer. Something was very wrong, and she couldn't understand what it was. What it was that was causing her aunt to move like that. And why didn't she speak? If something *was* wrong, why wasn't she calling for help or anything? She wasn't even crying. Her face looked blank, mouth agape, eyes staring at the ceiling.

Without warning, her aunt's head snapped to the side and continued its fish-flopping, banging her cheek against the low arm of the couch and staring straight at Marcy. Marcy began to cry, putting her trembling hands up to her face and feeling herself fill, top to bottom, in complete terror. And then Aunt Lily started gasping. Wheezing. Like a rough cough coming in and going out, mouth clapping closed, wrenching open again, repeating.

Marcy was in a full cry by now, panicking and asking her aunt what was wrong. "Aunt Lily, I'm sorry! What's wrong? Aunt Lily, what's wrong with you? How come you're doing this? I'm sorry! How come…"

And after another minute that seemed to last several hours in her young mind, her aunt's eyes focused in on her and widened. She looked like she was afraid all of a sudden. Very afraid of something. Maybe something behind where Marcy stood. Like someone coming in the door. Marcy turned and looked behind her, but seeing the screen door full of sunlight didn't assuage the terror she suddenly felt. She had to move somewhere to put her back against something solid. She moved over in front of the TV, bawling, now in a state of complete shock. Her sobs wracked through her tiny chest like waves of electricity. Her panic was completely immersive.

And then Aunt Lily's teeth closed together and her lips started making this weird movement – a gesture that looked like she had a bad taste on her tongue, and Marcy noticed her face was turning purple. She now had both hands over her own crying face, peeking between her fingers as she wailed, calling her aunt's name over and over.

And then it stopped. All movement stopped. The flapping arm, the snapping head, the left arm pistoning up and down behind the cushion, getting blood all over the place... Aunt Lily's knees relaxed and her legs fell flat onto the cushions. Her right hand slapped down on to the carpet beside the couch. Her face relaxed and her mouth opened slowly. And then she was completely still.

Marcy screamed and ran into the first room off the hallway, which her uncle used as an office and study, and slammed the door. She crawled into the space under the desk where Uncle Lloyd would put his feet while he was typing and pulled the chair in to hide herself. And that's where she stayed for the next two hours, on the edge of complete hysteria, terrified beyond her ability to function normally. Not even her body functioned normally. Later, when all was said and done, she came away with wet pants, though Marcy had no memory of having wet them. *Catatonic*, they had called her later. It wasn't until years later that she knew what this meant.

The funeral, held four days later, was the second time she saw her aunt dead. And in Marcy's mind, at any moment, the woman in the casket at the front of the sanctuary would sit up and look at her – or start convulsing again, snapping her head back and forth against the fine white silk. She clung tightly to daddy's arm, spending the entire ceremony in a state of passive horror – knowing she was trapped, she had to be there – and forcing herself to be a good girl and not scream and run out. As an adult, Shawn would look back on this sixty-minute period as one of the most stressful events in her life. Her stomach in knots, her hands trembling and her mind racing a million miles per hour – but just watching how everyone else in the church was behaving, knowing if they could get through it, she could. Why they weren't scared themselves was beyond her.

Marcy never went to another funeral. And when she grew up and made the decision to start referring to herself by her middle name, Shawn politely excused herself from every funeral invitation she ever received. She was so traumatized by her aunt's death that she couldn't even think back on it without her anxiety going through the roof. This would be accompanied by a wet stomach and trembling hands, alarmingly fast heart rate and thoughts of escape.

She had made great progress in her childhood by going to counseling for what seemed like many months. But that was all on paper. Progress in her handling stress and death meant being able to say the right things to a therapist. It was theory. The practice of actually facing death never really changed for her. At least she didn't think it had. Because up to now, she had just simply avoided ever seeing it again – partly by luck, but also by her own strict avoidance policy when she knew it was waiting somewhere. Like a funeral home.

Again, in her twenties, she had sought counseling, and was actually told by more than one therapist that she may *never* fully recover from the trauma she suffered as a little girl watching her aunt leave this life right in front of her eyes. Had she had the proper adult support at the time of the incident, she might have fared better. But disremembering something like that was usually handled automatically by a brain that simply can't take what it's seeing, and must shut itself down. Well hers had not done that, for whatever reason, so she was left with full, sickeningly detailed memories of the event. She remembered every sound, every movement – every little scrape on her aunt's arm and the look on her old face as she passed.

What Sameer could not have known when he asked her to join his *raise-the-dead* project, was that Marcella Shawn Stedwin was the absolute perfect antithesis to the helper he was looking for. Almost no one knew this about her, though. Death was simply not something she brought up very often.

She had been lucky – or blessed, depending on how one looked at it – in her life to have never had to face it again, at least not yet. Somewhere in the recesses of her subconscious mind, she surely knew she would face it again someday. But why try and prepare for such a thing?

But what she did not know was that a psychologist, with her best interest at heart, might tell her that she *was* the perfect candidate for the project. That facing death – in whatever capacity Sameer Singh was offering it – would be worlds more beneficial to her than any fifty-minute therapy session could ever be. Facing it in a controlled environment could help her see what it really was. Perhaps. Only, were she to have this conversation, and were they to use the word 'controlled' she would have something to say on the matter of whether it was actually controlled, and the extent to which they exercised said control. She had no idea what they would be dealing with in the structure of the project.

As for now, she had called off work the next day, hoping and planning to spend the day relaxing and pointedly *not* thinking about death – but somehow trying to think about his proposition in a mature and logical fashion. How she would achieve this stunt, doing splits over the awkward dichotomy she was trying to dance around, was beyond her. But she did feel she owed it to the man to give him a fair hearing on the matter. And this was, of course, without any further information about the project. Maybe she should hear him out first and then try to make an informed decision. But what she did know was that if death turned her off in every sense of the word, and it did, then it might not matter what her level of engagement would be to it. Simply put, if she couldn't come to terms with that somehow in and of itself, then it probably wasn't worth listening to his spiel. Shawn certainly didn't want to waste anyone's time – hers included.

"You look like you've seen a ghost all over again. What's wrong, Shawn?" said Cory.

She sighed and looked down at her hands, with which she was performing her ritual in her lap. "I guess we need to talk."

"Okay," Cory said. Then he raised the remote and turned off the television. "Like I said, I'm all ears." After a brief pause, he added, "Well, part mouth, if you're inclined to my advice on something."

She smiled wanly at him. "Have you experienced death at all in your life?" Shawn asked him, looking up to make eye contact.

She saw him consider for a moment, breathing in deep, like he was about to take on a heavy weight. "Yeah. In fact, I have. My little sister died when I was ten. She was six. We were swimming, and…" he stopped suddenly. Then he frowned. "I'm sorry. Did you want to hear what happened? Or were you just asking if I'd been around it?" he said, holding out a calming hand.

"You can tell me. If it doesn't hurt too bad."

"Oh, no. I still love her and miss her. Every day. But the hurt has long since passed." He leaned back on the couch and grabbed one of the square decorative cushions, pulling it onto his lap. "Well, anyway, we were swimming and I watched her drown."

"Oh my God," Shawn said, putting her hand over her mouth. "How terrible. I'm so sorry, Cory."

He shrugged. Forced a smile. "Yeah. It was pretty terrible. The worst part was that I had to stand there and watch it happening. I was screaming at the top of my lungs, trying to get my mom's attention, but she was inside, and she couldn't hear me. I couldn't get in the pool because I had a cast on my leg. I wasn't supposed to get it wet. And at ten years old, I hadn't yet developed the discernment that would have allowed me to say 'fuck the cast, I'm saving my sister'."

"Oh my God," Shawn said again. She was shaking her head. She had tears in her eyes. With a little coaxing, they would be streaming down her cheeks, followed by many more. "Cory, that is so awful. How helpless you must have felt!"

She could see he was fighting back tears now too. "Yeah. So you can probably see why I blame myself. I could have easily saved her. I was a good swimmer. I was just too fucking naive to know I was allowed to."

Shawn stood up and leaned over Cory, taking him in her arms. She put her chin atop his head as she hugged him. He had his arms around her waist, sitting awkwardly with his head against her chest. "I'm so sorry. That is so awful," she said again. "Cory, you know it's not your fault. You know this logically, right?" She stood up straight and crossed her arms, still in front of him and not quite ready to retake her seat.

He shrugged and made a face. "I don't know. I mean, I've gone through many years'-worth of counseling where they've told me that, but I can never make the leap to believing it. It wasn't my fault that she drowned. It was my fault that I didn't save her though. And therefore, it was my fault that she drowned," he said, moving his hands as he spoke, clearly reliving the event on some scale in his mind.

"Cory," Shawn said, reaching for his hand with one of her own. He took it and looked up at her. "You have to accept that you can't control everything that happens. The only way you'll heal is to believe that you couldn't have saved her."

He scoffed at this, took a deep breath. But maintained eye-contact. "How is that?"

"Think about it, Cory." She took her seat again, sitting on the edge of the sofa so as not to have to let go of his hand, which she now covered with her other as well. "You had a cast on your leg. You could have gotten in there and drowned yourself trying to save her. Then your parents could have lost two children that day."

"Holy fuck, Shawn," he said, a look of sobriety falling over his face. "You're the first person who's ever said anything about that."

She lifted her chin a little, tilted her head. "What, you hadn't considered that?"

He shook his head. "No. I never thought about that."

"Well, feel free to adopt it as your own. How high up your leg did the cast go?"

Cory pointed to his thigh, right where it met his groin. "Here. They were trying to keep me from bending my knee. It was a full-leg cast."

She took her top hand off of his and turned it over. "See? You probably would have drowned, too. Or maybe you could have saved her, then you would have drowned instead."

He took a deep breath, then let it out in a shuttering exhalation of emotion. And then he was crying. Shawn quickly moved to the other couch, right beside him, and took him in her arms again, this time from the side. Just holding him. She pulled his head against her chest and kissed the top of it. "Let it go, baby. Let it go, finally. Her death is not yours anymore."

The only other experience Shawn had with death was as an adult, only a few years ago, and it was so indirect as to almost not even count. She had been alone in a hospital room, waiting for the doctors to come in and stitch up her thumb from where she had sliced it open while cutting a tomato. She was sitting up in bed, a large gauze pad wrapped round the wound, holding it up against her chest and feeling sorry for herself as the pain throbbed sickeningly through her hand.

A murmured conversation was taking place on the other side of the wall, in the room next to Shawn's. And though she couldn't hear what was being said, it had the soft but stern sound of someone giving bad news. Then she heard the door close and the wailing began. There was simply no cry like the cry of someone having lost a loved on. The desperation in the woman's voice made it crystal clear what she had just heard from the person who had left the room.

Shawn had suddenly felt selfish for having thought of complaining about her cut thumb and wanted nothing more than to sneak into the room next door to try and comfort the sobbing woman. The deep belly wrenching cries coming from that room were horrible in their humanity and suffering, and it brought Shawn to tears herself.

When a nurse had finally come in to redress and clean Shawn's wound in preparation for the doctor, they had met eyes across the room, and Shawn had asked, "Did she lose someone?"

And knowing that the nurse couldn't answer due to ethics codes, there was no doubting the look the nurse gave her. The woman swallowed and stared at her for a moment, then looked away. As she was rifling through the top drawer of the cabinet looking for supplies, she looked back at Shawn and nodded – just a quick, subtle, double pump of the head – before returning her eyes to the drawer. Shawn's heart had sunk with the confirmation. Knowing that this woman, this nurse – this fellow *human being* – was sharing a complete stranger's grief with her, in silence.

When the nurse had turned and asked to see the affected hand, Shawn had seen the tears in her eyes. Instead of offering the hand, she had opened her arms and the woman had allowed Shawn to hug her. A completely unprofessional posture – one that might even get her in trouble, were she caught in the act – but one that was necessary in the raw and painfully hard-to-look-at face of life. They hugged for a few seconds before the nurse patted Shawn's back a couple of times – the universal sign that a hug is over – and then she stepped back and addressed her wound. Tears streaming down her cheeks and pain in her eyes, the nurse resumed her duties. How many of these personal tragedies must she be exposed to on a weekly basis? Shawn was thankful for people like her and the doctors who had to face it head-on as part of a job.

So though she had not seen evidence of the death, her suspicions had been confirmed and she had heard the soul-crushing pain in the woman's cries in the room next door. And it had hit Shawn hard. It had stayed with her for several weeks after the event, and she had cried several times about it. She had never seen what the woman looked like – and maybe that was a blessing itself. Seeing the pain in the woman's eyes might have been too much to bear. But without that meeting, her encounter had been limited to a wall-muffled cry. Shawn knew she would never happen upon the woman again in life. Or if she did, it would be by ridiculous odds, and they would each never know they had once been next door to each other in a hospital. One bearing grief, the other wanting so badly to offer consolation.

After a long period of crying, shedding himself of the guilt he had carried for over twenty years, Cory finally wiped his eyes and leaned back on the couch, pulling away from the embrace Shawn had wrapped him in. She sat up straight as well, knees together and feet tucked in behind her, facing him. She ran his hair back off his sweaty forehead, then reached down and picked up his glass of vodka and handed it to him. He nodded a thanks and took a long pull from it, then handed it back to her waiting hand. She took a thoughtful sip from it herself, then returned it to the table.

"Cory?" she said. He looked up at her. "Can I kiss you right now?"

His eyes widened, then he swallowed. "You want to kiss me?"

She squinted, half-smiling and nodded her head. "Your vulnerability is beautiful. A man crying in front of a complete stranger is very attractive to me." She continued to run her fingernails through his hair on the side of his head. He was still looking at her. "It doesn't have to mean anything. It's nothing sexual. I just wondered if it might bring you comfort."

Cory nodded, almost imperceptibly, then leaned his head back against the couch, closing his eyes. Shawn leaned in and put her lips against his, softly, not moving, for a long time. Then finally she twisted her head and kissed him a little deeper. And after a few seconds of this, he finally started responding. The kiss was coming from both directions now. She felt more comfortable in it because he did. She put her hand behind his head and kissed him deeper – more passionately. The breathing intensified and she felt his hand on her knee, thumb and first finger separated over it, his thumb rubbing softly in little circles. The kiss lasted more than a minute before she finally broke it, keeping her lips millimeters away from his own as she breathed in and out through her nose, regaining her calm. Then she licked her lips and sat back, picked up his vodka glass off the table again, and drained it.

"Thank you, Cory," she said. "I maybe needed that as much as you."


After a break they probably both needed, where Shawn went to the restroom, splashed some water on her face and refilled her vodka glass, they both ended up back on the couch. It was well after eleven o'clock now, and Shawn was starting to wonder what the arrangements would be for the night. Obviously she was not going to spend the night with Cory, but the worry was there that she might be keeping him up past a normal bed time at this point.

She was back in her corner of the couch, her arm up on the armrest, fingers twirling a lock of hair as she faced him across the corner between the sofas. She was not sure where the kiss had come from. She had acted completely on instinct. But it had not been instinct based on experience. It wasn't like Shawn had kissed a series of guys who had cried in front of her. It also wasn't like a series of guys had cried in front of her. In fact, Cory was the first guy she had ever seen cry. It had just hit her in a way that caused her emotions to speak for her. Of course, the kiss had awakened other parts of her psyche entirely, but that just proved they were compatible kissers. She had not set out hoping to turn him on – or herself for that matter. And was now a little bothered that she had. Because she could feel it in her pajama pants. She had carefully avoided looking in his direction, hoping not to see if he had responded physically or not. That just wasn't a direction she was wanting to go just yet.

"So, uh, you said we need to talk," Cory said after a pregnant pause. "Were you planning on doing any talking during our talk?" He smiled at her.

She giggled and sipped her vodka. "Yeah. Well, I was kind of wanting to hear if you had experienced death at all. And crazy enough, I had an experience not too different from yours. I watched my aunt die right in front of me when I was seven."

Cory shook his head, chewing his lip.

"I'm not that good at talking about it, but just know that it was an incredibly traumatic event. It sent me into shock, and I had to have therapy for many years over it. I still have PTSD, in fact. Like literal, real-thing, not just looking-for-attention PTSD."

He smiled weakly, tilting his head. "Why do you feel like you have to qualify that, Shawn?"

She shrugged and made a face. "I don't know. I think it's overused. People carrying those stupid yipping fuckin' dogs onto airplanes calling them 'emotional support' animals because they got yelled at by a teacher one time."

Cory laughed out loud at this. His laughter was contagious. She laughed with him easily. She was picking at her fingers on the armrest now, where both hands lay fidgeting as she looked at him.

"Anyway, I guess I just feel like I have to say that before someone rolls their eyes at me. Her death was very violent to me. Not in a murder-type violence sort of way. She had a brain aneurysm and convulsed to death right in front of me."

"Christ!" he said, mouth hanging open as he stared wide-eyed at her.

Shawn nodded. "Yeah, her lungs seized and she asphyxiated as I stood there watching her." She closed her eyes and shook her head, holding her hands up beside it, trying to wipe away the memory. "Sorry. I still can't talk about it. I'm just trying to say that I watched it happen and didn't do anything. I didn't know what to do. I was seven. I had no idea she was even dying. Just something didn't look right and I was too scared to act. My fear was the cast on my leg."

Cory nodded soberly at this. Then raised an eyebrow, clicking with his mouth. A gesture that said, 'what are ya gonna do?' "Well, I'm sorry you had to go through that."

Shawn wiped the corners of her eyes then took another drink. "Yeah. I can't say 'I'm over it' now, because I'm still not. But I think it's important for people to know how traumatic it was when I say I'm freaked out by death. I still am today. And now you know why."

"And why you can't watch horror movies. God. So sorry."

"No, I can watch them. I just didn't want to tonight because I'm a little freaked out. Hanging out with you has helped greatly. I hope I'm not keeping you up too late."

"Please," he said, waving a hand at her dismissively. "I stay up late anyway. Do you know what I do for a living?"

Shawn stared at him for a moment, head tilted, frowning. "No. I guess I don't. I've never thought to ask. What do you do?"

He chuckled. "I'm a locksmith."

"Whoa, kick ass!" Shawn said, raising up on her knees on the couch. She clapped her hands together, smiling widely at him. "That sounds really cool!"

Cory smiled back at her. "Yeah, it's cool. But it means I get to sleep whenever I want. I only go to work when my phone rings."

"Well doesn't your phone just ring constantly?"

He shrugged and tried to hide some of his pride. She leaned forward and slapped at his arm.

"Come on! Tell me!"

"I'm a corporate smith. Meaning," he said, holding a hand out, palm up, as if to take a little weight off the topic, "I only get called out for major lockouts. And it's not just picking locks, like you might think. It's breaking into bank vaults. It's reprogramming entry access for an entire facility. Lock-down procedures, badge reader audits, the whole nine." He was being humble in some respect, and she couldn't quite tell why – or what it was he was hiding.

"I guess the money is good?" she finally said, taking a chance.

He nodded, forcing a smile. "Yes. I might only get one job a month. But that one job sometimes pays fifty, sixty grand."

"Holy smokes, Bat man!" she said, bouncing on her knees and clapping again. "That is so exciting!" Her exuberance was rubbing off on Cory. He was giggling right along with her. "Well, some day you'll have to tell me some stories of things you've done for work."

"Yeah, sure," he said. He rolled his wrist a little. A gesture someone might do if he were wearing a watch. But Cory wasn't. The way he looked at his wrist was telling though. It meant the same thing in Shawn's mind. Never one to ignore a good hint, she stood up and grabbed her vodka glass.

"Well, as for tonight, it's time for me to shuffle off to bed and let you get your sleep. Thank you for letting me crash here for a while, Cory. It's been wonderful getting to know you a little. Thanks for letting me unload."

"Sure thing, Shawn. You're welcome to crash on the couch all night if you want. I mean, if you're not comfortable going home yet."

"Thank you, angel," she said, stepping forward and bending over to hug him goodbye. "But my daddy taught me better manners than that."

# T W O

When her eyes popped open the next morning, Shawn realized that she had just had an epiphany, right before waking. Somehow, talking about her aunt's death with someone who had suffered a traumatic death as well, had been helpful. She found that touching the memory lightly wasn't quite as sore just now. Of course, she was only five seconds awake, but even just the thought of fingering that wound before had been enough to avoid ever recalling it at all. She dabbed at it a little, pulling up thoughts of the scene from twenty-two years ago – the look in her aunt's eyes as they went out, the smell of the room she had stood in while it happened… That particular nimbus, whenever she encountered it anywhere in life, always brought her back to that death room immediately. And wherever she was, she would have to find egress quickly, lest she face a breakdown that could cause serious embarrassment and emotional trauma. But right now…

With that thought, she considered again Mr. Singh's offer of joining a project that would somehow involve bringing back the dead. She felt like she should at least hear him out. Shawn had touched on that thought the night before, wondering if she should ask, or just flat-out reject him, and had not been sure. But this morning, she did feel sure. Number one, because he was a kind man and he had always treated her with respect and dignity. But also because there was a part of her – primal or otherwise – that she had to admit, was crazily attracted to the idea. Even if just slightly. Her curiosity was definitely strong for it. Something about the idea was alluring in all its creepy glory.

She shook her head suddenly, the ideas of bringing back stale hundred-year-old corpses suddenly flashing into her mind, and stretched her arms above her head. She must be going fucking crazy if she were entertaining joining a project like that. Well, just because she attended the bake sale didn't mean she had to buy the baked goods. She could listen to his sales pitch at the very least. At the very least, she owed that to him.

So with that in mind, she changed the direction of her day, which had initially been to sit on the sofa and read all day. On days when she *wasn't* blessed with the opportunity to read all day, she would watch a little TV in the evenings. She loved running through entire series, but not quite binging them. She wouldn't, for instance, spend all day on a Saturday consuming a whole season of Dexter. She did, however, prefer to watch it the way she wanted to watch it. Which was sometimes as many as three eps per night, but at least one a night until the season was done. And that was another requirement: it had to be a show that had run its course and finished. She had no interest in catching up to current episodes and then having to wait a week for the next one. Gone were the days of waiting, being interrupted by commercials for shit she didn't want. This was not her father's television.

But today, having changed her mind about listening to her boss's speech about the project, she hopped into the shower for a quick fresh-up, brushed her teeth – one of the seven or eight times she would do so throughout any given day – and then put on actual work clothes. She would be driving up to the office to talk to him, so she would dress as if she were working.

After her shower, sitting on the couch in a stretch bra and her underwear, a towel piled atop her head, she pulled her phone out and curled her feet beneath her. She checked her OuterCircle wall. Nothing new or exciting there. Instagram, same thing. Tanis was in London. Gwen had a baby. Johnny and Amber were still at it. Same bullshit, different day, and Shawn realized she was stalling. Sighing and looking up through the sliding glass door that led to her tiny balcony, she reminded herself that this was the right thing. The 'right thing'. What the hell did that even mean? Right to whom? What if she was wrong about who was right? What if the wrong guy was right? Or the right guy was wrong? What the fuck? Again. Stalling. She rolled her eyes and opened her SMS. Scrolled down to Sameer Singh and tapped it.

*Hey, boss. I'm sorry for the way I acted last night. I have a history that*

She looked up. Should she go into that right now? Maybe not. Erase the last line.

*I'm a little freaked out by the subject because of a personal experience I experienced at*

Fuck. Repeating words. Sigh.

*I'm a little freaked out by the subject because of a personal trauma I experienced as a child. But I do owe you a listen. Are you available today for me to pop in*

Pop in? Was that too casual, having just mentioned that she had experienced a traumatic experience? She giggled at this. *F sake.*

*Are you available any time today for me to swing by and hear what you have to say?*

There. That should do it. *Send.*

She pressed the sleep button then tossed her phone on the couch. *Wonder what Cory is up to.* Why was she thinking about Cory? Last night had been nice. Opening up and being opened up to by a new friend was wonderful. Talk about experiences. She felt good about it. She also felt good about the kiss she had put on him. If he was gay then he was only '*just*'. She had felt his breathing get heavier along with her own. That part of the kiss she was not necessarily proud of, but she didn't regret it. She was pretty enough that she got compliments sometimes. Compliments gave her confidence. And knowing she was pretty made her confident that he wasn't disgusted by the kiss in retrospect. So she could probably feel okay about the whole thing. But she definitely felt good about the initial phase of the kiss – the one she had meant to do. The end part had been ad-libbed. The kiss she had meant to give him had been nothing but rewarding him for a breakthrough. A nice little pat on the back to a fellow soul going through this not-necessarily *easy* journey called life. That it had turned into something sexy was just a perk. Maybe misplaced under the circumstances, but he had not pushed her away, either. And now, here she was overthinking the whole thing. But what was he up to this morning?

Shawn picked her phone up and checked it for messages, even though she had not heard it vibrate. Whatev. She made her way into the bedroom and slipped into her work clothes. A knee-length sensible black skirt and a red blouse with a black cardigan. Nice. She put the hat on that she had worn last night with her pajamas. Perfect.

She grabbed her phone and poured herself a cup of coffee, then wandered across the breezeway. As she held her fist up to knock, she stopped herself, then frowned and turned back to her apartment. A minute later, she was back – this time with two mugs of steaming coffee in her hands. She kicked lightly at the base of the door. After a spot, he opened, frowning and looking down. Then his eyes found her hands and he smiled.

"Ah. Hey, Shawn! Come in," said Cory.

She was all smiles as she came in with the coffees and turned to hand him one. "Didn't know how you took it. Or, well, even if you took it at all. Or if you'd already -"

She was interrupted with a kiss. This time there was nothing left to doubt. It was all romance.

Shawn stood there with her eyes closed, stunned, holding two coffees, for a long time after the kiss had ended. Finally, she mouthed the word *'wow'* and breathed in deeply. When she finally opened her eyes, she saw that he was standing there staring at her – a sly smile on his face. She held the stare for a little bit, just waiting for her heart to slow a little. Then she finally said, "So I guess you're not gay."

On the way in to the office, Shawn was all smiles. She was listening to Lorde on her streaming service, singing loudly along and beating her steering wheel like it was a nine-piece set of Ludwigs. She was getting some looks from people in other cars around her. They weren't used to seeing someone so happy on these roads. But a hot girl in a hot Jeep with a hat on, singing with her eyes closed and full of smiles... What was not to love?

So what did this mean? She had to take a moment to dissect what had happened with Cory. He had initiated the kiss this time. Which meant he felt comfortable enough with last night's happenings to repeat the gesture. Did this mean he now thought of her as his girlfriend? Whoa. She gripped her steering wheel with both hands, knuckles white in the bright morning light.

What about her? What did Shawn think? Did she think of Cory as her boyfriend now? After a couple of kisses? She had not stayed long enough to settle into anything else. There was no petting, no removing of clothes, certainly no sex. But what about it? What about sex? The big S word. What if the kiss were to linger next time? Get a little deeper? What if it started involving hands and tongues and shirts being pulled off? What if it went horizontal? Would she object? Did she steadfastly stand against sex with men she barely knew? Of course not. She had a history that disproved the proof.

Well, she was smiling from ear to ear. So there was something going on below her head – above her pelvis – in that place where small fires turned into big ones with the right air mixture. And she wasn't sure she felt bad about it in the least. He was a good-looking guy, self-sufficient and had so many things in common with her that it was crazy. She wasn't into astrology, but she also didn't think it was complete bullshit. When someone had almost the same birth date, drove the same model of vehicle, and had experienced a traumatic event in his childhood, watching a loved one die… Good God. What percentage of people had even had that happen to them? It surely meant *something*. She believed in that.

About fifteen minutes after she had stepped into Cory's apartment, she had gotten the response from her boss, saying he was available now, and could she come in right away? Like a good little soldier, she had said, "Welp, there he is. Sorry, Cory, but I gotta jet. Wish me luck, though, okay?" Cory, like a good little soldier himself, had smiled and nodded, sticking his fist out for her to bump.

Now she was pulling into the parking garage of the BlueBird building. They only had one floor in the fifteen-story building, and only six parking spots assigned to them in the garage. So she had her own preferred spot. The first three spots on the floor they were assigned to park in had a concrete rafter running above them that her Jeep would barely fit beneath. She was always afraid of scraping the top. So she took the fourth spot. Everyone seemed to fall into taking the same one every day, making it feel like they were assigned spots. So Shawn always got her preferred spot.

Shawn turned the key off and stared at the dull concrete wall in front of her for a minute. She jiggled the keys in her hand. Did she need to go over this, yet again? Did she need to steel herself for a conversation that might not even be intimidating? The logistics of such a ridiculous project would surely be scary, no matter how light or heavy the actual engagement would be. Right? Like an under-water welder, it didn't matter how big the welding job was, you were still under the fucking water. Her only worry was that she would have a panic attack in the meeting. She could always say no to joining the project – at least she thought. That was assuming he wouldn't fire her. Lay her off, saying he no longer had a need for her position... But that was overthinking it entirely. That was another conversation on a topic they hadn't even broached yet. She needed to take a step back and reassess where she was. She reminded herself that even if it got scary, she always had two possible exits. One, she could stand up, hands up, and tell him that she needed to stop. She was getting anxious. And two, she could just stop him politely and tell him *why* she was uncomfortable. She could tell him about that traumatic event she had suffered as a child. Surely he would understand. Right?

Taking a deep breath, Shawn popped the door handle and grabbed her purse and phone.

The elevator smelled like piss. How an elevator in a pretty nice upscale building in downtown Arlington could smell like urine was beyond Shawn. Did the homeless come in here at night and use it as a restroom? Did they sleep in here? She had to pinch her nose closed and pull her blouse up over her mouth to use as a filter in order not to smell it. When it dinged and opened on the fourth floor, Shawn stepped out, paying more attention to her phone than her surroundings. She stopped a few feet outside the elevator, smiling as she read the text her mother had sent her. In response to last night's cry for potential need for help text, her mother had replied in a very motherly fashion. A whole bunch of 'I'm proud of you' and 'I know you'll be careful' and 'you don't really need my help' shit. Always the same. Momma would always preach about the dangers of the world, about always locking her car doors and pushing a chair against the doorknob of strange hotel room doors. But then when she took these precautions, she was over-reacting and taking things a little too seriously. Shawn didn't mind it though. She wouldn't stop practicing what her parents had taught her. She loved these texts from her mother, knowing they wouldn't come forever.

When she looked up, there was Sameer standing there staring at her, waiting patiently for her to finish. "Sorry," she said, then realized she wasn't. She had the day off. She was here of her own accord, as a courtesy to the man selling death.

"It is no problem, Miss Marcy. Would you like to join me in the office?" he said, holding a hand out toward his office.

"I would, Sameer. Hence my coming in on a Tuesday, of all days," she said. He turned and frowned at her, not catching the joke. "Never mind."

She pulled the chair out and dropped into it, straightening her skirt and checking herself as anyone in charge should do. Shawn had trained herself for this moment – preparing herself to think from the perspective of one who was in charge. Someone granting a few moments to an underling proposing a project he or she might decide to work on – were it okay with the boss to approve the funding. In this manner, she could stay disconnected enough to be able to stand up and stop the meeting at any point, were it to become necessary. She felt calm, but knew the heartburn was just under the surface of every word. The fear was lurking in the shadows, right next to the boogeyman he was about to tell her about.

"So, Miss Marcy, you are wanting to hear what I am thinking, yes?" Sameer said, steepling his fingers above his desk.

Shawn thought this much had been obvious, coming in on her day off to hear it, but replied, trying to keep her good nature in front of her. "Yes, I want to hear more about it. I can't promise anything, but I felt like you deserved to be heard."

"Well, that is very kind of you, Miss Marcy," he said. "So I told you what I am wanting to do with this project. Do you have any questions?"

She blinked, looking around the room. Had she just blacked out for twenty minutes, missing entirely the presentation? "Huh? No, you didn't tell me what you wanted to do!"

"I told you last night. I am wanting to bring someone back," he said. He was frowning at her again like she was indeed missing something here.

"Yes. But that's *all* you told me, Sameer," Shawn said, leaning forward and gripping the fronts of the arm rests. Window washers were outside his window, slapping squeegees against the glass and pulling away streaks of soapy bubbles. She tried to focus. "What am I missing here?" she added.

"Are you calm enough, Miss Mar-"

"Stop calling me that!" she almost shouted. Then she raised a hand, resetting. "I'm sorry." She took a deep breath and closed her eyes. Shook her head. "Will you please just call me Shawn?"

"I am sorry, but I am not understanding this name."

"My name is Marcella Shawn. I go by Shawn. I made this decision in my teens. It's what everyone calls me." She stared at him for a moment, squeezing the armrests as the man outside sprayed a small spot and scraped it away with the rubber squeegee. She shook her head again. "Or Marcy, if you like. I'm sorry, Sameer. Marcy is fine. But please, can you leave off the Miss?"

Sameer furled his lips and nodded slowly, as if this was all a new concept to him. "Okay then, I shall try, Mis-" he said, stopping short. "I shall try, Shawn." He said it slowly as if tasting a new fruit.

She tilted her head, pulling her chin in, then breathed in deeply. Blinked purposefully. "Okay. So let's start over. Tell me about your project. What's in it besides the one sentence you've told me so far?"

Sameer leaned back in his seat and tapped on the ends of the armrests. "I asked you if there were any questions you wanted to ask."

"I'm sorry I freaked out last night. I don't deal with this stuff very easily. Not naturally, anyway. But yeah. I have questions," she said. She stared at him for a moment, trying to sort out in her head which question should come first. She had so many. After a while, she breathed in deeply and shot from the hip. "Okay, how about this: who are the subjects?" She turned her hands over, palms up, then slapped them back down on the armrests. This was like an arm-wrestling match where the contestants tried to make the biggest impact with the fewest hand gestures. Extra points for keeping contact with the armrest. She almost smirked at this thought.

"That is a good question," he said, nodding. "We have a grant from the University of Texas from Arlington. People who donated their bodies to medical science will be the first we would be using."

Shawn took a deep breath, steeling herself again. Keeping her resolve. So far, so good. He had not said anything too creepy, but – and there it was. The chills crept up her spine. They had at least taken a minute to start. There was that much to be thankful for. But they were still there. Maybe she wasn't as steeled as she had thought. At this point, there was no way she was going to be able to say anything but a loud, resounding 'No!' to his offer. First question answered and she was already wigging out.

"You look uncomfortable, Shawn."

She appreciated the effort, but every time he said her name, he was pausing ever-so-slightly before and after the word, emphasizing it in an almost condescending reproach. And it was probably completely subconscious to him.

"I am. I have told you that, Sameer. I'm not trying to pretend I'm not. I'm just trying to be respectful of your time and your offer."

"Well, thank you. I am appreciating this."

"You know what? I don't think I have any other questions," she said, suddenly. Then she grabbed the armrests again and leaned forward, ready to stand up. "Wait. One more. How long are you planning to keep them alive? What's your goal here? Do you want to ask them a question? Have a full conversation with them? Make them perform a stunt?" she said. Then she shivered, hard. "Oh, God," she said, involuntarily.

He raised his eyebrows at her, but did not comment on the gesture. "These are good questions. I am wanting to start with just a seeing if we can get anything to happen at all. We just record what we see. I do not have a necessary 'goal' other than reanimation."

"Oh, God," she muttered again and looked up at the ceiling. She leaned back in the chair again. Looked out the window. Somehow, the window cleaner had finished the window she could see, and had moved on, all without her even noticing. She must have been entranced. "And this is real? This is not a joke, Sameer? Because Christ on his throne, this is the creepiest shit I have ever heard of," she said. After a moment of locking eyes with him, she added, "Pardon my French."

He smirked at this. "Is it okay, Miss Mar- … Shawn. I know it is coming as a shock to some people. Most people have never heard of such things as this. Or at least not having imagined them to be a reality."

"Exactly that," she said, pointing at him. "It's a very popular movie theme." She took a deep breath and looked at her fingernails. How in the world could this be real? "I will personally never watch *Pet Sematary* again. Jesus." She shivered again.

"I have not seen this movie," Sameer said.

"Uh, well, that's probably a good thing. Don't get any ideas from it. By the way, where are you planning to do this? I mean, bringing cadavers into a building must surely be covered by some code or something…"

Sameer smiled. Then he scooted back and stood up. "Would you like to see the lab?"

"Oh, Christ," Shawn breathed. "You already have the lab set up?"

"Don't worry, Shawn. There are no bodies in there right now."

She closed her eyes and steeled herself, then willed herself to stand up and follow him. Until yesterday, she had never been thoughtful about the half of the fourth floor beyond the wall by the elevators. From the outside of the building, one could see the building was a certain width. It was hard to take in from the inside, but she knew the elevator shafts split the building just about in the middle, because she had been on other floors. And now that she thought about it, she had never paid attention to the fact that half the floor was walled off from their offices. Now she became aware of it. There was a simple badge-controlled door out in the elevator lobby.

Sameer waved his badge at the reader and pushed the door inward. Lights flickered on as they entered and Shawn was immediately aware of the smell of cleaning products. It smelled sanitary.

"You see, this entire side of the building is for our use. I have been setting it up for the last two years. We have direct access from the service elevator, which is through that door," he said, pointing at another door on the same wall as the one they had entered.

Shawn nodded. Glanced around the place. This didn't look so spooky. It was not brightly lit like a typical hospital room, or what she thought a science lab might look like. In fact, the lighting was in the warm color temperature range. They were not under the harsh white, sterile glare of fluorescents. That was a bonus. The large area that covered this half of the building was separated into rooms with windows covering most of the walls, so one could almost see all the way across the space. On the lower corner of the windows that fell beside doors, there were large white letters. She was currently beside the one labeled D. It seemed to go up to room J. Sameer had been hard at work here.

"Two years? Good Lord, Sameer, this is incredible. How does no one know about this?"

He shrugged, hands in his pockets. He was now following Shawn as she meandered about the place, poking here, lifting a cover there, opening a drawer. "Mostly I am working on this after hours and on weekends. And when I am sending people home early on a Friday I come in here."

Shawn nodded, a knowing smile crossing her face. "Gotcha. I'll be damn. But Sameer, seriously," she said, coming to a full stop and turning to face him. "Do you really need all this space for it?"

"Oh, no," he said, waving dismissively. "It is not only for this project, Shawn. It is for other the other things I am working on too."

She raised an eyebrow at him and he simply smiled. He would perhaps tell her about some of that when he was ready. Need-to-know. She continued her tour, looking into the windows of just about every room, but not actually entering them from the wide hallways that separated them all. Then when they finally came to a room with a padded table in the middle of it, Shawn instinctively knew this was where it would happen. Brown leather belts crossed the vinyl pad of the table. Instruments sat atop a counter on the back wall, the only wall with no window in it. There was some machinery she recognized – a centrifuge, for one – but most of the other things looked as foreign to her as the idea of raising the dead sounded to her innocent ears.

Shawn took a deep breath and opened the door to this room. She stopped just inside the doorway, looking this way and that – taking it all in. The lighting was warm in this room as well. Not the standard operating room sterile white, but a nice orange, cozy illumination. "What's with the lighting?"

"Ah, you are noticing this. Very good. I am thinking it is best to comfort a guest if we are having success."

Shawn closed her eyes and breathed deeply. Any time an image of a dead guy's eyes popping open would enter her mind, she would have to take a breather. And this was just the thought of it. What if she did join the project, and they *did* get it to work? What if she actually saw a dead guy reanimate? Good God. Nope. Nope, nope and nope. There was no way.

"Hasn't this been tried before, Sameer? I mean, aside from in Hollywood."

"Yes. But I have pretty good science researching to say that I might be successful."

As they walked back to the exit door, Shawn turned to him again and said, "Thank you for the tour, Sameer. I have to leave now. Please don't be taking offense to this, but I need to think about this. I'm not saying no yet – though I probably will," she said, pointing at him. "But please give me some time to work through my own demons, okay?"

"Okay, Shawn. This is okay and perfectly fine," he said, nodding. His hands were still in his pockets.

She adjusted her purse on her shoulder and turned the knob on the door. As she pulled it open, she spun back around. "You're serious."

He nodded. There might have been the hint of a smile in his eyes.

She nodded too. Okay. At least one thing was put to rest here. He was serious. All other things considered, and whether or not she would join him – whether or not she would *survive* it if she *did* join him – at least she knew it was not a joke. Sameer was definitely serious about bringing someone back from the dead.

As she came through the door, Shawn tossed her keys on the kitchen bar and went into the bedroom to get out of her work clothes. It was still cool outside, but she was ready to let her legs get some air. She put on some short jean shorts and a hoodie, then stepped into the bathroom to relieve her bladder and brush her teeth. Now that it was almost noon, the thoughts of her spending the entire day reading were pretty much shattered. Ah, well. She could watch a couple of episodes of Dexter tonight and maybe do some knitting while she watched. She had a sweater she could work on. Or maybe she would see what Cory was up to today. Ever since he had taken her by the shoulder and moved her across that landing to point out his own Jeep, she had been parking back there right next to him. Jeep parking existed, she found, anywhere there was more than one Jeep. And his had been moved this morning between the time she had left and when she had returned. He had gone somewhere. But he was back now.

She made herself some lunch and sat on the couch to eat it, flipping through her phone. OuterCircle. Reddit. Instagram. Same bullshit. Different day. As she dropped the phone on the couch and picked up her sandwich, there was a knock on the door. Well, only one person it would be, right? She only knew one of her neighbors. She was a little curious about the excitement she felt when she thought about who it might be. But thinking it better to be safe, she went ahead and called out, asking who it was. She heard the muffled voice through the door, confirming her suspicions and smiled. Then she told him to come in.

The door creaked open and he came waltzing in looking suddenly like the hottest thing she'd ever seen. "What in the hell?" she said, eyes going wide. She dropped her sandwich on her plate without looking, shuffled any crumbs off her hands and turned around on the couch, coming up on her knees to look over the back at him. Cory was wearing dark jeans over black boots and a black leather coat zipped up. He had black leather gloves on and shades raised up onto his hair. A matte black helmet was tucked under his right arm.

"Hey, Shawn," he said, looking a little out of breath.

She was now staring with mouth agape and huge eyes, with a hand over her heart. "What the heck is this?" she said, unable to mask the excitement in her voice.

"I didn't tell you I have a motorcycle?"

"Uh! No!" said Shawn, dramatically drawing out the long O. "You look hot as fuck!" she said, then slapped a hand over her mouth. "Did I just say that out loud?"

Cory grinned widely and said, "Well, thank you ma'am. Would you like to go for a ride?"

"You bet your sweet ass I would!" she shouted, and vaulted over the couch, running to her bedroom. She was out of the shorty shorts in a flash, and pulling on a pair of jeans. As she hopped from foot to foot, she bounced to the doorway to see him, suddenly not caring if he saw her bare thighs and panties. "I've never been on a motorcycle before!"

"Well, I have an extra helmet. Do you have a coat though?"

"Uh huh," she said, nodding. She buttoned the jeans and ran up the zipper.

"Good. Boots too, if you have any. I have to warn you though, this isn't a touring bike."

She raised her eyebrows and stared at him. "I have no idea what that means, but I'm all ears." Then she went into the closet and dug around for those cute black boots she hadn't worn in a few months.

"Well, you know those big motorcycles that have a proper back seat? And the big shroud up front, where it almost looks like a car? Stereo and all that?"

"Okay," she said. Shawn had never much paid attention to different motorcycles on the road.

"Well, mine isn't one of those. Mine's a cruiser."

She stopped and turned toward him, holding her boots down by her sides, one in each hand. "What's that mean? That you don't have a back seat?"

He chuckled. "Well, I do. Not like that. But a pillion. It's just a little black pad on the fender. There's no seat back or anything."

Shawn thought about this for a moment. Then frowned. "How am I supposed to hold on?" she asked.

"You have to lean forward and wrap your arms around me," said Cory. He was jiggling his key in the gloved hand.

"Oh. Well, okay. I can do that." She stood there for another moment. "Is it safe?"

"Well, not really. But it's fun," said Cory.

As they went down the stairs, he turned her away from the parking lot and pointed back to the space underneath the staircase. There it sat in the shadows. She had never looked *through* the stairs as she had gone up then, and thus had never seen the bike. It sat beneath the stairs she used to go up back before she had started parking next to him in the back lot. She walked up to it and looked at it with wonder. "What a beautiful motorcycle, Cory!" she said. It was matte black all over, including the engine and pipes and everything. On the gas tank were matte silver letters spelling Indian.

"Thank you. Let me get it down into the parking lot, then you can get on with me, okay?" said Cory.

Shawn nodded excitedly. He had handed her a helmet. She now put it on and followed him as he walked the bike back toward the lot where their two Jeeps stood. She had no trouble figuring out the buckle. One piece slid into the other and clicked through several detents until it was snug under her chin. She had zipper her jacket all the way up like Cory had his, and was now standing on the curb watching him gently roll it off the sidewalk into the angled stripes of the handicap overflow spot. She was trembling a little. She reckoned it was only half fear. The rest was pure excitement.

Then Cory sat on it and reached down with his left hand, turning the key. He flipped a switch with his right hand and Shawn heard a humming noise. And then he started the bike and it roared to life. It had a throaty rumble to it that sounded mean and sexy, just like it looked. He turned halfway around on the seat and waved her over. God, he looked sexy in that helmet and those gloves and jacket. How had she not known he had a motorcycle?

Shawn stepped up to him and leaned in close as he told her how to get on. She swung her leg over then found the pegs with her feet and wrapped her arms round his waist, leaning forward and pressing her chest against his back. The seat had an exciting vibration coming through it. It felt like serious power between her thighs. He pulled forward slowly, turning right and came to a stop outside of the parking space. Then he cranked his head and lifted the visor of his helmet and spoke to her again.

"Don't try to fight me when we turn, okay? You lean with me. Stay attached to me. If we're leaning right, put your head over my right shoulder. Leaning left, go left. Got it?"

Shawn gave him a thumbs-up without pulling her hand out from in front of him. There was no way she was going to be letting go. She was scared shitless right now. And then he took off. Nice and easy, he meandered through the parking lot until they got to the main road. He turned up onto Brown Boulevard and then put on some gas. She felt herself being pulled backward by the inertia and tightened her grip around him, laughing out loud at the same time. *Holy shit, this is awesome!*

The real fun came with the went down some curvy roads. The leaning was intense. It felt as it the bike would just sweep out to the side, dumping them onto the asphalt. But the tires stuck and it whipped round the corners, pulling her stomach toward the opposite direction. Every time he would accelerate, her stomach felt like it lifted up into her throat and she would laugh out loud again. At one stop light, she was grinning from ear to ear with her helmet pressed against Cory's back as she rested her head. A couple in the car next to them at the light saw her and smiled at her. She must be a sight. The man rolled down his window and shouted at them, "Nice bike, man!"

Cory looked over and waved, then made an OK sign with his hand. Shawn released her death grip on him for a moment to make the same hand gesture. The man laughed, then rolled his window back up, waving at them before the light changed to green. For a lot of the rest of the ride, Shawn was screaming with glee and laughing like a schoolgirl. She was having the time of her life. This was exactly what she had been needing. Having to lean forward far enough to wrap her arms around him put her in a position that made it hard to look over his shoulder, because the chin of her helmet got in the way. It was easier for her to just turn her head to one side or the other and lean it against his back. This meant she didn't get to see much, but it made the ride arguably more exciting.

Cory finally slowed and turned into a parking lot and Shawn recognized the landmarks. She released her grip a little and let her hands slide back onto the sides of his coat where she was able to grab his pockets and look around a little. They were at Cino's, a fifties-style drive-up diner, and there were a ton of bikers standing around in the common area, some leaning against their bikes, others in the parking lot between them. Shawn's excitement went up another notch. Was this the lifestyle he lived on the side? Was Cory a biker? *Oh my God. I think I love this man.*

Shawn had never given much thought to the biker guys she saw occasionally. She wasn't necessarily attracted to them. She just never paid attention. But having gotten to know Cory over the last six months, seeing him a couple of times a week between their apartments or in the parking lot, she had never seen him in biker gear. So the sudden appearance of it came at her from a different angle. It was almost like being handed a gift to unwrap. Easy on the senses. Already having known him made her think differently about it than it would it that's how she would have seen him the first time. She might or might not have thought of him as hot. But this, this was like a paradigm shift. And it was remarkable how quickly she adapted to the thought of being a biker's girlfriend. She wasn't even his girlfriend. But daydreams had whipped through her mind like lightning bolts. And the idea did not turn her off.

They pulled into a slot and he killed the engine, then told her she had to get off first. She swung her leg over, standing up and feeling the stiffness in her thighs immediately. She reached up and fumbled with the helmet as Cory dismounted and pulled his own off, hanging it on the handlebar. He unzipped his coat and removed that too. Then he started pulling his gloves off. All this while Shawn was still trying to get the chin strap off. Her breathing was loud in the helmet as she tried over and over to find the trick.

A man had come across the center area and walked up to Cory, holding a hand up. They clapped their hands together and the man pulled him in for a man-hug. So Cory knew these guys. Or at least some of them. *Even hotter.* She finally gave up on the chin strap and called out to him, her voice loud and dead in the helmet. Cory turned and came over to her.

"Hey, sorry, Shawn." He reached up and yanked something and the chin strap fell away. Immediate relief poured in as she pulled the helmet off. "Hey, come meet these guys, will ya?" he said.

She came around the bike to the big burly man who was standing there staring at her. "Hello," she said, wondering if she was cool enough to hang out with guys like these. He wore a vest with patches all over it. And now, turning to look at Cory, she saw he had one on too. *Holy shit, batman!* The wonders never ceased.

"Hey, young lady. I'm Road Kill," the man said, extending a hand to her.

"Oh. Hi. I'm Shawn," she said, reaching out and delicately taking the man's hand. Road Kill pulled her in almost violently for the same hug he had given Cory a minute ago. She might have yelped as he did so, then burst out laughing. She reckoned it wouldn't have been so violent had she been expecting it.

"Good to meet you, Shawn," he said. "This over here," he started, then turned to look for someone. "Where the fuck she go?"

Cory pointed and Kill turned in that direction. "Daisy Duke! Get your pretty ass over here." Then, turning back to Shawn, "This is my wife, Daisy Duke."

A tall, knockout of a woman came walking up the sidewalk, all smiles. She wore a vest covered in patches as well. Shawn saw that indeed, hers read Daisy Duke above the left breast. They shook hands and Daisy pulled her in for the same hug, though a lot more gentle like. "Hi there. My real name's Catherine. They say I look like Catherine Bach, so, well, you get it." The woman smiled as they pulled apart. "What's your name, darling? Wow, you're gorgeous!"

Shawn blushed. Introduced herself.

"Good job, Hunter!" said Daisy, reaching out to shake his hand over the bike. They leaned in and hugged. Shawn, almost frowning, but quickly turning to glance at Cory's vest, saw that it read Squirrel Hunter above the breast. *Ah. I see. I'll have to ask him about that later.*

Cory's eyes shot over at Shawn. She tilted her head down ever so slightly and bit her bottom lip, then raised an eyebrow. It all happened in less than an instant. But Cory caught the message. He looked back at Daisy and said, "Thank you, Daise. Just started dating." He was rubbing his hands together as he looked back at Shawn. "Last night, actually." The four of them laughed. And Shawn felt a sudden warmth inside that she had not felt in a long time.

Cory introduced her to ten or twelve other guys and their wives or girlfriends. Every one of them were friendly and welcoming, completely dispelling the myth in her own head about bikers. She had been pleasantly surprised to learn they were normal human beings. Especially Lo. Lo had been standing with a big burly guy who went by Nine Lives, and she wasn't wearing a cut. A cut was what these people called a vest. She had learned that by whisper in the ear between one of the introductions and the next, after Shawn had said, 'I like your vest' to one of the ladies. It had been pink camouflage and worthy of comment.

When Cory brought Shawn over to meet Nine and Lo, Shawn had been instantly attracted to her. Not by anything sexual, but rather just an unusual connection in the eyes. She had learned since childhood that when that connection happened, she could tell they were going to be good friends. That had happened here. Cory made the intro and Shawn and Lo had locked eyes. Lo was smiling, and that smile had been visible even in her hazel eyes. It had made Shawn immediately want to smile as well. They shook hands and almost instantly clicked.

What had initially drawn Shawn's attention to the woman was how normal she looked. As in, not like a biker's girl. And with that realization, Shawn had suddenly not felt so odd, or at least not like the odd woman out. They had stood talking for a few minutes while Cory and Nine Lives had done some catching up.

"My name is Laura, Shawn, nice to meet you," said Lo.

"So is Lo your biker name?" Shawn had asked.

"Nah, this is my first time to come to something like this. I just recently met Heath," she said, smiling and looking at Nine Lives. Shawn made a mental note to file this man's name with the road name. "I've gone by Lo since I was a little girl. I guess since these guys are big on their nicknames he thought he should introduce me as that."

Shawn nodded and they stood smiling for a moment before Lo asked, "Is Shawn your real name?"

Shawn nodded. "Middle name. Marcella just doesn't fit. My parents call me Marcy. I prefer Shawn."

"I get it. I like that. That's a kick-ass name for a gal, ask me."

"Well, thank you," Shawn said, bowing slightly.

Lo stood almost her same height, same build but a little bigger in the chest, and had reddish-brown hair cut in a bob, almost exactly the same length as her own. She was wearing jeans and a white t-shirt with a pale pink cardigan buttoned halfway up. Completely out of place at a biker rally.

Cory finished his catch-up talk and asked Shawn if she was ready to move on. But before they walked away, she shook hands with Lo again. And Lo said, "Hey, let's tap our phones together. I'm new in town, maybe we could hang out sometime."

Shawn's chest filled with excitement at this. Not just with meeting a new friend, but the fact that trading phone numbers had been Lo's idea. It made her feel like maybe she wasn't so much out of place at all. Or that maybe they both were, and they should stick together.

"Oh yeah, that sounds like a great plan. I'll look you up sometime," said Shawn.

"Look me up, pup!" Lo said, pulling her phone out of her purse. "Did you know dogs can't look up?"

Shawn laughed out loud. "That's got to be the silliest thing I've ever heard. Like 'birds aren't real'."

"Oh no, look it up!" said Lo. They held their phones together and tapped the trade feature button. "Look it up, pup!"

Shawn smiled and then leaned in as Lo spontaneously held her arms open for a hug. When they separated, Lo winked at her and Shawn smiled again. Could it be that she loved that girl already? When she and Cory finally stood alone in front of an order station, Shawn slipped her arm through Cory's not even shocked at how natural it felt, and stood up against his arm like she had been his girlfriend for ages. She stood up on tiptoes and whispered in his ear, "Is this one of those outlaw clubs like on *Sons of Anarchy*?"

Cory giggled and looked down at her, hands in his pockets, and said, "Nah, this isn't a club. It's a group."

Shawn rolled her eyes and shook her head. "Club, group, gang, whatever."

Cory turned a little, forcing her to pull her arm out and stand up straight. He held a finger up. "Actually, it's an important distinction. Clubs have territories. Rivals. All that shit. A group is just a group of guys who ride together."

Shawn looked around, taking in all the patches and vests before meeting eyes with Cory again. He was smiling. "In principal, we operate the same as a club. There's a hierarchy. Dahmer is our leader. He has a tail gunner and a wing man, a sergeant at arms… everything. But we don't earn money and commit crimes and whatnot."

"Well that's refreshing."

Cory reached up and pinched her nose lightly, then said quietly, "I'll tell you all about it later, if you want."

"Where did you get the name Squirrel Hunter?" Shawn said, smirking at him.

He smiled back at her and shook his head, rolling his eyes. "Everywhere I go, it seems squirrels have it out for me. They always dart out in front of me and shit. Well, I was talking about it at a pool party last year and Dahmer overheard me. So it stuck."

"I think it's cute," Shawn said, and tiptoed up to kiss him on the lips. A car hop walked up and handed them their food and thanked them. She seemed to make eyes at Cory a little bit. Shawn guessed they came here a lot, and the hops knew them all. She was cute.

"That your girlfriend, sugar?" Shawn asked as they found a bench and sat down with their food.

"Yeah, I guess she would like to think so. That's Misty," said Cory.

"Well she's a cutie pie."

He looked up as if looking for Misty, then nodded. "Yeah, she's cute. A little young though."

Shawn smiled. They unwrapped their burgers and dug in.


Back at the apartment, they separated on the landing, Shawn promising she would come over to see him after she cleaned up. She smelled like exhaust, highway and sweat. Altogether, she found she wasn't turned off by the scent. In fact, smelling it on Cory when she had stood up to give him a quick kiss before they parted ways had turned her dials a little bit. She thought he smelled like a man should smell. Well, at least after a ride across town on a motorcycle. She did still enjoy the thought of a soapy-fresh scent being the typical aroma.

When she came into her apartment she realized she had left her half-eaten sandwich on the couch. She collected the paper plate and dropped it in the trash then went into her room and undressed. Standing naked in front of her full-length mirror, Shawn looked herself up and down, wondering if Cory would like what he saw when he finally saw her naked. Finally being a funny word, as she was beginning to feel like it might be sooner, rather than later. Then she wondered why she was even wondering what he would think. Wasn't it a little soon to be thinking about him all the time? Had he already gotten in? If so, then she really only had herself to blame. That one kiss she had planted had turned into something a little deeper than just a consolation kiss. Though blame was not a good word either, because she didn't feel the least bit unhappy about it. She cupped her breasts, pressing them flat up against her chest and then letting them go, seeing if they bounced or jiggled. They didn't. She made a face. Maybe she was a little self-conscious about them. The rest of her looked great. She knew that. And having Daisy Duke tell her she was beautiful today had really left its mark. But she always worried about her cup size. She knew a lot of guys liked big boobs. And she was not the type to get bolt-ons. Oh well. *We shall see, we shall see.*

She stepped into the steamy shower and washed off the road, eyes closed and humming through a smile the entire time.


After her shower, as she was about to head across the patio, her phone rang. Hoping it was Cory, then realizing she had not actually exchanged phone numbers with him yet, she leaned over the couch and grabbed the buzzing device. It was her mom.

"Hey, mom!"

"Hello, Marcella. I haven't heard from you in a few days. I was just checking in to make sure your neighbor friend didn't end up being an axe murderer."

"Well, I don't know yet, momma. He still could be, I guess. But I haven't seen any axes yet," Shawn said, grabbing her glass of water off the kitchen counter then coming around to sit on the couch where she curled her feet up behind her.

"I hope you're being careful, Marcella."

"Mom! We're not having sex. Why would you think that?"

Her mom sounded positively indignant. "Why, Marcy, what in the world makes you think I'm talking about sex? I'm talking about being careful not to get axe-murdered!"

Shawn laughed out loud, putting a hand over her mouth, closing her eyes. "Good word, mom. Why does it always have to be an axe? How many people have actually been murdered by axes in the last century, anyway?"

"Well, you might be the first."

"Yeah and Socrates is a lion," Shawn said, rolling her eyes.

Her mother ignored that. So I guess you've been spending time with him then?" she said.

"Yes, in fact I have. He took me for a motorcycle ride today and I got to meet some of his motorcycle friends!"

"Oh, dear God. You're not making me feel any better about this."

"Stop, mommy. I'm almost thirty years old now and I've never been on a motorcycle until today. He was a very good, safe driver. And we had a lot of fun."

"Well, I'm in my sixties and I've still never been on one. Maybe I should talk Gavin into getting one," said her mother.

Shawn laughed out loud. "Mom! Dad wouldn't buy a bike if he found the money! Anyway, we went on this one ride, and I'm already hooked. It's such a rush. And, oh, mom, he's in a motorcycle club. Group. Wait. I keep getting it mixed up. He's in the one that's not illegal."

Her mother sighed at this. "Why can't you just meet a nice boy like Monica did. Someone who does *safe* things."

Shawn shook her head. "I promise I'm safe," she said. *Dying for a subject change.* She took a sip of her water, then looked at the clock above the telly on the wall. "Okay, mom, I'm about to go hang out with Cory now. So can I call you tomorrow?"

"Sure you can. Talk to you then."

"Okay, love you, mom," Shawn said, and hung up. She dropped the phone on the couch and stared out the back door at the sunset, happening just behind the building that was blocking her view of it. She was absentmindedly playing with her toes, gazing off into the distance. Sometimes she would daydream like this for a half-hour before popping back into reality and realizing she had gone away again. It only lasted a few minutes this time, though. She picked her phone up and looked at the screen, then remembered her plans to go see Cory. *Oh, shit! How long has it been?*

She hopped up off the couch and dashed to the bathroom. Brushed her teeth, then looked at them in the mirror. "Okay. Good," she said, then flipped off the light and ran back to the living room where she grabbed her phone off the couch, her hat off the hook by the door, and whipped out, locking up behind herself. Two quick knocks, then she heard him say, "Come on in, Shawn."

She opened the door and stepped in, eyes wide and excited. "I brought you something, motorcycle man!"

"Oh yeah?" Cory said, looking back over his shoulder from the couch. "What's that?"

Shawn held up a bottle of bourbon. "Do you like bourbon?"

"I don't know how to answer that. I have a love-hate relationship with it," said Cory, getting serious.

"Oh, no. I'm sorry. I can go grab the vodka," she said, pointing toward the door.

Cory stood up and turned to face her. "I love bourbon. And I hate myself when I drink it."

Shawn scoffed. "Okay. What's that mean, silly man? Do you want some or not?"

He came around the couch and took the bottle from her, inspecting the label. "Yes, Shawn. I want some bourbon. Are you going to drink some with me?" he said. He put his hand on the bottle, his bottom two fingers touching her own, stepping close enough to kiss her. He looked down at her. She stared right back up at him, feeling a little weak in the knees.

She swallowed and breathed in deeply. What was his game here?

"Do you like Etta James?"

"Mmhmm," she hummed, nodding at him.

Cory reached into his back pocket and pulled out a remote and pointed it at the stereo behind him without ever breaking eye contact. And of course, the stereo clicked on, and of course, Etta James was singing about the man she loves. *How the hell do people do that? How do they click one button and have a stereo turn on to the song they want?* Shawn swallowed again. She was getting butterflies in her stomach. His standing this close to her and just looking her in the eyes was really turning her on. He reached back with his right hand and took her by the waist. Then he started slow-dancing with her to Etta. The bourbon bottle acted as chaperon between her right and his left hand. *Oh my God.* Now she was tingling in her special place.

He tilted his head and whispered, "Love the hat." He then reached up and gently removed it, tossing it on the table behind her. Then he pulled her in very slowly, closing the gap between them. She was forced to turn her head and rest her cheek against his chest as he pulled her right up against him. His hand came up off her waist and went to the middle of her upper back, taking up a lot of the real estate there. She loved that he had big hands. It made her feel secure. She closed her eyes as they swayed back and forth to the music, the bourbon bottle all but forgotten.

They danced like this for several long minutes, covering several songs before he finally pulled away a little and took the bottle from her hand. The relief of suddenly being short the weight of it was remarkable. She had not realized it was so heavy, but now that it was gone, she could feel it in her wrist. Cory went to the small kitchen and pulled two old-fashioned glasses from his cabinet, then poured a couple of fingers of bourbon into each. Shawn stood catching her breath. She felt warm in certain places of her body. She felt like she was sweating in others, but she wasn't. She shook her head. *Oh my God. He could have every bit of me tonight if he just asked for it.*

When she was finally able to break free of her statuesque enchantment, she turned and joined him in the kitchen. Cory handed her a glass. They clinked them together then sipped from them. The bourbon burned her from the inside, supplementing the burn she was already feeling in her loins. She couldn't take her eyes off him, either.

"So how long have you been riding motorcycles, Hunter?" she asked.

He chuckled and took another sip. "I hope you don't mind if I drink your bourbon tonight."

She shook her head, smiling. "That's why I brought it, goof ball."

"No. I mean, like all of it. I can't really stop once I start."

Shawn shrugged and made an *oh-well* face.

He licked his teeth and said, "Since I was about ten. My pop bought me a dirt bike. I transitioned to street bikes in my twenties. I've been on them ever since. I love the high."

"Why do you live here, Cory?" Shawn asked, shaking her head.

"What do you mean?" he said, frowning and smiling at the same time. He took another sip.

"You can clearly afford to live anywhere you want. Why here?"

He shook his head and looked into the room over the bar, then leaned on the counter, setting the glass down and crossing his arms. "Really, I like the simplicity of apartment living. I'm not a big 'things' guy. I don't need a lot of 'things'. But I love my Jeep and I love my motorcycle. I don't have to mow a yard. It's cheap."

Shawn was staring at him as he spoke, trying not to be distracted by this sudden attraction she had found.

He returned his eyes to hers. "I know, it sounds lazy, but I'm not. I promise." He waited for her to answer. She shook her head. "I know I'll buy a house someday. Right now, I'm throwing ninety percent of my earnings into savings, so when I'm ready, I can just pay cash for a house, retire, and never have to work again. Unless I just want to."

"Oh my God," Shawn said. "Well, just remember, I liked you before I knew you had money."

He smiled broadly. "Do you like me, Shawn?"

She nodded, sipping from her whiskey glass.

"I caught your look today. When Catherine called you my girlfriend. It looked like you looked at me and gave me approval to go with it."

"That's exactly what I did, Cory," she said, reaching out and putting her hand on his arm. "Which is why it's okay for you to call me your girlfriend. Because you can obviously read me."

He nodded, pursing his lips. "Well, then I guess you're my girlfriend?"

"Only if you're my boyfriend."

He chuckled and raised his glass to his lips. She stopped his arm with her other hand. "No. That's not funny. I'm not being cute."

Cory's eyes met hers again and the smile fell from his face. He swallowed. "What?"

"You have to be my boyfriend. If I'm gonna be your girlfriend, you have to be mine. Mine," she said, pointing her thumb against her chest. "All mine."

After a long moment of staring at her, glass suspended a few inches from his mouth, he swallowed and nodded. "Yeah. Of course. I'm a one-at-a-time guy anyway."

# Three

It was Wednesday morning and Shawn was back in the office. She had already caught up on all the emails from her day off, and had returned two phone calls to clients. Now she was poring through lines of code, her face only a foot-and-a-half from the screen. The screen was giant, as far as computer monitors went. A thirty-two-inch curved panel that blocked out almost everything else in her vision whenever she sat this close. The software she used to edit code was language-based, and color-coded the different syntax for convenience. It made coding a lot easier. If something was gray in color, it meant the tag had either not been closed correctly, or there was some other error in the syntax. This saved potentially hours of extra staring at the screen, and thus, her eyes as well.

Every line she scrolled brought her closer to the truth. She knew all it took was one tiny misplaced apostrophe to screw up a whole application. She had been scanning the lines for almost an hour, continually having to blink her eyes and refocus, when Sameer knocked on her doorjamb.

"Hello, Miss Marcy," he said. Back to that again. She rolled her eyes, aware that he couldn't see them from his angle by the door.

"Just a sec," she said, holding up the index finger of her left hand. She scrolled on with her right hand on the mouse. "I am sooo close to finding this booger," she added after a minute, drawing out the words. She finally got to a section of code six inches tall on her monitor that was all gray. "Annnnnd, I got it." She highlighted it with the mouse and pressed CTRL and C on her keyboard. Transferred the block to a new page and zoomed in, so the font stood a half-inch tall on each line. Now she could dissect the code without squinting, and find the error pretty easily. And since it was lent to a new page, when she made the change and saved, it would update the code on the original block. Upload to the production server, then she was done.

Shawn spun in her chair, putting her hands in her lap. "What's up, boss?"

"Good morning. I was wondering if you had spent any time thinking about the project offer," said Sameer, putting his hands in his pockets as he leaned against the door.

She shook her head. "To be honest, no, I haven't. I haven't thought about it since I left here yesterday. I told you I would need some time though." She tilted her head back and forth, rubbing her neck. "How quickly do you need an answer?"

"I am hoping to start next week. So I am needing an answer by today, Miss Marcy. I am sorry."

"Today?" she said, incredulous. "Well, then I'll have to say no! This is a serious obstacle for me."

"Okay, this is fair," he said, nodding. "But do you know that there is a stipend if you join me on this?"

Shawn was forcing a smile, just to be polite. She took a deep breath and said, "What kind of stipend? Look, Sameer, this can't be all about money. Okay? I seriously have a really hard time with-"

He cut her off with a finger over his lips, stepping forward. "Shhh! Please, do not speak it aloud," he said, holding his hands up in front of him.

"Yeah. Sorry. Almost forgot," said Shawn. She wanted to finish telling him that it wasn't anything against him, but that she didn't think she could ever get comfortable being around death. Or dead people, specifically. But he spoke again.

"I am willing to double your salary. One part for your current job, one part for the other."

Her heart stopped in her chest momentarily. *Holy smokes! Double?* Her mind instantly started going over what that meant. The ramifications of an instantly doubled salary. Shawn blinked and furled her mouth, looking at him from the sides of her eyes. "Are you serious?"

Sameer nodded, but didn't say anything. He was still standing a couple of feet in front of her, but had returned his hands to his pockets. He now turned and gently pushed her office door closed, then came and squatted next to her, his arm resting on the edge of the desk. She sat in her office chair, hands in her lap, staring down at him with wonder in her eyes. He definitely had her attention.

"Listen, Miss Marcy. Shawn. We can make this as easy as you want to. You do not have to be diving right in to the full scale of the project."

She was shaking her head. He closed his eyes and nodded. He knew what she was about to ask.

"I am not expecting you to overcome your 'demons' over night. And if you need breaks or breathings… Breathings… How do you say-"

"Breathers?"

"Yes, breathers. Then you are always welcome to take them. I am not ever wanting you to be uncomfortable."

Shawn stared at him for a long time, chewing her lip. This changed things. Much as she might say it couldn't be 'all about the money', this put her in a completely different playing field. That amount of money might make it worth the stress and the fear of working with the dead – of facing her demons. One thing was for sure: she was certainly not willing to turn it down now just on general principle alone. She looked down and noticed that her hands were trembling slightly. Sameer reached over and put one of his hands over both of hers. She looked up at him. He was smiling at her.

"Please. Consider it."

Shawn nodded. Then she nodded again. When Sameer was gone, she blew air out with puffed cheeks, shaking her head. The money was very attractive. Though she was not typically driven by money alone, when one started considering a windfall such as this, it was hard to sneeze at it. She was getting by so comfortably right now, not really wanting for anything, that she could effectively just start funneling the new amount directly into savings and never feel it. And if she didn't put the whole amount, but seventy or eighty percent, she could still do the same with the added benefit of paying off some debt in a very rapid time frame.

She didn't have a lot of debt. Just a Macy's card she couldn't quit using, no matter how hard she tried, and her Jeep payment. Vehicles were damn expensive these days. And even stretching the note to seventy-two months had only brought it down to a barely-manageable amount. With double-sized paychecks, she could pay it off in a few months. Holy cow. And what was to stop her from taking the job and just trying it out? If it didn't work, surely she would be able to back out. Right? Sameer was a pretty good guy. He would surely understand if she just couldn't make it work. She could give it the ol' college try and if it didn't work, or she was just too freaked out, then she could tell him, 'Look. Sorry, I gave it a shot, but I can't do it.'

But he had also said he was willing to work with her sensitivity. To help her acclimate. That was fair. More than fair, actually. He didn't expect her to come right in and get to work on a dead body. That thought caused her to suck in a quick breath. She closed her eyes though, and worked through it. She might could do this. She knew she was strong in other areas. Why couldn't she get stronger in this one? Anything was possible. And with a whole bunch of extra money in her pocket, she might could get used to anything. That much money would buy a lot of whiskey. Or weed. Whatever it took to calm her nerves on bad days. She found herself nodding as she returned her hands to the keyboard and mouse.

She reopened the page she had been working on and almost instantly saw it. The very first character, a greater-than sign, should have been a less-than. That was it. That had caused an entire section of code to turn gray. Everything in the code from that typo up to the next less-than sign on the page had been affected. She swapped it for the correct character and hit CTRL and S. The document saved, then the window closed. Back on the original page, she saw all the lines of syntax change to their appropriate colors. Bingo. Done. Shawn wished they could all be that easy.

Now it was Shawn's turn to knock on Sameer's office door. She had spent the last hour and a half browsing the internet, not quite paying attention to the videos she was watching, just wasting time and thinking. It was honestly the most she had thought about the offer since he had made it. And she didn't want to be shallow, but it kept coming back to the dollar signs. Was that shallow? She wanted so badly to call her mom and ask her for advice. But there was just no way she could ever talk to her mother about this without spilling what the project was about. And she knew darn well that mom wouldn't be able to keep the secret. She would be on the phone with her best friend, Dorothy, as soon as Shawn had hung up with her. And she obviously couldn't tell Cory. Well, not obviously. He might be a better candidate for spilling the secret – were she going to share it at all – than anyone. Shawn thought she could trust him. That wasn't the problem. It was just that… Well, it was that he… Shawn realized there was no logical reason she couldn't tell him. Except for the fact that she cherished the value of her integrity. Mental health would have to come first though. If she started developing traumatic stress from this, then she would have to talk to someone. And she knew Sameer was not going to pay for a therapist. Not for this. She would have to take that matter into her own hands. For now, though, she was going to give it a fair shot without thinking of all the negatives up front. Without dwelling on the 'creep factor'. And who knew? Maybe it wouldn't be so bad. She actually smirked at that thought.

Now, here she stood in Sameer's doorway. He leaned back in his office chair and put his elbows on the armrests, steepling his fingers beneath his chin. "Hello, Shawn. So you are ready to get started?"

A smile crept across her face. That was one thing she liked about Sameer. He could read people really well. She nodded. Then Sameer nodded, smiling himself, and offered her the chair on the other side of his desk. He leaned over and opened the bottom drawer to the cabinet on his left and pulled out a file, slapping it down on the desk. He opened it and flipped through the pages until he found what he wanted, then slid a couple of papers out.

"These are standard non-disclosure agreements. They are very necessary for the safety of this project. Please sign them when you have read through them. Feel free to take your time," he said.

Shawn glanced through them and looked at him. "You're sure you want me on this, Sameer? Jeremy out there could probably be a lot more help."

Sameer lifted his chin. "How so, Shawn?"

"Well, for one, he's bigger than I am. Strong. He's a dude. If you ever needed help lifting a…" she paused and swallowed. Sighed. "A, you know, a body. If you ever need to lift a body up onto the table or something…"

Sameer nodded slowly. "Yes. This is what I was thinking, too. That is why he has already signed the NDAs. He will be joining us too."

Shawn was a little shocked, having thought she was the only one Sameer had said he could trust. Maybe she had misheard him. Was this a little tinge of jealousy she was feeling? Here, she had been ready to turn down the offer and walk away, and now she was jealous to find she wasn't the only one who had accepted it? What was wrong with her?

"Oh. Well, yeah. That's good then," she said. And she felt like she meant it. Now that she thought about it, the physical benefits of having another man in the room were obvious. But it also gave her someone else she could talk to about it if she ever needed to. This could be better than she thought. Plus, it might take some of the pressure off of her, if she was needing to move a little more slowly than Sameer was willing to wait. And after just that long, she found she had flipped on it. This would make things a lot better. Jeremy was a big teddy bear of a guy. A tall, jolly fellow with a thick beard and a huge smile. He was always friendly and fun, and always had that smile on his face. What little professional interaction Shawn had actually shared with him, Jeremy had proven to be quite intelligent, too.

On a couple of occasions, she had needed help with a web application – when she came up with an idea, for instance, that she had never seen done before – and he had been able to spit out the code for it while she stood there and waited. Not the entire code, obviously, but a framework that she could fill in with details. That was pretty insane. So having him on this project would be nothing but a benefit, as far as she could see.

She dropped the papers on the desk and grabbed a pen from the cup Sameer kept on the desk, and signed them. When she handed them back to him, he slipped them into another folder and stacked them neatly to the side. Then a thought occurred to Shawn. If Jeremy was so brilliant, and so physically strong, then what did Sameer need Shawn for? What particular talent could she bring to the project that wasn't already covered? She decided to wait to ask him though. Sameer had his reasons, and they would probably reveal themselves to her before too long anyway.

"Shall we go take another tour then, Shawn?"

They stood in the main operating room. Though the white letter on the window read 'D', Sameer called it the

Lab. Shawn could think of other things that more aptly went after the D. She, of course, kept her comments to herself. Sameer wheeled a tall cart away from the wall so they could stand close to it. It was a machine of some sort on a single steel pole that in turn was mounted to a steel plate that had six casters on the bottom of it. The top piece – the actual gadget itself – was covered in a semi-translucent plastic cover that felt like a mixture of nylon and wax. It was very satisfying to the touch to Shawn, who was a very tactile person. She loved the feel of different textures, and often bought purses based not on style or color, but texture. Thus when she would walk through the aisles of a store, or through a mall, her fingers would constantly be rubbing it.

Sameer pulled off the cover and revealed a very simple looking machine, if not a little out of date. It looked like it might have been made in the nineties. The distinct difference, Shawn thought, between an electronic device made in the eighties and one made in the nineties, was that they looked essentially the same. But in the nineties they figured out how to make them look a little smoother. The eighties pieces looked like they just threw some shit together because it worked, and would worry about presentation later. In the nineties, to be precise.

It had several buttons on it: flow, meter, speed, volume and a few others. There was a square screen marked around its edges with tiny gray numbers and letters. It had a thick hose hanging from its back side that ended in a series of small tubes, each with a needle on its end. This part looked someone like a jellyfish.

"This is the autotransfusion machine," Sameer said, patting the top of it like a favorite child. "This is what pumps blood through the brain to bring it life."

Shawn was chewing on her jaw, staring at the machine as he spoke, determined not to let that statement get past her defenses and into her thoughts where it would create its own ideas about how this would look.

"There are two major arteries which bring blood to the brain. These are the internal carotid artery and the vertebral artery. They branch off inside the brain and send blood to all of the parts. All we do is plug this machine into the arteries at the base of the neck," Sameer said, holding up the two needles that had blue bands around their bases. "The rest of the needles go elsewhere, and bring the blood back to the machine. Since we will not be using heart and lung function, we have to clean the blood and inject fresh oxygen into it as it is recirculating."

Shawn nodded. "With you so far," she said, and actually felt a tinge of excitement. The subject matter notwithstanding, she was so close to the edge of something scientifically magnificent that its monumental importance in her life could not be ignored. Whether it creeped her out or not, she would get to be part of something no one had ever done before. Or at least not that she had heard about. Maybe it had been tried for decades, but no one had gotten it to work. *Or maybe they had...*

He hung the jellyfish back on its hook so that the needles didn't touch the ground. Shawn noticed they were capped with clear covers. Then he put the cover back on the machine and wheeled the stand back out of the way. "Now," he said, putting his palms together in front of his chest. "Here is where you come in. We are injecting nanobots into the brain via the bloodstream."

Shawn's eyes widened. Her mind went to images of *Fantastic Voyage*, the movie from the mid-sixties, where people were shrunken to microscopic size and injected into a man's bloodstream. Surely that wasn't what Sameer was talking about though.

"These nanobots will attach themselves to parts of the brain we would like to be stimulating. We can send electrical impulses to these parts and activate motor functionality," Sameer said.

"Like talking."

"Sure. Like talking."

Shawn tilted her head, looking at him through squinted and serious eyes. "Well that isn't so creepy. That's science."

"Yes, it is very much science. What were you expecting, Shawn?"

She stood there looking at him for a long moment. "I guess I don't know. But that takes a lot of the creep-factor out of it for me. Like, we're energizing parts of the brain to come alive. So it's kind of like he's not really being woken from the dead. We're just using parts of his brain to do things."

Sameer bounced his head around a little, holding his palms up. "Yes, this can be somewhat true. If you want to think of it like that, it might help you."

"So what did you mean by 'this is where I come in'?"

"You will write the program that controls the bots."

"Oh my God," Shawn said, as her entire body went over in chills. These were the good kind though. These were the kind you got when you were filled with excited. And just like that, her entire perspective on the project went to complete and total enthusiasm.

The nanobot penning trap was fascinating to Shawn. They were held in a large rectangular box that had a solid white top, steel around the edges. It looked much like an old-fashioned x-ray viewing board, where the white would light up to shine through the film. But this white lit up like a monitor. One could literally control the bots from it. He had turned it on and shown her how easy it was to use. The bots were represented by pixel-size dots on the screen, and he could lasso in a few thousand of them by dragging his finger across the screen, then tapping a button. That group suddenly changed to blue and developed a line around it. He had then done the same thing with another group and it changed to red. Then he could move the group with a joystick-like set of keys that had appeared on the screen. It seemed pretty rudimentary, but he assured her the control system she would be using was much more like a computer. This was just the control built into the trap itself. "And," he had said, "of course the bots don't actually change color."

Duh.

Shawn had managed to keep from rolling her eyes. She had to humor him. This was fantastic science. Cutting-edge technology would be at her fingertips. And all the other tech-jargon cliches she could think of. Though most of the code had been installed natively, she could adapt it to fit their specific needs. The excitement of working with such fascinating technology was something about which she would not be able to keep quiet. Shawn would definitely be telling Cory about getting to work with nanobots. Maybe even her dad.

Sameer showed her a few other instruments that were not quite as critical to the reanimation exercise, but had other importance. The one that held the biggest creep-factor for her was the large helmet that felt like it weighed as much as a car. He said it was filled with electromagnets. Were something to go wrong, this helmet could be clamped around the subject's head and turned on. When the magnets were energized, they would instantaneously disable all the nanobots. This was a last-resort device, Sameer had said. And he had stressed it by saying it more than once. He obviously did not want to have to use it. Nanobots were apparently very expensive, and in somewhat limited supply. They would be working with a few thousand on each project, and only had a few hundred thousand.

"So you're planning to get started next week?" Shawn asked.

"Yes. This is when our first subject will be arriving," said Sameer. He was leaning back against a counter top with his arms crossed.

"Ah. So we'll be calling them subjects," Shawn said, standing directly across the room from him. The death bed, as she had come to think of it almost immediately, was right between them. Maybe anti-death bed would be more appropriate... Assuming they had success.

"Yes, I am thinking this is more professional then calling them bodies or cadavers."

Shawn nodded, making a *duh* face. "Yes. Of course. So do we know anything about our first... subject?"

"Yes, of course," said Sameer. He pulled his phone from his pocket and thumbed through it momentarily, then slid the phone across the table to her. She picked it up and saw an *app* of all things, with a man's face in a thumbnail image at the upper right. It listed the man's vitals and his cause and time of death (cardiac arrest, this morning) and a few other details. Not his name though.

"You have a freakin' app for dead people?" Shawn said. Part of her wanted to laugh. The other, and she'd like to think the better part, was completely incredulous. *A fucking app?*

"Yes. Why is this shocking, Shawn?"

All she could do was shake her head, her mouth agape. She had no words.

"It is how they check out bodies – subjects – from the university. It is how we will be selecting our subjects because we can choose just the right one."

"How many of them are there? I mean, to choose from?" Shawn said.

"Not very many. We are being lucky with this one being a heart attack. But the person who dies must have been listed as wanting to donate his or her body to medical science. Not very many people are doing this."

Shawn shook her head again. "So we get him next week?"

Sameer nodded, collecting his phone from the table and stepping back to lean against the counter again. "They must have the funeral and release him through the proper channels before we can use him."

Shawn put a hand over her mouth, her eyes still wide. The reality of this whole thing had still not set in yet, and thinking now of this 'subject' she realized they would be dealing with an actual human being. A recently deceased man. He would be having a funeral. His loved ones knew, presumably, that he had donated his body to science. But did they know what BlueBird would be doing with him? For God's sake, this was insane. She tried to put herself in the shoes of this man's wife – assuming, of course, he had had one – and wonder how she would react if she found out a company was trying to reanimate her dead husband's body. And here came the goose flesh. She shivered and stood up straight in an effort to try to mask it. She had been doing so well and not letting her mind wander.

"What the heck do we do with him when we're done using him?" she asked.

"We send him back."

"Okay, I guess I have a lot to learn about this," she said, running her hand up to the back of her head, where she ran her fingers into her hair at the base of her skull.

"Yes, Shawn. But these are logistical details you won't necessarily need to be knowing if you would rather not."

She shrugged. "Yeah. Maybe. Either way. Can I scroll through the list of the subjects they have?"

"No, this is not how it works. We have filled out certain criteria for these subjects. When the office gets one that matches our request, they alert us and send us the subject's details, as you are seeing in the app."

Shawn nodded, understanding.

"I had to sign him out, so that we get to have him before another company is beating us to him."

*Oh my God. This keeps getting uglier!* Shawn was growing more disillusioned by the industry by the minute. These were human beings, for God's sake! Well, the tense of that statement seemed to be the key word. *Were.* Now they were science experiments. Lab rats.

"Okay, so I guess we need to discuss work schedule and whatnot. This will be a second job, right? What kind of hours do you expect me to work? And when do I start? I guess I should get started coding the nanobots, huh? This is all a little overwhelming, to be honest."

"We start small, Shawn. This is not to overwhelm you. We will first be infusing the brain with oxygen-rich blood for forty-eight hours. Then we will inject the bots."

Shawn was nodding. "And when do we bring in Jeremy? Or you, I guess. When do *you* bring in Jeremy?"

"Jeremy will be playing very little role in the lab, Shawn. His work is mostly on the outside. He mapped out the entire brain for the system. He is uploading the master index to the nanobot colony so that they can find their way to the proper parts to stimulate our desired functions."

"God, this is awesome," Shawn said under her breath. "Really incredible."

"I do not expect you to work double the job, Shawn. This will be your primary job. But you can see now why I hired you."

"Wait. What?" Shawn said. She didn't know whether or not she should be offended. This was the reason he had hired her? "What would you have done if I didn't sign onto the project?"

"Then you would still fix client code errors. This is like our business front. Though what we are doing is not illegal, it can kind of look like the same setup as an illegal front. You see? I hire people for talents and get to know them to see if I can trust them to see the secret project."

"Wait. Okay, so the whole business is a front? What the heck does Jeremy do?"

"Jeremy is a code operator as well. But more on the application programming side. He works with high-tech machinery."

Shawn shook her head. "How the hell did he map out the brain then?"

"He was brain surgeon in his previous career field. He lost his license to practice. But his skill is still valuable, as you can see."

"Incredible."

"So you will still answer customer calls for your support job. But we are not expanding the client base, Shawn. You should not ever have too much work. I hope this is acceptable to you," said Sameer.

"You're asking if I find it acceptable that you hired me to do very little work unless I join your secret project."

"Yes," he said, nodding. "This is why you must always work in the office instead of working from home."

"I see." Shawn took a deep breath and thought for a moment. There was really nothing to think about. It wasn't insulting, as such. It was a little off-putting at first, but really, there was nothing inherently offensive about it. If she had not decided to join the project, she would still make the original salary, and would never have much work to do. What she had assumed would be a growing business that would finally overwhelm her and force Sameer to hire more support engineers like her was actually just there to give him the pretty office space. Appearance was everything. She supposed she could get used to it either way. She shook her head, furling her mouth. "Whatever. I don't think it matters. I mean, I'm fine with it. I'm happy either way."

Sameer nodded, a very faint smile just showing itself. He stepped forward. Shawn stepped forward. They shook hands over the death bed. "Good. Welcome, Shawn."

Back at her apartment, Shawn turned on the shower and undressed, walking around the place in the nude while she put things away and waited for the bathroom to get steamy. Sameer had sent her home with a couple of books on the human brain and the nervous system. They looked like medical texts from a brain surgeon's bookshelf. Well, technically, that's exactly what they were. She wasn't sure why he had given them to her, and was hoping she wouldn't actually have to read them. Just thumbing through and glancing at captions and select paragraphs, she could tell the subject matter was a little over her head. A lot, in fact.

She popped a TV dinner in the microwave and wondered what Cory would be doing for dinner. If she had gotten his number, she could text him and ask him. There was something attractive about having not yet traded numbers though. This way, when they wanted to talk, they had to see each other. Was that weird? She shrugged to herself. Maybe. But it was sexy too. And sweet. It made her look forward to coming home so she could sneak across the breezeway and check up on him. They had not spent the night together yet, but she reckoned that would come in due time. Hell, she was already calling him her boyfriend. Well, she was *about to start* calling him that. She hadn't actually said it to anyone yet. The thought gave her a little thrill in her belly, where it felt good. And there was a point in favor of trading numbers: she could put him in her phone as BOYFRIEND ♥ and smile every time he called her.

She tossed the phone on the couch and stepped into a bathroom so full of steam she almost couldn't see the shower. This brought a smile to her face. Just the way she liked it. She brushed her teeth with a toothbrush and paste she kept in the shower in a little cup above the faucet, and let the scalding water run down her hair onto her back.

When she finally came out, hair and body wrapped in separate towels, she collected her meal from the microwave and peeled off the plastic. It had cooled while she was in the shower, so she could dig right in without burning the roof of her mouth. She stood in the kitchen forking out pieces of Salisbury steak and powdery potatoes while she scrolled through OuterCircle with her other hand on her phone. Same bullshit, different day.

A knock at her door made her jump. "Just a minute!" she shouted. *Oh my God.* Obviously, there was only one person it could be, but she was in no way presentable yet. She went to the door and opened it a few inches. "Hey, boyfriend!" she said, smiling. Cory stepped back and covered his heart with his hand, smiling widely.

"Hey, Shawn," he said. "If I'm still the boyfriend, then I get a kiss, right?"

"Well, I'm eating, so you'll have to wait until I finish so I can brush my teeth."

He looked her up and down. Then he pushed the door open and stepped up to her. She had just enough time to mutter an "Oh!" before he had her in his arms, kissing her full on the mouth. Her belly lit up with a nice fire. When he let her go, he stepped back and saluted her with a finger, before turning on his heel and heading for his own apartment.

"Well, that was nice," she said to herself as she closed the door, her entire face feeling like it was involved in the smile she had going. She finished her dinner then dried her hair so it wouldn't look frizzy in the morning, then threw on some pajamas and her boater hat. She stood with her back to the door while she looked around the apartment, wondering what she was missing. *Phone, keys, vodka...* Oh, shit! She set everything down on the floor and dashed to the bathroom to brush her teeth.


Cory yelled through the door for her to come in. Shawn came in, arms wrapped round her stash, smiling widely at the man on the couch. "Boy, you surprised me with that nice kiss!"

"Yeah, I wasn't ready to take no for an answer. Teeth brushed or not," he said. After a second, he frowned, then added, "You're not one of those, are you? Who has to brush her teeth every time we're gonna kiss?"

Shawn looked up at the ceiling, pursing her lips.

"Oh, God. So anyway, when are we going to start Seinfelding it?"

"What's that mean?" she said, rounding the couch and dropping into her favorite spot.

"You know how in Seinfeld, all his friends always pop in without knocking?"

"Yeah, but they had to be rung up first. So he knew they were coming," Shawn said.

"Not Kramer," Cory said, holding up a corrective finger.

"Oh. Yeah. Him. So you want me to just start walking in whenever I want?"

Cory shrugged. "I think I could get used to it pretty quick."

"I don't think I'm there yet at my place. I keep my door locked, anyway. I'd have to give you a key. And my momma says I have to make sure you're not an axe-murderer first."

He raised his chin. "Ah. Is a machete-murderer okay? A piano-wire strangler?"

Shawn leaned over the corners of the couches and kissed him, laughing.

As she sat back down, she crossed her legs, Indian-style. "So, listen. I have some good news."

"What, you've figured out that I'm not a murderer?" said Cory.

"Ha. You wish," she said, fake-smiling at him. "I got a raise today."

"Well, shit yeah! That's bad ass. We should toast to this," he said, grabbing her vodka bottle off the table.

"Oh. Yeah. Glasses. Shoot," she said, and hopped up, bounding over the arm of the couch to run to the kitchen. When she got back, she went the way she had come, then handed him the glasses. He filled them and handed her one.

"Cheers!" she said. They clinked them and took a sip.

"So I'm guessing it was a good percentage," Cory said, holding a hand out, palm up.

"Yeah, you could say that," she said, trying not to smirk too much.

"Okay," he said, nodding, "what percentage?"

"Try a hundred."

He frowned. "A hundred percent raise?" He shook his head. "What the fuck? Dude doubled your salary?"

She nodded slowly, letting her smile show itself fully.

Cory held that hand out again. "You're going to have to tell me about this. How does one get a hundred-percent merit increase? Unless you weren't making enough to begin with…"

"Nope. I was making great money. Now I'm making double-great money." She sighed and twisted her mouth. "I took this extra job. This one that's been freaking me out lately. And check this out: I don't have to work double shifts or anything. In fact, I have to prioritize this new project as my main job."

"And you're going to tell me that you can't tell me about it, right? Like some CIA agent shit or something?"

Shawn shrugged and took a swig of the plain liquor.

"Wait. It was freaking you out? All that talk about death… Are you a mortician now?"

"Let's just say yes. But here's the exciting part – the part I planned on telling you. I don't care what anyone says, this is too cool and I have to talk about it," she said, holding her hands up in front of her. "I get to work with nanotechnology."

Cory didn't say anything. Instead, he just stared at her in wide-eyed amazement. Shawn could tell he was mulling over in his head what could possibly link death and nanotech together. He might get it eventually, too.

Shawn nodded again. "Yeah. Seriously. Nanobots. I get to write code that controls them!" she squealed and clapped her hands together quickly, bouncing on her rump.

"Okay," Cory said, nodding. "Okay. Well, congratulations on that. That sounds effing amazing."

He held his drink up to her again. She clinked it again, then winked at him.

"So, can I ask you a personal question, Shawn?"

"Of course. What's up?" she asked.

"Did you brush your teeth before you came over?"

She frowned and twisted her head. "Yes. Of course. Why?"

"Because I'm going to need more of those kisses."

Shawn smiled widely at him, then set her glass on the table. She climbed on top of him, straddling his legs on the couch and putting her hands on his shoulders. Then she pulled her hair back behind her ears and tightened her hat on her head and leaned in for the long kiss.

When they finally came up for air, she sat up straight, hands on her thighs and said, "Cory, I really appreciate how much of a gentleman you've been being." He nodded slowly, looking at her with curious eyes. "I just mean you're letting me take my time with this. Thank you for not trying to touch me yet."

He breathed in deeply and made a face that spoke of exasperation. "Well, that's getting kind of hard, to be honest. But yeah, I understand. I've been waiting until you tell me you're ready."

"Yes. Thank you for that. It'll happen soon, I'm betting. I won't be able to resist." She sat staring at him for a moment. "I hope you know, it turns me on as much as it does you." He looked down at her chest briefly, then back up to her eyes. She looked down herself and noticed why he had made the obvious glance. Her nipples were poking through the pajama shirt like two little erasers. "Yeah. See?" she said, reaching up and grabbing them with her whole hands. "Anyway, thank you. It means a lot to me."

"You're welcome, Shawn. You're worth the wait."

This made her smile. "Aww! That's so sweet. Okay, I'll let you touch 'em through the shirt just for that." Then she leaned down to kiss him again, and said, with her lips against his, "Just this one time."

She could feel him smile, but he made no move to touch her. So she reached down and pulled his hands up to her chest. She guided his large hands in exactly the manner in which she wished to be touched. She didn't fill his hands. Not even close. They covered her entire chest, but it felt like heaven. She had not been touched in a long time. She hoped it felt as good to him as it did to her. This was her test, to see if her breasts were big enough for him. Though she wasn't sure he would pull his hands away and say anything as obvious as 'that's it?' or some other comment. But this was it. Shawn would know when she stopped him.

The kiss was, obviously, more passionate and intense than their others had been thus far. A lot heavier breathing and deeper diving with the lips and tongues. They were both feeling it, and of that she was sure. His hands were now working without her guidance. He had them on her rib cage, thumbs moving up and down across her breasts. And while it wasn't hurting her, it wasn't the softest of touches. Cory was putting a little pressure against them as his thumbs trekked up and down, up and down. It was pure ecstasy. If she were to let him keep it up too much longer, there would be no turning back. Her nipples felt like burning coals.

Shawn finally sat up, breaking the kiss. He stopped his motion, but his hands lingered a moment longer. She swallowed and took her hat off, then ran her hair back with both hands. And he finally took his off of her. "Cory, are they big enough for you?"

Cory didn't frown. He tilted his hand and stared at her. It was a different look. An inquisitive gaze, but not a frown. "Yes, Shawn. They feel absolutely perfect. I can't tell you how bad I want them in my mouth right now."

She tilted her own head now, staring intently into those bright blue eyes. "Yes, you can."

Now he did frown. "Say again?"

"You said you can't tell me. Yes. You can."

He breathed in deeply and swallowed. He was being so good. Maybe her little reward had been a bad idea after all.

"Okay, I won't make you tell me. Why don't you show me instead," Shawn said, reaching up and unbuttoning her pajama top. When she got three buttons undone, she leaned forward and pulled his face into her. He took them into his mouth, one at a time while she leaned her head back and closed her eyes. If his touch had felt like ecstasy, then what was this? This was rocket fuel. She was in complete euphoria now. *My God, this was a terrible idea.* She shook her head and pulled back, rolling her eyes.

"I'm sorry, Cory. I, uh…" she started.

"It's completely fine, Shawn. I understand. No pressure at all," Cory said. His hands were on her hips now. "I can take care of myself later."

"No, you didn't let me finish. I was going to say you're going to have to have sex with me now. I hope you're okay with that."

# Four

Thousands of lines of code awaited review. It wasn't quite accurate to say it was a blank slate, because there was code there already. But the nanobot manufacturers had embedded them with basic code, called HiveMind that enabled them to be controlled at all. Together in groups of as few as four, they were able to be controlled with a wireless communication protocol not unlike Bluetooth. Far simpler and less weighty, it allowed them to communicate between the controller and the bots, as well as between the bots themselves. One could set about lining them all up into a column, for instance. Shawn had asked the question, 'How does this one or that one know that it's supposed to be in column one, row one instead of, say, column four, row twenty-nine?' Jeremy had answered her with the very simplistic response, 'HiveMind!'

The truth was that he didn't know either, because the firmware was not open-source. No one knew exactly what made them work. No one but the designers, that was. But they were able to be programmed with any number of drop-in functions that were available from the company website, and the basic behavioral software embedded from the factory *was* open-source. The difference between firmware and software was the key. So with the generic pattern software installed, they could be told to form shapes and act as individuals within the group, without necessarily having to worry about telling which one to go where. Delegation of specific tasks was left to the bots themselves, which made it far easier than having to lasso four at a time and give it a name and a function. Instead, Shawn had selected four thousand of them and had clicked on a menu option called 'Enumerate' and they had assigned themselves their own numbers. Then if told to form a square, for instance, each one would therefore know its position within. That was HiveMind.

Jeremy's mapping of the brain had been brilliantly helpful. He had over a hundred functions labeled and numbered in menus. Some others beyond the initial hundred or so were labeled with EXP- meaning it was an experimental function. 'EXP-Distill' was one. Another, in the experimental section, but not prefaced with the EXP was called 'Kick.bat'. Interesting. She had no idea what most of them meant, but assumed they were probably proprietary and would never get used. Like the bloatware that came installed on a new computer. While interesting, most were probably not useful for what they would be doing. Which, Shawn had to admit, she still wasn't even sure of herself. All she knew was they were attempting to reanimate a human. She couldn't even say body, because she didn't know how much of the body was wanted. She assumed they would start with the face. But the mapping program Jeremy had coded, affectionately called BotMap, made assigning functions to the bots a cinch. In practice, then, if Shawn wanted to have the subject blink his eyes, she could literally select a menu option from a drop-down list, and assign it to the bots. The bots themselves would then determine which group got the designation. By Jeremy's explanation, these bots would then know which path to take through the blood vessels to get to the part of the brain that controlled that function, and attach themselves to the nerve root. Then by rearranging themselves within the quad-group, they would create an electrical shock so tiny it replicated the firing of a synapse. This was fantastic technology she had her hands on, and found herself with mouth gaping open at several points during the introduction from Jeremy. It furthermore rendered the books Sameer had lent her completely useless. Jeremy had taken her need to know the brain right out of the equation. He had literally done all the hard work.

So she sat staring at her computer screen playing with the bot controller. Since the steel-edged x-ray box she had seen yesterday was physically wired into the company network, she could control it from her desk back in the regular office. This is where she would do all her work on the code. When she had learned this detail she had squealed with joy, having previously believed she would have to sit in that spooky lab to do her hours and hours of line-combing.

Shawn had already gotten the hang of quickly controlling multiple groups of the nanobots to do certain things, just based off the HiveMind options alone. She could have them bundle in groups of a hundred or more and physically light up, as they formed tiny but visible light emitting diodes. She had laughed out loud when she stumbled onto that function by accident and seen it happen. The monitor on her screen had flashed, showing her real-time that they had indeed lit up briefly. And she was getting paid for this? Holy cow! Had she known from the beginning that her job would mostly involve coding – which she was already doing anyway – she would have been far less reticent to accept the offer. But on the other hand, she had found herself wondering if Sameer would have offered her the large 'stipend' if he hadn't needed to. Of course, there was the redeeming fact that he had immediately gone to doubling her salary. He had not tried to negotiate by starting at the bottom of the acceptable offers list. Either way, here she was, a new day at work and a completely new project to work on.

And of course it didn't hurt that she now had a boyfriend. Jeremy had noticed, too. One of the first things he had said to her when he came and sat on an empty chair and rolled over to her desk was how she appeared to be glowing. "Someone must have gotten laid last night!" he had said, his typical grin making it hard to be offended. Not that such a comment would have offended her anyway, but she could see how the blunt, point-blank approach could turn certain corporate types the wrong way. Jeremy was hard not to like though. Just an all around good guy.

Her answer had been to raise her chin a little and smile, closing her eyes and jiggling her shoulders. It had been answer enough, because he had high-fived her. Then he'd gone right back into professional mode. "Let me show you HiveMind," he had said.

Shawn's assignment from Sameer was to get the bots ready to wake the vocal cords of the first subject and to call on several functions that would hopefully awaken some of the last memories made by the prefrontal cortex. This stimulation, along with the communications aspect of the firmware, would hopefully trigger the subject to start talking. The fact that this creeped Shawn out beyond her ability to comprehend was irrelevant. First of all, it was unlikely to work. She couldn't imagine getting results until they had been at it for many months. And they wouldn't get to keep the subject for any longer than a week. She guessed it had to do with decomposition, although Sameer had assured her the subjects would be coming to them already drained of their blood. Secondly, if it did work, she planned to be sitting at her desk and watching on the screen, the same way she had seen the success of the ad-hoc LED. Unless she was misunderstanding her role in this whole thing, she would never actually have to *see* the successes with her own eyes.

By the time she learned that she had been misunderstanding her role, she was already so deeply involved that she couldn't have turned back or backed out anyway. When she got grabbed by the science, it wrapped its intrigue around every muscle in her body. Scared or not, there was simply no way she could be talked out of continuing.

After playing with the code for several hours and honing down some functions she knew they would actually use, she thought she had a pretty good set of instructions to upload to the controller. She was getting coffee in the break room when Sameer came in and asked her how she was liking it.

"I've never seen anything so fascinating in my life, Sameer," she said. And she was happy to know she had not embellished her answer at all.

"Good. This is very good. I am happy you are enjoying it. Your part will be priceless in this. I am hoping you are knowing this, Shawn," he said.

She smiled, holding her mug up to her mouth and blowing on the black coffee. "I am happy to be a part of it. Thank you for bringing me in!"

"Yes. Of course. Do you have a moment? I want to show you something," he asked.

Shawn followed Sameer into C Room. She could see the death bed through the window in the room next door and nodded, proud at herself for not getting the creeps as she looked at it. This room was not as eerie. It was filled with shiny steel wire shelves full of support equipment. Most of it was separated into plastic bins, which were labeled with printed bar codes and titles. Sameer stopped at the back wall where, like the rooms on either side of it, there was no window. Along this wall were two giant steel boxes that looked like deep freezers. As she got closer, she realized that's exactly what they were.

Sameer was standing beside the freezer on the right, patting it like a prized possession. "This is a controlled-access freezer. No one is to open these freezers without authorization. I will be giving you an access code of your own, Shawn. But only I will ever tell you to collect something from here. This is very important, Shawn."

"Yeah, okay," she said, nodding. She stared him in the eyes, catching the gravity of his statement. What the hell did he keep in these things? Dead babies?

Sameer keyed in a six- or eight-digit code and pulled the freezer lid open. The control panel on the front next to the keypad beeped. The temperature was reading a nice balmy thirteen degrees Fahrenheit. When the steam cleared, she saw red and her heart skipped a beat. She had initially been anxious to see what was in here that was so important. Now she was rethinking that.

"Mostly bags of red blood cells," Sameer said, picking up a flat package and handing it to her.

"I didn't know you could freeze blood," she said, feeling the consistency of the plastic between her fingers. It had a satisfying feel to it.

"You can if you separate it into its components. The blood cells can be frozen for eight to ten years. Other components have to be more fresh. But these carry the oxygen. This is the most important part for what we are doing in there," Sameer said, pointing toward the Death Room. Shawn closed her eyes for a moment, telling herself that she would need to make a serious effort to stop thinking of it by that name. Thinking of it like that would eventually cause her to call it that aloud. She did not want to leave that impression on her boss. Especially not when she was being paid such a handsome salary. Part of that surely covered discretion.

He took the bag from her and returned it to its place in the freezer. "Nitrogen bottles," he said, pointing at some black canisters standing in a rack in the corner by the blood bags. "A lot of these other things are for medical purpose. Think medicine. Not strictly able to be taken by living persons, but okay to use in our situations."

She breathed in deeply. Still trying to maintain her steel. She had been doing well until he had said that. The ridiculous image of giving a dead man a Tylenol popped into her head, and the creep turned to a giggle. Thank God.

"Any questions?" he asked, putting his hand on the lid, ready to close it.

"What's in the other one?"

Sameer looked at the freezer on the left. "Mostly empty. It is to be for overflow if we need it. Emergency backup. The usual. As you see here everything we has is redundant."

Shawn nodded. "Okay, makes sense."

"One is of course always hoping not to need the backups. But I have learned this lesson the hard way by not having them before." He held his hand out toward the door and Shawn turned to leave the room.

"Was this all you wanted to show me?"

"Yes," he said. "I will not be in the office in the morning. I will need you to get a bag of blood from there and put it in this little refrigerator so that it will begin the thawing process. It will be ready by Monday this way."

"Okay," Shawn said, looking at the fridge. It looked like a normal college dorm fridge but for the keypad on the front.

"I will make your code the same for both systems."

Outside the room, he turned off the light and pulled the door closed. Shawn stopped and turned to him. "Sameer, can I ask you something?"

"Of course, Shawn," he said, nodding. He put his hands in his trouser pockets.

"Why. Why are you doing this?"

"Doing what?" he asked, raising his eyebrows.

"This. This whole thing. Why do you want to bring someone back to life?"

He smiled at her. "It is not to bring a full body back to a living state. It is to bring a brain back to a semi-conscious state for a temporary amount of time."

"Okay," she said, leaning her head forward a little. "Still. Why? What do you hope to get from it?"

"I have always been fascinated by death. I want to see what is beyond the pall. I want to know what happens after death." He shrugged. He sure looked like he was taking this lightly. "It is just an interest of mine. I am a scientist, Shawn. And I want to investigate death."

"Fair enough. A little weird," she said, putting her hand on his arm and smiling, "but I get it."

Shawn was exhausted by the time she got home that evening. She reckoned it was not so much the *amount* of code lines she had dissected. But rather, the content of the lines. It looked completely different to her eyes, and she was reading it like text from a book, lining up one with another, making sense of syntax and putting together a sensible program. It was different than the foreign gibberish that made up web applications, though it was made of the same characters. Shawn likened it to beer. Someone without the cognizance or the eloquence would say all beer tastes the same. She would say, 'No, all beer tastes like *beer*. But each style and brand has its own unique flavor notes.' One knew he was drinking beer when tasting it blind. No doubt about that. But they did not all taste the same. All code, likewise, looks like code. But this new program she was working on had its own flair and flavor. It was exciting, but it had strained her eyes in a different way than she was used to.

She had dropped on the couch as soon as she got out of the shower and laid her head against the headrest. She didn't feel like checking her social media, straining her eyes, so she just closed them and relaxed, replaying the things she had accomplished during the day. She had her body towel laid open, letting the fan cool her naked body, still red from the scalding shower. When her phone rang, she didn't even look at the screen. She just swiped her thumb across the bottom, her muscle memory putting it right where it needed to be after a hundred thousand practices.

"Hello," she said, phone resting lazily against her head.

"How's my little monarch?"

"Hey, daddy." She sighed audibly. "I am so tired. How are you?"

"Well, I'm doing what I love best, so I am well."

"Sitting on the pier, drinkin' beer. I wish I was there with you, dad."

"Me too, darlin'," said he. Shawn could picture him in his folding lawn chair sitting on the edge of their pier, staring out at the lake while the sun set. She had seen it enough times to recall it in perfect detail, the orange sun twinkling in a billion separate crystals on the water. They lived right on Lake Hamilton and he sat down their most evenings, watching the sun set and having a beer. He never had two. But he always had one. Shawn missed it like something removed from her.

There had been many boats through the years. Dad would come home with some used boat or another and would set about fixing it up. It would last a couple of years or he would just get bored of it, or it would just die… In one case Shawn remembered, one of them just sank. But he had long since given up his dream of having a running boat. Now they had the boat slip, the pier, and that's where they held their parties. In the eighties, Gavin had built a roof over the slip and it served as a party deck. Kids would jump off the edge into the lake. Now the kids were all grown up, so the adults would do the jumping.

Shawn had not been home during the whole six months she had been here, not wanting to take the weekend trip to see home. She wanted to accrue some vacation days first so she could actually stretch her legs when she got there. Not just spend a night or two. Her parents had come to see her one weekend a few months ago and had stayed one night. It was nice to see them, but she thought she might miss the house more than the people who lived there at this point.

"So I heard there might be a new dark horse in the running," he said after taking a sip of his beer.

"Well I don't know how dark he is, but he's definitely a horse," Shawn said, then slapped a hand over her mouth, eyes popping wide open. "Oh my God, dad. That came out completely wrong."

"I see," he said, giggling.

"I meant like, yes, there was indeed a running. And runnings obviously have to involve horses. I was just trying to illustrate that he wasn't a dark one."

"So you're saying he's white, then," said dad.

Shawn laughed out loud, rolling over onto her side on the couch, collapsing in the laughter. "Dad, no! God!"

"Well, I'm just trying to get it right, butterfly. You should send us a picture."

"Yes, dad. He's white. But – okay, let's just drop the animal references," said Shawn. She heard her front door open then close quietly. Her eyes popped open again. Cory came around the end of the couch and stared at her. "Oh my God! Hang on!" she said, dropping the phone and grappling with the towel. It was stuck beneath her, in the most useless orientation possible for privacy coverage. She finally had to stand up to get it off the couch and wrap it around her.

"Cory, what the hell are you doing?" she squealed. "Don't you knock?"

"Sorry," he said, holding his hands up in front of him. His eyes were wide as well. "I was trying that whole Seinfeld apartment thing we talked about."

"Cory, I said it would take me a while to get ready for that!"

"Shit. I'm sorry, Shawn," he said, turning and putting his hands on his head. "Dude. Really. So sorry." He slipped out the front door.

Now Shawn mimicked the gesture, putting her hands on her own head and growling. "God!" She shook her head and dove back onto the couch, trying to find where her phone had got off to. She found it on the floor between where the sectional sofa pieces met. "Dad? Sorry."

"You okay, hon?" he asked. "You sounded like you may be in a little trouble."

She breathed in deeply, closing her eyes. She put her hand against her forehead. How much had he heard? "I'm fine, daddy. Just had a surprise."

"Your white horse got out of his stable?"

She shook her head, trying not to admit that she was smiling. "God, dad. I thought we were dropping the animal references."

"What, you don't like me calling you my little monarch?"

"Of course, dad. I'm not talking about that." She chewed on her thumb while she walked back to her bedroom, locking the front door on the way. She let the towel drop on the bathroom floor then sat on her bed. She spent half an hour longer on the phone with her dad. He would call her about once a week and talk to her about whatever progress he had made on his projects. He was currently restoring a 57 Chevy Bel Air. He spent many hours in the garage during the days and would go through all the minute details with her. He probably knew she didn't need that level of granularity but he was also wise enough to know he didn't have a lot to talk about otherwise. How did a sixty-year-old man connect with his thirty-year-old daughter? Gavin Stedwin knew his daughter loved to hear her daddy's voice, and of course, hers was like a sonata to his ears, so these calls were as important to him as to her.

When they finally hung up, Shawn stood up from the bed and took the towel off her head. Her hair was almost dry. She ran her fingers through it as she stepped into the bathroom. Now she would have to do something drastic with it.

With nothing to do tonight and Cory being away, Shawn decided it would finally be a good night to catch up on some TV. Cory had told her when she left last night that he had to run to Prosper for a job, and would be gone for a night or two, maybe into the weekend. This had stung Shawn pretty badly, as they had just opened an entirely new door in their relationship – which, she had to admit was moving quite quickly – and now it was all she could think about. She also had to admit that she had been the instigator of all that had transpired between them so far. Part of that could be attributed to the long eerie silence she had braved. Two years without a boyfriend. Without any male contact, if you wanted to get technical. She had broken up with her boyfriend, Rich, because it wasn't going where she had thought it should. And they hadn't even slept together for the last two months of their relationship. This era of loneliness, as she referred to it privately, had perhaps awakened a little more than just her normal levels of desire.

The other thing she could blame it on was Cory's aura. She had never been with someone so confident in his placidity. He wasn't outwardly arrogant or proud about anything. But he carried himself with such coolness that it left little doubt who he really was. At least to those who would look for it. She had only seen him interact with other men the one time, at the Cino's, but even that had been enough to see that he had no problem meshing and mingling with men she would typically think of as alphas. The way Cory moved about with such social grace made her sure that wherever he went, he was most certainly the coolest guy in the room, and the alpha all the way. He just wasn't one of those guys who had to make sure everyone knew it. It was as if his confidence was so deeply ingrained in him that he just knew it. There didn't need to be a competition. He would let all the other cocks strut their walks.

Something about this confidence was so sexy to Shawn. And it wasn't just that he was so manly, either. It felt to her that nothing fazed him. He didn't flinch. He didn't worry or scare. She felt pretty sure he could well handle anything he was faced with, and if she was behind him, she would be protected. Not to mention his big hands. God, his hands were so nice. The veins and muscle definition in his forearms was enough to make her mad. And when they were on her body…

Cory had come along at exactly the right time, and was exactly the right thing for her. So when he had told her of his trip to Prosper, she had immediately been flooded with disappointment. Hell, it might have been more accurate to call it despair. It certainly felt that way. What in the world would she do without him? It was ridiculous. She had not even spent the night with him. They certainly didn't live together. Why was she so enamored of him so quickly? Was he a player? A con man? Was he fucking magic?

Shawn shook her head and ran her hair back with her hands. Her head was starting to feel hot, thinking about him. As she dropped onto the couch and opened her phone, *same bullshit; different day,* she realized she had not even taken any pictures with him. By now she should have made a few selfies. Something she could look at. Maybe she had taken him for granted, and now that she would have to spend a night or two without him, she had nothing to look at. For that, she could kick herself. Oh well, maybe digging in to *Dexter* would take her mind off of Cory. Cory, who actually kind of looked like Michael C Hall. Good God. No, this was not going to be easy. Shawn came to realize she had to admit one more thing: she was smitten.

She reached for the television remote on the cushion beside her but instead found the two fat books Sameer had given her to read. Shawn rolled her eyes and sighed. If she didn't at least glance at them then she would feel guilty. Sameer had put sticky notes on some of the pages that stuck out like book markers. There were obviously a few things he had wanted her to see. She reckoned she could at least have a look at those tagged pages and see if any of it made sense. She picked up the first one, titled "The Human Brain". Holy shit, that sounded exciting.

Shawn turned to the first page he had marked with a pink sticky note. The page was a chapter introduction called Neurons. He had highlighted several paragraphs.

> Scientists estimate that the human brain has somewhere around 86 billion neurons, which provide storage capacity for thoughts,

memories and innate bodily functions, to name a few. When these neurons form connections, the storage capacity is increased. Healthy brain exercises like crossword puzzles and word searches cause the neurons to combine.

There is virtually an unlimited amount of connections that can be made between these neurons. A fully functioning, healthy brain can have as many as a quadrillion of them. The more connections are formed, the higher the storage capacity. Diseases like Alzheimer's can destroy these connections, which mainly affects the memory.

The neurons themselves are considered pound-for-pound to be some of the most powerful things in the universe. A piece of brain tissue the size of a grain of sand can contain as many as 100,000 neurons and over a billion synapses. It is therefore vitally important for a body to maintain its supply of oxygen to the brain. As these neurons lose their oxygen, the brain cells die, which can affect abilities performed by that particular area of the brain.


Shawn stopped reading and looked up through the glass of the sliding door. Didn't this mean a brain that had died wouldn't be able to be brought back to life? What was all this about? If brain cells died and prevented functionality, then shouldn't they be working with live patients? She shook her head and sighed. Obviously, this must be what he was trying to achieve with his project. Sameer wanted to see if he could bring the brain cells back from the dead. The bottom line of the whole project seemed to be hung on that very thought.

The thought of the brain cells seemed to take up residence in the back of her mind. Surely, this most obvious of revelations had occurred to Sameer. He had highlighted the damn passage. How could he not know that dead is dead? She had to laugh at that. This whole project stood spitting in the face of that statement. Shawn had her doubts about bringing a body back to life, but she had accepted it with a pleasantly easy attitude. So why was she getting hung up on the death of a cell?

It seemed almost too obvious to her, but she couldn't pinpoint it. Of course, you start with the basest, most simplistic element in any hypothetical. If it can't stand on its own, then there was no point in arguing for the completion of the project. If the cell couldn't be brought to life then no amount of electricity or oxygen would bring the body back. That very element was why Darwinist evolution couldn't be real. Darwin himself had said that he knew this, and that if someone couldn't come along and find the missing piece, his puzzle would never make a picture. Shawn had to roll her eyes every time she heard someone else hanging an entire belief system on something its own founder had disclaimed.

But, as Darwin had pointed out, how can a system that doesn't function progress and take a forward leap in technological stature? A dead cell, therefore, could not effect function in a living system. It could certainly *affect* it. Dead cells slowed things down. Caused defect. Deformity and chaos. Not harmony. But… But. There was that word. Sameer had *wanted* her to read this very set of paragraphs. So he had seen them too. Of course he had. Unless that was someone else's yellow highlighter on the paper. What was he calling on her to see here? Something different than he had? Or to read between the lines and figure out how to defeat the death of a cell? Well, if that was the case, she had four days to figure it out. Holy fuck.

She picked the book back up and sat down on the couch, gaining a sudden interest. She had lost interest in watching Dexter Morgan put people to death. Shawn Stedwin was now on a mission to figure out how to bring them back.

An alarm was going off somewhere in the distance. But there was a loud snoring blocking most of it out. Once she became aware of the snoring, she was able to put an end to it. But the alarm was still blaring. Would someone please shut that fucking thing off? She rolled her eyes and slapped her head in exasperation. In real life though, this equated to her arm flopping uselessly out to her side. Not to her head. Her hand made contact with something solid. Something hard. That brought her head forward. "Someone get that please!" she said, eyes popping open.

Shawn sat staring at nothing for a long time before she finally realized it was her alarm. And it had been she who was snoring. She blinked and looked around carefully, like a cat observing a room full of new strangers. She must have stared at her phone for another ten seconds before she finally shouted at it, "Oh, shut up, will you!" Then she picked it up and swiped the alarm dismissal. What the hell was going on here?

She was sitting on the couch with her legs crossed under her, what she used to refer to as Indian style as a child. She had a book open on her lap. She stared at that for a few moments too. *Oh. Okay. I see. I have fallen asleep on the couch, reading these fuckin' brain books.* She rolled her eyes, then wiped the sweat off her forehead and looked around the room. She should probably go crawl in the bed and get some good sleep before she had to get up and go to work.

When she stretched her legs out in front of her, she realized two things simultaneously: her legs were harder asleep than they had ever been, and everything from the waist down was soaking with sweat. Shawn cried out as she stretched them out and rubbed them, waiting for the pins and needles to pass. *Oh my God! How did I sleep like this? I didn't even drink anything!*

She finally stumbled to the bedroom and dropped into the bed, slipping under the heavy covers and rolling over to grab a pillow to slip between her knees. She should probably close the curtains to keep the sunlight out. Fuck it. She slipped her phone under the other pillow and closed her eyes. That was when they finally popped open with some clarity. Sunlight? What the hell? Alarm? She looked at her phone again. For real this time. It was now six-eleven. *Oh my God!*

She had stayed awake until after two, reading – even covering more of the book than the pages Sameer had marked with sticky notes and highlighters. She had maybe gotten four hours of sleep, and now it was time to get up and go to work.

As Shawn stood in the shower, extra hot this morning, she let her hair hang down over her face and let the water bang on it. She thought about how long her day was going to be, but then was reminded that Sameer wouldn't be in the office this morning. Because she had to get blood out of the freezer and put it in the fridge. And that meant it was Friday. Oh thank God. *Glory, hallelujah. There is a God, and he made today be Friday.* And Shawn saw it. And she saw that it was good.

The access code for the freezer was in her email inbox, along with some other instructions and some other tasks he wanted her to complete today, in preparation for Monday's exciting experiment. Yay! Working with our first dead body! He said he would see her early Monday morning. Wait. This meant that he wouldn't be in at *all* today. Why had he said it like it was just for the morning? *Woohoo!* "Cat's away, girls!" she said out loud and almost danced to the freezer, shaking her hips and snapping her fingers as she walked.

After moving a bag of red cells from freezer to fridge and speaking the access code to herself about a hundred times, she shook her way into the break room to get coffee. She was snapping her fingers and singing *My Name is Human* at more than just a whisper as she entered the room. Jeremy turned and smiled at her.

"What's that?" he said, turning to face her, stirring his coffee with a straw.

"My Name is Human? You haven't heard it?"

Jeremy shook his head, still smiling.

"Oh, hell, Jeremy. You have to go listen to it right away. Do you not know what we will be doing here Monday?" She took him by the shoulders and looked him in the eyes and quoted the chorus to him. "See?"

He shook his head, still smiling.

"Oh my God, you're hopeless. Move. I need coffee." Jeremy complied and she poured herself a cup of steaming black coffee.

"You should be singing *Bring me to Life* by Evanescence, shouldn't you?"

Shawn looked back and him and rolled her eyes, smiling. "Nice," she said, nodding.

"So Monday's the day, huh?" Jeremy said.

Shawn frowned at him as she took her first sip. "Huh? Do you not know what's going on?"

"Well, of course I do. I just…" he started, then paused. "Well, I guess not. What's going on?" He was now furling his eyebrows, but that goofy smile still hadn't left his face. Sometimes Shawn just wanted to reach up and squeeze his chipmunk cheeks. He had a cute smile.

"Jeremy. The project?"

"Oh. Oh! That's Monday?"

Shawn widened her eyes at him and tilted her head. "Good Lord boy, do you not know?"

Jeremy shook his head. But he didn't speak.

"We're getting our first body! We're starting the…" then she drifted off as a thought occurred to her. She felt the blood flush from her face. Maybe Jeremy didn't know…

Maybe she wasn't supposed to share with him! She covered her mouth with the hand not involved in delivering coffee to her system.

"Oh, wow. That's Monday? Cool!" Jeremy said. He reached out and touched her shoulder and said, "You know I'm not part of that, don't you?"

Shawn shook her head, suddenly mortified. "Oh God."

"No! No, don't worry about it. I know all about it, Shawn. I'm just not part of the actual experiments. I do the background programming. I won't be in there for the Awakenings."

"Awakenings," she said coldly. "You won't?"

He shook his head, his smile growing even wider. "No, I'm not part of that part." He looked at her thoughtfully for a moment, then said, "Shawn, it's okay for you to talk to me about it. I'm cleared to know everything you know about it. I just won't be in there. Sam wants to keep it minimal in there."

Shawn turned, looking for a table. She found one right beside her and set her mug down on it so she could cross her arms. She was suddenly feeling a little cold. "Minimal? Whoa, dude. Sameer said he brought you in on it, so I thought you would be part of the... the 'Awakenings'?" she said, phrasing the last bit like a question. She made quotes with her fingers, then recrossed her arms.

"No, I will be at my desk 'watching the numbers'," he said, making his own quotes.

Shawn leaned in a little closer to him, tilting her head and lowering her voice to a near-whisper. "You're okay with that? What a gyp!"

"Oh, no," Jeremy said, waving his hands in front of him. "I want no part of that. I would rather not be anywhere near the action. I don't mind what you're doing in there, but I'll be fine at my desk, thank you very much!"

Shawn nodded slowly and took a deep breath, staring at him with raised eyebrows. She had to let this sink in. This meant she would be alone in there with Sameer. She would have to help him lift the… "Wait! Aren't you going to help lift the cadav- the subject up on to the death bed?"

Jeremy frowned. "Death bed?" He giggled. "Yes, Shawn, relax! It's all under control!"

By the time Shawn was back at her desk, her coffee was cold. She spit it back into the mug and pushed it away, then put her head in her hands, staring down at her keyboard and trying to search herself. Was she ready for this? Now that she knew Big, Strong Jeremy wouldn't be in there, was she still ready to take it on? *As much as sixty percent of the human brain is made up of fat.* She shook her head. Visions and flashes of the text she had read for so many hours last night were popping into her mind at random times this morning.

She finally leaned back in her chair and checked her agenda to make sure she had completed everything she needed to get done today. The biggest line item she had not been able to check off was sleep. She needed to get the heck out of here, go home and crash on her couch for a few hours. *It is a common misconception that humans only use ten percent of their brain.* Hands back in her hair. *Oh, brother.* This book was invading her brain, and she knew it would continue to do so until she had gotten more sleep. Where was she? Oh, yes, the agenda. Nope. She had already checked it. She had literally checked the agenda, what was it? Ten seconds ago? And she had already forgotten. *Oh my God*. She really needed to get out of here. *The average human brain weighs between three and four pounds.*

F this. Shawn stood up and stretched, then grabbed her jacket and purse. Pushed her chair in. Then she pulled it back out a little. It might fool someone into thinking she was still here somewhere if she left it out. She looked around the office. Since there were only two other employees, they would notice sooner rather than later. No one cared. She knocked on the short wall separating her from the rest of the office space. "Later, Jer," she said. "I'm getting out of here."

"You wrappin' up? Okay, cool. Have a good weekend," he said, a friendly smile on his face and a wave in her direction.

"You, too, sweetie," said Shawn. She pushed her chair in and swept out of the office. She leaned against the elevator's back wall as it descended. She was scrolling through her OuterCircle feed, *same bullsh-*

Her phone rang. She held the phone to her ear before she even looked at who it was.

"Hellooo?" she said.

"Hey girl, it's Lo. What are you doing?"

"Hey, Lo! Oh my God! What's up?" said Shawn, squealing.

"Nothing. I'm bored. I thought I might invite myself over for drinks and a movie," said Lo.

Shawn's heart sank as she thought about having to try to fight falling asleep all evening, but she also felt the levity of excitement and decided to give it a shot. "Absolutely. I'll text you my address! What time do you want to come?" The elevator dinged and the door slid open.

"I'll leave as soon as I get done with my chores. I'm waiting on the washer to finish a cycle. Maybe thirty minutes?"

"Perfect!" said Shawn. She hung up and almost skipped to her car, giggling with excitement the whole way.

The hot shower woke her up a little bit, at least for now. She started a pot of coffee and popped around the small apartment making sure everything was in order for her guest. Just as she finished, standing in the middle of the living room with her fists on her hips and looking out the sliding glass door, she heard the knock on the front door. Then her fists were up by her face, shaking with excitement as she bounced over to the door squealing. She flung it open to see Lo standing there with her arms wrapped around a brown bag.

"Come in, my lady!" Shawn squeaked. "I'm so glad you came!"

"Yes! Me, too," said Lo. "I've been thinking about calling you ever since we met, but I've been so busy. I got off early today, so I thought, why not call my new friend, Shawn!" she said, setting the bag down on the kitchen counter.

Shawn stood still for a moment and put a finger over her mouth. "I have to admit something, Lo."

"Uh oh," said the other, stopping with her hand in the bag.

"I had actually forgotten we traded numbers. I am so glad you called."

"Oh. Ha! Yeah, well, here I am!" she said, and pulled out a bottle of tequila. Then she pulled out a bottle of vodka.

As she was reaching back into the bag again, Shawn said, "Good Lord, woman! How much did you bring?"

But this time she pulled out a couple of limes. "That's it. That should be enough, right?"

They both laughed. Shawn said, "You know, you didn't have to bring all that liquor. I have plenty."

"Well, I wasn't taking any chances. Besides, I always bring something. My daddy taught me right."

"Holy F," said Shawn, play-shoving Lo on the shoulder. "Get out of here. My daddy taught me that too."

"Are you close with yours still?" asked Lo, peeling the cap seal off the tequila.

"Oh, yes. We talk about once a week on the phone. He calls me his little butterfly."

Lo stopped in the middle of opening the bottle, staring Shawn in the eyes. "Get out of here."

"What? Does yours too?" Shawn asked, covering a huge smile with both of her hands.

"Yes. I have a tattoo of a monarch on my shoulder," said Lo. She turned and stretched the neck of her sweater over her left shoulder, showing Shawn a beautiful blue monarch about three inches across.

"Oh my God, that is beautiful, Lo!" she said. She still had her hands on her mouth. As Lo let the sweater snap back into place, she said, "Wanna see mine?" She was grinning widely.

Lo was shaking her head. "You have got to be fuckin' with me."

Shawn shook her head too. Then she unbuttoned her jeans and pulled the fly open, pulling down her panties with one hand while she lifted her t-shirt with the other. Lo stared in amazement.

"You know, this is almost creepy, Shawn."

Shawn nodded, mouth open in a silent laugh. "I know. It's like we were meant to be friends."

"Exactly what I was thinking. Now let's get drunk together, butterfly sister!"

Over the next few hours, they sat Indian-style on the couch facing each other with the bottle between them on a couch tray, just getting to know each other. It was fascinating to Shawn how much they had in common. Lo was like a long-lost sister. They told stories, talked about family and their boyfriends, and moving to Texas – Lo had moved to Texas four years before, but had just migrated from Dallas to Arlington a few months before. Heath had been the first person she had met. So, aside from the motorcycle group, Shawn was the second.

They had drained quite a bit of the tequila by the time Lo asked what movies Shawn had. Shawn had furled her lips and said, "Who has movies anymore? I have streaming stuff, but I don't even have a DVD player."

"Let's find something on Netflix then!"

Lo made it about twenty minutes into the movie. Shawn might have made it five.

When she woke in the middle of the night, having to pee, Shawn realized she had fallen asleep with her head in

Lo's lap, and Lo had lain over backwards at a funny angle that was sure to make her hurt the next day. Shawn stood up and pulled Lo's legs up onto the couch, then helped her straighten her hips and covered her with a blanket. Then she clicked the light off and went to her the bedroom to get some real sleep.

Once they were both up and done with their morning duties, they stood in the kitchen drinking coffee and making plans for the day. They had already decided they would be going to Larry's for breakfast and then they would hit the flea market over by the ballpark. The relief of letting go the burden she had been carrying on her mind for the last five days was a welcome break. Shawn believed in herself, sure. But it was hard to believe in oneself doing something one didn't necessarily strictly believe in. She still wasn't sure where she stood on the whole issue of bringing someone back from the dead. And since Sameer had not been at work yesterday, she had not gotten to ask him about the cell death thing. If it *was* real, and if they *could* be restored to a living state, then she believed she could make it through whatever trials it threw at her. It was still a new concept. So it was nice to be able to relax with a friend and forget about the whole thing for a while.

After breakfast, they went to the flea market. Hundreds of booths covered the ballpark parking lots. They took their time browsing the booths for farm-fresh products and homemade crafts, having discovered another shared interest. It didn't really matter to either of them what someone was selling. If the booth was setup and the face was friendly, they were looking. They spent an especially long time at the record seller's booth, as he had four six-foot tables forming a square around him with five crates on each, all full of pre-loved records. Lo ended up dropping over two hundred dollars at that booth alone. Records, she said, were one of her few vices. She simply couldn't get enough of them. She had almost a thousand in her apartment music room, which she had told Shawn all about. They planned to end up there after the festivities of the day had played themselves out. Why not? Shawn had nothing planned for the weekend, and both of their boyfriends were gone. Of course she would spend the night at Lo's!

As they walked the parking lot, stopping at interesting booths, Shawn told her of the stresses she had been dealing with over the last week – without getting into specifics. She spoke of the stress of having to read the text book and try to divine what it was her boss was wanting her to latch onto. Shawn had not thought to put the text books in the coffee table drawer, so she was unable to fudge around with the subject matter when Lo asked what she was doing with books about the brain and the nervous system. In the end, it hadn't mattered though, because, as it turned out, Lo had a shelf full of science books at her place as well. She had, as she called it, a borderline obsessive interest in astrophysics and cosmology. She had books on her shelf that spoke of the beginning of the universe and how Einstein had died trying to combine the science of the big and the small. All of these things fascinated Shawn too, but she had not been exposed to them yet. They agreed to trade some books so they could widen their knowledge. Another shared interest.

At lunch time they bought fried turkey-leg drumsticks, like one would find at a Renaissance Faire. Shawn had been so tickled to see they were selling them that she had run up and bought two of them without even bothering to ask Lo if she was interested in one. When Shawn had returned to Lo, after telling her to hang tight and running off to buy them, Lo had been looking at her phone, and was thus surprised to see the food in front of her. She had then told Shawn to stand by, and had jogged off to fetch two tankards of grog, which she found just as easily. So they stood drinking beer out of wooden mugs and eating turkey legs, the way God intended Saturday lunches to be.

At around three o'clock, they were both starting to grow tired. They decided to pack it up and head for the Jeep, which was parked close to a mile away on Nolan Ryan

Boulevard. As they dragged their feet – and their bags of loot – across the wide parking lot in the hot May sun, Shawn said, "Thank you for calling me yesterday. I might not have ever taken that first step. But I'm so glad one of us did."

Lo looked at her and smiled, then ran her thumb across Shawn's cheek – much as a lover would do – pulling her hair back behind her ear. "Shawn, you wouldn't believe if I told you how much I needed this. How much I've needed you. I've needed a friend so bad. It's so nice to have found you."

They stopped in the middle of their trek, and hugged.

Shawn had a bag full of clay spice jars for the kitchen, and a large ebony-framed shadowbox with a giant orange monarch butterfly in the middle. It was so perfectly appropriate for her wall that she didn't even bother to ask how much it cost. She had just handed the vendor her credit card while she stared at the tiny details of the wings and talked to Lo about what an incredible find she had made.

Lo had her own bags of things needed – mostly records – and walked with the handles of them strung over her forearms, causing her to walk with her arms bent at the elbows. They both now had wooden mugs that they may or may not ever use again. Of course if they ever came to the flea market again – or to a Ren Faire – they would come in handy. But would they even remember to bring them? Shawn wouldn't bet on that.

They finally walked through Lo's front door at nine-thirty, well after it had gotten dark. They were tired and sweaty and drunk, but they were laughing. The apartment, Shawn saw, was almost the same layout as her own and she guessed there weren't terribly too many floor plans to choose from when designing an apartment complex. Efficiency was key. So she was able to easily find the bathroom to relieve herself before joining Lo in the kitchen to prepare for another round.

Shawn stood watching as Lo started with some sophistication, shaking margarita mix and tequila in a steel canister with a handful of ice. Then reached into the freezer and grabbed a handful of ice from a Sonic bag, and her cred dropped a few notches. But dropping that Sonic ice into a couple of Solo cups she pulled from the cabinet put Shawn into hard laughter. Lo couldn't help but giggle, herself, but she kept saying, "Hold on! Don't laugh yet! Hang on!"

When she finally finished, she turned and handed Shawn a plastic cup full of what she promised was one of the best drinks she would ever have. "Trust me, babe."

Shawn pursed her lips, nodding at the concoction like a proud mother. "Well, I'll try anything twice!"

"This is my famous White Trash White Girl Rita," said Lo, holding up the red cup for a toast.

Shawn tapped her glass against Lo's, laughing so hard she almost spilled the drink. Then she tasted it, and the laughing – even the smile – faded. "Holy fuck, Lo!" she said. She took another sip, then licked her lips, staring at the cup. Then she sipped again. "This tastes like…" she said, and had to sip again. Her eyes finally got wide and she shook her head. "Dude. Seriously, Lo. This is the best margarita I've ever had."

Lo was smiling widely during her whole buildup, just sipping her own drink. "I told you not to knock that shit, bitch," she said.

Shawn raised her right hand, eyes wide, and shook her head. "I swear, I'll never laugh at your bartenderism again."

Lo laughed out loud. "It's good, huh?"

"Oh my God," Shawn said, drinking again. Then Lo reached up and put her hand on the bottom of Shawn's cup, tilting it back for her. Shawn lifted her hand to her chin, pushing her head forward to keep from dribbling. She kept drinking.

"Atta girl!" Lo said. "Yes, mama, drink that shit!"

Shawn finished the juice in her cup, then licked her lips and looked at Lo. "Are you serious? You just made me slam that shit!" She shook her head again and wiped her mouth, feeling a little scared. Was Lo trying to achieve something here? Was there an ulterior motive she needed to be aware of? Because she had been drinking with her all day, so it was getting a little late to start thinking about having to watch herself around this woman. She was already highly buzzed. And with this last swallow, drunk would shortly follow. "Are you wanting to get me drunk?"

Lo nodded.

And suddenly, Shawn's fears felt more real. Her chest suddenly felt cold. The smile slid from her face. She gulped and set her cup on the counter. "Huh?" she asked, maybe trying to buy some time to think of what to do, or maybe to reaffirm that she heard what she thought Lo had said.

"Why, Lo?" she asked.

"Because we're letting go, sister! We're supposed to be having fun! Why are you worried all of the sudden?"

Shawn cleared her throat and breathed in deeply, crossing her arms. "Because you're making me drink alone."

Lo looked her in the eyes with a straight face. Then slowly, she let a smirk creep onto her lips. She held her cup up, then tilted it toward Shawn's eyes so she could see down into it. Lo's cup was empty as well. The wash of relief through Shawn's body was so immediate and profound that she almost fell forward. Lo saw the relief in her eyes.

"Are you okay, Shawn? I'm not trying to push anything over on you here."

"Okay," Shawn said. "Maybe I was freaking out a little bit there." She gulped again and felt the need to wipe away tears that might or might not actually be dripping from her eyes. She couldn't even tell at this point. Why was she so shaken by this? Was there something in her past that she couldn't recall? Something that had scarred her a little? Well, maybe or maybe not, but she was really starting to feel the drink tonight. She hadn't been this drunk in a long time.

"You don't need to freak out, darling. If you don't want to drink any more, you don't have to. I was just trying to make it feel fun," Lo said. She reached up and put her hand on Shawn's chin. "I'm sorry, Shawn. Really."

Shawn took another deep breath and shook her head. "No, it's okay. I just lost my composure a little bit. Maybe I'm a little drunk."

Lo smiled at her. "Well, good! That's the point here! We're supposed to be having fun! Drinks! Dancing!" She turned and unscrewed the cap off the tequila, refilling her glass sloppily. It sloshed all around, some of it splashing out of the cup. And Shawn saw in that sloppy pour that Lo was actually quite drunk herself, and was just being a goofball. She wasn't trying to be hurtful in any way, she was just drunk and didn't know how to act. Completely normal. Shawn held her own cup up.

"Are you sure?" Lo said, holding the bottle sideways just above the lip of her Solo cup.

Shawn nodded. Lo poured. They bumped them together again. They drank.

"I'm ready…" Shawn said after her first big gulp, and had to cover her mouth for a belch that might turn into something more if she wasn't careful. "Ooh! Excuse me! I'm ready for some of that dancing you talked about."

Lo's eyes got really wide as if she were surprised. "Oh, yes! Let's make that shit happen. My neighbors are cool, don't worry," she said, looking over her shoulder and waving at Shawn dismissively as she walked to the stereo in the other room. Shawn followed her into the music room she had heard so much about. When Lo flipped on the light switch, the lights that actually came on took Shawn by surprise. They weren't the standard bulb-in-the-ceiling-fixture. They were a series of hidden LED strip lights placed all over the room behind things, which made the ambiance of the room explode with pure awesomeness. Orange lights came on behind a cabinet against the far wall. She had lanterns on the side walls with bulbs in them that mimicked flickering flames, and strips under other surfaces that lit up the floor. The room was no longer dark, but washed in the colors of a campfire. It was wonderful. Shawn put her hand over her mouth.

"Oh my fuck!" she said.

Lo nodded, smiling widely. "You like that?"

Shawn nodded, bouncing up and down on her feet and squealing in delight. She leaned forward and reached out to hug Lo. During the embrace, Lo stopped and said, "Oh, shit! I left my records in the car!"

"Well, you better go get 'em!"

They listened to all the records Lo had bought that day, dancing and singing and drinking tequila. When it finally got time to say goodnight, Shawn was so sloshed she could barely stand up straight. She noticed that Lo was as well, though, so she didn't feel like an idiot. They had dropped to the floor, sitting facing each other on a round rug in the middle of the room, knees to knees, feeling like they had to get it all out tonight, lest they never talk again.

Having run out of new records, Lo had finally put on a streaming playlist, blasting the music loud enough they had to shout to hear each other. But Shawn liked it that way. Somehow it was comfortable. She wondered momentarily about how the neighbors felt about the loud music but remembered Lo's saying her neighbors were cool. Her unease dissipated. Occasionally they held hands, or one of them would grab the other's wrist and lean forward, shouting extra loud when she was about to say something extra important. And it was all important. They shared more than Shawn would have imagined sharing with a new friend. But it all felt right. The music was loud, the tequila was still flowing, and the mood lighting was perfect. There was nothing Shawn could have thought of that would have made the night better. Just having a new friend after six months of knowing almost no one in the area was such a reward that she didn't want to be anywhere else. Not even with Cory. She missed him like crazy, which was something she reminded herself to revisit when she was sober, but she was so enveloped in this warm little space with the music and the liquor with Lo. She was so happy all over. New boyfriend, new friend, new job... It was perfect.

And that's when she spilled it.

Shawn reached over and grabbed the remote, pointed it in the general direction of the stereo and turned it down a few notches.

"Hey, Lo, I need to tell you something."

# Five

Shawn stood at the counter, hands trembling as she watched the last of the blood drip into the reservoir. She was filled with a nervous excitement that wasn't quite fear – wasn't quite as bad as she had expected it would be. The body was already in the other room – Room D – lying on the table under a white sheet. How appropriate. She was happy for that. As clinical as Sameer was with his project, he wasn't completely immune to the immodesty of leaving a dead, naked body lying exposed on a table. Shawn could be okay with the nakedness from a strictly clinical perspective as well, but why? They only needed the head. No point in having the whole body uncovered. Not to mention the respect it showed for the decedent.

Shawn, of course, realized that nervous energy was not the only culprit involved in causing her hands to be jittery. Sunday had been a recovery day for her. In her life, she couldn't remember ever having drunk so much liquor in one night, much less, tequila. Tequila was not her drink, so she didn't know how it reacted with her body chemistry. Well, she had learned yesterday all throughout the day and into this morning that it wasn't a favorable reaction. As she sat up yesterday morning and blinked against the sunlight streaming in through the back window, hair in her face and head pounding, Shawn made one of the many promises one makes throughout life that this would be the last time. *Never again. Dear God.*

How had she thought those last half-dozen drinks were a good idea? Especially on top of all the beer they had consumed at the flea market? Not wanting to wake the still sleeping Lo, Shawn had sneaked out the front door, turning the lock on the knob before pulling it closed. She couldn't remember everything she and Lo had talked about Saturday night into Sunday morning. But she did remember one thing. Every time she remembered *that* part of their many-hours conversation, she got a little tense in the stomach.

The blood finished its trek from wax bag to reservoir and she snapped it closed. The rez would slide into the circulation machine and thence came the wonder of life. Or so they hoped. The circulation machine had a tube that connected to an oxygen tank, and kept that blood infused with a fresh supply of O2, in much the same way a heart and lungs did it naturally in the human body.

There was no escaping the fact that Shawn had spilled the secret of the project she was on. It bothered her like a bad cavity in the back of the mouth. She hated so much the cringe that came with admitting to herself that she had broken her word to Sameer. Her integrity, her most important asset, was no longer complete. So what if she had been possessed of the demon called alcohol? It had made her do other things as well. She had spoken of many things without the filter her normal conscience could provide. But it hadn't made her change any other beliefs. She had not suddenly decided, for instance, that she needed to climb on top of Lo and live out some dark fantasy she had never had. So nay, there was no denying, she was in charge of her own faculties enough to know she had slipped in the ethics. And now she had to dance in the eggs.

She made her way back into the Death Room and pushed the rez into the housing machine with a comforting snap. The hoses were already hooked up, as she could see them disappearing under the white sheet that covered the dead man. The subject. Apparently there was no amount of ethic that could make her remember to call a dead human being a 'subject'. It just seemed so impersonal. So disconnected from the reality of the situation. Even the word 'patient' sounded better. But having brought this up to Sameer, she had been reminded that a patient was a *living* person. Once life left the room, there was no patient remaining.

The worst part of the conversation with Lo was *not*, however, the fact that Shawn had spilled the secret of the project. It, at least in Shawn's eyes, was that Lo had been more than a little interested. Of course she was interested in what it meant – bringing a brain back from the dead for a little while – but that wasn't the part she was *most* interested in. The part that had fascinated Lo had been the ability of someone to make the decision to donate her body to medical science. She had been instantly interested in finding out how she could make that pledge. Her eyes had even gotten wide, and Shawn remembered this vividly, and taken both of Shawn's hands, and said, "Ooh, I could be in the project!"

"Do you have the nanobots penned, Shawn?" said Sameer from the other corner of the room. The lights, a part of the project that still creeped her out just a little bit, were not bright. The room was almost covered in a pall – like the dimly lit visitation room in a mortuary, where a loved one might lay in a half-open casket, eyes closed and hands crossed on the chest like some statue celebrating its new peace. She walked over to the penning trap and flipped on the surface light. It did nothing to help the ambiance of the room. If anything, it made it worse: the indirect lighting from the white surface of the trap reflecting off the ceiling. She held back a shiver as she answered in the affirmative.

She had rounded up and assigned the functions of those bots over two hours ago, sitting in similar darkness at her desk.

"You do understand that this project is for people who have died, right?" Shawn had asked Lo that night. "You're literally saying you want to be dead if you're wanting to participate." The comment had triggered a thought in her head as well, right then, staring at her new friend: would it be easier to set about the task of reanimating a dead brain if it were a friend? Or would it be harder? Lo had not shown the slightest bit of hesitation. She had nodded with an excited smile. And therein, they had perhaps found their first disagreement. The first interest they did not share. Lo had no fear of death like Shawn did. And Shawn's was not a fear of dying. Not herself, at least. Just a fear of being around others who had. Lo had no such reservation.

She slipped a long cylindrical tube into the side of the trap until it clicked. It looked like a glass cigar case, but very thin. A new option illuminated on the back-lit top of the device. It read very simply, 'SEND'. She touched the red square with a finger tip and an animation showed the little bots following the command, a little train of dedicated soldiers lining up to file into the tube. The tube was filled with a saline solution that was not necessarily sterile, and Shawn had to remind herself that sterility did not matter nearly as much here as it would in a hospital, where the goal was to keep someone alive rather than not.

They had not talked about whether or not Lo had experienced death in a personal way, but she had shown great interest in the exercise of bringing a brain back from beyond. Asking it questions. What would it say? Would the person be able to describe where he or she had been? The very things that brought hard chills up Shawn's spine seemed to be the things that made Lo giddy with excitement. "Yes, I understand that, Shawn! I don't want to die, but if I do, how cool would it be if you got to work with me?" Lo had said. Shawn, shaking her head, rolling her eyes, and doing just about every other passive thing she could think to relay the point that she was against this idea from the very top all the way down.

"Okay, Shawn it is time to turn on the circulation system," said Sameer, startling her back to the present. To say her mind was elsewhere this morning was understatement. But it might have also been a blessing. If there was one way to soften the blow of being in the same room as a dead body, it was to be in it with half of your consciousness on vacation. She wasn't trying to be absent-minded, but having not fully recovered from Saturday night's engagement was making her foggy in ways she wasn't used to being. She flipped the switch to the on position and listened to its near-silent hum as it immediately started moving the blood through the away tubes. She reached down and twisted open the oxygen valve then stood back with her hands on her hips just observing the machinery at work. Deep breaths.

The passive hints were not taken by the ever-indulgent Lo. She was either ignoring them entirely or just completely unaware they were hints to begin with. Alcohol could have been blamed for some of that. Shawn knew her friend was not socially awkward in the least. She knew how to read people. "We should come up with some code words!" Lo had said. When Shawn had frowned and shaken her head, Lo had said, "Yeah, like you ask a question and I give you some cryptic answer. Then if I'm ever on your table, you ask that same question that only I would know the answer to and see if I answer the same after I've been dead!"

Tiny bubbles pushed up the return tube, followed by a dark liquid that didn't quite match the product going into the brain. It was amazing how much difference fresh oxygen made in even just the color of the blood. Shawn's mouth was a tight and tiny representation of its normal size, pinched by the urgent feeling of horror lurking just beneath the surface of her conscience. She was staring at blood that had run through a dead man's brain and come back with no oxygen. Some part of that man lying under the sheet was now present in the blood in that tube, that reservoir. His essence now existed in their lab. "Are you okay, Shawn?" asked Sameer, smiling gently. She looked up at him and nodded, forcing a smile of her own.

As freaked out as she had been by the concept of a challenge/response scenario, she had also been oddly turned on by it. It had an ethereal curiosity about it that excited parts of her brain otherwise frightened by such things. She had stopped talking for a moment, pursing her lips and staring at Lo while Lo just sat there wide-eyed and nodding at her. "Yeah!" she would say. Then, "Yeah! See?" And Shawn had to admit after a few minutes that yes, she did see. It was attractive in spite of its eerie foundation. She had asked what such question and response would be, and Lo had gotten a mischievous smile on her face, looking up at the ceiling in the near-dark room, raising her arms into the air. "How deep is the darkness?" she had said. And Shawn had instantly known the answer.

"This is good. You can insert the injection tube into the circulator, but let us hold off on release until we have saturated the brain for two hours," Sameer said. Shawn raised a finger in the air and waved it as an acknowledgment of his direction. She noted that the display board of the penning trap now read 'Safe to Remove' where it had read 'Standby...' a few moments before. She clicked the tube out of the edge of the contraption and looked at it against the light of the display. Of course, she couldn't see anything in the saline. But they were in there. Four thousand of the little boogers. *What an amazing piece of technology this is.* She took the tube to the circulator and slid it into its proper channel, again with a satisfying click. A green light illuminated on the front of the display under the label 'Catalyst Ready'. Typically this is where they would insert plasma or bulk dosages of heavy medication in the machine's normal use in a hospital.

"It is endless. It is complete. It is perfect," she had said, and Lo had tilted her chin down, looking back at her through the tops of her hazel eyes. She had nodded slowly, then held up a hand in front of her. Shawn, without looking, slapped it and rolled her eyes. They had their challenge and response. "So if you end up on my table, which, God for-fucking-bid you ever do, I will ask you that question. And if you say that response, I will know you're still with me." Then she had shaken her head. "Remind me, Lo, why the hell piss are we talking about this like it's going to happen? If your ass dies, I will kick it for you. There is no way you're going to end up on that table." Had she known then the truth of the matter, what might it have changed?

"Can I pull the sheet back?" Shawn asked. Sameer nodded and stepped up to the side of the table. They stared at each other over where a dead man lay coming back to life. "I want to see him. And I want to know that I'm able to look at a dead person, Sameer." He nodded his understanding and grasped the corner of the sheet closest to him. Shawn did the same, and then slowly and carefully, they peeled it back, folding it over to lay on the man's chest. Shawn got her first glimpse of the man's face, pallid and gray like some left-out meal. Her immediate instinct was to gag at the sight. She was able to restrain herself, staring down into the man's lifeless eyes with a forced calm, breathing slow and heavy. Why did his eyes have to be open? And no sooner had the thought entered her mind than she saw a minute twitch in the edge of the man's eyelid, and she physically jumped back, yelping and knocking over a stand on which hung rags and towels for God knew what purpose. Covering her heart with a now badly trembling hand she stood looking at Sameer levelly. "I'm sorry, Sameer. I just saw a flutter in the window."

The processes that were taking place in that brain in the lab were so infinitesimally small that Shawn had trouble believing anything would happen. She was back at her desk now. No need to stand in the lab over a dead man, waiting for the oxygen-enriched blood to penetrate all the capillaries in the brain. She had asked Sameer how every single cell could possibly be affected by the blood. Surely there were not that many vessels and capillaries. They couldn't touch *every* part of the brain, right? All those billions of neurons? "Osmosis," he had said simply. "That is why we are having to be waiting for some hours before we try our experiments."

She checked and rechecked her functions, reading each line carefully to make sure she had assigned the proper functions. It was exciting to Shawn to see that the four thousand nanobots were indeed marked as separated from the home base. The label read 'Transit Colony'. Neat. She hoped she had gotten all the right groups of functions they wanted to achieve. Not knowing what to expect at all could either make her more careful or more reckless. She would have to wait to see which it would be. She had involved functions for the eyes, the vocal cords, the tongue and jaw and the ears – among basic awareness functions that hopefully would hitch a ride under the 'Awareness' group that Jeremy had created. He had auto-mapped about a hundred tiny brain functions that would create situational awareness in the subject without Shawn having to map out each individual function every time they ran a new series of tests.

Shawn was proud of herself for how she conducted herself in the lab, her freak-out from the eye twitch notwithstanding. When one sees a dead body move, is it not a natural response to flinch? She didn't know if Sameer had flinched – hell, he might not have even seen the twitch happen – but maybe he was more familiar with death and little things like cadavers suddenly moving didn't faze him. But what about that eye twitch? Was that shit normal? They had not even injected the nanobots yet! The blood was just providing oxygen. There should not have been anything telling any parts of his body what to do. That was freaky. She wondered not only what had made that happen, but if it would be happening again. Hell, there might be parts of that man's body coming alive in the other room right now, still covered by the sheet. Proud of how she had acted or not, there was no controlling the chill this thought gave her. A body reanimated without scientific instruction was a zombie. That's what it was, if he was twitching and moving fingers and feet in that room, he was a fucking zombie. Shawn had to stand up and go to the break room. Coffee. A cinnamon roll. Anything to get her mind off of that shit.

Two hours later, they were back in D. Sameer was standing over the subject with a clipboard, scanning down a document with a pen, looking for something while Shawn waited quietly by the penning trap, trying to act busy and build her courage back up. She had not seen the sheet doing any moving or twitching, which was a relief, but the thought would haunt her until well into the night if she didn't get rid of it soon.

"Okay, Shawn we are ready to inject the bots, please," he said behind her. Shawn nodded, took a deep breath, then turned and moved to the circulation machine.

She put both of her hands on the unit, steadying it as well as her hands, then pressed the round button labeled 'Inject Catalyst'. A light started blinking and the machine hummed lightly as it sucked the nanobot solution into the blood reservoir. *Here goes nothing,* she thought and tried again to think calming thoughts. Not sure what else she could think about, she didn't get too far with that. Her mind was completely here now, and maybe that was good. Her morning distractions had faded.

"Sameer, why do people donate their bodies to science?"

He smiled at her, a genuinely friendly response to her question. It helped relieve a little tension. "Interesting question, Shawn. A lot of people do it to help allay the cost of a death. This way the university handles the cost of the burial or cremation when we are finished with the project. But not all people for this is true. Some are just altruistic," he said. He hung the clipboard from a hook beneath the table and leaned his hands on the edge. Shawn wasn't quite ready to be that close to the cadaver yet.

"So do people get to request what their body gets used for?"

"Yes, in some cases they are specifying to go to cancer research or Alzheimer's or whatever they are interested in helping to research, absolutely. Why do you ask, Shawn?"

She shrugged. "I'm just curious, really. I was just wondering if something like what we're doing could be specified."

He nodded slowly, looking at her for a moment before speaking. "Well, it is not likely because we do not disclose our research to the family. Most families want to hear back about how their donation has helped advance science. A lot of them are used just for training new doctors. They can learn how to perform surgeries and insert catheters or other sensitive tasks that might put a living patient in danger." He looked over at the machine that stood quietly pumping blood through the brain. Then he returned his gaze to hers and said, "What we are doing here is classified as non-invasive brain research. But it is private because I have stated that our research is for proprietary technological advancement."

"That's smart," said Shawn. She took a deep breath and glanced at the subject's face. She felt like she needed to make these little looks obvious to her boss, so as to show him her bravery. Her progress, at least. The man's face was still pallid, but it looked a little more flushed somehow. Like maybe some of that blood had leaked into the veins that livened someone up. It was refreshing not to be looking at someone who looked so dead. The ridiculous nature of that thought almost made her giggle. *I'm sorry sir, death is okay here, but could you just look a little* less *dead for us please?*

"Okay, so when should we start seeing something happen?" asked Shawn.

"You have activated the routines for the nanobots, yes, Shawn?"

"What do you mean? They automatically find their places in the brain, don't they?"

"I am assuming so, yes," said Sameer. "But they will not activate their tasks until you tell them to do so."

"Oh. Yeah. Okay, well are you ready for me to do that?"

"Whenever you are ready, Shawn. I think we have saturated the brain with blood long enough."

"Okay," she said. She bounced on the balls of her feet a couple of times, then said it again. "Okay." She turned to the counter where her laptop sat. She could not control functionality of the Transit Colony from the penning trap itself. It could only control the bots within its enclosure. She opened the application and saw dashed lines around several functions, awaiting activation.

Unsure about which ones to activate first, or if it even mattered, she selected the first one on the screen and clicked the 'Activate' button with the cursor. The first function was Jeremy's 'Aware' routine. She kept her back turned to the subject for the time being, scared to death to see if Aware meant aware like she thought it meant. Like, would that guy on the table wake up and start looking around? Dear God, she hoped not. Then she clicked the sensory functions which would open up the aural and visual passageways in the brain.

Here, Shawn steeled herself and clicked the 'Vocal' function and finally turned around. Nothing was happening. *Thank God.* She didn't exactly wish for the failure of the project. Of course not. That would likely put her out of a job. Not to mention crushing the hopes and dreams of Sameer Singh, who had this wonderful vision. She did an inner eye-roll at the thought of that. But nor did she mind if it took a little time to get it right.

Of course, that could come with its own set of horrors. If things worked, but in the wrong way. Like a subject sitting up and screaming at them, or getting violent or anything else. She had to remind herself that these things were not able to happen, because they had isolated functions of the brain to those they wanted to see happen. In theory, a subject should *not* be able to twitch his foot like she had thought about earlier. He should, in fact, be effectively paralyzed from the neck down as far as their project was concerned.

But still. They were messing with the human brain. She realized peripherally that she sure was putting a lot of trust in Jeremy's ability to map the human brain. And what if every brain was different? There were trillions of variables if that was the case. And she knew that from a hundred years of science in studying the brain, there had been advancements to the point where they were pretty sure what they were dealing with. Pretty sure. She did roll her eyes at that.

Standing next to the table, she began to feel a little better, because nothing that wasn't supposed to happen had happened yet. Or again, rather. Considering the eye twitch she had seen earlier to be a complete fluke, she was happy to see it wasn't just happening constantly at this point. Sameer pulled a digital voice recorder from his pocket and put its lanyard around his neck. Then he held it up and looked at it for a minute. He slid a switch on its side, then waited another moment. Then he dropped it gently against his chest, making sure it was facing the right way.

"Okay. Today is Monday, May twenty-second. The time is," he said, and held up his hand to look at his watch, "it is eleven-eleven. We are starting on Subject Number One. We began circulation at eight o'clock this morning. We injected the nanobots about fifteen minutes ago, and just activated them. We are seeing no signs of response visibly."

Shawn took a deep breath. She had been staring at Sameer as he spoke into the DVR. Now she glanced at the face of the dead man, just to confirm to herself that what Sameer had said was true. It was. No signs of life.

"Okay, Shawn, would you like to address the subject?"

Shawn blinked. Shaking her head, she looked up at Sameer. "Excuse me?"

Sameer nodded patiently, then put his hand on the DVR on its lanyard, sliding the switch on the side. "We will have to ask him questions to see if we can get a response," he said.

"You want me to talk to a dead guy?"

Now Sameer closed his eyes, tilting his head and sighing – the effective equivalent of an eye-roll if she ever saw one. "Yes, Shawn. Unless you can think of any other way to try to make him respond."

"You know what? Maybe we should have had a meeting about this before we came in here," Shawn said, waving her hands above the cadaver like she was about to perform a séance.

Sameer nodded again. She could tell his patience was wearing thin, and what remained was now mixing badly with a little bit of disappointment. "Okay, I will start it off. You do not have to speak to him until you are more comfortable. But yes, we will have to find a way for you to get that way if you are to be being on this project," Sameer said.

Shawn shrugged and held her hands up at her sides. "Yeah, I get it. I was just completely unprepared for this. You didn't really give me a game plan, you know?"

"Yes, I understand. This is all experimenting, Shawn. We will have to find what is working and what can be improved. I am as new to this are you are, Shawn." He reached up and slid the switch back to the record position, then carefully held it to his chest by the inch of lanyard just above the device so he could lean in close. He got his face uncomfortably close to the subject's ear and spoke softly so as not to jar the dead man.

"Hello, sir. Can you hear me?" he said. Then he stood up. After a few seconds he repeated the whole process. Shawn realized she had been tensing up, almost holding her breath while she awaited results. The suspense and anticipation of something happening – or not – was taxing her nerves. "Sir, my name is Sameer. Feel free to speak to me if you can hear me."

"Oh my God, this is freaking me out," Shawn said. She had balled her hands up into tight fists and was shaking them by her sides subtly. "I'm sorry, Sameer. May I step out a moment?"

Sameer stood up straight, losing the patient smile he had been wearing only a few seconds before. Then he nodded. "Please don't be long, Shawn."

Shawn nodded back and turned to exit the room. She walked to the break room with her hands in her hair. Jeremy was standing by the fridge with a cup of coffee in one hand and a magazine in the other. "Jeremy, move out of my way. I need coffee," she said as she came into the room.

He stepped out of the way, never losing his smile. "How's it going in there?"

Shawn reached the counter and pulled a mug from the open cabinet above, then poured herself some of the brew. She could tell it was fresh by the smell. And any time Jeremy was in the office, there was bound to be fresh coffee. That guy didn't have any concept of time of day. If he was breathing, and at work, he was drinking coffee. Easy formula to remember. "I don't know," she said, turning to face him while she blew across the mug. "I mean, well, it's not, yet. Not yet."

"Not yet?" he said, still smiling. He sipped from his coffee. If Shawn liked hers black, Jeremy's could be called 'white'. Lots of cream and sugar. Yuck. She had no idea how he wasn't diabetic from this mixed treat alone. The man knew nothing of moderation, at least as far as coffee was concerned. "So you're confident."

"Jeremy, how do you feel about all this? I mean, does it bother you at all what we're doing in there?"

"How do you mean? I mean, duh, I know how you mean. But in what way? Like are you asking from a spiritual standpoint?"

Shawn stopped mid-thought and considered what she had been asking. "You know what, I hadn't even thought of it from that angle. You're a Jew, right?" Shawn had seen his Star of David necklace many times, gold standing out against the black hair on his chest.

Jeremy nodded, his mouth open in an almost grin. "Yeah. I don't practice very much, but I still believe."

"So does it bother you that we're trying to wake the dead in there?"

He made a sour face and shrugged. "Not really. I mean, it's a body. I believe in the afterlife, but I don't think that has anything to do with what you're trying to accomplish."

Shawn sipped from her steaming coffee mug again. "Mmhmm. So what's that mean?"

"What do you mean, what's that mean? It means I think you're trying to reanimate a corpse. It's not like the soul is going to pop back into the body from its reward and join the living just because you shock a few nerves," said Jeremy.

"That's an interesting take," Shawn said.

"Yeah? Well what do you think then? Obviously I'm okay with it. I'm working here."

"What, are you saying I got here under false pretense?" she said and chuckled. That was what she loved about Jeremy: he had a knack for calming her nerves just by his good-nature. She sighed and took another sip. "I'm a non-practicing Christian myself. I believe just like I always have. I just don't live in a bubble. But I hadn't thought of the spiritual aspect of this project."

Jeremy nodded, smiling at her.

"I guess you're right though. It makes sense, if we as believers believe in an afterlife, then sending electrical pulses through a brain does not bring back the spirit. Interesting take. I'm glad I came in here," she said and patted him on the shoulder as she strode out the door. "Sorry, Jer, I have to get back in there."

"See ya," he said.

Back in the lab, and re-energized with the coffee and the smiles from Jeremy, she had a new take on this whole thing. If they were able to reanimate a corpse, it would be a soulless thing. A happenstance of science meeting technology. Well, a little bit of biology would be thrown in there. You mix those three things and you might get a word or two out of a dead guy. But looking at it from that angle meant that Jeremy was right: there was nothing about this that interfered with her Christian principles. Those beliefs that had been so strong on her mind when she came in here that she had completely failed to even consider them over the last eight days. That deserved a smirk. Sameer saw the smirk and asked if she was okay now. "Better?"

"Yes. I'm sorry, Sameer. I'm still trying to get used to this. This is literally the second dead body I've ever been in close proximity to. It might take a while," she said, setting her coffee on the counter and returning to the bedside. Tableside. Was this a bed or a table? Another good question. She found herself seeing a completely different angle on everything now, apparently. "Thank you for being patient with me," she said.

"You are welcome," said Sameer, not without a touch of incredulity in his countenance. "So I have been asking questions over and over and nothing is happening."

"About that," Shawn said, leaning on the table with her hands only inches from the cadaver. "I have been meaning to ask you about the dead brain cells. You highlighted that part in the book, where it talks about a brain starved of oxygen dies because the cells die. What was – or is, for that matter – the plan for dealing with the dead cells."

He crossed his arms and looked at her, the patience seeming to have rejoined the conversation. "It is my opinion that anything can be brought back to life. Cells are dead from lack of oxygen. But intrinsically, nothing changes. Nothing breaks inside them that cannot be repaired with a renewed supply."

Shawn nodded, squinting at him as she considered this. "That sounds reasonable."

"I have done tests to this very matter. Under a microscope, I have seen cells come back to living status after having been oxygen deprived and technically dead for several years. Frozen. Back to living," said Sameer.

"Wow," Shawn said. Again, this was something she felt like maybe he could have made her aware of. She felt like all involved parties should have access to the same knowledge. "That's significant."

"Yes, I am thinking so. I am not seeing why we cannot translate that to our project here," he said, pulling a hand away from the arms-crossed posture to wave at the dead man's face. He stared at her for a long time, then said, "Did you come up with any ideas out there, Shawn? I am almost ready to shut this down and send him back."

Shawn frowned and scoffed. "Really? So soon? We've only been at it an hour. No, to answer your question – no new ideas. But what about this," she said, holding a hand out toward Sameer. Her comfort level in being around this cadaver had multiplied exponentially, and it was showing in her gestures. Just being this close was a step in the right direction. So to speak, anyway. "What if we left him hooked up overnight. Let that blood pump through the brain for twenty-four hours and see if that makes a difference?"

Sameer was nodding very slowly and subtly as he stared at the dead man's face. "This is not a bad idea, Shawn. There are billions of cells in the brain. Maybe they have not yet received the blood and oxygen because they are not directly in contact with the capillaries."

"Osmosis," Shawn said, pointing at him.

Shawn skipped up the steps with a smile, purse banging against her hip, as the excitement grew in her chest. For when she had pulled out of the parking lot this morning, there had been no sign of Cory's Jeep. But when she had pulled in just now, it had been there. She had parked right next to it with a yelp, raising a fist in the air. She opened her apartment door and slung her purse up onto the hook, then slid her phone across the bar as she dashed to the bathroom to wet and brush her teeth. She performed these two tasks simultaneously to save time, and did the latter with great vigor, as she knew she was about to be handing out long kisses.

When she finished, she whipped her sweater off and pulled on a t-shirt, then looked down at herself. The khakis weren't doing it for her. So she kicked them off as well and went ahead and donned a pair of soft cotton pajama pants – these with coffee mugs and saucers on them. She immediately felt better. In the kitchen, she grabbed the vodka bottle, then stopped, standing and frowning at the fridge. "Nah. Not tonight," she said to herself, and put the bottle back on the counter. She grabbed her phone and was out the door.

Three hard knocks on his door, and a fifteen-second wait later, and the door finally swung open. Shawn didn't wait to jump on him and shower his face with kisses. "Cory! Oh my God, I missed you!" she said. Then she growled as she kissed him on the lips. He wrapped his arms around her and picked her up, kicking the door closed behind her and carried her to the couch, piggy-front style. She was proud of herself when he dropped her down onto the couch on her back, because she never let her hands come out of their position around his neck. She did squeal as she fell backward, though he was right there with her all the way. Cory's weight knocked her breath out as he landed on her, but she didn't let that stop her. Her tongue was in his mouth and they were already breathing heavy. Hell, they had three days of kissing to make up for. These mouths weren't going to kiss themselves.

After several long minutes of necking, hands seeking and squeezing what they found, and moaning, Cory finally, and abruptly, sat up. Shawn stretched her arms up above her head, reaching for the arm of the couch, smiling widely.

"So, how you doing, girlfriend?" Cory asked, raising his eyebrows and turning to lean against the corner of the couch. He was clearly bothered. Shawn was glad for this. Any time someone had his hands on her chest, she was going to be monitoring his mood afterwards. That was just the way it was. It always had been, and it always would be. There was no getting over that for her. Self-doubt was a powerful toxin in the blood, and couldn't be boiled out without major therapy. But his hands on her had been that therapy.

Shawn put her feet against his leg and pushed herself up to a sitting position, then straightened her pants underneath her. She tilted her head and smiled sweetly at him. "I'm fantastic, boyfriend of mine!" she said, pointing at him playfully. She stuck her tongue out, mouth open and reveling in her happiness. She had only used the word once or twice before, when referring to Cory. It still felt new and fun to call him that.

"You'll have to tell me all about your trip," she said, rubbing her toes against his leg.

Cory shook his head. "It's actually not that interesting. A new system install. Access lists. Entry badges. Shit like that. Pretty boring to talk about. How about yours?"

Shawn sighed and looked at the ceiling. "Well, I had a breakthrough at work today. This guy, Jeremy, who I work with, he made a really good point about something I hadn't thought about. So the whole rest of the day went a lot better."

He stared at her for a beat, the ghost of a smile on his lips. "Really? If you were any more cryptic I'd think you were a Dan Brown novel."

"I know, I know," she said, holding her hand out in front of her face so she could look at her fingernails. It had been almost two weeks since she'd had them done, and it was starting to show. "I'm – OH! You know what?" she said, suddenly sitting bolt upright. "Oh my God, I can't believe I almost forgot to tell you this!" She leaned forward and came up onto her knees, tucking her feet behind her, then sat on them, putting her hands together in a clap. "You know Laura Carter?"

Cory looked at her sideways for a minute. "Wait. Is she the gal we met the other day at Cino's? The one Heath's dating now?"

"Yes. Her. Dude. We are like best friends, Cory. You wouldn't believe. I love this girl so much," she said, clasping her hands together in front of her heart and raising up on her knees again. She looked up at the ceiling, smiling dreamily. "We are like two peas from the same pod."

"Wow. That's great. You've been hanging out, I guess," Cory said, raising his eyebrows.

"Uh huh. She came and spent the night with me Friday, then we went to the flea market almost all day Saturday. Oh my God, we drank so much beer. Bought a bunch of shit," she said, waving her hand toward the new butterfly shadowbox on her wall, "then we crashed at her place that night. But we stayed up late into the night drinking tequila and listening to records."

"Tequila? Whoo. Girl, keep me away from that shit," said Cory, shaking his head.

"I know, right? Especially after drinking so much beer. Cory, I love this girl so much. She has to be my best friend."

"Whoa, that's awesome, sugar! I'm glad you two met, then!" he said.

"I am so glad we met." She put her hand on her heart. "I am *so* glad we met," she said, shaking her head. "Oh, and plus, also too, as well, she's the only girlfriend I've met since I moved here. I really needed a girlfriend. She's only like eighteen months younger than me. And we like so much of the same stuff."

"So how'd you two hook up?" he asked.

"Well, we traded numbers at Cino's that day. But she called me Friday right as I was getting off work. I had actually forgotten that we traded numbers." She fell back onto her rump and stretched her legs back out, putting her ankles on Cory's thigh. "Crazy. So I am so glad she reached out. Anyway, she invited herself over for drinks and a movie. I had a rough day Sunday, I'll tell you that."

"Yeah, I can imagine. Tequila on beer? Sign me up for that!" he said, waving his hands and looking off to the side guiltily.

Shawn giggled. Then she sat looking at him for a minute, just smiling and taking in his good looks. "It's so good to see you, Cory. I'm so happy you're back."

"Me too," he said, nodding. He put his hands on her ankles and rubbed them. "I missed you something fierce."

"Hey, look," she said, "we need to talk."

He raised his eyebrows, pulling his head back on his neck. "Okay…"

"Well, I'm not sure why you pulled off of me a minute ago, but I'm on fire right now. I really, realllllly need a fireman."

Thirty minutes later, and sitting naked on the couch, side-by-side, Shawn leaned her head on Cory's shoulder. His hands were clasped behind his head, feet up on the ottoman and breathing heavily. Shawn had her hand on his chest and was rubbing slowly, just feeling his chest hair beneath her palm. Her mouth was open, mouthing different shapes subconsciously as her mind went back over what she needed to tell him. When she finally spoke, she was hoarse, and had to clear her throat and start over.

"I told Lo what I do at work."

"Yeah?" Cory said, being polite. Very interesting subject matter, that tone said.

She slapped his chest lightly. "No. I mean, about the secret project."

"What?" he said, trying to lean forward. They looked at each other. "Seriously?"

"Please don't be insulted, Cory. I was really drunk and not making good decisions." They had returned to their previous posture and she was rubbing his breast again. He was rubbing her shoulder now, pulling her in closer. Her hand was very large in her vision, her eyes pressed right up against his skin under his arm. "Anyway, I've been thinking about it. And I will tell you if you want me to, Cory."

Cory didn't say anything. He just kept rubbing her shoulder.

"I've already told her. So I've broken my word." She shrugged. "I don't even really feel bad about it anymore, either. What we're doing is private. But that doesn't have to mean secret."

"Yeah. Well, I don't want to make you feel worse about it. But if you're already feeling better about it, then yeah. I would love for you to tell me. All this mystery has made me deathly curious."

"Funny you should say that," said Shawn.

"What?"

"Deathly."

She sat up and looked at him. Her face was half a foot from his. She looked it up and down, studying the shape of his lips, his nose. "God, you're handsome," she said.

"Well, thank you. You know I think you're pretty gorgeous yourself."

She smiled and patted his chest. "So you want to hear what we're doing up there behind the curtain?"

He raised his eyebrows and nodded. "Yeah. The anticipation is killing me."

Shawn rolled her eyes, feigning exasperation. "Will you quit with the death metaphors?"

He smiled lightly at her, then put his hand on her chin, cupping it. He rubbed his thumb on her cheek. "I know, Shawn. I already know."

Shawn finally said yes when Cory invited her to stay that night. Why shouldn't she? She wanted to sleep with him. They had already had sex, so the only new ground to be broken was the actual sleeping part of it, and she couldn't find any part of her that objected to being his small spoon, his thick arms wrapped round her and protecting her from the night. She only hoped he liked to snuggle.

After having spent her first weekend away from him since they had become an item, she realized she had missed him terribly. She had not spent the whole weekend pining over him, but that might be attributed to her having Lo to hang out with. When she had finally taken a moment to process what she was feeling for him, during one of her midnight excursions to the bathroom to pee, she had realized it wasn't just a little thing she was feeling. Sure, she knew infatuation came before the big show. But she also believed infatuation – that sweet puppy love that spins up the heart like the capacitor on a high-powered motor – was a gift from God. It was like kindling to get the fire started. During the honeymoon phase of the relationship, she believed was the best time to get all the getting-to-know-each-other stuff covered. Because when the flames took and the real wood started burning…

It was also not lost on her that she had been making a lot of references to fire during her internal metaphorical monologue. And on the heels of that, she realized she really felt something wonderful. Like, maybe more than just infatuation. She really had it bad for that boy.

At the breakfast table the next morning, Shawn was beginning to feel the stress of being up against the clock. She felt like she had so much to tell Cory, so much to catch up on with him, but knew she had to get to work soon. And then, of course, there was the thought of what was waiting for her when she got to work. She felt like maybe that disconnect between spiritual and science that had helped her overcome so much yesterday – well, maybe it was just new-car smell. Nothing had changed and she had fallen back into the discomfort zone. Now it felt like no matter how many times she reminded herself this was just science and tech doing crazy things with biology, she still couldn't talk herself into believing it wasn't a big deal. And it was, by God! Bringing a dead person back to life in *any capacity*, spiritually disconnected or not, was huge! It was unnatural! It was peeking behind the curtain, asking someone what they had seen. There was a reason it was referred to as the Great Divide. Man was not supposed to have affair with someone who had been there and back. New car smell or not, whether she had strengthened her resolve or not, she was going to have to get used to standing in a room with a cadaver that may or may not open its mouth and speak to them. Focus its eyes on them. And maybe the possibility that it could happen without warning spontaneously was the worst of it. How does one prepare for that?

While she drank her coffee, her toast now so many tiny crumbs on the white plate, she asked Cory how he had figured out the secret. How had he known, and why had he hidden this knowledge from her?

"You asked about my experience with death. You told me about yours and how it had scarred you so badly." He shrugged, forking the last bit of egg into his mouth. Then he wiped his mouth and crumbled the napkin, dropping it on the plate. "You kept talking about how freaked out you were by what your boss was doing. It didn't take a giant leap to make the connection," he said. Then he leaned forward, reaching across the table and taking her wrist. "Listen, Shawn, your secret is completely safe with me. I'm here for you. If you need to talk about it or anything. I know it's probably insanely scary for you. But you don't have to worry about me talking."

Shawn nodded at this, sipping her coffee. "Thank you, Cory. That means a lot." She stared at him for a moment, watching as he cleaned the inside of his mouth with his tongue. "Cory, what do you think of Lo's excitement about the project?"

"What do you mean? I can't blame her. I'm excited too!" he said.

"Oh, no. Not you too," she said, shaking her head.

"What? What are you talking about?"

"Don't tell me you're going to donate your body to medical science now. Fuck sake. I can't handle it."

Cory frowned and chuckled at the same time. "Hell, no! I'm not saying that. Not that I have anything against it in principle. But no, I'm not wanting to be on your table."

"Well, I think she is. She does want to be."

He waved a hand at her, shaking his head. "Nah. I think you're reading into this. She's having fun, late-night ghost-story talk with her friend."

Shawn put her hands between her thighs in the chair and took a deep breath. "You think?"

"Sure. Haven't you ever stayed up late as a kid with your friends, trying to spook yourselves?"

"No."

Cory widened his eyes. "Oh. Okay. Well, I'm sorry, but you're the exception. Not the rule. Everyone does that shit."

"Well, I didn't. Maybe I didn't have those kind of friends. I have had this aversion to doing anything that involved thinking about death though," she said.

"Yeah. Well, I wouldn't read too far into that. She's just having fun. I'll be surprised if she actually registers for whole-body donation," Cory said, shaking his head. He picked up his mug, then scooted out from the table to go refill it, putting a hand on her shoulder as he passed by. "Besides," he said from behind her, "wasn't there a lot of alcohol involved?"

Shawn sighed, looking up at the back door. The sun was spilling in at a beautiful angle, turning one side of his living room into a billion shades of white. "Yeah. I guess so," she said. Then she leaned over the back of the chair stretching her arms into the air. "Okay. I gotta go," she said, scooting away from the table. She handed her plate to Cory, who stood next to the sink with his hand out.

"Okay, sugar. I'll see you tonight, right?" he asked. She liked his use of the pet name.

She nodded and stepped forward, kissing him quickly on the lips. "My place tonight, okay?" Then she shuffled across the breezeway to freshen up and get dressed for the day.

The office had a buzz about it. Everyone seemed excited about something. This made Shawn's stomach drop. She had barely set her purse on her desk when Sameer was breezing by behind her, saying, "Shawn, we've had success! Hurry to the lab!"

Oh God.

She slung her coat off her shoulders and onto the back of her desk chair, then made eye-contact with Jeremy, who stood behind his own desk smiling, a cup of coffee up to his mouth. He gave her a thumbs-up. Shawn smiled weakly back at him and gave an even weaker thumbs-up herself. Then she turned and followed Sameer's burning path to the hidden side of the building.

When she came in through the secured access door, she looked straight through all the glass rooms back to where D Room was, hoping to see something and hoping not to see anything at the same time. All she saw was a slightly distorted version of Sameer walking around the room with a fair amount of purpose. There was extra pep in his step, that was for sure.

Shawn followed the glass-surrounded corridor back to the lab and pushed open the door. The first thing to catch her eye was the fact that the cadaver, though still mostly covered in the white sheet, had been strapped down with the leather belts attached to the bed. Oh dear God. Had that been necessary? Her heart was beating madly in her chest. "What's going on, Sameer," she said, a look of worry and fear evident in her visage. She thought her voice might have betrayed the same.

Sameer turned and looked at her, smiling broadly. He reached up and adjusted his wire-frame glasses and said, "We have had breakthrough, Shawn. And I must give you credit for your idea."

"My idea?" she said, still standing by the door. There was no fucking way she was coming any farther into the room until she knew there wasn't a damn *Walking Dead* character in the lab with her.

"Yes!" he said, coming around the table and taking her by the shoulders. He looked as if he might want to kiss her cheek, squeeze her in a fatherly hug. *So proud of you, darling!* "What? What is wrong?" he said, his smile finally giving way to the realization that Shawn was not celebrating with the same celerity as he.

"What kind of success are we talking about here, Sameer? Did the man get up and walk around?" she asked, looking past him to see that the body still lay still on the table.

Sameer frowned and dropped his hands from her shoulders. "No. Shawn, this is impossible. We do not activate those parts of the brain."

She looked past him again and he followed her gaze. "Shawn, I strapped him down as precautionary measure only. You can be assured."

She swallowed and nodded, still staring at the lump in the white sheet. "Okay. So what was this great success then?"

"Come!" he said, turning and pulling her by the shoulder. "Come to look at his face!"

Shawn steeled herself and stepped forward, heart slamming even harder now, double-time. She felt faint with fear and excitement, and hoped she didn't lose her footing. As she approached the head-end of the table, she immediately saw what had Sameer all bursting with excitement. The man's eyes were moving rapidly around. His cheeks were twitching and lips separating by only millimeters. It looked as though he were in a deep REM-powered dream, but for the eyes being open. Shawn stared in horror at the tiny movements going on in the man's face. His physiognomy looked alive. She swallowed again and looked up at Sameer. "Has he spoken or anything?"

"No, but the awareness protocol seems to be working!"

"You think he looks aware?" she said. If anything the man looked like he was having a nightmare and needed to be put out of his misery. She didn't want to say 'awakened' because fuck that. He needed to be put back to death and sent back to the university for cremation. Right now. But no, he did not look 'aware' to Shawn. He looked alive somehow, God help her, but not aware. If this was the success Sameer was talking about she wasn't apt to get on board with the celebrations too quickly.

"His senses are reacting to external stimuli, Shawn. Watch this," he said, then snapped his fingers loudly in the man's right ear. There was a marked change in the subject's tiny twitches. They almost *leaned* toward the right side of his face, and looked as though if the corpse had the proper faculties about it, it would definitely turn its head away from the loud noise. This flicker in the pattern she had seen had only lasted an instant, no more, but it had been well obvious that it was indeed a reaction. She stood shaking her head.

She took a deep breath, trying to calm herself. Well, this wasn't *that* bad, was it? All things considered, if this was the worst that had happened, she could come to terms with it. It was by far easier than accepting a corpse coming to life and stomping around the room breaking shit. She put her hands on her face, wiping away the stress, then stretched her hands out by her sides, concentrating on slowing her heart rate. "Okay. I see. This is good news, Sameer," she said, nodding. When he looked up at her incredulously, she smiled wanly at him.

Ever the model of patience, Sameer smiled back at her. God bless him, he was being extremely tolerant of Shawn's extreme discomfort with the dead. She knew it was written all over her face, and had been, probably, every time she had been in this lab. And he was pointedly ignoring it, treating her with respect and dignity. No need to talk about it if she can't help it. Shawn was thankful for this.

"Has there been any other breakthrough?" she asked.

"Only the sensory response to stimuli. You can wave your hand over his eyes and see," said Sameer. Shawn understood that he was offering her the chance to participate in the project for which he was paying her a ridiculous salary. She also understood it wasn't an offer she could refuse. He was not asking, in other words.

She gave a minute nod and stepped forward gingerly, then opened and closed her hands repeatedly by her sides. Her palms were sweaty. She took a deep breath in, then blew it out through a small O. She then raised her hand above the cadaver's incessantly moving pupils. She held it still for a moment, just building the courage to do something else. Sameer waited silently, an exercise in patience and understanding. She met his eyes momentarily, then looked back at her hand. That was when she noticed that the eyes that were rapidly darting hither and yon only seconds before, were now staring straight up at her palm. The pupils were still shaky – it was not a perfect static focus, but they had stopped their erratic shifting. She felt a cold chill run down her spine as she realized what was happening here. This was reanimation. Granted it wasn't a full 'sit-up and have a conversation with them' reanimation, but it was reanimation. They had brought this man's brain back to life enough to have his eyes and ears respond to stimuli. Her blood felt cold in her veins. It wasn't completely borne of fear, either. This was something new to consider. She would have to spend her own hours thinking about what had happened here – which was a brand of excitement. Acceptance and curiosity, learning and experimentation. Her mind would have to process this. But no, the cold blood was not all from fear. It was from possibilities opened to the world of science. It was from the recognition that maybe all things were possible. It was from understanding that maybe the Great Divide wasn't so great after all. Maybe it was only a small step across a very deep, but very narrow chasm. Had they defeated death here? Certainly not. But they had gotten its attention. It now looked headlong at them over its shoulder, knowing it had been tapped.

Shawn moved her hand from left to right, toward the subject's chin and back toward the forehead, very slowly. The eyes played catch-up. They followed her movements, a split second behind. The eerie feeling she had had settled in her stomach. And during this entire time, from the time she had seen Sameer snap until now, the dead man's lips and cheeks had never stopped their tiny minute twitches.

She met Sameer's eyes again, breathing deeply, still focusing on her calm. Her courage was gaining traction, winning out over the unsure. She was staring at him, steeling herself, knowing what her next move was to be, and wondering if Sameer could see it in her eyes. He never looked away. The ghost of a smile still lingered on his lips. That knowing smile, backed by an intelligence founded on successful experiments just like this. He nodded very subtly at her – just the one dip of his chin, ever so slightly as to almost be invisible – and she licked her lips. Then she looked at the dead man's face and leaned very slowly down toward his ear. At this close proximity, she could see the tiny veins in his face – burst capillaries from stress or other, from another lifetime. She could smell him. He smelled like the grave. He smelled like flesh that had once been vital, but had run its course. She could see the long gray hairs in the man's ear and wondered if the man had had a wife in his other life. Had he kept his hair trimmed for her? Did someone love this man as a husband? She focused on the man's eye – only the left was visible from this angle – and she could see the minute twitches in his eyelid as well as the erratic darting motions of the pupil. With a calm she could have never guessed she would possess, Shawn spoke softly. "Hello. My name is Marcella. Can you hear me?"

It wasn't something she had planned out to say in her mind, but the feminine and proper version of her name might have been received better by a mind on the brink of existence, brought back by so many tiny shocks just on the edge of a false consciousness. Hearing the soft purr of her feminine voice speaking a name typically reserved for a man might have caused some adverse reaction in the chemical science taking place in that man's reawakened brain.

Again, much as it had after Sameer's snap in the other ear, the face reacted. Only this time it didn't look as though it was trying to get away. If anything, it looked calmed by the calming voice. Like now it was trying to stop its tiny insignificant and wasteful movements. As if they had all been by design somehow, a never-ending search for something to latch onto. The lips looked stiller. The eyes, now shifted ever so slightly toward his left ear, had taken on an eerie calm as well. The movement of his cheeks was subtler.

Still in the same position, hands resting on her knees, Shawn spoke again. "I see that you can hear me. I am here as a friend. Are you aware of where you are?"

The eyelids looked strained for a moment, as if they were trying to force a focus in the eyesight. It looked, for all intents and purposes, like the man was blind and trying to see. She wondered briefly if he had been blind in his past life, and was that something they would know? Something disclosed on the death certificate details to which they had access through the university app? For the first time since entering the room, Shawn noticed that the man had not and was still not blinking. How his eyes were staying moist was a wonder she would have to reflect on later. Then suddenly the movements stopped. All the minute, almost imperceptible twitches and shifts in the man's face – not controlled by muscle but, rather by nerves – were suddenly replaced by a perfect still. She pulled her head back a notch and frowned. She looked up at Sameer without moving her head. Sameer stood stoic and faceless, arms crossed in complete detached observation.

Shawn stood up, looking between the dead man's now static visage and Sameer's live but contemplating one. He, too was staring at the face of the subject. She saw him chewing the inside of his lip in concentration. After a full minute, Sameer sighed and pulled the sheet up over the cadaver's face. Shawn watched this with solemn curiosity. Part of her felt sad, for it looked as though the man had just died all over again. Had he experienced two deaths? If they could hook him up again and get him to talk, would he describe both deaths? Would there be any cognizance of the time separation between the two, if there were two?

When she looked back at Sameer, he was staring at her. He nodded once, curtly, then tilted his head to the machinery. Shawn nodded back and went to the head of the table, turning off the circulation machine. She knew Sameer would later deal with disconnecting the tubes from the needles, removing the needles from the base of the subject's skull, and disposing of the now dead blood. She bent down and turned off the oxygen supply. Knowing their use of this man's body for the project had reached its conclusion, she felt strangely at peace. It had not been a terrible experience for them. She hoped it had not been for the reanimated man, if there was any consciousness to be had there. She felt good knowing that the last thing he had heard before he shut off completely had been her calming, soft voice whispering friendly assurances. There had developed a sort of bond with this twice-living man and she was thankful for the peace she now felt, rather than some mixed sort of horror and repulsion – which is what she had expected to feel. She looked at Sameer again and he nodded again, subtly, closing his eyes for a moment. She was finished here. Before she turned to leave the lab, she took another bold step in the direction of her acceptance of death and finality: she reached up and gave a respectful pat on the chest of the body that lay beneath the white sheet.

Tuesday evening was even better than Monday had been. The stress of having to face death in such an odd and personal manner was off her shoulders and she had made it through. Granted, she had only been exposed to the body for a total of only several hours, but she felt like baby steps were an appropriate way to face such a traumatic fear. She was proud of herself, regardless of how long or short her interactions had been, and especially considering the hurdle she had made it over in the last few minutes of the last session this morning. That had been a huge step for Shawn. Though she had to admit to herself that if that man had turned his head and looked at her, she would have walked out of her sanity. She wasn't ready for that yet. Baby steps.

Fresh out of the shower and sitting on the sofa with her towel opened up, she lay under the fan cooling off. It had occurred to her before that if she didn't take such hot showers, her cool-off time wouldn't be so dramatic. But she felt cleaner – more sanitized, even – when the water was so hot it turned her skin red, the fact that her armpits and lower back were already sweaty before she even grabbed the towel notwithstanding. She had made sure the front door was locked this time so as not to have her cool-down time disturbed. She may have a long and happy future with the man next door, but that didn't mean she needed him walking in while she lay cooling. It was almost an anxiety when she was cooling off that someone would walk in. The fact that he had done just that last week had only gone to strengthen her resolve about it. Not help her get over it.

She opened her phone and pulled up the OuterCircle app. *Same bullshit, diff- wait!* There was something different here… A friend request! *Ooh, nice!* She had a pretty good feeling it was Lo, and was rewarded with the answer. She accepted immediately, smiling and squealing to herself. Then she had to look at Lo's pictures and profile. That took fifteen minutes or so, and by the time she was satisfied that she knew everything she needed to know about her new friend, she had sufficiently cooled to the point of shivering under the fan. Mission accomplished. Sleep the phone, wrap the towel, stand up and head for the room to get into her pajamas. It was starting to warm up outside, finally, so she chose the black silk shorts and camisole.

After drying her hair, she unlocked her front door, taking a quick peek through the peephole to see if by chance Cory was already on his way over. The chances were, she knew less than one in a thousand trillion billion, since he only had about fourteen feet from door to door, in which she would be able to see him through the peephole. But sometimes you got lucky. No one ever wins the lotto, but someone always wins. She went to the kitchen and made herself a drink.

When she got back to the couch, she picked up the Big Book of Brains and fingered through it to the next sticky note. Was there something else in here that could help them on the project? She couldn't see why there would be. Unless Sameer had assigned her the reading as just a second set of eyes. Maybe she would catch something he didn't? But then why had he highlighted exactly what he wanted her to read? There was no way she would catch anything he hadn't. Maybe Jeremy could. She looked up at the sliding glass door. Jeremy. He was the brain surgeon. Hell, maybe *he* had been the one to do the highlighting, originally intended for Sameer's eyes! That sparked a thought and she flipped to the front of the book to look at the inside cover. And there it was, written in black ink at the top of the inside cover, Jeremy Gaylin. So this was his book. That did make a little more sense. So it was likely – or at least possible – that Sameer had not even read the book at all. He knew his stuff, that was for sure. But it was well understood in the office that the brain guy was Jeremy. Not Sameer. Interesting. Without asking why he lost his license to practice, Shawn sure wanted to ask why he had lost his license to practice.

She flipped back to the next section marked with a sticky.

Though the brain only forms a small percentage of the host's total mass, it consumes as much as 20% of available energy and oxygen. Thus, the more one uses his or her brain, the more calories are being burned. Even at rest, the brain consumes 20% of a calorie. It is always active, and never sleeps, even when the host does. While the person is sleeping, the brain is reorganizing, regenerating connective neural pathways and learning. Scientists have long thought dreams are the product of these involuntary exercises performed by the brain while the body is asleep.

*But what the hell is sleep?* Shawn thought. Some part of the brain must surely be shutting down during sleep, because it is a different phase of consciousness, is it not? She looked back through the window. A quick knock on the front door, and it was suddenly coming open. "Hello in here," said Cory as he came in.

Shawn turned and smiled at him, then patted the couch beside her. "Hey there, my man. Wanna drink? Come sit!"

"I'll get one in a minute," he said, rounding the couch and dropping into his normal corner spot. He leaned back and put his arms on the sofa back, then yawned. "What's up, buttercup?"

"Hey, I wanted to ask you a question," Shawn said, slapping the book closed and turning in her seat to look at him.

"Hit me," said Cory, slapping his knees.

"How did you really know about my project at work?" He started to answer but Shawn held her hands up, "Hang on. Hear me out. I thought a lot about it and I just can't get there. Just because someone mentions death and being freaked out by it, then says something about her boss creeping you out… How would someone make that leap from this to that? Bringing someone back from the dead? That's like my telling you I'm working on something small and you just guessing I'm building an atom bomb."

"Shawn, I promise, I'm not lying to you," he said, shrugging. "I mean, I know this guy. Sameer Singh has been in magazines and shit. I mean, once you know who he is it's not a giant leap to think he could be working on something like that," said Cory. Shawn's face fell and he saw it. "I mean, after hearing you say the thing about death and all. I mean, perfect storm, right? It all just sort of added up." Then he stared at her for a moment longer. "What? What'd I say?"

"You've read about him? What do you mean? What magazines?"

"Shit, I don't know, Popular Science? You don't know who your own boss is?"

Shawn was staring at him like she'd just seen a ghost. She swallowed, holding her glass in front of her now, and looking at it like she might have made a mistake in pouring it. "I guess not, now that you say that. So you've read about him? What did you read? Who is he?"

"Oh, man, he's an innovator. He's always trying new brilliant experiments. It said he spent time working with a quantum computer, trying to manipulate matter in a way that would make it invisible. Said he had some success at it," Cory said, holding a hand up. "Crazy stuff, really. But it's all pretty cool. He was the guy who invented the active matrix monitor."

Shawn shook her head. "I don't know what that is. None of that sounds very interesting to me. Like, nothing as shocking as bringing someone back from the dead."

"Well, you should read the article. It's hard to remember all his failures because they never became anything. But he worked with some really weird shit. I think his daughter had some rare disease or something and he was trying to do some experiments on her brain. All through strobes and loud noises or something. I can't remember all the details."

"I didn't know he had a daughter. I guess I really don't know my boss," Shawn said.

"Anyway, I'm sorry if it freaked you out. That wasn't my intention. I was just thinking you were talking so much about death and that what he said had shaken you to the core. I made the logical leap: if anyone would work on such a thing, it would be him."

"I guess," she said, turning her left hand over to look at her nails. It was getting time to have them done again. Maybe she would go by tomorrow after work. After a minute, she sighed and started twirling a lock of her hair with that hand. The other hand pulled the martini glass up to her mouth. "When are you gonna take me for another ride on your Indian?"

"Whenever you want, babe."

"I think the four of us should go somewhere together on your motorcycles."

"Four of us?" Cory said, frowning.

"Yeah. You and Heath can take me and Lo," Shawn said. "Like a picnic or something."

Cory scoffed. "A picnic? Uh…"

"Shush, you," said Shawn. "You know what I mean. Maybe a dinner or something."

Cory nodded. "Yeah, we can do that. Set it up."

Shawn talked Cory into sleeping at her place that night after a little coaxing. He had initially said he wasn't sure he could sleep in another bed, not with his only thirty feet away, at least. Then Shawn, standing at the edge of her bed, had frowned at him and said, "Oh yeah. You said you hadn't seen my tattoo yet."

Cory, leaning against the doorjamb with his hands in his pockets, had shaken his head, pursing his lips. Maybe he was interested.

But when Shawn had whipped off her camisole and pulled her shorts down a few inches, acting like she wasn't standing there half-nude, his eyes had perked up. She was acting so casual that someone listening from another room would have had no idea the state of dress she was in. "Yeah, see, it's about to take flight," she said, running a finger down below its little feet. She didn't have to pull the waist band down more than a couple of inches to reveal the whole butterfly, but the gesture of holding it down with her thumb made up for whatever wasn't actually showing. Cory was staring, his mouth hanging slightly open. Shawn was loving the attention.

"I mean, I guess you could kiss him if you wanted to," she said, pulling her shorts down another inch or so, revealing the top of a patch of stubble that hadn't been tended to in a couple of days. The tattoo fell directly behind where her waistband would sit under normal circumstances, so there was no need to show her pubis. But with her top off and her nipples standing out now, it felt good to be sexy. "See?" she said, pulling them down just a tiny bit more. She was staring at the butterfly herself, twisting this way and that to show it under different angles of the light from the bathroom. "But you would have to be in the bed with me, because that's the only time I can let him out of his cage."

She looked up and met Cory's eyes, which had almost glassed over. He was chewing on his lip.

"Does he like to be kissed?" he said, almost without inflection.

"Oh, yes. But so does his friend," she said, pulling just the middle part of her waistband down several long inches. This revealed her to him in a way he had not yet experienced. Cory's only encounter had been a completely tactile one. Not visual. She wiggled the shorts band back and forth with her thumb, twisting her hips slightly. "You could make them both very happy if you would come to bed and kiss them for me. I reckon about thirty minutes of kissing would do," she said. She looked into his eyes tilting her head down. "Though I don't think the butterfly would need more than a few seconds of that."

# Six

Wednesday morning, Shawn woke up peacefully during a natural break between REM cycles. She rarely used an alarm, preferring instead to let her own brain make the decision about when it was ready to join the waking world. Alarms were so jolting. And having practiced the routine of just getting up when her eyes opened, she woke up at roughly the same time every day. Her life had been worlds better since ditching the klaxon.

So her eyes had drifted open to a brightening ceiling, the overhead fan lazily running its repetitive course, and she had instantly remembered that her man was in bed with her. She lay on her back naked, arms stretched out to the sides, and Cory was on his stomach, head up under her right arm, breathing on her rib cage just inches from her breast. His right arm was strewn across her ribs, his ankle entangled with her own. She felt no urge to get up just yet. No urge to end this blissful waking moment. This was wonderful. This was what life was supposed to be about. This peaceful feeling would be smashed as soon as she walked out the front door. As soon as she merged into traffic on her way to the office. As soon as she slipped out from under Cory's arm to go relieve her bladder. She knew that anything she did beyond just lying here, right here, right now, would ruin the moment. So she lay still.

Staring at the ceiling, she felt more at peace than she had in as long as she could remember. She could tell by the sound of the traffic on 360, only a few hundred yards from her window, that it was not yet 6:30. The sound of the traffic told her when it was six, and then seven. She usually woke up at 6:04. Almost without fail, when her eyes popped open and she checked her phone, that's what time it was. So it was likely only a few minutes after that now. She had always been a fan of waking a couple of hours before it was actually time to roll out for work. That way she was alert on the road, fully awake and ready for the day before she ever left her door. Not to mention not having puffy eyes. So she still had plenty of time before she had to put her feet on the carpet. And she was reveling in this wonderful life. How could it be so perfect?

Shawn rolled her neck to look down at the sleeping beauty whose head was almost buried in her armpit. All she had to do was bend her arm at the elbow to reach down and lightly run her fingernails across that strong, muscular, manly shoulder. When she did, she saw his breathing change ever so slightly. But they had spent a few nights together now, so his unconscious awareness had let her in – had gotten used to her being part of his proximity. No alert necessary, it would tell him. If you feel the touch of a hand in the night, it's safe. It's only Shawn.

She stared at the top of his head, his brown shaggy hair making curls against her upper arm. She could feel the thin layer of sweat that stood between his arm and her rib cage. She was aware of many things this morning, lying in her own bed with a man snoring softly beside her. She watched his back muscles flex ever so subtly as he breathed, the pattern of light from the window changing, creating different shadow patterns with each breath. His muscles and – well, just his *manliness* made her wet. She could feel it now, in fact. She thought about waking him up before it was time to go. Roll him over onto his back and climb on top of him, riding him like that motorcycle he kept parked under the stairs. She smiled at this thought, fingernails still gently caressing the part of his back her hand naturally fell upon with her arm in this position.

Shawn felt at peace for another reason as well. When she went to work this morning, it would almost be like it had been ten days ago, before Sameer had ever come calling her to dinner, asking her if she wanted to bring people back to life. The body would be gone this morning. The thoughts of what had gone on, and project review, notes, a meeting with Jeremy, all of that would happen still. But at least there would be no corpse in the lab. She was getting closer to being okay with it all, of course. But it was going to take time. *Baby steps.*

She breathed in deeply, then picked up her phone from the table beside her bed, which her hand could reach without dislodging the sleeping man beside her. She woke the screen and swiped in her security pattern. She had a text message. From Sameer. Strange, that. He never texted this early. It had come in at 5:04 this morning. She hoped everything was okay.

> Shawn. Plz feel free to take the day off. Troubles with return of corpse to uni. Jeremy and I will be out all day. Enjoy the day

And just like that… the day got even more perfect.

There was no way she could go back to sleep now. Once her eyes opened for the day, Shawn never fought it. She never rolled over and tried to get back to sleep. That was not only a fruitless endeavor, but a waste of time. She did intend to stretch this moment a little longer. She thumbed through her social media, looked at the weather for the day – a high of 85° - and texted her mother and father, in a group text feed they all contributed to almost constantly.

She typed 'Good morning! I love you guys! It's gonna be a wonderful day!' then dropped her phone on the nightstand. Then she rolled over onto her right side, pulling Cory's face to her chest and wrapping her arms around him. He moaned and adjusted under her, but didn't try to pull away. After her extended hug, which involved a lot of kissing the top of his head, she finally got up and started the shower.

With a whole day to do whatever she wanted, Shawn tasked herself with coming up with what that would be. She sent a text to Lo asking if she happened to be off today. Lo responded almost instantly saying no, calling her a lucky bitch, and telling her to enjoy herself. She had also added kissy faces. That was okay though. Cory was always free to do something unless he got an emergency call, which he said didn't happen very often.

She sat at the kitchen table and ate a bowl of cereal with a pen in one hand, jotting down thoughts and ideas as they came to her. The biggest, boldest note on the page was 'Motorcycle Ride!' She underlined this several times and drew stars beside it. The sweater she had started knitting months ago sat on the chair next to hers, as she thought maybe she would get a wild hair this morning and actually add a little to it. It was already forgotten though. She pushed her cereal bowl away and rested her chin on her fist, staring out the back window while she twisted her pen in the other hand. She found herself suddenly and abruptly reminded of something Cory had said the night before, about truly knowing who her boss was.

Having completed most of her interview process on the phone and over video meetings, Shawn had accepted the job before she ever even met Sameer in person. So the name had never stuck out at her. She usually did a fair amount of research on whatever company she was interviewing with, believing a job interview should a two-way discourse. She had liked what she read about them, he was friendly and intelligent, so the phone calls and meetings went smoothly, and he had passed her interview check as she was passing his. There was nothing to indicate she needed to do any further research on the man. But now she was curious.

Cory had thought the man was interesting enough that he remembered his name. Furthermore, he had somehow made the jump from her mentioning death to divining that it was a resurrection project. No logical human would make that leap unless the man was known for pseudoscience shit like waking the dead already. So Sameer must have worked on some pretty outlandish things, and probably with some fair amount of success, to be mentioned in a magazine like PopSci, for God's sake. How had that escaped her knowledge?

She opened the browser on her phone and typed in his name. Hundreds of results were immediately ready for clicking. Hmm. Interesting. She went to tap the first one and the screen changed: incoming call from dad. She smiled and pressed the answer button, putting him on speaker and setting the phone on the table. "Hey, daddy! Good morning!" she said, standing and picking up her cereal bowl. She walked over to the sink to do away with it, running the water at a very low stream to keep quiet.

"Hey, butterfly. How's the weather in Texas?" said her dad.

"Ha, ha. I guess you've already looked it up if you're asking me that. So you're about to ask me if I miss Arkansas, right?"

"Honey, I already know you're Miss Arkansas."

Shawn rolled her eyes, and made a gagging motion with her finger. "Dad. Oh my God."

"That's what dads do when they retire, honey! They polish up on their dad-jokes," he said.

She sighed loudly enough for him to hear her. "You're right. You always make me laugh. So what's up, Papa?"

"Well, your mother and I have been talking, and we think we're going to come down there and see you for a while."

Shawn stopped what she was doing, widening her eyes and said, "Really?" And then she squealed with excitement.

"Yes, doll. How does this weekend sound?"

"Daddy, are you serious? I'm so excited!" she said, her voice breaking into unknown territory. "This weekend would be amazing!"

"Okay, little monarch. Make sure you make sure the weather's good for us," he said.

"I'll do what I can," Shawn said, raising a finger in the air. "Love you guys!"

"We love you too."

They disconnected and she dropped the phone on the table, bouncing up and down with her hands balled into fists in front of her. This was too good. She could not let Cory sleep through this news. He was finally going to have to wake his butt up.

Shawn was laughing again. Her face pressed hard against the side of her helmet, which was in turn smashed up against Cory's back. It was the only way she could comfortably put her arms around him and feel safe on the back of the motorcycle. She had tried sitting up straight and holding onto his waist a couple of times, but each time was quickly reminded not to do that again. A quick release of the clutch would send her backward – probably less than an inch – but instinct would kick in, causing her to bolt forward and grab him like her life depended on it. It probably did. It sure felt like it did.

There was a place around the lake that was nice riding, as Cory didn't like to spend too much time on the highways, what with all the idiots who treated it like their own personal Grand Prix track. And a Scout was not the most comfortable bike for highway riding anyway, as it weighed so little. Just the wind displacement from big trucks would send it all over the lane. Shawn was okay with whatever he decided on for their destination, knowing he would always keep her safety in mind.

Today, she wore a backpack because she had won him over about the picnic thing. Thinking she had achieved great victory when he finally agreed to it, namely because they were not meeting up with anyone else, she had shouted with glee and thrown her hands into the air. Then she had hugged and kissed him. Cory had said, "You know this means you have to carry it all, right?" Oh.

Still, though, they were heading to a nice spot on the other side of Joe Pool Lake where there were tables and benches under the shade of large elm trees. She had packed a tablecloth and some sandwiches and fruits. Thinking she was being fancy and unpredictable, she had sneaked in a bottle of vodka. Standing there watching her put it in the backpack, Cory had said, "Wanna pack something I can drink too?" Oh.

Knowing he never drank when he was handling the motorcycle was another thing that made her feel safe about it. Shawn could not see over or around him enough to get a look at the speedometer, but it sure felt fast to her. She, who had never been on two wheels until she met him, still had not gotten used to the road around her feet, and everything felt fast and exciting.

When they got to the other side of the lake and she finally stepped off the bike, thighs tight and tingling from the extended exposure to motor vibration, Shawn immediately shrugged off the backpack and went to work pulling out their lunch.

They had found the table and bench arrangement to be impractical and uncomfortable. The benches were old wood and were coming apart, giving plenty of places to catch clothes or give someone splinters. So they spread the tablecloth out upside-down on the grass and sat on that. Lunch had not been very exciting, in and of itself. Sandwiches – arguably the most boring food item – and some chips and sodas. Shawn was lying on her back now, looking up at the tree coverage above, her, hands up in the air as she told Cory how much she loved being on the back of his motorcycle.

"Are you sure you're happy riding pillion? You sure you don't want your own bike?" he said.

"Oh, no, no. Not me. I'm scared to death of motorcycles. But I don't mind riding with you," she said, swinging her arm down to point at him. Cory was leaning back against the tree, one arm resting across his knee.

"Yeah, well I think you'd look good on your own Indian. Maybe a white Chief."

"A white motorcycle?" Shawn said, frowning.

"Yeah. They have a matte white model. It's slick."

"That does sound pretty. Maybe we can go look at them this week," she said. "Or this weekend. Ooh!" And suddenly, she was rolling over on her belly and propping herself up by the elbows. "Cory! My parents are coming into town this weekend!"

"Hey, kick ass. Am I gonna get to meet them?" he asked, pulling a long draw from his plastic bottle of Coke.

"Well, of course you are, darling!" she said, reaching out and putting her hand on his leg. She squeezed and he put his hand on hers. After a minute, his smile faded. "What's wrong?"

"Are you sure you're ready for me to meet them?" he asked. "Isn't that a big step?"

"No!" she said, slapping his knee. "Silly. I've never understood why that was a thing. Unless," she said, getting real serious, "you plan to ask my daddy for permission to marry me." She closed her eyes and turned her face up to the sky, fluttering her fingers in the air.

Cory laughed out loud. "I love ya, Shawn, but I don't think we're quite there yet."

"Yet!" she said, rolling back and sitting up, crossing her eyes. "I heard you, Cory Klein! I heard you say 'yet'!"

Cory rolled his eyes and shook his head.

"You know I'm kidding, right?" Shawn said after a pregnant pause. "Though Marcella Klein does have a nice ring to it…"


That night in Cory's bed, they talked more about the motorcycle. And amazingly enough, Shawn found herself not just running from the idea. She tried to imagine what she would look like on a white bike. Obviously, she would get an Indian. If Cory said they were good, she believed they were. Knowing nothing about motorcycles herself, she had to take someone else's word. And frankly, there was nothing that turned her off about the idea of having the same brand as her boyfriend. Plus, she just liked the name. *Indian*. It sounded wonderful.

She tried to picture herself pulling up somewhere and swinging her leg over a white motorcycle, then pulling off her helmet. Could she rock that look? Would she need to get a few tough-looking tattoos to match? She had to smile at that. She was a butterfly girl, and that's about as far as she was willing to go with the ink.

After they had made love and she lay with her head on his chest, Shawn realized she was going to do it. She was going to buy a motorcycle. She thought it would be the coolest thing she had ever done. Plus, what better way to spend a little of her new salary? Why not? Of course, she would have to take a class and learn how to even ride one. Then she would want to practice and get proficient before she started daring the highways and byways. But yeah, sure, why not?

And with these thoughts in mind, she drifted to sleep with a smile on her face.

Shawn had offered to pick her parents up from the airport, assuring them it was no trouble, and her boss would have no problem letting her off a little early to make the trip out to D/FW international. But no. They insisted on renting a car so they could get around throughout the weekend. Offering her Jeep to them hadn't even gotten a response from her mother, who had trouble even climbing into it. "When are you going to get something more practical, Marcy?" she had asked, not without a little condescension. Shawn had to roll her eyes every time she got that talk from her mom. She just didn't understand, there was nothing like a Jeep.

She had indeed gotten off a little early Friday, which still wasn't a problem. Her job had defaulted back to the code wrangling she had been doing before the subject of awakening the dead had been broached. And since her workload was still relatively light – only a few customers to support – there had been little for her to do on Thursday.

She and Sameer had spent a little time talking about their successes with the project, which did involve, she was happy to say, a little patting on the back from the boss about her advances in being exposed to the dead. Shawn asked him when the next subject would be available. He told her there was no way to tell, what with the lottery-like system the university made bodies available to cooperating research labs. It could be a week, or it could be months, in other words. This excited her as well as giving her a little anxiety. Knowing that this could be sprung on her at any moment wasn't the most comforting of arrangements. But that was the nature of the system, she supposed. So with nothing further to report Thursday, Friday was even more of a breeze at work. When she asked permission to leave a little early to welcome her parents into town, Sameer had smiled and told her she was the queen of her own domain. She knew her workload, her customers and their demands. Which almost made it sounds like she could just not show up on days when they weren't blowing up her phone for code repair. Almost.

Shawn was now hustling about the apartment lighting candles and placing fresh flower arrangements, because she knew how much her mother loved them. She had stopped into the Tom Thumb on the way home and grabbed four or five arrangements, vases included, not paying much attention to price or type. Shawn didn't care much for flowers and plants herself. For one, she wasn't good at keeping them alive. And secondly, she always tended to forget they were even there, each piece becoming a part of the background of her daily meanderings. Thus, she forgot to water them. Which was why she wasn't good at keeping them alive. She had created her own personal catch-22 the first time she ever brought them into her home.

The counters were clean, everything was in its place, and it smelled like fresh flowers. She was sweating under her shirt and needed a shower, but was pushing it to the very last minute, wanting to make sure everything was perfect so they would see for themselves that she was doing well for herself. Her sister Monica already owned her own house by the time she was twenty-five. Shawn's apartment living would never hold a candle to that, no matter the fact that she could actually *afford* a house, but was just too uninterested in keeping up with it to bother. She always felt like she was competing with Moni even though her mother would always wave a hand and look away and say, 'Oh, stop that,' any time Shawn would bring it up. She had stopped bringing it up years ago.

When everything finally looked and smelled as good as it was going to look and smell, she stood in the middle of the floor, fists on her hips, turning in slow circles and telling herself she had done well. Shawn was wearing a tank top and gym shorts, her hair back in a messy ponytail, and she was covered in sweat, top to bottom. Billy Joel was blasting through the soundbar speaker, singing about Brenda and Eddie. She nodded. "Yeah. Good. I think we're good."

She finally got in the shower at ten past five. Her parents should be pulling into the parking lot around six. Mom had just texted saying they had landed. Perfect timing.

When they walked in, mom immediately noticed the flowers. Dad came strutting in with his shades on acting like he was the cock of the walk. Sixty years old with a beer gut and bad posture, her dad was still the coolest guy in the world. She laughed out loud as he oiled in through the front door looking like he was considering an investment opportunity. Then she ran up and hugged him. Sixty or not, he still had the strength to pick her up with one arm, twisting her back and forth while she kissed his cheeks.

"Hey baby doll! Wanna see a magic trick?" he said.

Shawn backed up and nodded, smiling and biting her bottom lip in excitement. He called her close with two of his fingers. She stepped forward and he leaned in close and said in a dramatically low voice, "I bet I can make your mom's cheeks turn bright red."

"Are you talking about me, Gavin?" said mom, making her way around the room and smelling the flowers.

"No, honey, just keep doing what you're doing," he said, looking over at her like he was exasperated. "Marcy, dear, your mother was the prettiest woman on the entire plane," he said, standing up straight and making a serious face. "And I know. I checked out every single one of them."

Shawn laughed out loud. Her mother didn't. But her cheeks did brighten. She was shaking her head. "Marcy, your father and I are going to need a drink."

"Yes, ma'am!" she said, and kissed her dad on the cheek again before dashing into the kitchen. She started pulling bottles out and setting them on the counter, right where they always were, pretending they hadn't just been put in the cabinet ninety minutes ago. "What would you like, Queen Estelle?"

Her mother came to the bar and rested her forearms across it, dropping her purse by the stool. She sighed. "What are you having, darling?"

"Oh, mom, you know I'm a vodka gal. I have all these little water bottle flavor things. They're like the perfect size for a water bottle, and they ma-"

"Just pour me something strong, honey, please."

"Sure, mom," said Shawn, losing a little spunk. *Grapefruit. That's what we'll have.* She opened the box of grapefruit flavorings – one of the ten boxes of flavors she had bought just for this visit – and ripped the top off of one of the foil packets. "I think you'll like this one, mom," she said.

Her mother waved a hand dismissively and turned toward the glass of the back door. Her dad, meanwhile, was stopping at every picture she had hanging on the wall, hands in his pockets and leaning in close, studying each one of them in turn. After Shawn finished mixing some vodka with the grapefruit flavor and pouring it over two glasses of ice, she rounded the bar and handed one to her mom. Her other hand, hidden behind her back, held a bottle of craft beer she had just purchased for the occasion. She loved trying to find beers she thought her dad had never tried. Back when she still lived in Arkansas, she would pick up a six-pack on her way to visit him most weekends. It always made her happy when she handed him one he hadn't yet tried.

"Daddy, you want a beer?"

Dad turned to her, raising his eyebrows. "Am I ready for the surprise?"

Shawn's face lit up in a smile. She nodded and held the bottle out in front of her, one hand below, one above, as if she were showcasing a fine piece of sculpture. He leaned in and squinted, then took the bottle from her. He fished his optics out from his shirt pocket and held them up in front of his eyes. "Ah, Conspiracy Pale Ale." He then tilted his head and smiled at her. "New to me!"

"Yay!" she squealed, hopping up and down and clapping her hands. She then handed him the opener she had put in her pocket. She took his bottle cap and went back to the kitchen to get her own glass. "Come on, come on, sit!" she said, offering her couches to them. Shawn dropped onto the corner of one where it would naturally force a separation of her parents. It was her favorite spot anyway.

Her dad put his hands on his knees and lowered himself into the seat to her left. Her mom continued standing, sipping her drink and looking out the back door. Oh well. She would sit when she was ready.

"So, I think we need to talk, you and me," dad said, leaning back into his own corner and crossing his legs.

Shawn sat up straight, pulling her feet under her, Indian-style, and straightened her shoulders. She was smiling. Her dad's talks were never serious anymore. Not since she had moved out. She had nothing to worry about.

"When are we going to get to meet the not-so-dark horse?" he asked and took a meaningful sip of his beer.

"Well," Shawn said, smiling bashfully, "I told him I would let him know when it's the right time for him to come over."

"Well, shouldn't you go ahead and let him know, sweetheart? Your father and I don't want to wait around all night for him to show up! Your father is going to have to eat soon," said mom.

Dad rolled his eyes, but only Shawn could see it. "I'm fine, Stel, just you stop your fretting," said dad.

"Mom, he lives across the breezeway anyway!" said Shawn.

"Oh my, I didn't know that. Did you know that, Gavin?" her mother said, some real concern in her voice.

"Well, yes, in fact, I did. I just didn't make a stink out of it, because our daughter is almost thirty years old," he said, leaning forward and putting a hand on Shawn's knee. "Well, we're ready whenever you're ready, my little butterfly."

Shawn couldn't help but smile. The excitement she felt for getting to let her dad meet her new boyfriend was right up there near the top. Be damned whatever propaganda she had spewed to Cory the other day. It *was* a big thing. It didn't have to mean anything, but it sure was fun.

"Mom, are you ready for me to go get him?" asked Shawn.

Her mother grasped the pendant of her necklace and looked worriedly at her husband. Was she trying to spoil this encounter? Why did she have to be so obviously uncomfortable meeting a boy? Big effing deal! Shawn knew that her dad had partly planned this trip just to meet Cory. And it wasn't because they necessarily cared who he was. If she was happy, they were happy. But her daddy knew it would make her happy to get to introduce them, so he had made it happen. She knew this because he had just about told her. As good as he was at telling dad jokes, he wasn't very good at hiding his intentions from her. Her mother, on the other hand, didn't even bother to try.

Gavin looked back at Estelle and raised his hands off the couch back, then dropped them. "What are you looking at me for?" Then he looked at Shawn and said, "Of course, she's ready, butterfly. Go get your man for us." He smiled and winked at her.

"Okay, daddy."

Cory was nervous. He stood inside his door, dressed for the occasion and fidgeting with the buttons on his shirt, his hair, popping his knuckles… "What are you worried about?" Shawn said, stepping into his apartment and taking him by the arms. "You're going to love my dad! This isn't an inquisition!" She stood on her toes and gave him a quick peck on the lips.

"Your dad? What about your mom?"

"Don't worry about her, sweetie," Shawn said, stepping closer. She put her hand on his cheek and looked him in the eyes. "She's not that bad. She's not going to eat you," she said softly. After a moment, she added, "as long as my dad is there, anyway."

Cory straightened his look at her. Then he smirked. "Okay. Okay, do I look okay?"

"Yes, you look amazing! I think you're way overdressed, but that's okay. You will make a great impression!"

"Okay. Do we have time for a quickie before we go over there?" he asked with a pleading look in his eyes.

Shawn matched his look and shook her head slowly. "We don't, I'm so sorry," she said, putting her hand on his cheek again. Then again up onto her toes for a quick kiss on the lips. "Let's boogy!"

She pulled him across the breezeway by the hand and dragged him into her apartment like a parade trailer with a flat tire. "Helllllooooo!" she said with more verve than absolutely necessary. "Mom and dad, meet Cory Klein!"

Her father got to his feet and crossed the room to shake Cory's hand, and Shawn could instantly see the approval on his face. Her mother waited patiently for her turn, standing with her hands clasped together loosely at her waist and a better-than-you smile threatening her lips. When it was her turn she did not step up and hug Cory like Shawn would have done were their roles reversed, but instead offered her hand to be shaken (kissed?) and looked down her nose at him as she introduced herself.

"It's very nice to meet you both. You did a wonderful job raising this one," said Cory, turning to look at Shawn.

Dad put his hands in his pockets and nodded. "So am I to understand that you take my daughter out on a motorcycle?"

Cory glanced back at Shawn, unsure how to react, then back quickly to her father. "Ah, she told you that, huh? Yeah, we've been on a couple of rides."

"I see," said Gavin. "I never could get the hang of being on two wheels myself. I was always wary of the difference in tire ratios between bikes and cars."

Cory shook his head and said, "Ratios?"

Her dad leaned back a little, nodding with his whole body as he rocked on his feet. "Yes. If you have a blowout in a car, for instance," he said, holding a hand out, palm up, "you still have seventy-five percent of your rubber on the ground." He stood smiling at Cory.

Cory nodded. "Yeah, I see your point. Half your tires gone in one swoop," he said, sweeping his hand across him like a golf swing. Shawn rolled her eyes. Why were they even having this conversation?

"Well, you just make sure she always wears her helmet," said her father, putting a hand on Cory's shoulder.

"Oh, yes sir," said Cory. "I never even have to tell her to."

"So tell us, Cory," her mother said, as if she had just been waiting for her turn to speak. "What do you do?"

Shawn's stomach dropped. *God, mom! Is that all you care about?*

"I'm a corporate security specialist," said Cory, surprising Shawn. She had not heard him use that term before. It sounded like a fancy way of saying locksmith.

"Ooh," said mom, looking over at Gavin to see if his approval was in line with her own. "Well, that's nice."

After the introductions, everyone made their way down to the parking lot to load into the rental car her father had acquired at the airport. The men sat up front, Shawn and her mother in the backseat, and headed for The Big Taco on south Division Street. Shawn had scoped it out a few weeks ago, but hadn't had a chance to try it yet. She considered herself a Mexican food connoisseur, which involved – at least in her mind – trying every dining experience at least once.

Dinner was not uncomfortable. Mom got a margarita with Shawn and she loosened up a little bit. She stopped the interrogation after she realized that all his answers were better than her questions, and by the end of the meal, finally came to a sort of stalemate. She seemed to get more comfortable accepting that he wasn't going to leave her daughter alone just because she asked him the right combination of questions.

Her dad, of course, was aiming for the fences with the dad jokes, as always. With such location-appropriate winners such as 'I know a little Spanish. *Deliver*. My doctor told me to slow down on the liquor because it's bad for *deliver*' and 'How about *shutter*? Estelle needs to learn to *shutter* mouth when I'm watching TV.' Shawn guessed the groans to him were like roars of laughter for a stand-up comic. When Cory asked Gavin what he had done when he was still working, her father hadn't missed a beat – or an opportunity – and said, "Well I got to retire early on because I invented a new kind of broom." Estelle and Shawn both had stopped eating to look at him before he said, "Oh yeah. Honest truth. It swept the nation." The eye-rolls were almost palpable. But Shawn could tell Cory liked him.

Gavin paid for the dinner even though Cory tried to object, and even tried to steal the bill from the waiter. Alas, he lost that battle and Shawn sat smiling at her dad while she leaned on Cory, her arm looped through his. On the way back to the apartment, she rode in the backseat with Cory while her dad spent most of the trip looking for something on the radio. "Who's in charge of your radio stations down here?" he had said. He finally found a station playing the Traveling Wilburys and sang along loudly. He was nobody's singer, but he didn't sound bad. For a dad. Shawn found she couldn't stop smiling, having her two favorite men on the planet in the same vehicle.

Her parents dropped them off in front of the apartment stairwell while Shawn begged them to stay. She had pulled fresh sheets onto her bed this afternoon just for them. She had offered to sleep on the couch for the weekend. But her mom was having none of it. They had already booked a nearby hotel and would come back in the morning and spend the day with her. Her excitement dashed, she walked up the stairs holding Cory's hand. But then she remembered she had fresh sheets on her bed, and Cory and she could sleep on them tonight, and the excitement returned full-force.

The next day Shawn spent the entire day away from home, taking her mom to all the little niche shopping joints, having lunch at the greasiest burger joint on the planet – a place called *Simply Burgers & More,* where by the time they got back to the park where dad awaited, the paper bag had a grease spot in it the size of a fist – and ducking into dive bars to have a drink and get out of the heat for a snap. At one point, Shawn got a call from Lo asking what she was up to. When Shawn told her she was out with her parents and that Lo should meet up with them at the next stop, Lo agreed immediately! "Cool!" she said, and that was that.

And of course, Shawn's mother loved Lo. Roll-eyes. Not that she didn't approve of the reciprocated approval, but it was just too perfect. Her mother loved everyone but Shawn herself, it seemed. Lo made her laugh and knew the exact moments to raise her glass for yet another *'Cheers!'* and when to lean in and put her arm around Estelle, making her feel young again.

The rest of the weekend blew by in a blur. It was memorable, if nothing else, but Shawn found herself in a funk on Sunday afternoon when her parents left, and couldn't seem to get out of it. She and Cory laid up on the sofa watching reruns of *Western Wagons* and drinking some of the beer she had bought her dad. Cory had offered to put on the *Dexter* series for her, but she didn't want to think. She didn't want to expend anything other than carbon dioxide for the rest of the night.

So she lay curled up with her head and shoulders on Cory's lap, her legs covered with a blanket, sipping occasionally from her drink through a straw so she wouldn't even have to lift her head. She might have drifted to doze a time or two but would start awake when there was gunfire or a rearing horse on the show and watch a few more minutes. *Non-committal television,* she called it. Anyway, who the hell actually watched the *Wagons* for anything more than just a laugh?

When she finally drifted off for the final time that night, she lay wrapped in Cory's arms again, in her bed and memories of the weekend drifted away with her. Memories of her excitement about getting her own Indian followed closely behind them. The only thing that stuck with her was her daddy's smile and Cory's warm embrace.

# Seven

It was three weeks later that they got the next body. Shawn had no premonitions about it. No weird feelings, no nervousness that she could feel in her stomach. All good reasons not to have advance notice, but she might not have guessed that without experiencing it. She had initially thought she would always be given the heads-up, given time to prepare herself. To get a good night's sleep – if that was possible – and do a little meditation before she had to go in and deal with the dead. But the night before the second body came in had been a night just like any other. Shawn reckoned that was the better option, though she doubted it would always be that way. Likely there were others to come where Sameer would give her plenty of advance notice.

Shawn was doing a little reading on the evening before. The books on the brain and the nervous system, while still daunting in their heft and size, were a little less intimidating now. It wasn't like she picked it up and read several chapters, either. But a paragraph or a page here and there could only be good for her, right? While she sat with the book in her lap, a little classical music coming from the sound bar beneath her television, she would turn to look out the back window occasionally, soaking in the last bits she had read. She doubted understanding in this field would ever come without effort.

A butterfly swooped onto the balcony and flew directly into the sliding glass door. It fluttered around the top corner, banging its wings and body into the glass repeatedly. Shawn stood up quickly and ran to the back door. She stared in wonder at the small creature, resplendent in its simplistic beauty. As she got closer she realized it was fighting entanglement in a spiderweb. She slid the door open and went out, reaching up and pinching its wings together, freeing it from the snare before the wolf spider could wrap it up.

She set the bug on her finger and smiled at it as it unfurled its wings. The dark orange made itself visible and she gasped. "Oh, you're a monarch! Hello, beautiful!" The butterfly did not immediately fly away, but rather sat on her finger extending its wings and drawing them up. After a few moments, it raised its body and took flight. It hovered around her face for a moment. She closed her eyes, smiling and feeling it patter against her lips, her nose and eyelids. Then it flew away. "Bye bye, sweet monarch," said Shawn.

She finally turned and looked at the spider. "And as for you, Mr. Stupid, you should be ashamed of yourself," she said, wagging a finger at it. Then she made a face at the spider and went back inside. Having grown up on the lake and spending most of her childhood down on that boat slip, Shawn had seen her fair share of spiders. She was no more bothered by them than she was the butterfly. He had his place in the window. And as long as he didn't set out to trap the monarchs, she would leave him be.

After the butterfly rescue, Shawn spent the rest of the evening watching some television. The books had lost their interest for the time being. By the time she went to bed, she was feeling it behind her eyes. That text was so tiny. It seemed like the publisher had tried to fit as much as he could on those pages, as if to try and save paper. Then the TV had just lulled her eyes to a state of blur that could only be alleviated by a good night's sleep.

The next morning, the second body was there when she got to the office. She was more tired than usual, having been awakened sometime after midnight by the sudden bright flashing of colored lights outside her window. Shawn had crept to the blinds and peeked out, heart slamming in her chest with the adrenaline of coming awake so quickly. There had been an ambulance parked a few buildings down to the right outside her window. The downfalls of living in a cheaper part of town, she supposed. Her insomnia prevented rapid return to the peaceful slumber she had been enjoying. Hard-start awakenings like that could sometimes keep her up for hours.

Dragging her tired bones into the office, she had set about her normal routine of finding Sameer and checking in with him. He was usually either in his office or in the hidden half of the floor behind the elevators, and today was no different. The only difference between this Tuesday morning and every other morning was that the table he stood behind now had a white sheet on it. She instantly recognized the shape beneath the sheet as that of a woman. Shawn's heart sank as she walked into the room.

"Good morning, Miss Shawn," said Sameer, looking up from his tablet.

"Well, hello. What have we here?" Shawn asked, trying to sound casual.

"I got the ping on the app this morning saying she became available late last night and it was a special circumstance case."

"Special circumstance?" Shawn probed. That didn't sound comforting.

"Yes. No family will be claiming the body. There will be no funeral." He set the tablet down on the table beside the leg-part of the hump and turned to the counter behind him where stood his mug of still steaming coffee. "She died of exsanguination."

Shawn's eyebrows went up. Sameer stared at her as if waiting for her next question. She nodded. "Suicide?"

He closed his eyes respectfully and nodded.

Shawn moved to the head of the table and pulled back a corner of the sheet, revealing the face of the woman beneath. She was pretty. Young. Dark hair and pale eyes. She looked to be in her early twenties at most. Maybe even as young as eighteen or nineteen. Shawn was sad for this woman – this girl – because there was no one else to be sad for her. *No family?* Good God. She stared into the dead eyes for a moment, then shook her head and pulled the sheet back up.

"They didn't have to perform an autopsy?"

"Apparently not."

"It seems like there would at least be an investigation or something. Like, how do we know she killed herself? I mean…"

"We do not get to know these things, Shawn," said Sameer, returning to the table. He placed his hands gently on the table next to the body. "Is this going to be upsetting you too much – this subject being young and female?"

Shawn pushed out her bottom lip and looked back down at the sheet, then shook her head. "No. I don't think so. I'm sad for her, but I can professionally disconnect. I'm okay." They locked eyes for a moment and then Shawn nodded. As a signal of her ability to do what she had assured him she could, she asked, "Shall I get the blood ready?"

"I pulled out a bag from the freezer this morning, but it is not thawed yet."

Shawn stared at him for a moment, then crossed her arms. "Okay…"

"We may not be needing to use our blood, Shawn," said Sameer, looking levelly at her.

"I thought you said exsanguination."

"Yes. I did. But that does not mean all of her blood is lost."

"So they didn't, I don't know, drain it?" Shawn asked. She was almost horrified by this. It was coming on too quickly for her to tell yet. She would have to think back later to see if this should be something she needed to be concerned about. Meanwhile, she needed to focus on being the professional she had pronounced she was.

"No, Shawn. This is the way it is. So I will setup the machine to start drawing before it starts pumping."

Shawn spared him the dumb question this put in her head. *You can do that?* She had not seen any buttons on the device that divulged that feature. "Okay," she said, putting her hands down by her sides and feeling a little inadequate. "So we have twenty-four hours?"

"No, Shawn. I want to start in two hours."

"Two hours?" she said a little too loudly. "What happened to the day of oxygenation? We-"

"Shawn, she died less than twelve hours ago. I would like to see if we can get results. Please get the nanobots ready."

Shawn sat at her desk, frantically clicking and opening routines and subroutines, trembling as she exhibited every symptom of being completely flustered. She needed time to prepare for these things! She had just walked into a fire and been told to get her sunscreen on. And how the hell had this girl come to them so quickly after death? Was there not some legal process that they had to follow before releasing her to the university? *Special circumstance* sounded pretty special indeed. She got a sudden coldness in her blood that shook her to the spine, and hoped it was all above the board. She didn't know how much liability she could be held to if things went down, but she guessed it wouldn't be a case of Scott-free skating.

And what about that? Obviously there were regulations in place to prevent abuse of the system – even abuse of the bodies. And regulations meant oversight. So did they conduct random, routine audits of the facilities on the donor list? This almost surely had to be the case.

Something just seemed fishy about getting a body so soon after death that they hadn't even gotten the chance to embalm it. Maybe there were different procedures for bodies donated to science. She would need to have a talk with Sameer at some point – if for no other reason than just to make her feel better about the ethics and legality of her part in it. But that conversation would not be in the lab. She didn't want him to feel attacked. It needed to sound casual. Like over breakfast one morning. Or coffee in the break room.

She used the same basic set of routines she had used on Subject 1, planning for speech and cognition. In one of her talks with Jeremy about the first experiment, he had mentioned how difficult it would be to regulate nervous function to affect only the physiognomy. One might pin down the nerves for facial control, but they would surely come with some bleed-over into other areas, such as the neck and chest, or even the fingertips. But physiognomy – the facial gestures that told of someone's character – was a desirable feature to involve in their project, when trying to read emotion during a conversation. Those had been Jeremy's words, almost verbatim. It had creeped Shawn out more than just a little to realize that she sat across the break room table from a literal brain surgeon who was talking to her so nonchalantly about the possibility of holding discourse with a cadaver. Like, not only was it possible, it was no big deal. Hey, we do this shit all the time here! Wanna talk to the dead? Wake 'em up!

But creepier than allowing the facial nerves to fire – at least in Shawn's eyes – was the possibility of that bleed-over causing the fingertips to suddenly start fluttering by the subject's side. Here, Shawn's imagination brought her the damnable vision of a corpse sitting on a piano bench, playing Chopin as its head lolled around its neck, mouth and eyes twitching and rolling.

At the end of the allotted two hours though – and she knew that wasn't an 'about' from Sameer – she was ready. She had even had time to check her routines enough to feel comfortable that she had gotten them all, even in a rush as she was. She uploaded the instruction set to the nanobot terminal on the penning trap and rolled back in her chair. She didn't stand up yet though. Shawn sat with her arms extended, hands gripping the edge of the desk, and looked down at the floor, then closed her eyes and said a little prayer.

"God give me the strength to compose myself in there and be professional. Remind me that I've done this before." She took a deep breath and looked up, then finally stood up, straightening her blouse and then her hair. "Oh. And forgive us if we're playing in your attic," she added as she stepped out of her workspace.

The familiarity of the stage was eerie. It felt like a secret life Shawn had already adapted to. Just another office she popped into occasionally. The lights above were comfortably dim – enough to sleep by, in Shawn's estimation – and the ambient temperature was a cool 68°. The light shined brightest on the white sheet that covered the body in the perfect center of the room. This made access attainable from every side of the table equally, with plenty of room on all sides. As if showcasing the dead, like an Egyptian tomb in the time of electricity and air conditioning.

As Shawn came into the room rubbing sanitizer on her hands, she immediately went to the penning trap and flipped the switch that turned on the back-lit top and ran her fingers across the touch screen. Sameer was not in the room yet, so she took this alone time to get herself ready to deal with the dead. Again. She wanted to pick up with the same boldness she had seen in herself during the last few minutes of interaction with the first subject. Having attained that level of steel made her proud of herself as if she had overcome a major milestone in her life. In a way, she supposed, she actually had. Having witnessed her aunt's death was otherwise going to haunt her for the rest of her life. Maybe she could start to file that away appropriately, to where it belonged.

As the penning computer ordered and filed the bots into the injection tube, Shawn walked over to the head of the table. She looked around through the windows to see if Sameer was on his way down one of the halls. She could not see him. She rested her hands on the edge of the table, touching the white sheet. Took a deep breath. Rolled her head around to loosen her neck. Then she peeled back the cover. Shawn had made a silent commitment with herself that she would look into the face of every subject they wheeled through here. Out of respect for the dead, as sort of a thank-you for their donation to the research field, and just to help her establish and remember that she was dealing with a human being. Alive or not, these used to be people, and deserved the respect and dignity of being treated like one, even in death.

This particular woman – this girl – Shawn had not gotten a good look at before. She wanted to stare at her for a while – to get comfortable seeing the perfect stillness that only the dead were capable of. And this was the perfect time. The girl was striking. She had black shoulder-length hair and pale blue eyes. Her skin was milk-white and Shawn didn't know if that was because of the blood loss, her expiry or if she was just pale-skinned. She had on dark eyeliner and heavy eye shadow, but not in a gothy way. Her lips were full and pink and slightly parted. Shawn felt sad for her, knowing the girl had died less than twelve hours ago; she was also sad that she didn't have anyone to claim her. No one to come to the morgue and identify the body. No one to plan a funeral or to hold her one last time. Maybe that was why the girl had taken her life.

Shawn shook her head. Here lay a young woman who just last night had been a living, breathing person. While Shawn had been watching television with her head in Cory's lap, this girl had been going through the worst low of her life. And she had not made it out. God, what a waste.

She realized she was discriminating against the man, their first subject. Was it because of his age – because he had lived a lot longer life? Or was it because he was an unattractive man? Was it simply because she had just not yet come to terms with what their project actually entailed? Well, whatever the case, Shawn had certainly not had the intention of feeling any differently about the man. But this also *was* different. This young woman could have been her friend. She looked like someone Shawn would hang out with. This made her think of her new friend Lo. She sighed.

"Why did you do it?" she asked quietly. Shawn reached up and pulled the girl's hair back from the side of her face. Running her fingers through it, she could feel an oily substance, and realized immediately it was the residue of soapy bathwater. She closed her eyes with the sudden knowledge of how she had ended it.

Shaking her head, she turned away from the table and checked the status of the indicator on the penning trap. It had been plenty long for the trap to have transferred all of the nanobots but she checked anyway. It read 'Safe to Remove' so she clicked it out and took it over to the circulator. As she was inserting it into the injection port, Sameer entered the room. "Are we ready, Miss Shawn?" he asked casually.

"Yes. I am. We are," she corrected. "Want me to release the bots?"

"Yes, please," he responded, setting a coffee mug down on the back counter and taking off his jacket. He approached the table and stood beside Shawn. She inferred that this was to be his side of the table, and that she should move across to the other side like she had been on before. She turned and pressed the 'Inject Catalyst' button on the circulator. Blood had been pumping through this woman's brain for two hours. Now there would be microscopically tiny robots going in with it. Arterial technology. She rounded the table to her side and stood with her hands on the edge of the sheet-covered steel. Just like Sameer. She looked up at him. And then she nodded. Sameer pumped his own chin once in a slow nod.

"Today is Tuesday, June twentieth. The time is nine thirty-six. Present are Sameer Singh and Marcella Stedwin. Subject is young female, Caucasian, twenty years old. Time of death was established eleven hours, thirteen minutes ago," Sameer said into his DVR. Shawn frowned at this and did the quick mental math. Apparently the girl had been pronounced dead at 10:13 the night before. She wondered what else he knew that she didn't. Obviously he knew her age as well. Did he know her name? Even her first name? Shawn felt like she should know that. She wanted to know this girl's name. This poor darling who would never take another breath. Never see another sunrise or open another Christmas gift…

"We begin," he said, and dropped the DVR carefully on its lanyard where it hung around his neck. "Will you please check for aural sensitivity, Miss Stedwin?" said Sameer. She noticed he was being a little more thorough this morning. Maybe the results of the last experiment had re-energized him; maybe it had made him want to be more professional in the hopes of getting even further in the project.

Shawn thought it harsh – maybe even rude – to reach over and snap in this girl's ear. Then she shook her head, closing her eyes. She had to remind herself that the girl was dead. She had had her chance at life and had given it up. Snapping in the ear of a cadaver wasn't rude. It wasn't impolite or unthoughtful. It wasn't *anything.* So Shawn took a deep breath and reached over and snapped her fingers.

Instantly, the girl's eyes became aware. A cold chill shot down Shawn's back, like iced stilettos being hammered in her spine. She drew in a breath and stood still, waiting for the eyes to stop moving. They didn't. But nor did they look like the man's had. These pale blue eyes were not twitching and quivering like someone's who'd had too much coffee. These eyes were darting around the room like she was looking for something. Shawn stood perfectly still for a moment, trying to catch her bearing. She glanced up at Sameer, not moving her head. He was staring at her with the look of near-amusement. Like he was waiting to see what she would do.

He spoke aloud, "Subject has reacted visibly to the snap. Eyes are scanning the…" he started, then stopped as they both saw what was happening. The girl's eyes had settled on him. The brain was alive. Not having motor control of her neck though, the girl's head was not moving. But it was very clear where she was aiming those ice-blue eyes. And they were fastened on him. Shawn licked her lips and looked back at Sameer, wondering what to do. What was going on? What if – just *what if* – their project had actually brought this young woman back to life? What if she was here now? Like, fully, really, totally alive again?

The thought was not to be laughed at or dismissed out of hand, in Shawn's eyes. God, no. This girl was looking at the man who had just broken silence with his voice. Shawn's snap had brought her here, and now she was focused on the only voice she had heard.

Softly, slowly, Sameer spoke again. "Can you hear me? Miranda, can you hear me?"

Miranda? What the fuck? Sameer *did* know her name? Shawn had not known that was part of the information he had in the app. She was both thankful and horrified at the same time. She was happy to be able to call this poor girl by her name, associating it with the memories she was forming right now. The girl deserved that. But Shawn had not known it was an option. Had Sameer known the man's name too?

She looked up at Sameer, giving him a look of disbelief mixed with a tad bit of anger, but he was staring intently at Miranda's pale visage. That countenance was looking back at him. Shawn realized she was holding her breath in anticipation. Was this girl about to start talking?

"Miranda, my name is Sameer. I am here to talk to you. I have come as a friend. Will you let me know if you can hear me?"

An eyebrow moved. The movement had been so subtle – so minute – that it was almost indecipherable from the still of the dead. But those tiny muscle twitches that people's eyes and faces made a billion times a day without ever being noticed – those movements that separated the dead from the living – they were what made it uncomfortable to stand over a casket in a funeral home. Because dead people's faces didn't do that. The dead had that perfect irresolute stillness that persisted through any potential breath-holding or trickery that could ever be imagined by the living. Shawn knew she could stand staring into the casket of a dead loved one for an hour or a day or even a week waiting for just one little twitch, and she would never see one. Miranda's face was a collage of them.

"She can hear you," said Shawn, and she wasn't sure why. She felt like she might be annoyed with Sameer. Annoyed that he had not shared the name of the dead girl with her. Annoyed that he was asking the same question over and over. Could he not see the 'subject' had reacted to his voice? She almost considered telling him to remember the girl was just a subject. Why was she so upset by all this? Well, because it was wrong. This beautiful young woman had taken her life. She hadn't even gotten settled in on the other side yet and here they were waking her up, asking her questions. And she was looking at them. If this wasn't the very definition of wrong, then Shawn didn't know what the word meant. This was disturbingly fucking wrong, and every bit of her conscience was rebelling against it. She felt her stomach turn like she might be sick and had to hold her hand up to her mouth.

Sameer was looking at her. "Are you okay, Shawn?" And just like that, she was calm. His soft, patient voice reminded her that he held no ill will. She had never known a nicer man than him. Well, maybe except for her dad. But she suddenly remembered Sameer was not the type to withhold information from her just to spite her. Especially on a project he had asked her to join. What would be the point? He was just trying to get results. Maybe he had separated himself from death enough to be okay in thinking the girl lying on the table was a subject. But to Shawn, she was still a person. And here she was exhibiting signs of life.

It was actually almost terrifying in and of itself to see the face alive with these minute movements while the chest stayed perfectly still. Miranda was most certainly not aspirating. And with that thought, the girl's lips pulled back and a growling, gargling sound emanated from her mouth.

Shawn's eyebrows went up and her skin once again crawled in terror, but she didn't step back. She breathed in sharply through her nose and tightened her lips, looking down at Miranda as if for answers. Shawn either wanted this to end quickly, or to even itself out somehow – maybe throw off its cape and reintroduce itself as something less nightmarish.

Sameer stepped up to the head of the table, completely unfazed by the vocal outburst and leaned in close to the girl, much the same way Shawn had at the end of the last session with the man. He was close enough to kiss the subject's cheek. "Very good, Miranda. You can talk to me. I am your friend. My friend Marcy is here, too. Can you talk to us?"

That was when the body on the table very clearly said the name Marcy.

Shawn was in the break room, head in hands, elbows on the table. Jeremy was sitting across from her, speaking in a calming voice, reminding her that it was just science. Just technology with a little help from some bio-matter. "Come on!" she had said, looking up at him with her hands still in place. "How the hell can you sit out here and tell me this and *not* want to go in there and see a dead girl talking?"

Jeremy had only looked back at her patiently, shaking his head. It was a 'when will you ever learn?' gesture. "Seriously. Have you no interest at all in what's going on in there?" she asked, twisting her wrist down to point toward the lab.

"Shawn, I can't get involved."

"Why? What the hell is this? I mean, this never fuckin' happens, you know that right?"

Jeremy flinched at that.

"Sorry. I didn't mean to curse. But you know what I'm saying? We're in there playing Dr. Frankenstein and a girl is talking. A dead girl. Is talking." Shawn stared at him for a long moment, head hovering between her hands. And then finally she shook that head and put it back in her hands. And that's where she had been sitting for the last several minutes just listening to him explain why he had no interest. None of it mattered. He was either full of shit, or he had seen it before. There was no way she could stay detached, had she not just gotten the soul scared out of her at least. Her curiosity would have eaten her alive by now.

"Are you going to go back in there?" asked Jeremy when he finally realized she wasn't responding to his other questions and comments.

"Ghahahhshsshha!" said Shawn, and scraped her fingernails down her cheeks, leaving red marks. "Jeremy. I need you to talk to me like a scientist right now."

His eyebrows went up. He wasn't even quite smiling. This might be a momentous occasion. "I'm not a scientist."

"Jeremy. You're a brain surgeon. You're the scientist of the medical field."

He stared at her for a moment and then said, "What are you wanting me to say, Shawn?"

"Tell me this is science. Not séance."

"Well, technically, that's *all* it is, Shawn. There is no magic going on in that room. Nothing paranormal is happening."

That got her attention. Shawn looked up at Jeremy and finally dropped her hands onto the table. She took a deep breath. Jeremy responded to her looking at him. He saw that he was getting through.

"Shawn, you've got blood which carries oxygen, and technology in the form of tiny robots…" This he said flicking his fingertips as if to dry them. "Tiny little robots shocking parts of the brain that make these things happen."

She stared at him for another long moment. Then she finally stood up, scooting her chair back with the backs of her knees. She leaned on the table and chewed her lip. Then she shook her head and stood up straight, putting her fists in the small of her back and leaning back over them to crack it. "Then how is she coming up with words?"

Shawn dragged herself back toward the lab, a fresh cup of coffee in her hand. It was only three-quarters full. She had been discerning enough to understand that her shivers might spill it. She was walking stiffly, like her knees were taped, breathing through her nose with a steady sense of purpose, forcing herself to keep calm. *This isn't real. This isn't real.* She kept repeating the mantra even though she knew it didn't make sense. What made sense was her getting up on the roof of the building and shouting through a megaphone to the people below that they were cheating death. They were playing God, and sooner or later, God was going to get tired of it and put an end to it. That this wasn't right and they were tapping into something that man had no business playing with. That when someone was dead, they should accept it. Bury them, weep and move on. She wanted to run up to someone on the street and shake him by the shoulders and tell him that they had cracked the code! They had death's number now, but also that they should lose that number; they should pretend they never found it. She and Sameer and Jeremy and anyone else at BlueBird who had their hands in that code should participate in a book-burning: they should shred their documents and destroy their code, smash their machines and send the dead back to the graveyard. Death was not a toy meant for the hands of man. Her insides were trembling with this knowledge. But her feet were still moving, bound and chained by duty and integrity, curiosity and the need to earn a living. At what cost was she trading her living though? Was this worth it? She had now bridged the chasm between death and life, bringing together the two sides and putting an end to the greatest mystery of man.

Shawn didn't believe she *should* feel right about this. She wondered, of course, if she would get used to it. Adapt, change, grow. Would she eventually be okay with the artistry they were performing in there? Would she find routine in tearing asunder the great curtain that hid from them a darkness man should never see? Or would she unveil an unrest that would bury itself so deeply into her soul as to guarantee a life filled with sleepless, terror-filled nights? More importantly, had she already encountered this unveiling?

She wished badly for someone to talk to about this. Sameer. A Sameer. That's who she needed. Not him, specifically, but someone *like* him. Someone who had stood there in that room with her while she witnessed these abominations, but also had her love and respect. A friend or family member. She could never relay appropriately the thoughts and emotions she was experiencing to someone who had not seen it himself. This was a bedtime story to scare the children. A tale told around a campfire. Not something that really happened. How could she get the therapy she was surely going to need after facing this, if she could not refer to specific instances inside the lab? She could recount them all day, with the greatest attention to detail, telling every word of it in perfect recollection, and it would still never be the same as having witnessed it. Somehow in her mind, the bottom line was that a barrier that cannot be crossed, had been crossed. Like a law of physics that was accepted universally as something impossible to break, this barrier was tall and strong and unyielding. And yet…

She pushed open the door to the lab and met eyes with Sameer, who still stood near the head of the bed. There were no condescending looks or remarks. No impatient sighs or glances at his watch. Just a man who patiently awaited her return. Though he had not stopped his inquisition, he had obviously not lost faith in Shawn. He understood her discomfort with the project's underlying subject matter and was allowing her space and time to gather her steel. And she had come back each time. That was her saving grace. It was okay for her to step away. But she had come back each time. And she knew she would overcome. She felt this steel in her blood now – right now. And she knew she would at least be able to go as far with this girl as she had with the man. Maybe because she felt a connection to her. Maybe because she was just a young girl, and deserved a chance to be heard. Whatever the case, Shawn's resolve was strengthened, knowing she would bury whatever selfish fear she had of encounter and carry on for the good of the – the what? The Project? The girl?

"I want you to know," said Sameer, standing up straight and putting his hands behind his back as Shawn approached the table, "that nothing further has happened since you left. As you can see, her eyes are still very alert. But she has spoken no more."

Shawn didn't know whether to feel relieved at that or mortified. Did that mean Miranda was *saving it all up* for Shawn? That she *knew* Shawn had stepped out for a bit to get some coffee, maybe grab a smoke, and she'd be back shortly? And following that, did she, therefore, *know* that Shawn was back now?

She stepped to the head of the table, directly across from Sameer, and they held each other's eyes for a long moment. Was there a mind-reading going on here? Shawn felt calmed by these times when Sameer would look her in the eyes, sub-verbally communicating with her. It wasn't quite telepathy, but she did truly understand his look. Like a sign language for the brain, she knew he was asking if she was okay and ready to proceed. So she sent him back a signal in plain universal sign: she nodded.

Then she breathed in deeply and closed her eyes, slowly tilting her head up to the ceiling and taking several long, deep breaths. She gathered her will, her emotions and her resolve, then clasped her own hands behind her back and leaned over, getting close to the dead girl on the table. She ended with her mouth a few inches from Miranda's cheek, exactly like she had done with their first subject – the man with no name.

Again, from this angle, Shawn could see details not visible from two feet taller under these soft, warm bulbs.

Tiny blemishes in Miranda's skin; the oil of an unwashed face; the scar from an acne outbreak, likely from her teens… At this proximity there was no debating that the woman on the table was real. She was very human. And at this close tolerance, it was indistinguishable from the subtle living characteristics of anyone living: her face was full of life.

Shawn tilted her head and tried to reset her brain. Instead of thinking of Miranda as a subject – instead of thinking of her as a science project – a girl awakened from the dead, she would think of her as a friend. A living person lying on this table. There had perhaps been an accident that rendered her unconscious and maybe she was coming around now. She was awakening, little by little, and ready to start receiving questions – the kind of questions a doctor might ask someone just back from the coma vacation. She set her mind to think of Miranda as a girl who'd had an accident. Nothing more. Let's take death completely out of it. This girl is no more dead than I am. Or Sameer. She's just had a bad fall and I'm trying to help her come out of it.

"Miranda. My name is Shawn," she said, then looked up at Sameer through the tops of her eyes, not moving her head. She was staying his objection without words. "I know my friend said my name was Marcy. And, well, really, it is. But I go by Shawn. Can I talk to you, sweetheart?"

The girl's jaw started trembling. Her eyes were staring straight ahead at the ceiling. Her mouth was still slightly open, lips making tiny gestures that represented life, but not movement.

"I…" Shawn started, then had to choke back her emotion. She suddenly felt overwhelmed with sadness. Here she was, alive – vibrant and full of everything this girl would have someday grown into had she not ended her life – and trying to communicate with someone no longer strictly 'with them', and she was worried about how she would be perceived. "I think you're beautiful, Miranda. I'm really sad that you…" she trailed off. She thought better of finishing that line of thought. Glancing at Sameer and seeing the same stoic visage he had displayed through the entire thing, she continued on her own.

"Miranda, I would like it if you would talk to me," Shawn said. She realized that if Miranda's face was full of living sensory then she could probably feel touch, so she reached up and ran the girl's hair back with a fingernail – the same way she had done on the other side of the table an hour ago. Miranda's eyes closed.

Shawn then squatted again, resting her hands on her knees, and hovered near Miranda's face. She looked up at Sameer. "Get me a stool, please," she said. Sameer immediately complied, though he had to leave the room to do so.

Within a minute he was back, carrying a doctor's stool. He bent over and set it down behind Shawn, then gently pushed it forward until it touched the backs of her legs. Shawn didn't even look back. She was so focused on Miranda that nothing else existed. She didn't dare break away now.

Shawn lowered herself onto the stool and scooted it forward with the toes of her shoes, then put her right arm around the top of Miranda's head and rested her hand on the woman's far shoulder. With her close hand, she cupped Miranda's chin. If the only nerves alive in the girl's body were ones associated with the face, then Shawn was going to give that face as much comfort as she could provide with her skinny little arms. She had wrapped Miranda's entire head in her embrace, and now rested her chin on the steel table, an inch away from the girl's left ear.

"Miranda, I'm here with you. You're safe here. I just want you to talk to me," Shawn said, and then she made a little bit of a show of breathing in and out, ensuring that whatever hearing was available would hear her aspirations. "Can you talk to me, sweetie?"

Miranda's cheeks moved. Shawn popped her head up an inch or two, just to get a better perspective on the woman's face. It looked like she was trying to smile. The twitching muscles looked as though they were trying again and again, failing again and again, to do nothing more than create a simple smile.

"It's okay. It's okay. I'm here. Can you talk to me? My name is Shawn."

Miranda's mouth opened wide. It was the simple movement of her jaw, dropping an inch or so. And then her eyes closed again. "Hello, Shawn."

The exchanged look between Sameer and Shawn was brief but meaningful. They had both been startled by the sudden response, in such a clear voice. The initial vocal rendering of the subject had been a deep-throated gargling sound as if something was rooting around back there on her vocal cords. This response had been staggeringly clear. Shawn had somehow been able to get out in front of her flinch and stop it before it happened, though the frozen hand that reached in and grabbed her heart had gotten through without a fight. The chill of having heard her name from the mouth of the dead girl lingered long after the quiet had returned to the room, but still, Shawn maintained her calm. If Miranda did indeed have access to feelings of comfort from Shawn's surrounding arms, she wanted to maintain that through the entire encounter if possible. She was not only surprised by her ability not to have jumped out of her skin, but also proud of it. Progress was being made, and at a pace she would not have believed had she been told beforehand.

Another thing that surprised her was Sameer's seemingly standoffish approach to the interview. This was his show, after all. His project. His money had funded the equipment purchases, the lab setup and the licensing from the state to perform medical research. Did he not want to be a bigger part of it? Maybe it was just that the only true responses they had gotten from either of the subjects had been from Shawn's soft soothing female voice. Maybe it was his dialect. There were any number of reasons a subject might respond favorably to her voice instead of his, but she had no idea which – if any – was the right one.

Of course he had been the first to speak this morning – and with the last subject. But once Shawn had built the nerve up enough to participate, she had pretty much taken over. Unwittingly and inadvertently she had become the moderator of the interviews. This was how she thought of the experimental encounters now: interview sounded more personal and closer to what they were actually trying to effect than anything else. It wasn't that Shawn had a problem running the sessions, but she wasn't sure where she was supposed to go with it. Since the only thing missing in the multi-million-dollar facility was a game plan, she had no real idea what Sameer's intentions were once the subject started talking. He was free to step in and start talking any time he wanted, surely. But she had yet to see that happen where he took the reigns back from her. So Shawn carried on with her own gut feeling about how to get them to talk and what to say, what to ask and where to go with it. For now, she would just move forward with the idea that if they could get a subject talking at all, she would just roll with it and Sameer would be happy. Maybe he had no real plan, in other words. Maybe he just wanted to see what they could achieve, and they would both figure it out as they went along. Playing by ear.

Shawn lightly squeezed Miranda's shoulder and nodded subtly – mostly for her own benefit -then said, "Good. Good. I'm glad you can hear m-"

"My friends call me Randi so I have a boy's name, too," said the girl.

Shawn's eyes again shot up to look at Sameer, who now stepped in closer and stood at the head of the bed. Shawn mouthed at him but was sure he wasn't getting it. She started making motions in the air behind the girl's head as if she were scribbling something down on paper that wasn't there. He got that, nodded and held a finger up, then turned and quickly fetched a small whiteboard off the counter. He handed it to Shawn above the subject's head and she took out the connected dry-erase marker.

*USING PRESENT TENSE!*

Sameer nodded, raising his eyebrows and gave her the universal sign for 'keep it rolling' by twisting his hand in the air. Shawn smirked and shook her head then stammered a bit, trying to get back into the same groove she'd been in a minute before. "Uh, okay, um, Randi… Would you like me to call you Randi?"

"Where am I, Shawn?" she asked.

Shawn breathed out and sat up straight, looking up at the ceiling and shaking her head. Fantastic. This was what she was worried about. They had not gone over any pat response options for something like this. What was this girl asking? Was she asking about her geographical location, or where she was in the process of moving to the afterlife? Was she seeing purgatory? No. Of course not. As Jeremy had stated before, there was no soul here. Nothing about this was spiritual at all. She could literally insult this girl until she was no more and it wouldn't mean anything. It was like talking to an intelligent fence post.

At least that's the way Jeremy had made it sound: so many nerves and synapses firing because of a technological implement working under source code they had written in-house. What they were seeing was the brain doing its own communicating with no connection to anything beyond the grave. So technically speaking, it shouldn't even realize it's alive again. Or that it had ever been through death at all, for that matter.

Shawn didn't necessarily feel that way, of course. She would no more insult the dead than she would have if she had known this young woman in life. There was no place for it. No reason for it. But it was hard to separate what she knew versus what she felt in her heart. The fact that these words were being generated by latent impulses and leftover intellect and not some intrinsic knowledge of her own existence made no difference to Shawn. The vocal cords were the same, so the voice was the same – presumably – as it had been in life. No reason to think otherwise. So this, in essence, at least to Shawn, was the same person lying here communicating with her now as would have been fifteen hours ago. Or a week ago.

"Can you see the room?" Shawn finally asked. Miranda seemed to be infinitely patient in her waiting for response.

"Yes," said Miranda.

"Good. Very good. We are in a comfortable room just having a friendly talk."

"How do I know you?"

Shawn looked up at Sameer again. She shook her head. *What the heck am I supposed to say?* This time he read her lips.

Sameer took the whiteboard from Shawn and wrote something down, then showed it to her. Shawn nodded and spoke the words to Miranda. "We're just meeting. Do you know why you're here, Miranda?"

Her eyes suddenly looked like she was trying to form a frown. "No. I still don't know where I am," she said.

Sameer nodded when Shawn looked up at him again. "We're in a lab. What is the last thing you remember before our conversation?"

Miranda was silent for a very long time. Shawn was sure she wasn't going to answer. And then she finally did. "I don't remember anything."

"Do you not remember being in the bath tub?" asked Shawn. She ran her thumb across the girl's cheek. Miranda's eyes squinted, then started moving like she was looking for something. It looked as though she wanted to use more than just her eyes. Like she wanted to turn her head. Shawn could imagine her scampering about, lifting this, turning over that, looking frantically for something she had misplaced. Her lips were now trembling as well.

This went on for a few moments. Shawn was beginning to get concerned because the subject suddenly looked very uncomfortable. "Are you okay?" Shawn asked her. She wasn't sure if this would translate, or what it would mean to the girl, but what else could she do?

Miranda did not answer. Her eyes continued to dart around, limited by the width of her static vision. Unable to turn her head or shoulders, the poor girl had a very small view of the room. Shawn suddenly got an idea and put her hand on the girl's cheek. She pulled gently, turning her head to face Shawn. As Miranda's eyes met Shawn's, it was well obvious that the girl was able to see her. Her pupils dilated. Her eyelids raised slightly and her lips stopped trembling. She was focusing on Shawn's face.

Shawn now rubbed the other cheek with her thumb, still resting there. She smiled gently and mouthed '*Hi*'. And then Miranda's eyes lost that focus. She suddenly looked very worried. Her cheeks starting quivering and her lips trembled. "Harrison? Harrison? HARRISON!" she cried, as loudly as her vocal cords would allow without the aid of aspiration. Shawn realized the that if Miranda had use of her lungs right now, she would be shouting. She immediately let go of the girl's face and scooted back, standing up. Sameer rounded the table and came to squat in front of her, obviously trying to observe what was going on in the girl's visage. Her eyes had changed somehow. It was as if she was no longer seeing at all. Then her tongue started making small movements between her teeth, coming out as far as her lips and shivering as it moved about. Her facial muscles were twitching – those same muscles that normally flexed to pull a smile – and her lips were trying to make weird shapes. Shawn stood staring, hands clasped between her breasts, horrified and not knowing what the hell she should do. What was that poor girl seeing? What was she thinking? And who was Harrison?

Sameer, ever the clinician, was peering into her eyes, shining a pen light and watching the focus and movement of the pupils. He was very close to her, and yet the girl didn't seem to notice the violation of that precious dimness he had claimed was all for the comfort of the subject.

"Oh my God, Sameer, stop! Please just stop!" Shawn said, probably a little too loudly. "Stop, Sameer! She's obviously terrified! Can't you do something?"

He turned toward her, pivoting without removing his hands from his knees, and looked over the tops of his lenses at her. "What would you suggest I do, Shawn?"

"I don't know! Just end it! Put her out!"

Sameer stood up and put his hands on his hips, clearly dissatisfied with the options he was being presented. He didn't want to lose his precious research subject, but he also didn't want to upset the balance too badly. Shawn was part of that balance. He had to know that if he turned her against him, he would lose her. He sighed and shook his head, then reached over and turned off the circulator.

Shawn covered her mouth with her hands. *Oh my God! He's just going to let her brain die of asphyxiation!* But all she could do was stare in horror. Meanwhile, Miranda's mouth was still twitching and jumping, open and closed, tongue shooting in and out of her lips while her eyes switched between terror and fascination over and over again. It was incredibly unsettling to Shawn, who had come to some sort of peace with this whole thing only a few minutes before.

"Sameer, turn it back on!" Shawn said. "I'm sorry, turn it back on! You can't just let her…" she started and then thought about how she was about to end that sentence. Sameer turned and saw the distress on Shawn's face. He gently put his hands on her upper arms, looking straight into her eyes.

"Shawn, it is too late. We have lost her," said Sameer.

"No!" cried Shawn, trying to see past him to look at the girl on the table – the girl who was dying again. Already. She'd only died eleven hours ago, and here was going through it again already. "No, Sameer, we have to save her! We can't just let her die!" Her hands were covering her face now, and she was holding back tears. "Sameer, please turn it back on!" she said, but her voice hitched as her cry grew more intense. And quickly, tears were pouring down her face, over her hands. She was shuttering, bawling loudly and trying to keep it all in, but nothing was working together. "God, no!" she bawled. And Sameer finally stepped forward and took her in his arms. Shawn buried her face in his shoulder and let him hug her. It was the first time he had ever put his arms around her. She was crying so hard now that she couldn't breathe, body wracking with the muscle spasms that happen in a deep sob. Then she finally pulled her face back and looked over his shoulder and saw Miranda once more. Her face looked a little softer, somehow – as if her own muscle spasms had finally subsided – but her eyes were wide as if in fear, and her jaw was twitching slightly, mimicking the motions one would make as if she were gasping for air. She looked like she was asphyxiating, and worst of all, she looked as though she was completely and perfectly aware of it.

Shawn turned and ran out of the lab, her face buried in her hands, and sobbing so hard she couldn't breathe.

# Eight

The next three days were a blur of emotions, weeping and grieving for a woman she had never known in life, and had spoken less than a hundred words to. She spent most of her time in bed just trying to focus on what was real – what was stable in her life. Death did not seem to be on that list any longer. She couldn't even count on that to be a permanent fixture anymore, apparently. There now existed a gigantic chasm in her own existence. On one side lay everything she had ever known and believed in, and on the other… Well, that was where Shawn seemed to be standing now. She realized, at least on a subconscious level, that her anguish had not been solely based on the second death of the woman named Miranda. Part of it had most definitely been the undoing of what she had known all her life to be a solid system. Death had now seemingly become a choice. It appeared it could be a non-persistent state. She would never have believed that something so basic as the definition of death could unravel so much of her life with its undoing. But here she lay, sobbing in confusion and anger and hatred and sadness. Every time she thought she might be about to come out of it, she was reminded of that girl's face and how it had suddenly shifted from relief or peace to absolute terror. And the last thing she had ever seen before she went into that state was Shawn's smile. Surely that had not been what had sent her there.

It was Friday before Shawn began to see a light in the tunnel. Sameer had gracefully given her the rest of the week off, and she had taken it without argument. He knew true distress when he saw it. She had made incredible steps in her short journey to existing comfortably in the same room as the dead. She would just need to be exposed to – or at least prepared for – every aspect of its undoing before she could be as much of a soldier as he was in its sometimes ugly face. *Baby steps.*

On Friday afternoon, she finally resolved to dissecting what had gone wrong. Not just with the subject, or the experiment, but with herself. Why had this affected Shawn so harshly? Was it because she had tried to make it personal? Had her efforts to keep from treating the dead like the dead backfired on her? She obviously had felt a connection of some sort to the decedent, but it couldn't only have been that. Shawn believed there was something about witnessing death being overturned, only to be returned so quickly. Perhaps part of her conscience had associated the resurrection with a full return to living. And maybe somehow that had caused her to forget what she was truly doing in that dimly lit room. Maybe from here out, she should focus less on being personally respectful to the subject, and more on being clinical like Sameer.

But part of this introspection would need irresolute evidence. She would need to hear the tapes. Shawn emailed Sameer asking if he could send her his recording of the session. She needed to listen to the changes. She needed to be reminded of exactly what she had said before the girl's demeanor had completely shifted gears. Something had changed in the room, and it had been palpable. The figurative climate had suddenly gone to the North Pole, but she couldn't remember what had caused it, nor what she had said just before it had done so.

Within fifteen minutes, Sameer had responded, the .wav file attached. She was thankful he hadn't found it necessary to remind her of the proprietary nature of the data contained within. She fired off a quick thank-you and saved the file to her desktop. Then she reached beneath her desk and retrieved her earphones from the hook upon which they hung. Slipping them over her head, she turned up the volume and double-clicked the file. Several clicks on the progress bar got her passed the introduction, then the long pauses of silence filled only with the eerie sounds of the lab. She could hear the minute hum of the circulator doing its job, and the scratch of the voice recorder against Sameer's shirt as he moved around.

She sat staring at a bright spot on her screen, not really focused on anything, her chin resting on her hand as she listened intently. When she heard her own voice suddenly, she jumped, and had to turn the volume down.

'Can you see the room?' she had said.

'Yes,' said Miranda. There had been no hesitation in her answer. That indicated to Shawn that her cognizance was very real.

'Good. Very good. We are in a comfortable room just having a friendly talk,' Shawn responded.

'How do I know you?' said the girl. Shawn pressed the space bar on her keyboard, pausing the playback. She leaned back in her chair. She wanted to think more about this. She remembered wondering what to say when she had been in the lab. What do you say to something like that? This had been when she had looked up at Sameer and waited for him to write something down on the whiteboard. Shawn remembered what he had actually written. *Be honest! But be careful…*

But what had she wanted to say? Had she thought of saying something about wishing they had known each other in life? The thought did spark something of a memory. But she had bitten her tongue, still unsure that she should bring attention to the fact that the girl had died. That was the great mystery, wasn't it? Maybe that's the first thing they should be asking. Maybe she should stop focusing on making the subject feel comfortable and just start getting 'clinical'. Maybe that was the whole fucking point of the project, after all: to learn what was actually going on in the reawakened brain. *'Are you aware that you were dead for a time? Do you know that we have brought your brain back to life? Can you tell?'* That's what a disconnected scientist would ask, for sure. But could Shawn actually rid herself of that human kindness and compassion just to get answers for some damned project? She shook her head.

She pressed the space bar. This is where she heard the shuffling of the DVR against his shirt. She could see him in her memory vividly, taking back the whiteboard and writing an answer to her. The whole exchange took maybe ten seconds before Shawn spoke again, and she was reminded of how patient the subject had been. There was no, 'What's going on? Are you guys still here?'

'We're just meeting. Do you know why you're here, Miranda?' Shawn's voice said from the recording.

There was only a slight pause before the girl answered. 'No. I still don't know where I am.'

'We're in a lab. What is the last thing you remember before our conversation?' Then ensued the longest pause of the interview.

Shawn paused the playback and leaned back again, crossing her arms. That was it. That was what she had forgotten about. Her last question had called attention to the time before the reawakening. If the human memory was capable of spanning that gap between two sets of consciousness, then this is where the girl was likely remembering taking her own life. Shawn had not been so blunt as to pull the sheet up to check, but her strongest suspicion was that Miranda had slit her wrist – maybe both of them – while lying in the soapy water of her bathtub. She had felt the soapy residue in her hair. No woman would step out of a tub knowing that had not been washed out. One could further pursue the question of why she had washed her hair at all if she had intended all along to take her life, but that was the lesser point, in Shawn's estimation. Her newest question was, how had someone found her so quickly if she had no family?

What had Shawn expected her to say at this point? That was the material question, in her mind. If they could have gotten an answer, would that not check some box on their achievements list? Something – even unspoken – that they were hoping to get out of this project? Like, if she had said, 'I remember sitting in the tub, and then…' would that not have fulfilled some wonder? Answered some age-old question about whether the conscience remains even interrupted by death? Well, Shawn didn't know what she had expected. But she did remember her heartbeat had increased at that point. She had anticipated something. Something meaningful. She pressed play.

'I don't remember anything.'

There it was. The non-answer that was potentially more of an answer than anything else she would get for the rest of the interview. If it was the truth, it was every bit as telling as a complete recollection of the events. Saying she didn't remember anything could mean several different things. The most obvious in Shawn's mind was was that her memory was gone. Her brain had reset. She was literally awakened from death. What would a normal person think of if presented with such a reality? A normal person, in Shawn's mind, would expect a brain awakened by scientific method – *science over séance* – to be nothing *but* blanked memory. Now if the soul were brought in to the equation – a conscience – then the answer might be different. But what did she know? This is why she needed…

*Jeremy!*

She picked up her phone and called Jeremy. He answered on the first ring. "Hey, Shawn," he said. She could hear the smile in his voice.

"Hey, Jer. Can I ask you a question?"

"What if I say no? Then you got away with one."

"Shush, you."

"Hey. Gotta try."

"You and my dad would get along swimmingly," she said.

"Whatchu got?"

"Here's the thing, Jer. Do you think the soul is what retains memory?"

"No. Of course not," said Jeremy, not a little condescendingly. "Why would I think that?"

Shawn did the equivalent of a mental shrug. "I don't know. I'm thinking morals. Conscience. Right and wrong. Do you think that's all in the brain?"

Jeremy sighed. "Are you asking if I think someone reanimated could exhibit signs of moralistic aptitude?"

Shawn sat still for a moment, fingertip against her lips, considering what he was asking. Considering, therefore, what *she* was asking. "Well, I guess, but now that you say it like that, I think I may have answered my own question."

"What did you see in there today?" asked Jeremy.

"I don't know. I don't know how I got off on this tangent," she said, rubbing her brows with a thumb and index finger. Then she took a deep breath. "Okay. Here's the thing: I asked her if she remembered what had happened right before she joined us." Shawn gave him a moment to see if he got it.

"Okay," he said. He got it.

"She said she didn't remember anything. In your mind, does that mean her memory has been reset, or do… Or do…" She shook her head.

"It sounds, Shawn, like you're asking me if there's a spiritual tie-in here."

She pursed her lips and exhaled. "I guess so."

"I stand by my answer. And I think you have yours."

"I do?"

"Well, yeah!" said Jeremy. "Don't you see? If there's no memory, then that means that maybe the spirit *does* carry the memories across the boundary of death."

"Yeah! Aha!" she said, and actually pointed a finger at her monitor – as good a stand-in for the person as anything else.

"You got me."

"I got you!" she said, shaking her fist.

"Do you see the fallacy?" asked Jeremy?

There was silence. Then, "I didn't get you."

She could almost hear him shaking his head. She turned to look out the back window. It was cloudy and gray. Like it might rain tonight. That would be nice. Then she wouldn't feel so bad about staying in on a Friday night. About pushing Cory away for one more night.

"Shawn, if there's no memory, and we are to believe that the spirit carries those memories across the boundary, then that would speak of the existence of a spirit. Right?"

"Yes!" she almost shouted, standing up from the chair. She frowned then, thinking she might be missing something. She put the tip of her thumbnail in her mouth. Ran it against her teeth.

"So if we agree there's a spirit, and we agree it's the only thing capable of transporting memories across a gap... Then can't we say that spirit is absent in the lab?"

Shawn's heart skipped a beat. "Oh my God."

"Well, let's not get carried away. I mean, I'm pretty good, but..." Jeremy said.

"Shush, you!" she said.

After they hung up, Shawn didn't even bother returning to her desk. Instead, she turned on her stereo and started a streaming playlist and undressed right there in front of the sound bar. Then she thought to herself, *How will I go on?* This wasn't a question of life and death. It was only a question of logistics. The most literal definition of that particular string of words in that exact order. What exactly was her plan for moving forward? What had she been hoping to discover there? Had she already known what he would say? Had she already known the answer to the paradox herself? Maybe she had. But yet, she didn't feel any relief from the revelation. It felt like she should feel really good right now, having proved one thing or another. But instead, she felt like she might not have proven anything.

And what did it prove if she *had* proven something? If she had proven there was no spiritual persistence after death, then what of the project? It certainly didn't prove the spirit carried the memory. Science had found where memories were stored in the brain. Jeremy had even mapped it out so that her nanobots could follow the bloodstream directly to the point of interest, attach themselves and dance upon its dead cells until it came back to life. Memory was strictly a biological function. Not a spiritual one. No one could say how true that statement was for memories carried across the gap of a temporary death. There was no science on that yet. That's why she was standing here asking this question.

She danced across the floor, swinging her arms gracefully, moving like a ballet dancer. She had quit ballet a quarter-century ago, so it now only existed in her alone times. Dancing naked through her small apartment was one of the few top-secret joys she would miss if she ever lived with someone else. She was alone now, though, and there was such freedom in the act. She spun and hopped across the floor, allowing her arm to swing out like a swan and touch down on the tiny target of the space bar of her keyboard. She twirled and came to a stop behind the chair. And listened.

'Do you not remember being in the bath tub?' said her own voice from the recording. Her shoulders drooped as she sighed and rolled her eyes at her own idiocy. There was no need to hear any more. She pressed the space bar again, stopping the playback. Then she walked across the den to the stereo and stopped that too. *Fuck sake.* Why not just ask the girl, 'Why did you kill yourself?'

That had been when everything went south. Right after that was when Miranda had started calling for someone named Harrison. It was now very clear what had sent the poor girl into another state of panic. The end of the interview had been precipitated by that very outburst. That was what had taken her over the edge of sanity – if that were even a realistic word in the world of resurrected brains. Shawn had been the sole proprietor of that downfall. No wonder the poor thing had locked up and stopped talking. She'd gone into a near seizure. She stood still now, hands in her hair and staring out the back door at the setting sun trying to beat its way through the cloudy evening sky, and wondering how she could have been so thoughtless. Miranda, God rest her soul, could have had a much better experience in rejoining the living, had Shawn only known what to ask. They needed an agenda. A schedule of questions and responses they were allowed to ask and tell. This experimenting simply couldn't go on without some absolutes. This wasn't fair. Not to the living, who were conducting the experiment – but nor, to the dead. What if Miranda now lay in everlasting anguish because her last few minutes of life – bleeding out in that tub peacefully, listening to her favorite music – was replaced by this travesty in waking? What if it did persist into the afterlife somehow? What if the last few minutes of life stuck with you for eternity? And what if Shawn had just overwritten Miranda's last few minutes with a horror story?

Saturday morning, Shawn awoke to the sound of the rain hitting her windows. It was a perfect, steady patter, consistent and incessant – the kind of rain that sounded like it would last all day. She got up from her bed and dragged her feet into the bathroom and brushed her teeth while she sat to pee, staring at the shower curtain. When she finished, she spit and washed her hands, then looked in the mirror at her puffy cheeks, the bags under her eyes. She looked like she had spent the last three days crying. She would need to be ready for work Monday though. She felt fine about having taken the three days she had been given – though

Sameer had not numbered it at all – but any more than that felt like she was milking it.

She swept up her blanket and wrapped it round her shoulders and put her feet in her slippers, then went out the front door. She crossed the breezeway, mist wetting her face, and knocked on Cory's door. It took him a full minute to answer. But when he did, he just took her in one of his arms and led her to his bed, as if this had all been prearranged. She tossed her phone on his nightstand and crawled under the covers with him, not even bothering to take off her pajamas. Cory had his bedroom windows open and she could feel the cool rain-soaked breeze blowing into the room. She fell back to sleep quickly under the comfort and security of his embrace, his breath warming her back, and didn't wake up until almost eleven.

At the breakfast table, Shawn recapped the last few days for Cory. He had respectfully given her the space she needed without questioning her. Knowing her hang-ups with death and the dead, he told her he had figured it would be a traumatic experience for her if they started getting results in the lab. He had also allowed that it would probably have been too much for him. He didn't know anyone who *wouldn't* have that reaction to something so inhuman. It was the farthest thing from normal any person could ever be exposed to, and to be emotionally overwhelmed by it was a completely normal thing to expect.

"How the hell is Sameer so okay with it?" she said, staring out the window as she took tiny bites of her dry toast. Her stomach was trying to reject the food, but knowing that she needed it, she was forcing herself to eat. No way those runny eggs were going down though. As soon as she had slid them from the skillet onto her plate, she had regretted it.

"You don't think he did some experimenting with it before he ever invited you in?"

Shawn looked at him. She chewed slowly as she thought about it.

"I mean, maybe that's what made him invite you in to begin with, right? He discovered that he was going to need help? Like, he realized he couldn't do it all himself?"

She swallowed, her eyes locked onto Cory's with something like fascination. "Oh my God."

"You hadn't thought of that? Really?" asked Cory with the hint of a smile playing his lips.

"I guess not. But it makes sense. Makes too much sense." She sighed and dropped her napkin on her plate, then stood up and went to the sink. "Cory, I've been thinking about something. This girl we had in there was so young. And she had no family."

"What do you mean, no family?"

"No one came for her. No one to identify her. No one to plan a funeral for her or bury her," said Shawn. She ran water over the plate then slipped it into the dishwasher. She leaned against the counter with her arms crossed. Cory turned sideways in his chair to look at her.

"That's sad," he said, nodding slowly.

"It is. But here's the thing. If I let this go, it's gone."

Cory now shook his head. "I don't…"

She closed her eyes and shook her head, signaling him to hear her out. "Sameer treats them all as subjects. Nothing more than part of the bigger project," she said. Then she raised her eyebrows. "I mean, rightfully so, right? He doesn't get emotionally attached like I do. Right? But still. Once they give out, he's done with them."

Cory looked at her through furrowed brows, trying to catch what she was implying.

"I'm not saying anything bad about that. I'm just saying, he's clinically detached. This is a project for him. Fine. Whatever. So when he sent that girl back Tuesday, that was it for him. He won't get hung up on what she said or who she was or anything."

"Right…" said Cory, tentatively. He was now looking at the cabinet door by her knee, obviously thinking over what was being said.

Shawn squatted down in front of him and took his hands in hers, forcing his eye-contact. "Cory, I don't want to let her go yet. I want to know more about her."

He breathed in deeply, eyes wide with concern, lips a tight line across his face. But he didn't speak.

"I'm not ready to let her go."

Cory shook his head. "What does that mean, Shawn?"

"She called out a man's name at the end. It sounded like she was looking for him. Or calling for him. Something. I don't know," she said, looking away. She tried to replay the event in her head. Tried to remember what it had been like standing in that dark room while the dead girl repeated the name. "Well, it might have been a surname."

"What was it?" Cory said, lifting his chin.

"Harrison."

They stared at each other for a moment. "Does that mean anything to you?" Cory finally asked.

Shawn shook her head. Then she breathed deeply and said, "But I want it to."


They had moved to the couch. Cory had opened the sliding glass door, keeping the screen closed so they could hear the rain and Shawn had made another pot of coffee. It was going to be one of those lovely rainy days that would keep them inside all day, allowing them to be lazy. The gray sky almost invaded the apartment through the back balcony, and they welcomed it in. Shawn sat in her favorite corner of the couch staring at Cory over the gap formed by the corner where the two sofas came together. Their hands bridged the gap, fingers lightly locked together.

"What exactly is it you're wanting to do, Shawn? I get that you don't want this girl's story to end. I mean, once it's over, it's done, right? No one will remember her?"

Shawn was shaking her head. "Yeah. I can't understand how she has no family to come calling on her. But maybe there's something to that. Maybe she lost both her parents. Only child. Whatever. But why didn't she have any friends?"

"Who found her after she died?"

Shawn pointed at him with one of the fingers she was using to grip her coffee mug, which she held suspended a few inches from her lips. "That was my question. I want to find out these things. She said 'my friends call me Randi' during the interview," Shawn said. "What friends?"

Cory looked up at the ceiling, a look of exasperation, then shook his head. "I get it. You're wanting to go to her house."

Shawn sighed and took a sip of the steaming coffee. "I don't know. That seems the logical place to start. But I don't even know where she lived. I don't even know if I could possibly find that out."

"Oh, anything can be found out, babe," said Cory.

She shot him a look. "What do you mean?"

"A couple of phone calls and you could find that out. It's not classified information. Deaths are a matter of public record."

Shawn was nervous. Standing at the window with her fingernails tapping a rhythm as she waited for the clerk to return. It was cold here. Or maybe she had just brought the cold in with her. She had been surprised to learn the morgue was even open on a Saturday, but Cory had reminded her that people died every day. They probably didn't have the same hours as a bank. She had rolled her eyes at that, but he did have a point. But to her own point, the clerk had apologized for the wait, saying they weren't fully staffed on the weekends. She had used the words 'skeleton crew' then widened her eyes at Shawn. Her next word had been 'Sorry.'

Now she stood waiting for that clerk to return to the window. The glass between her and the rest of the building – for the lobby of this place was about the size of her apartment kitchen and everything else in the building was behind the walls around her, protected by a steel door with a keypad on its handle – was thick and had hundreds of tiny, radial scratches that caught the light from the woman's desk lamp. Cory had opted to wait in the car, saying it might look less 'official' if multiple people showed up asking about the decedent. She figured there were probably several morgues across the city, but they had to share access to the same database.

When the woman finally returned and dropped into her rolling chair, she scooted up to the desk and dropped a thin manila folder onto the blotter in front of her. She glanced up at Shawn and gave her a weak apologetic smile. "Sorry for the wait. So what is it you're looking for?"

"Just any information you can give me as part of public record," Shawn said.

"Well, technically I could give you a copy of the death certificate," said the woman.

Shawn nodded and said, "Just a birth date and address is probably all I need."

The woman's face made a frown that lasted less than a full second, but Shawn had caught it. Was this making her look suspicious? Oh well, it didn't matter much because the clerk had not even asked who she was. Or who she was with. She guessed public record truly meant public.

"Okay," said the woman, slipping a fingernail down the paper as she scanned the tiny print. "Miranda Kate Struck. Died Monday, June nineteen at twenty-two thirteen. Twenty-six oh four Brown Boulevard, Arlington…" she said, and Shawn's heart dropped into her stomach. "Apartment fourteen-fourteen."

Shawn must have gone white as a ghost because when the woman looked up, she did a double-take, then asked if Shawn was all right. She blinked a few times then tried to force a smile. "Yes. Yes, I'm fine. Sorry."

The woman's gaze lingered on her eyes a few seconds longer before she finally looked back down at the paper and rattled off the birth date. Shawn had surmised the year of her birth based on Sameer's calling her twenty years old. But now she knew the birth month and day: December thirteenth. When the woman finally looked up again and asked what else she was looking for, Shawn tapped the counter in front of her lightly and said, "That's it, thank you very much. I just needed those details for the obit."

The woman raised her chin as if she were about to nod, but kept it high. Her mouth opened but Shawn said another 'thank you' and turned to exit, mouthing '*Holy fuck, holy fuck, holy fucking fuck*' all the way to the car.

When she popped the door open and ducked inside, she pulled back the hood of her raincoat and Cory looked up at her. The raincoat had probably been a wasted effort, as she now sat pooling on the cloth seat of his Jeep. She would be soaked through to the skin by the time they got back to the apartment. The rain was loud on the sailcloth top of the Jeep. She looked over at him and met his eyes.

"Cory, she lived in our apartment complex."

They had pulled into a parking spot in front of the deceased woman's breezeway. She lived on the first floor only two buildings down from Shawn's. The 'small-world' factor was heavily at play here, in Shawn's mind, and her heart was racing for it. "I really don't think this is a good idea, babe," Cory said. His left hand rested atop the steering wheel while he clicked his teeth with the thumbnail of the other. He was staring into the breezeway ahead of them, gaze interrupted every four-and-a-half seconds by the wipers clearing off a track through the blur of rain on the windshield.

"I just want to see. I just want to try the door. If it's locked, we go home. It if's open, I just go inside and have a peek." She looked over at him through the tops of her eyes. Why was she so interested in this woman's home life? This woman she didn't even know. Was it because she had gotten to catch just a glimpse of what it had been like to know her while she was alive? Had hearing her living voice, so natural and sweet – soft with a little husk to it – been enough to make Shawn wish she had known her in life? Well, something had. If that was truly what this was – a desire to have known someone she couldn't possibly ever know now. If she could go back in time, she would know her. She would walk down that sidewalk on a sunny Saturday morning and knock on that girl's door. And when she answered, Shawn would introduce herself and ask if she wanted to join her for a coffee at the mall. *'My treat!'* No need for it to be weird, even. *'I'm just looking to make friends in the neighborhood and I saw you walking up to this door the other day…'* Whatever it was, there was no going back now to reconcile that dream past with the real future. There was no past with her, and there never could be. But that didn't mean Shawn couldn't give the girl some dignity in her death. Find something she loved and do something special for her. Put some flowers on her grave if no one else on the planet cared enough to do so. The bottom line was that something had awakened in her the realization that she, Shawn, had awakened Miranda Struck from her permanent sleep. And then she had sent her back to the beyond with a head full of terror. If that did carry over – if there was a persistence of some sort – then by God, Shawn was going to reconcile that. She would do *something* special for her.

Cory was shaking his head. He took a deep breath, then leaned back and put his hands on his knees. "I just think you're prolonging your misery. Your grief, suffering, whatever this is… And I'm not trying to diminish it, mind you," he said, opening his hand toward her, "I know its, real… I'm just saying that you might be better off trying to let it go now. There's nothing you can change in her life, no matter *what* you might find in that apartment."

"I know. I know, Cory. I do. But something is calling me to look. Because I know that once they come and clean that apartment and turn it over, I'll never get the chance."

Cory shrugged. "I guess you've got a point. I just hope you don't find something that makes it worse for you." He looked over at her, then reached over and took her hand, resting on her thigh. She met eyes with him. "If it's locked though, that's where it ends, okay?"

"Cory, you're a fucking locksmith," she said, rolling her eyes. And before he could react, she had popped open the door and was shutting it from the other side. Shawn trudged through the river of rain that ran down the steep incline of the grounds and across the sidewalk. There was no grass under the giant oak tree. The place wasn't nice enough to pay for that kind of landscaping service. It was mostly hard-packed dirt and exposed tree roots, and it created whitecaps in the torrent that ran from the roof gutters all the way to the parking lot. Shawn didn't pay it much attention as she sloshed through it on the way up to the first door on the left.

The door was unremarkable in every way except that there was a notice to keep out. Management had scheduled a cleaning and the apartment was vacant until further notice. It didn't look to Shawn like a police document, or otherwise official in any way, in fact. It was a white piece of printer paper taped on its four corners. She looked up and down the breezeway for any signs of life. There was none. Taking a deep breath, she reached up and knocked lightly. She thought briefly of leaning in and saying, *'Miranda!'* through the door, but decided against it, just in case it traveled. She didn't want the neighbors to know she was here. If someone popped out and said, 'Uh, she's dead," it could seriously inhibit her ability to enter the premises with any sort of plausible deniability.

Shawn took the brass doorknob in her hand and stood there for a long moment, willing it to be unlocked. There were two locks on the door, as there were on all the units at the complex. A twist on the knob, and a keyed bolt above it. Her mind ran through each of the four possible combinations of the state of the locks, finally settling on the twenty-five percent chance she had of an open door being pretty good odds, and turned the knob.

The door opened easily enough, cracking away from its weather seal with a separation that sounded like peeling away from paint. The smell was immediately evident. It didn't smell bad, necessarily, but it wasn't a fresh smell. It smelled like wet carpet. Possibly a little mildew. Shawn stepped inside and turned on the light, closing the door gently behind her. Then she stood with her back against it, both hands behind on her on the knob, just taking in her surroundings. It was immediately clear that whoever the powers that be – whatever corporate entity was responsible for clearing out her personal belongings and cleaning the place up – had not yet gotten started. Everything was – presumably, at least – exactly the way Miranda had left it. She glanced to her right, into the breakfast nook, where a small round table stood with one chair pushed away from it and one leaning against it like someone would do at a bar to save his seat. Miranda's keys were on the table, next to some well worn magazines and a book, as if they'd been tossed there the last time she ever walked through the door Shawn had just entered. The kitchen light was already on. Or still on. She couldn't see over the bar that formed about a twenty-inch section of the wall next to the doorway that led in there, but it looked neat enough from what she could see. A vase stood on the bar. A dead rose hung its head over the edge of it, dried up and colorless, leaves long since fallen to the counter and swept away. Moving her head to the left, into the living room Shawn's eyes fell across the coffee table, standing a couple of feet in front of a lone sofa that backed against the wall in which the door stood. The coffee table was cluttered with the usual findings: a remote control for the television, a stack of unopened mail and a journal of some sort that lay open with a pen in its crease. Maybe the journal would hold some clue as to who this young woman was. Mention of a family, friends… someone? The eerie similarity between this apartment and Cory's nagged at the back of her mind. It was the exact same floor plan. She knew the one across the breezeway would be exactly like hers, a mirror of this one and Cory's. She was so familiar with the layout of this stranger's apartment that it almost felt like home, even with the foreign furniture and arrangement. Shawn noticed the smallish television standing on an ordinary glass entertainment cabinet, cocked at an odd angle and covered with dust. Clearly, this woman had not been a consumer of mindless programs. Shawn smiled at this. *So she had a life.* She nodded and stepped from the small patch of laminate flooring onto the carpet of the living room. That's when she realized whence the smell was emanating. The carpet squished beneath her feet. She looked down at her shoes and saw small puddles around them as they pressed in on the carpet. It was completely soaked. Flooded. Shawn covered her mouth with a hand and turned to look at the rest of the living room. She now recognized the odd luster of the carpet, full of near-standing water. It was so full that when pressed down upon by the weight of a foot, it spilled over. *Oh my God.* She was breathing heavily now.

She crept down the edge of the bar toward the bedroom, feet making squishing wet noises in the flooded flooring. When she got to the bedroom, she reached in and flipped on the light. Thunder rumbled outside, shaking the windows, perfectly timed to feel as though she had switched it on. The bed was immaculately made. Decorative pillows stood against the hump in the comforter made by the sleeping pillows. A stuffed monkey leaned against the middle square, staring dumbly into the distance between it and where Shawn stood. Shawn couldn't remember the last time she had taken the time to make her own bed this nicely. Her version of a made bed was a whipped-up sheet and pillows tossed toward the general direction of the headboard. A messy make. This was beautiful. Almost professional. It saddened her to see. It spoke of the desire to come home to something neat after a day of work. As if she had planned to live another day when she got up that morning. What had changed, then? What had made her want to slit her wrists, draining the life out of herself? She shook her head, staring at the bed, the monkey and the pillows. A glass of water stood on the nightstand next to a lamp and an alarm clock that blinked back at her. *3:04. 3:04. 3:04.* It had lost power at some point so that now it ran its bad schedule, keeping up with the minutes but not the time. A broken clock is right twice a day. This one would never be right until it was reset.

Shawn looked into the dark bathroom, fearing what she would see, but knowing that was her ultimate destination. She had to go in there. That was the whole point of this endeavor – this intrusion. All she could see from her current angle was the dim image of the toilet. She swallowed and breathed in deeply then took the few slow steps to the doorway, reached in and turned on the light. The mirror instantly caught her eyes. A lipstick message had been written on one side, out of the way but easily viewable when Miranda needed to see it. She instantly understood that Miranda had written it to herself. It read, 'Believe in yourself! You will change the world!'

Shawn's bottom lip trembled as she pulled it in to bite it. To hold it back, out of the way. Tears ran down her cheeks. She reached up and wiped them away, then exhaled, trying to hold back the deluge that threatened to come pouring forth if she didn't strengthen her dam. She tried to smile at the message on the mirror, imagining the hand that had written it. She had a sudden and startling realization: like a fool, she had been assuming this woman had killed herself – or otherwise died in whatever way – here. *Here*, in this apartment. What if she had been somewhere else?

The tub had been drained. There were shampoo and conditioner bottles lying in it, caps open. No blood. No blood on the floor outside of the tub, either. There were several wet towels on the floor pushed up around the toilet and up against the tub, though. They were probably at least partially contributing to the wet smell of the apartment. She noticed the drain plug lying on the floor beside it, its chain broken. One of the links was bent into a C shape and lying beside the rest of the intact links of the chain. From the faucet hung the other few inches. Someone had reached in and ripped the thing out to drain the water. *Exsanguination*. The word fluttered to her mind like a butterfly dancing on the edge of perception. How had this woman bled to death in a tub if there wasn't even a drop left over? They obviously hadn't taken time to clean the apartment yet. The wet towels and flooded carpet said so. But they had cleaned up the blood? She frowned and turned to look at the carpet in the bedroom, where her footprints clearly stood out. If she had filled the tub with blood, then presumably at least some of it would have spilled over as the tub kept running, filling the apartment. She pushed the closest towel over with her foot and saw it. The bottom was dark with blood. Her blood *had* spilled out of the tub. It was just so diluted that one couldn't see it across the apartment. Now that she looked down at the floor, she did see the evidence of it there as well. Tiny specks dotted the floor. Shawn shook her head and covered her mouth again. She dropped to her knees and pushed her fingertips gently into the drain hole, feeling for the razor blade. Her fingers came back unpricked and uncut. There was no razor. She looked up at the head of the tub, the end opposite of the faucet, and there it was: a tiny line of blood and flesh on the rounded corner of the edge. She inhaled sharply through her nose, then stood up and dashed out of the bathroom, grabbing the monkey off the bed and the journal off the coffee table as she made her way out the front door and back into the rain.

She stepped into the Jeep with the phone against her ear, already ringing. Cory turned to ask her something, but she held up a finger and let go the two items she had wrapped in her arm. She quickly grabbed the monkey and handed it to him. "Sameer! Were that girl's wrists slit?"

Back at her own apartment, Cory waited for her to get out of the shower, leaning against the counter with his arms crossed as she blasted some warmth back into her frigid skin. The rain-soaked clothes had finally lowered her body temperature enough that her jaw was trembling, clattering her teeth together. Now she stood in the shower, filling the bathroom with thick steam, and shouting over the din of the water at Cory.

"She didn't kill herself, Cory!"

He nodded, staring at the floor. "I mean, I guess you're going to tell me how you know that."

"Look!" she said, whipping the shower curtain back as if to give him a show. "Check this out."

Cory waved away the steam, but obliged. Shawn squatted carefully and dropped onto her butt, then leaned back as if she were taking a bath. She put her feet against the wall of the tub beneath the faucet, ignoring the fact that the stream of water from the shower head was now raining directly in her face. Her shoulders were just beneath the edge of the tub, her head against the first row of tile above it. "I'm five-foot-seven, Cory. Now watch this," she said, and slid down until her head rested against the back edge of the tub, where she had seen the blood spot in Miranda's bathroom. She looked over at Cory, spitting out the water that constantly ran into her mouth. She blinked a few times, then nodded, smiling at Cory. Then she sat up and whipped the curtain back into place before standing up and resuming her shower.

Cory held his hands up in question, unseen to Shawn. "I'm not following, sweets."

"Cory, she was shorter than I am. She was like five-foot-three. With her feet flat against the wall, her head would be right where she banged it on the edge of the tub."

"Uh huh…"

"She fell in the tub, Cory!" she shouted, again whipping back the edge of the curtain to stare out at him, hair hanging in her eyes. "She slipped and banged her head, then her feet hit the wall, keeping her from dropping into the water!"

"How could you know that?" he asked, frowning. "Can you even bleed to death from your head?"

"Sure you can! There are two arteries right there," she said. She pulled the curtain back to the wall. "Sameer said there was a pretty big wound on the back of her head, but no, she had *not* slit her wrists." After a few moments of silence, she finally turned the water off and reached out to grab a towel. She pulled it back into the steamy sauna behind the curtain to dry off. "Cory, this changes everything! I've been thinking this whole time that this girl killed herself, but she didn't! It was just an accident! A stupid unfortunate accident!"

"Shawn, I just don't want you to get caught up in this and get it wrong, babe. I mean, no offense, but you're not a detective."

Again, the curtain whipped open. She stared at him. Cory finally reached over and opened the door, allowing some of the steam to vent.

"I am a detective. How would I have this wrong?"

"What if you *do* get it wrong? I just don't want to see you latch onto something and get depressed again if you find out you're wrong. I just care."

"I'm not wrong," she said, spitting the water out that had run down her sweating face. "Why do you think I'm wrong?" Shawn stepped out onto the rug and readjusted the towel, giving him a brief glance of her glistening naked body. She saw his eyes go away for a moment. Good. He still lusted over her.

"I, uh…" he said. "Shawn, I just don't think there's that much blood in the head."

She held up a finger and got close to him, putting that finger up under his chin. "Aha! That's where you're wrong!" She raised up on her toes and kissed his lips, then bent over and wrapped the towel around her head, letting her hair fall into it. "The brain takes about twenty percent of the blood pumped by the heart. If my math is correct, that is one-fifth of the body's entire supply."

He held a hand out again. "Okay. No need to be snarky."

"Not snarky. Just letting you know, I know what I'm talking about. I've been reading all about the brain from that text book Sameer lent me." She stood up, whipping the towel back over her head, then grabbed another off the rack and wrapped it round her chest under her arms, noting along the way, the path Cory's eyes traveled from her breasts to spot where her legs came together. "Seriously. The brain requires so much oxygen that it takes that much blood. She laid there in that tub unconscious, bleeding out into the water, until the tub finally spilled over, flooding the apartment."

She swung the door to the nearly closed position and back to wide open several times, trying to force vent the poorly circulated bathroom. "Plus, also, too," she said, "think about this: ninety-nine times out of a hundred, medics find the razor in the drain when someone cuts their wrists in a tub or shower. There was no razor in her drain."

Cory shrugged. "Okay, babe. I'm not saying you're wrong. I mean, missing evidence isn't evidence at all. But let's say you're right. And," he said carefully, holding a peacemaking hand out to her, "I'm inclined to believe you are, but let's say you're right. What does this change?"

Shawn crossed her arms. She breathed in deeply, staring him in the eyes. "Likely nothing. But it gives me peace knowing this beautiful young girl, who never even got to reach my age, didn't kill herself."

Cory raised his eyebrows and rubbed his chin, adjusting his neck.

"She probably died quietly and peacefully. I can sleep at night knowing that at least she didn't die two horrifying deaths."

# Nine

Sameer had texted a group Monday morning at six o'clock, saying to meet at Ryan's Pancake Factory before coming to the office. Shawn had Jeremy's number saved in her phone, so he showed up as *Jeremy*. And of course, Sameer showed up as the sender. But the third number in the list only showed up as a number, so she didn't know who it was, but quickly, there were thumbs-ups and *got-its* being sent back. Shawn had sent, 'See you there!'

Now, Shawn sat sipping from her water glass and waiting on coffee while Sameer looked over the menu. "Who else was on that list besides Jeremy, Sameer?"

Sameer looked up at her and adjusted his glasses. "That's Chandra. Do you not have her number saved, I guess?"

Shawn raised her chin. "Ah. Okay. See, new surprises every day. I've spoken to her maybe three times in my life. Never had the need to have her saved." The waitress returned and slung a couple of coffee mugs onto the table, then filled them with the carafe and set it down.

"Still waitin' on the others?" said she.

Shawn looked up at her. "Yes, please. Thank you, sweetie." She smiled widely. When the lady walked off, Shawn said to Sameer, "What makes them think we're suddenly going to stop wanting to wait for the rest of our party? 'Oh yeah! They get here late, they lose they plate!'" she said, wiggling her head around and snapping. Sameer didn't get it. He raised his own chin now and looked at her.

"Are you okay, Shawn?"

"Yeah. It was just a joke. I'm fine. Sorry," she said, beginning to feel slightly embarrassed. He must have left his sense of humor in the car.

"No, Shawn," he said, lowering his chin and putting his hand over hers on the table. "Are you okay. Ready to come back to work." He said these like statements rather than questions.

"Oh," she said, slipping her hand out to scratch her other shoulder. "Yeah. Yes, I am," she said. Then she leaned in close and said, "Sameer, she didn't kill herself! She had an accident!"

Sameer stared at her for a moment. Suddenly the chair across from her was sliding back. Jeremy dropped into it and picked up his menu, smiling at the two already present at the table. "Good mornin' guys," he said.

Shawn and Sameer returned the greeting, then Shawn leaned back in, about to repeat what she had said. But Sameer, not leaning in, spoke first. "What is making you think she did not kill herself? The DC said she bled out in the bath."

Jeremy, without looking up from his menu, said, "The girl from the other day?"

Shawn shot him a look. One he didn't catch, because of his concentration on the menu. "Yes, Jeremy. I did a little investigative journalism this weekend. Well, without the journalism part. And I can tell you that Miranda Struck did not commit suicide." She looked up at Sameer, keeping a finger on the menu and said, "You said yourself there were no slits on her wrists, right?"

That got Jeremy to look up. Sameer was looking too, with a new intensity in his stare. "Why does it matter?" Jeremy asked. Then he looked at Sameer, probably to see if his questioning was out of line. "Have I missed something?"

Sameer took a deep breath, but gracefully did not say anything. He wouldn't betray Shawn's hangup about the subject. She stared between both of them for a long moment before she finally sighed and decided to burn the hole card. "Okay, remember how I called you the other night, Jer? Asking if the spirit carries memories across the void?"

Sameer frowned at this, then looked from Jeremy back to Shawn. *These people are having conversations without me?*

Jeremy smiled and said, "Yes, I remember." The waitress returned. Jeremy smiled at her too. He tapped on the rim of Sameer's cup, raising his eyebrows. God, that boy had a pretty smile. Shawn wished she could learn to use hers as much as he did. Well, she had to get confident in its beauty first, she reckoned.

"Well, I'm not gonna lie. I've been really beat up about this poor girl. No family. No one to claim the body. No funeral. No friends."

Jeremy looked at Sameer, who was looking down at his coffee mug. Without fully looking back at Jeremy, he saw the gesture peripherally and nodded.

"And this whole time we've assumed that she killed herself. So," Shawn trailed off and shrugged. "I just wanted to know more about her."

Chandra finally appeared, holding her purse strap with one hand and waving with the other. "Hey, guys, good morning," she said, pulling out her chair.

"Good morning, Chandra," said Sameer.

"Good mornin', boss," she said, smiling. Then she looked at Jeremy, who widened his own smile at her. Then she looked at Shawn.

"Hey. Good to see you," said Shawn.

Chandra winked at her. Chandra was basically the financier of this little outfit. She arranged for the permits that allowed the company to participate in medical research on the bodies. She filed all the proper paperwork with the university and the city morgue and paid the bills. She even kept her eyes on the app looking for new subjects that might fit their criteria. But she never came into the lab. Shawn couldn't help feeling a little proud that she and the boss man were the only two at the table allowed to actually get their hands dirty, so to speak. It felt a little like being at a party and having the host come up to you personally and thank you for being there.

Sameer steepled his hands in front of his face, his elbows on the table. He nodded toward Shawn and said, "So you are feeling better about the whole thing now?"

"Well, I don't know about that. But I'm feeling better about her. About Miranda." Shawn looked around the table briefly. "I guess-" she started, but was interrupted by that damned waitress doing her job again.

"Hey, sweetie, what can I get ya?" she asked, huffing like she had just finished a ten-K. She looked like she ate most of her meals here. And most of those were of the pancake variety.

Chandra sat up straight, raising her eyebrows as she glanced over the menu. Then she turned and slapped the menu into the waitress's hands and said, "Just give me a stack of pancakes, mama."

The lady chuckled, writing it down. "Anything to drink?"

"I'll take a mug please, my dearest. These two are in danger," Chandra said, reaching out and grabbing the two closest wrists to her – one of Shawn's and one of Jeremy's – "of having to share theirs with me."

She chuckled again, then went round the table taking the rest of their orders. When they finished with the ordering and handing in their menus, Chandra pulled a notepad from her purse and opened it to a fresh page, laying it on the table.

She held a pen at the ready, clearly in the know that this was about to get started.

"So, we are having some great success in the lab," Sameer said, looking at each of his employees in turn. Chandra nodded, Shawn saw, almost imperceptibly, and jotted something down. Shawn almost giggled, but was able to cover it with a well-placed hand and by raising her mug to her lips. What the hell could she be writing down already? *Great success in the lab?*

"I'm not sure you know, Chandra, but Shawn has been promoted to a director position," said Sameer.

Chandra looked over at her and smiled. A real, true, non-jealous smile. "Hey, congratulations, rock star!" she said, and held a fist up for Shawn to bump. Which she did. But Shawn was blushing, she just knew it. How had this escaped her? She knew she had gotten a raise. And a new set of job duties. But a promotion? A directorship title? Uh… That had somehow slipped by her.

"Yes. She is the Director of the Dead."

Chandra slapped her pen down on the pad and rolled her eyes at the ceiling. Jeremy laughed out loud. Shawn leaned back and shook her head. Okay. So she hadn't missed anything. And apparently Sameer had *not* left his humor in the glove box. He was smirking at her. Nice.

"I tease. But truly, I have promoted her to being director of this project. She has taken the reigns in every way when we are in the lab. Her ideas are forward-thinking and fresh. She has an emotional investment in the subjects that I do not have. It is in her hands that I think these subjects will be treated most humanely." This he said while lifting one of his hands toward the ceiling. "When working with the dead, it is sometimes easy to forget they are – or were – human beings. Shawn is not forgetting this. She carries the greatest honor with her into the lab. I think we are in good hands."

Jeremy nodded and clapped lightly. Chandra did the same. "Yes. It's good to know someone keeps in touch with that," she said.

Shawn smiled humbly and thanked them all, feeling her blush grow stronger. After a few more minutes of mostly small talk, the waitress came back and slid their plates in front of them. Everyone dug in except for Sameer, who only ate one bite every several minutes. Shawn didn't know how one was able to sit in a pancake house and take that much time. She wanted to squish the butter and batter and syrup all up into a tight ball and shove it all in her mouth at once, then quaff back a cup full of coffee to wash it down. His patience and restraint were on point, as always.

"Now, onto the real business," he said, clasping his hands behind his plate. "As I said, we have had some success. I would like to understand better what has changed between the two subjects."

Shawn, with a mouthful of pancakes, looked up. She held a finger up to buy a moment, then swallowed and chased it with coffee. Wiped her mouth. Dear God, why were they talking during eating? This would take forever. Unless the others talked with full mouths. Which would promptly cause her to stand up and excuse herself from the table.

"Sorry. Okay, I used the same routines. Unless Jeremy honed in some of the sub-functions of the general routines," she said, shrugging and pointing at him with an open hand.

Jeremy, still forking food into his mouth, raised his eyebrows and shook his head. He covered his mouth and hummed *mm mmm*.

"Okay, so functionally nothing has changed," said Shawn.

"So to what do you attribute our success on the second versus the first subject, then, Miss Shawn?" asked Sameer, picking up his fork and taking his monthly bite.

"Well, I can only think of a couple of things. One of them could be the difference in time spent post-life." She looked at Chandra, who was staring at her with her fork held a few inches above the plate, brown eyes squinting, mouth making mush of her pancakes. Again with that very subtle nod. "I mean, there is a difference," Shawn said, shrugging, "in the two patients as well. Cardiac arrests are by definition different than exsanguination when it comes to how the brain is treated."

Jeremy quickly swallowed and pointed his fork at her. "Explain that."

"Well, cardiac arrest actively deprives the brain of living blood. The brain even has functions that supposedly kick in, trying to sanction off parts of the body so it can get more of the blood. It has its own survival instincts." Shawn saw Jeremy nodding at her. That made her feel good. When a brain surgeon agrees with something you're saying about the brain, it has a tendency to elevate the confidence.

"Exsanguination is not the product of a fault of the heart. It's a sudden and traumatic depletion of the lifeblood of the entire circulatory system. The brain can't do anything about it. Functions be damned."

Sameer was nodding too. Chandra still stared at her with that 'amazed' look, chewing away at her food and nodding almost imperceptibly. Clearly she was no scientist. No dummy, for sure. But not the code-head these other three at the table were.

"So what is the upshot of this, Miss Shawn?" said Sameer. He was stirring around parts of his food now. Could he be full already? No wonder he was so skinny.

"Well, I think that might be part of it. Her blood loss was traumatic enough to kill her before her brain *could* react. Meaning, it died in a different way than did the first subject. Now forgive me, I'm speaking out my a- I'm uh, just making this up as I go along. But it's an educated guess. I have been thinking a lot about this."

Jeremy crumbled his napkin, waving his hand over his plate asking them not to continue until he spoke. His message was clear. Shawn was good at sign language. She waited. "You're right about their dying a different way. Depletion because of a system component will register differently than will depletion because of a sudden blood loss." He quickly took a sip of his coffee. A gulp, really. He held up his finger to hold his place in line. Again, asking them not to talk yet. No one was in a rush to interrupt the one true subject matter expert at the table. Shawn smiled.

"Here's my hot sports opinion on the whole thing," he said, leaning back and clasping his hands together across his substantial gut. His golden Star of David was visible against the black hair of his chest. "I think that since she was only dead for what, thirteen hours?"

"Close to eleven," said Shawn.

He lifted one hand off his belly, turning it over, then dropped it back into place. "Eleven hours. Brain death wasn't as absolute. We've suspected for many years that it begins at around five minutes without oxygen. But no one knows how quickly it progresses. Or how deeply. Or how long it takes before it's irrevocable."

"That might have made some difference, for sure," Shawn agreed. She noticed that Chandra's hand was working quickly as they spoke. She looked at each person as he or she spoke and jotted down notes on what each of them said, without ever looking at the pad while doing so. Somehow she managed to stay on the lines. She must be well practiced, Shawn thought.

"What is the one thing you would say you have learned on this subject, Miss Marcy?" asked Sameer.

From the corner of her eye, Shawn caught Chandra's flinch. She turned to look at her. "Marcella Shawn. He's still used to the other," she said, rolling her eyes playfully. Chandra lifted her chin, opening her mouth in an *Ah! I see!* She jotted it down. What the hell.

"This subject, being this topic? Or do you mean this subject, like Miranda, as opposed to Subject One?"

Sameer shrugged, smiling at her. Oh. Yeah. Mister enigma. *I could have meant either.* She went with the obvious. "I think she's different because like Jeremy said, she was dead for less time. And she still had a lot of her own blood in her. We didn't use any foreign blood. Her brain was used to her blood."

"This is good thinking," said Sameer, still stirring his eggs. *There are starving kids in China...* "I am wondering, then, why did we lose her so fast?"

Chandra finally had something to say. Looking down at her notepad, she held the pen up and said, "What do you mean by 'lose' her?" she asked.

"We only get so much time with the subject. There is no telling how long it could be. It might be ten minutes, or it might be two hours. Though we are yet to be seeing a two-hour session," Sameer admitted. "But when they drop away, we cannot get them back no matter what."

"How do you know that?" Chandra asked, frowning.

Sameer shrugged. "It is the way of it, Chandra. Jeremy has confirmed, the nanobots burn the neurons."

Shawn looked down at her phone, resting in her lap. It was almost eight-thirty. She looked back up and met Sameer's eyes. She could see he was waiting on her to answer this. "I think I scared her," she said simply. "I hate to sound like I'm making a joke, but I've thought hard about this over the weekend, and – well," she said, holding up a hand, "the extra days I took off – I think that the last subject I broached with her literally scared her to death."

Jeremy raised his chin, but didn't smile. He didn't laugh. He could see it wasn't a joke. And he was nodding in agreement with her assessment. She breathed in deeply, satisfied with her estimation.

They spent most of the rest of the day in the lab drawing on the whiteboard and talking about ways to improve the project. And Shawn finally got what she wanted in an aggressive list of things they should or shouldn't talk about. The topic was presented about whether or not they wanted to let the subject know he or she was dead – if it wasn't already known. Was it likely to send them back, like it had seemed to with Miranda?

Shawn had thought back about the first subject and remembered the last thing she had asked the man was if he was aware of where he was. That was kind of the same thing that she'd seen with Miranda, right? With Miranda, Shawn had told her she was in a lab, and then asked her if she remembered being in the bath tub. A huge assumption at the time, not even knowing for sure that she had died in the tub. Which could also lend more credence to her theory, now that she thought about it. If reminding the subject that the bathtub was where she had expired was what caused her to go into shock, then didn't that confirm she was right about it? Otherwise, it seemed to Shawn that the girl could have just said, 'What the hell about a tub? What's that got to do with anything?'

But somehow these two had to be tied together. Without having more compiled evidence, and without stepping out on a limb and asking Sameer if he had any research gathered from before when she joined the project, she was left with two instances of losing the subject to what appeared to be fear. One had been asked to basically accept – or to take in, observe, assess, discover – where he was, which was different than where his living brain should remember his being. The other had been asked if she remembered being in the tub. Same thing. Both questions would cause the subject to try to remember across the gap.

So, she decided, for now, this would be added to the list of things they should not discuss. "I'm going to try not to make any mention of anything that would cause the subject to try to bridge that death period. Maybe that's what brings the brain to a full state of awareness, and it can't reconcile where it is with where it should be."

"I am thinking this is a solid theory," Sameer said, and added it to the white board. He wrote 'No questions connecting death location and here' and turned back to her, marker in hand. "What else?"

"Well, I think along those same lines," Shawn said, pointing at the board, "we should consider whether we even talk about where they are now at all. Regardless of a connection to where they died."

"How is this different?"

Shawn shrugged and twisted, adjusting her pant leg. She sat with her legs crossed, hands clasped around her upper knee. "Well, maybe it's not. I won't ask anything about where they died. Right? But maybe I shouldn't even mention the lab. Not even answer if they ask. Confirming that they are in a lab is essentially confirming they are in a different location than the brain was when it died. It might make its own deduction from that."

"Okay," he said, and turned to write 'No confirmation of location'.

"But how do we do that? What if one of them persists in their questioning? 'Where am I? What is this place?' You know? How do we answer without answering?" asked Shawn, holding her palms up.

Sameer, snapping the lid of the marker on and off, said, "Well, I think if they are asking that, they have already realized they are in a different place. But it might be a temporary buffer. Like the brain is accepting it is in a safe space, and categorizes it as such – even temporarily."

Shawn shook her head, frowning.

"I mean, it might accept that without going back and checking its records to see if the safe space matches the location it should be remembering as current."

"Ah," Shawn said, lifting her chin and pointing at him. "Yes. So if they directly ask any details about the lab, or ask where they are…" She put her thumbnail between her teeth. "Well, no. That's location confirmation," she said. She looked up at him. "What should I do?"

"No details," he said, pointing the marker at her again. "Try to steer the subject in a different direction." Here, Shawn wrestled with the word 'subject' and its context. Steer the subject as in the person? Or the subject as in the conversation topic? Might be the same thing.

"So. Just answer vaguely, right? I could maybe kind of throw it back at them. Like, 'Well, where do *you* think you are?' or 'What does this place look like to *you*?' or something like that?"

"Sure. We will have to experiment. But I think it is better to try to avoid confirming anything. Rather just try to keep it moving and in a comfortable way."

"So what's the point then? If we can never learn more about that gap in their two separate conscious states, what's the point of the project?" asked Shawn.

"I think that if we talk to them long enough and keep it light enough – *safe* enough – they will grow more and more comfortable. If they finally come to feel that they are in a completely safe space, they may be able to talk about anything. We will just have to see," Sameer said. He stared at her for a moment.

"God, this could take months. Years, Sameer. At the rate we're able to get subjects, we could be doing this for years before we learn to improve our encounters."

Sameer shrugged. "Do you not want the salary to last years, Miss Shawn?" he asked, smiling.

She smiled back, waving a finger at him. *Tricky, tricky!*

"This, I think, is okay. We do not have to be in a rush to learn these things. There will always be bodies. But I think you are wrong about one thing."

"Oh yeah?" asked Shawn, raising her eyebrows. "What's that?"

"About our ability to learn from the encounters. Even the tiniest bit of information is knowledge. Each time we will get better and better. Look at us now, Shawn. We have only had two subjects on our table and we are already coming up with good ideas to keep them engaged longer."

She shrugged and nodded, pursing her lips. *Fuck it. I'm gonna just ask.* "Sameer, have you had subjects on the table before? Before I joined the project?"

He stared at her soberly for a moment. "Not in the way you are asking, no. Not for the purpose of bringing them back to life."

There it was. And it was sort of a non-answer, she realized. Not for the *purpose* of bringing them back. But that didn't mean he hadn't brought them back. By accident? By fluke? Purpose signaled intent. He had not *intended* to wake someone from the dead. But had it happened anyway? Shawn shivered at that. Imagining being part of a project where neural resurrection was *not* the goal, but it happened anyway? Jesus Christ.

"So how quickly do you think we will get another subject on the table?" she asked.

"You seem to be getting more comfortable with this, Shawn."

"I am. And I'm going to try to keep my emotions out of it. At first I thought I *should* get emotionally attached a little bit. So as not to disrespect the dead. If they're brought back to life, they deserve the same respect as the living. Right? But maybe I'm getting a little too personal."

"May I offer some advice, Miss Shawn?" Sameer asked, putting the marker on the tray of the whiteboard and leaning on the counter in front of her. She nodded. "I think you should keep doing exactly what you're doing. If you can do so without the depression part of it, I think your compassion is what will be bringing great success to our project."

Well that was a shocker. She found herself nodding. "Okay. Thank you, I guess. I will try to keep going like that. I'll just have to learn when to flip the switch off and let it go," she said, making eye-contact with him. He had a reassuring smile on his face, and he was nodding. "So... how long until you think we'll get another subject?"

"She will be here Wednesday."

When Shawn pulled into her usual parking space behind the apartment, she was happy – if not a little surprised – to see

Lo sitting on the stairs waiting for her. Shawn hopped down out of the Jeep and slung her bag over her shoulder, skipping up onto the sidewalk with a smile. "Hey, hot thing! What are you doing here?"

"Hey, sister!" Lo said, standing up and holding her arms out for the impending hug. "I haven't gotten my Shawn Fix lately. I need to see my friend!"

They met on the bottom of the stairs and hugged, then trotted up the stairs together. "What the hell do you mean, 'what am I doing here?'" Lo said, punching Shawn in the shoulder. "Do you not remember texting me yesterday, ya dork?"

"Oh. Oh, yeah. Have you been waiting long?" asked Shawn.

"Oh, about two weeks," said Lo.

"Shush, you."

As she unlocked the door, Lo threw a thumb over her shoulder and asked, "How's he doing?"

"Good as he's ever been," said Shawn and pushed into the apartment. "Need a drink?"

"Does the tin man have a metal dick?" asked Lo.

Shawn laughed out loud. "Got you covered. Vaka to the rescue!" she said, holding up a fist as she tossed her bag on the couch and went into the kitchen. "So how's Mr. Nine Lives?" she asked.

"Well, there's a thing about that," said Lo, pulling up one of the bar stools. "That might have run its course."

"Oh, no!" said Shawn. She slid a martini glass across the bar top to her friend. "What happened?"

"Nothing happened," Lo said, taking a sip. "More cran, please." She slid the glass back and Shawn tipped the bottle over its rim, allowing a little more, then handed her a stir stick. "That's the problem. Nothing ever happened. All he ever wants to do is ride."

"Ooh, but I have to beg Cory to take me riding," said Shawn, sipping her own drink, still standing in the kitchen.

"Really?"

"No. I guess not. He's up for it whenever I ask. But it just doesn't happen all the time. Which I guess might be a good thing. Anything in moderation, right?"

Lo shrugged. "I like Heath. And I love riding bitch sometimes. But you know, it's hot, and you always smell like the highway. Like you can't go somewhere nice for dinner because by the time you get there, you're sweating and you stink like exhaust."

Shawn chuckled. "Yeah, we don't go to dinner on his bike. But I get you. We plan our little outings to coincide with something we're doing outside already." Shawn took another sip of her drink, then added more cranberry to hers as well. Stirred it with a fingertip, then put the finger in her mouth. "Well, I'm sorry to hear that."

"Meh. It's okay. I haven't told him yet. I've just been politely declining his daily invitations for a ride. I mean, I like riding, like I said. But I could go without it. You know?"

"Sure. Kind of not your thing," said Shawn.

As they stood there talking something caught Shawn's eye out the back window. She squinted, putting her hand on Lo's arm to stop her for a moment. "What the hell. I think that butterfly is back, Lo," she said.

They both walked over to the back door and Lo actually gasped. "Oh my God, he's trapped!"

Shawn slid open the door and repeated the gesture she had done before, freeing the butterfly from the spider's web. When she let it go, this time it went right through the door and landed on Lo's face. She yelped in surprise, stepping back and raising her arms. Shawn came around the door smiling, and said, "Hey! Hey! Relax! He's giving you kisses. He's thanking us for freeing him!"

The butterfly patted around her face just like it had done to Shawn the other night. Lo cooed and moaned, keeping her mouth closed and her hands up in front of her, ready to strike if it bit her. Shawn finally grabbed those hands and held them. "It's okay! He just wants to kiss you!"

Lo was giggling as the butterfly felt her up on the face. Then he finally fluttered around the top of her head for a moment, and darted out the door, as if it knew the way like a well-traveled road. The two women stood there staring at each other, smiling. Shawn still had Lo's hands in her own.

"See? That's exactly what happened to me the other night! That's what I was telling you earlier."

"I don't know much in life, Shawn, but I know one thing: that was fuckin' wonderful," said Lo.

Shawn giggled. "Yes! That's what life is all about."

They made their way back to the bar and Lo asked, "So, how's your Frankenstein project going?"

Shawn said, "Well, it's been sobering, for sure." She proceeded to tell her friend all about the last subject, how she had grown some crazy attachment to her, gotten hung up and depressed, and cried for three days over the girl. She told Lo about finding out Miranda lived two buildings down, and going on a little B and E hunt.

"Well, technically it's not breaking and entering if you just turned the knob," said Lo, finishing her glass and sliding it back for a refill. They were still in their same assumed positions – Lo on the stool and Shawn standing in the kitchen facing her over the bar.

"True. But whatever. First time I've ever done anything like that. My heart was slamming in my chest. Part from unlawfully entering a residence, and partly because I had no idea what I would find."

Lo shook her head. "Yeah, that could be pretty stressful. Especially for someone who's had such a traumatic experience with death."

Shawn then told her about taking the stuffed monkey from Miranda's bed and the journal off the coffee table. Lo's eyebrows went up at that. "It wasn't premeditated. It was a spur-of-the-moment decision. I just saw it and grabbed it without really thinking. I haven't even opened the journal yet. Haven't gotten the nerve up yet, I guess."

Lo was nodding, hands clasped behind her drink on the bar top. "That may be traumatic in and of itself."

"Yeah. But see, I think I'm getting over her. Like maybe I wasn't really crying over Miranda, as such. But more just the trauma of the experience. Getting used to seeing death in a different way, banging it around in my head against what I went through with my aunt's death," she said, waving her fingertips around her head. "You know, just all of it coming together at once. But I think I'm better. Now I would just like to learn a little about Miranda to give her some dignity in her death."

"Cheers to that," said Lo, holding up her glass for a toast.

# Ten

"Today is Thursday, the twenty-ninth of June. The time is zero-seven twenty-seven. Present are Marcella Stedwin and myself, Sameer Singh. Patient is forty-seven-year-old African-American woman, died eight days ago. Blunt trauma to head."

Shawn looked up sharply at this. She had up to this point been staring at the dead woman's eyes, which were closed for a change. Both of the other subjects had come in with eyes wide open. *Of course, that could make it a little spooky when they pop open...* And what was with the word 'patient' there instead of 'subject'? Had that just been an innocent mistake, or was there more to it? Sameer met her eyes when she glanced up, and switched off the recorder momentarily. "Blunt trauma is not necessarily ruling out what we can achieve, Shawn. We can still learn something here. Maybe more of something."

Shawn shrugged and looked away. She stood looking at the shape on the table under the white sheet and after a long moment, realized he had not resumed his talking. She looked back up at him.

"Shawn, we could either wait another potentially long time, or take this one in yesterday who had head trauma. I thought it better to test some of our findings than to have to wait."

She nodded this time. Tried a light smile. "Fine," she said. She had her hands clasped together in front of her. What she found interesting is that all day yesterday – the day the subject had been brought in – Sameer had been in Room B, back here in the hidden half. Well, that part hadn't been the interesting part. A lot of times he was locked away in the hidden half while the rest of the company (all three of them) were in the office area. The interesting part was that he had not wanted to be disturbed, and thus had gone an entire day without speaking much to Shawn, or any of them for that matter. And so Shawn had not come to find out that the woman had died of blunt-force trauma. To the head. What the hell, Sameer?

"Bagged blood has been circulating for twenty-four hours. Nanobot transit colony injected, oh, about a half-hour ago. We are seeing the usual collateral skin twitches in the facial area. Marcella will be moderator." Sameer held the DVR near his mouth for a moment as if deciding on something internally, then added, "Marcella is also known as Shawn."

She rolled her eyes and smiled at him. "Well, thank you for that, Sameer," she said quietly. He returned the smile and lowered the lanyard to his chest where it hung naturally. "I'll start with our usual," she said. Then she began snapping the fingers of her right hand, down by her side. She stood by the woman's mid-section, so the snapping was not offensively close to her ear. She raised her hand slowly, still snapping. She got to the bottom side of the table and stopped her hand, but continued snapping. And Shawn was ready for it when the woman's eyes suddenly popped open. She stopped snapping. She glanced up at Sameer and said, for the benefit of the tape, "Eyes open."

"Hello…" then she stopped, looking up at Sameer and held her hands out to her sides, exasperated. "I'm sorry, Sameer, what is this lady's name?"

He raised his chin slightly as if to be heard better and almost whispered his answer. "Sonora."

"Hello, Sonora. Can you hear me?"

The woman's eyes shot down to find the source of Shawn's voice, showing the whites above her irises. It didn't make for a comforting sight. Shawn stepped up closer to the head of the bed. "Sonora, I'm here. My name is Shawn. Are you hearing me?"

Jeremy had realigned some of his brain-mapping protocols, tightening the tolerance of some of the general functions having to do with cognizance. Shawn wasn't yet sure whether the changes would yield practical results, but if the rapidity of this initial response time were any sign, things might be improving already.

The eyes followed her voice. This wasn't so bad. Weirdly, this part of it was starting to feel normal to Shawn. Standing here next to a table, upon which lay a dead person, whose eyes were *fucking following her* as she spoke. Completely normal. *Oh my God.*

What happened next, good or bad, was *not* yet normal to Shawn. Maybe she had begun to desensitize to eyes moving, lips trembling and cheeks quivering on a dead person. But never would she grow sensory apathy for this. The woman's face completely contorted in a rigor so fierce and violent that Shawn had to step back from the table, inhaling sharply. She instinctively raised her clasped hands, just beneath her chin as if she had been engaging in prayer. Every muscle on the woman's face was completely flexed in a desperate painful deathly panic.

Sameer stepped up to the head of the table and calmly rested his hand on the woman's forehead. The reaction this brought was not one of comfort but of fear or anxiety. The eyes were rolling back in her head and she began grinding her teeth. "Sonora, this is Sameer. You are okay. Can you tell me what you are feeling?"

The subject began squishing her tongue against her teeth and the roof of her mouth as if she were choking. Quickly, Sameer turned to the counter behind him and grabbed a spray bottle and returned, prying the woman's mouth open. He sprayed the water in her mouth, creating moisture where there had been none – where in life there had been saliva glands that were no longer working in death. Shawn stared in horror at the woman. Sonora's jaw moved up and down, but her eyes were staring straight ahead at the ceiling, wide open. She looked as terrified as Shawn felt in her heart. Like she was seeing death all over again. Maybe this wasn't getting normal after all. Maybe this project wasn't for her as she had thought. She had thought she could adapt. Get used to it. *Desensitize.* Maybe that had been false hope. If she had to see things like this, she wasn't sure she could make it through.

The woman started growling words from deep down in the back of her throat. She was pursing her lips as if to speak something – maybe something that started with F, but no vowels followed it. Just a jugular, repetitive expulsion of sound. *Fh fh fh fh…*

Was it a muscle contraction? A spasm like they had seen before? She looked like she actually might be convulsing. This was going from bad to worse. A convulsion where no muscles besides the facial were involved did not look right to Shawn. "What should I do, Sameer?"

"I do not know." He put one hand under the woman's chin, one on the top of her head, as if to try and force her mouth to stay closed.

"She's having a reaction. She's convulsing, Sameer! You need to do something!"

"Get the Phenobarbital from the freezer, Shawn!" he shouted. Shawn rushed to the freezer and hammered in her code with trembling fingers. She had to try twice to get it. When she hoisted the top, waving through the smokescreen of mist she reached down into the base where there were several boxes filled with vials of medicine. She remembered him telling her on her tour that they weren't necessarily approved for use in live patients. Or at least not anymore. Maybe expired. Maybe deemed ineffectual or dangerous. But this wasn't a 'live' patient, was it? Or was it? It was difficult to see through the frost on the bottles, and with such poor lighting in the freezer, she had to bring each of them out into the dim light of the room to see the labels. She finally found the one she was looking for and dashed to the first drawer in the counter, letting the freezer slam with an eerie thump. From the drawer she pulled a syringe and quickly popped the cap off, letting it fall to the floor as she rounded the head of the table. She jabbed the needle into the rubber film at the top of the bottle, then Sameer looked up, still holding the woman's head.

"No, Shawn! Warm it up!"

"Fuck!" she shouted, pulling the syringe out and looking around quickly for a place to put it. She finally slapped it down on the woman's chest and rolled the bottle between her hands creating quick friction.

After a few seconds, Sameer said, "It is good, let's go!"

She stuck the needle back in the jar. "How much?"

"One hundred fifty milligrams. Go!"

She pulled back on the plunger, spinning until she could get good light on the syringe body, and filled it to the specified amount. Then she started searching for somewhere to stick the needle.

"In the tube! Shawn, in the tube!"

Oh. Yeah. Duh. She reached over and traced the tube coming from the circulator machine to where it disappeared under the table. Her hand found the hub she was looking for, just under the opening in the table through which the tubes ran and connected to needles of their own, stuck in the woman's lower skull. She popped the needle into the inlet and pushed the plunger.

Almost instantly, there was a change. The grimace left the woman's face. A calm fell about her visage. Shawn took a deep breath. Removed the syringe and dropped it on top of the circulator, then covered her heart with her hand. It was slamming incredibly hard and fast within her ribs. "Christ on his throne," she said, almost in a whisper.

Then the face changed again. The woman squinted her eyes closed and began mouthing something. It was a repeating pattern. It sounded like words, but hadn't the strength of a vocal backing. Like the woman was talking without a voice box. Using only her mouth to enunciate the words. And without the aid of pulmonary aspiration, it was very difficult to discern. Shawn, whole body trembling from shock and adrenaline, leaned over, putting her shaky hands on her knees, and moved her ear closer to the woman's mouth. Then she repeated what she was hearing from the woman. "Full something. Kim? Full kim?" She turned to look at the mouth for a moment, frowning. "That's not right. What is she saying?" She turned her ear back to the woman's mouth. "Fucking…" she said, then waited for a few moments.

"What is she saying, Shawn?"

Shawn held up a finger to silence him, to buy a moment more to listen. Then she finally shook her head, breathing in deeply, and stood up. "Fucking kill me." She stared at Sameer for a moment. He looked as though he were about to ask her why she would say such a thing. Like it couldn't be *that bad*. "She's saying, 'fucking kill me', Sameer. She's repeating it." Shawn crossed her arms and stepped back, catching her breath. "She wants us to kill her."

Sameer sighed deeply, looking up at the wall behind Shawn. Clearly, he wasn't ready to give this one up. But Shawn, or at least the humane part of her that Sameer had claimed he was happy to have, knew when to call it. This was torturous. This poor woman was either experiencing death again, or was in such an incredibly intense state of fear and misery now that she was asking for it again. Either way, it was time to accept defeat and put the poor woman to rest. Her face was a concentrated picture of suffering and terror. How could that be strictly the result of the technology they had injected into her brain? Shawn understood, at least on a fundamental level, that the nanobots and oxygenated blood were forcing lifelike nuance into an otherwise dead face. How else would one explain that the face was the only part of the body actually reacting to the injection? Why weren't the feet moving? The legs and hands? The lungs – why weren't they suddenly contracting, pulling in wheezing, gasping breaths? They were electrifying tiny parts of the brain – only the parts they wanted, and only in the face and throat – to serve their purposes. This was manufactured life. If you shock something the right way, with the right amount of voltage, it's going to move. Biologically whole flesh will jump and skitter when voltage is applied to it. There's nothing magical or supernatural about it. It's forced science. Human beings had gotten so good at mapping the brain that it had brought them all the way to this. Shawn was literally seeing the results of scientific research performed on the generous hosts who had donated their bodies to this very thing. Just like Sonora. Sonora herself. Their research had gotten them to this point, where they could awaken synapse and circulation, and simulate living function in the areas that could make one believe the subject was alive. Shawn had thought more than once that this very technology could sell a hell of a lot of tickets to haunted houses. It was exactly what the creep movies had been going for. Though there was nothing about it that spoke of something beyond scientific and technological.

But not when it came to pain and suffering. Something was making that brain recall functions related to pain and suffering. Or simulating it. Either way, Shawn did not feel that she – nor Sameer – had the right to judge whether or not it was real. Whether it was the result of so many nanobots attaching to just the right neurons to falsify living torture. That was where she drew the line. If a brain was able to reanimate to a point where it was able to call upon a function that would literally *beg them* to put it back to death, she had to oblige it. And with every bit of haste she could possibly summon. It was not hers to argue whether they were seeing latent memory recall or true and new distress: it was hers to obey. This woman needed to be put to rest.

"Sameer. It's time. End it," Shawn said.

"But, Shawn, there may still be some valuable-" he started.

"I am moderator in this room. Put her to peace."

Sameer looked at her with serious eyes, but closed his mouth. Then he nodded curtly and sighed. He turned and walked to the corner of the room where the electromagnetic helmet device stood on its post. A fat tangle of wires hung from its base. He shook his head as he picked it up and returned to the table with it. The woman on the table had meanwhile opened her eyes again – again with that look of terror, staring straight ahead at the ceiling, eyelids pulled as wide open as they could go – and was still repeating the near-silent mumbling. *'Fucking kill me. Fucking kill me. Fucking kill me…'*

Sameer slid the helmet down over the front of the woman's face, where it conveniently rested on the tabletop, covering everything visible above the neck, and then reached beneath her head, lifting it up to put the strap around it. He then put his fingers on the control keypad and looked up at Shawn. He made a face, furling his lips, and pushed and held the red button.

Shawn didn't know what she had expected – a zapping noise? A buzz? - but it was completely silent. And when he took it off a second later, the woman's face was frozen in a still-image snapshot of what had been a moving picture of horror before. Sameer took the helmet back to its cradle and set it on the post, then returned and closed the woman's eyes. He had to hold them closed for a few seconds for the effort to take.

*Another one down,* thought Shawn. She was not excited about losing the subject any more than Sameer was. But enough was enough. It was sickening to watch that kind of contorted suffering. "Thank you, Sameer. We can talk about whether I have been insubordinate later. But that," she said, pointing at Sonora's face, "was painful. Unethical."

He sighed as he looked at her. "There was no impropriety here, Miss Marcy. You are in charge, just like I said you were. Your humane approach has ended something I might not have been able to end myself."

"Thank you, Sameer," said Shawn, covering her heart with a hand. She felt humbled. Empowered. Curious. A whole host of emotions played at the edge of her conscience. But above all, peace. Knowing this woman was no longer suffering – as an artifact from her former life, or a forced scientific encounter that bid the same results – she was able to feel okay for her. The woman was at peace now. Finally. And therefore, so, could Shawn be.

"What the hell was that?" Shawn said as she entered the conference room. She was the last to arrive. Jeremy and Sameer were already at the small round table when she came in with a fresh mug of coffee. Sameer looked up at her with an expectant hope in his eyes. Shawn didn't quite understand what it meant. She knew what it *looked* like. It *looked* like he was resentful about having to pull the plug. Like she had just wasted several thousand of his dollars on a colony of nanobots they would not get back.

Jeremy was shaking his head. He held a sheaf of papers in his hands and a pen between his fingers. "I've printed out the changes I made to the Awareness Routine, Shawn," he said, and slid one of them across the table to her.

She pulled a chair out and sat, sliding the paper up in front of her. "Am I going to understand this?"

"You're a developer. Of course you are," said Sameer. Yup. Resentment. *There it is.*

She glanced at him then back at the paper. Studied the lines of code. The code did indeed look legible, but the remarks under each were what made for the easiest reading. She scanned down the list of changes he had made. Most of them were very minute. "I don't know what I'm looking for,

Jer. Have you found anything you're waiting to surprise me with?"

Jeremy chuckled and said, "No. Not at all." He shrugged. "I don't think it's the routine. You say she never became situationally aware?"

"Didn't look like it."

"No, and she also never used her vocal cords," said Sameer.

"There was some growling at first that-"

"That was glottal."

"I thought glottal was vocal," said Shawn.

"Negative, Shawn. Not necessarily. It was a product of the surrounding muscles, much like clearing one's throat. This can be done sub-vocally."

Shawn shrugged and looked away. "Okay, so…"

"Nothing on here about the vocal cords," said Jeremy. "I didn't touch that region of the code."

After an almost palpable uncomfortable silence in the room, Jeremy leaned back, clasping his hands across his belly. "Listen. Have we not considered that the CoD was our problem here?"

Sameer looked up at him through the tops of his eyes. Shawn felt a surge of adrenaline in her blood. A tiny endorphin rush – a reward from the brain. Hearing from the brain surgeon in the house that the cause of death might indeed have interfered with their goal, well, that was nice affirmation. And she was glad Jeremy had said it. Because she had been wanting to say the same thing, but she had not wanted to sound snotty. *You're pissed because I made you pull the plug. But if you wouldn't have plugged in a subject whose* brain *was fucking damaged…* She maintained her composure without letting her joy show its smile. Instead, she sat in silence, allowing Sameer time to answer for it himself.

"It was, of course, considered. We acknowledged upon initiation that there could be some obstacles because of the brain trauma. But we agreed," he said, looking at Shawn, "that it was better to get a potentially unusable subject with which to experiment than it was to have to wait an indefinite time for a more desirable one."

Jeremy shook his head. "I'm not arguing your eagerness to get bodies on the table. I'm just wondering why you think the code changes had anything to do with it."

Sameer sighed. "I'm not saying they did. I'm asking if you are aware of any that you *think* might have caused issues. We are also in here to discuss how we move forward."

"Forward?" Shawn asked, eyes growing wide. "What do you mean?"

"Nothing, Shawn," he said, looking down at the table. "I think it is important we meet after each session to discuss strategies. Takeaways. Anything we could do better."

Shawn nodded. "Look, I'm sorry, Sameer, that I made the decision to end it. I-"

Sameer made a sour face and held a hand up a few inches off the table to silence her. He shook his head and dropped his hand. "Shawn, I am disappointed we lost a subject. But I am not displeased with your actions. For the record, as I said at breakfast Monday, I wanted you moderating the project because of your compassion. If you think it is right to end it then I will follow your recommendation."

He finally looked up at her. A weak smile touched his lips. Then he slid his right hand across the table, knocking her paper out of the way to rest his hand on top of hers, then squeezed it.

"Thank you, Sameer."

He nodded, the pulled his hand back. "I am not here to criticize your decision. You did the right thing by your heart. I want to review what we could perhaps try differently next time. To see if we could have prolonged it."

"Watching tape," said Jeremy, smiling. He leaned forward and returned his elbows to the table.

"Excuse me?" Shawn said, looking at him with furrowed brow.

"Like NFL teams do on Monday mornings. They watch the tape of yesterday's game."

Shawn lifted her chin, ready for understanding. Mouth slightly open. She was trying. Not getting it.

"It's… Never mind," said Jeremy, smiling.

Shawn stared a moment longer, her mouth clapping shut. Then she sighed and rolled her eyes for effect. Jeremy knew where her heart was. "Okaaaaayyy."

He giggled.

Shawn said, "I don't see how we could have prolonged it, Sameer. As soon as we turned her on, she started making that F sound."

"F sound?" asked Jeremy. So Sameer took the digital voice recorder – still on the lanyard around his neck – out of his shirt pocket. He unclipped it from the ribbon and set it on the table, then pressed play on the last recording. And they listened to the entire episode.

On her way home, Shawn called Lo to see if she wanted to meet for a drink. Lo said she and Heath were riding up to the Draft House to do just that, and asked if Shawn and Cory would like to join them. "Well, that sounds like a fantastic idea to me. I'll run it by Cory when I get home and see what he thinks," she said. Then she added, "He'll probably say yes. It feels nice outside."

"How long until you get home? We're gonna head out here in a few. I guess it doesn't matter. You guys can pop in later."

"I'm about fifteen out."

"Oh. Cool! Well give him a shout and let me know, k?"

"Well, I'll have to ask him when I get home," said Shawn.

"What's, his phone broken?"

"I don't have his number," she responded.

"What."

Shawn laughed out loud at this simple statement. "Lo, we haven't exchanged numbers yet."

"You've exchanged bodily fucking fluids, but you haven't typed in each other's numbers yet? What the hell is wrong with you two?"

"Weird, I know. We've just never gotten around to it."

"Oh, my God. Okay," said Lo, "whatever. Call me when you get there. Lemme know if you're gonna meet us."

"Okay, will do. Later." Shawn hung up and looked at her phone screen for a minute. Then she slapped it back against the magnetic dash mount. Why *hadn't* they exchanged numbers yet? She thought there had been a reason the last time she thought about it. But that had been a while, and it didn't seem to make sense anymore. Except that every time she got home, one of them went to the other's door pretty quickly. They had found a groove that worked pretty well, taking turns staying at one another's apartment. Every night, back and forth.

In that regard, there was no need to trade numbers. Cory knew she would knock when she got home, or after she had cleaned up and put on her pajamas. He always told her when he would be gone for work. It seemed to work for them. She knew it wouldn't last forever. Someone would need to call the other at some point. Shawn's one worry was that having his number in her phone would distract her at work. She might get into a text chat with him and forget she was on the company dime. This is one reason she avoided social media apps like Insta and OuterCircle when she was at work.

When she pulled into her normal parking spot, she saw Cory up on the landing, leaning over the railing smoking a cigar. In his other hand he held a short glass of brown liquid. He smiled broadly at her as she hopped down from the Jeep. It was infectious. She loved his smile. It always made her smile back. She waved. "Hey, good lookin'!" she said.

Cory held his whiskey glass forward, raising his eyebrows. *Cheers.*

"Whatcha doin'?" Shawn said, climbing the stairs with a jog.

"Ah, you know, sharpening the blade on the lawnmower."

Shawn stopped halfway up the steps and looked up at him, frowning. Then she rolled her eyes and sighed. "Shush, you." She carried on up the stairs. He turned and held his arms out to her as she approached. Both hands were full so the hug was weak, but she kissed his neck and put her cheek against his chest for a moment. That was good enough.

"Lo was asking if we wanted to meet up at the Draft House for a pint. But I guess you're already into the whiskey."

Cory shrugged. "Not really. I just poured this. I can stop. You wanna ride?"

Shawn looked down at his glass. "Yeah, if you're okay to," she said.

"Yeah. First one. Let's do it!"

"All right, let me put my stuff away!" she said. She trotted off, then stopped a few feet away and came back to kiss him on the lips. "There."

Shawn put on her black jeans and boots and a cute black top she had gotten at the flea market the day she and Lo had spent the entire day shopping. She pulled her hair back into a tight little ponytail that hung low enough to clear the back of the helmet but would keep the tiny wisps of it out of her eyes during the ride. She was excited, and felt like she looked more like the part of a biker's gal, even though they weren't meeting up with the whole group. She wanted to at least show Cory her dedication to what little role she played in the whole thing. She was at least trying. Maybe not ready for her own 'cut' yet, but she could dress a little less like she was going into the office.

Before she came out of the apartment, Shawn leaned out the door and called to Cory. "Hey, come in here for a minute," she said.

Cory set the cigar on the edge of the landing just under the rail and turned to comply. "What's up, buttercup?"

She pushed the door closed behind him and walked to the middle of the floor, then turned around and spread her arms. "Do I look a little more like a biker girl?"

Cory looked her up and down with a smirk on his face. "Yeah, I guess you do. You look hot as hell, I'll tell you that."

Shawn tilted her head, smiling. "Good. Thank you."

"Turn around. Lemme see the ass!" Cory said.

Shawn playfully complied, turning and squatting slightly to give him the most for his money, shaking her rump and holding her hands up in the air. She then stood up, laughing and went to the table to pick up her purse. Through the back window, she saw a fluttering of orange. The monarch was back. "Holy Eff!" she shouted, dashing to the door. Caught in the web again, it was fluttering against the glass, inadvertently entangling itself more with each twitch of its wings. The spider was out, waiting a few inches from the butterfly. Shawn shouted through the glass, "Hold on, sweet monarch! I'm coming!"

She flipped up the lock and slid the door open, rounding the sliding glass and jumping to grasp the wings of the monarch like she had done before. The spider moved in and she flicked it back with her fingernail. "Oh, no you don't Mister Buttface." she said. She couldn't get her fingers on the wings of the fly like she had last time. She was growling as she stood on her tiptoes, trying to reach it without having to jump. She finally got one wing and pulled lightly. The body was already stuck pretty strongly to the web. If she could just get that other wing she could pull without worrying she was going to break the one wing off.

Finally, as all hope was about to be lost, she reached up and cupped it out with her hand, caging the butterfly in and yanking half the web down. The spider came with it though, and climbed up the back of her hand. "Oh my God, you just don't know when to stop, do you?" Shawn said, knocking him off her finger with a cocked finger-flick.

As she came back into the apartment, she shook her head at Cory standing there watching her. "Is this your new pet?" he said, smirking again.

She rolled her eyes. "He's all webbed up. Stupid spider." Then she sat on the edge of the couch, knees together, and started gently pulling the sticky gossamer threads off the butterfly's body. Some of it was on its wings as well. That part was even harder to get off. It was slow going, but the monarch appeared to be patient, gently and slowly flapping one wing occasionally.

"That looks like a lot of work," Cory said.

She looked up at him briefly, then back at the work she was performing. "Yeah. I don't know why he keeps coming to visit me, but this is the second time I've freed him from that spider's web."

"Kill the spider."

"Shush, you," said Shawn, looking back up at him through slits. "He's taking care of his share of the mosquitoes and flies out there."

"Yeah, but if you don't want this little guy suffering, you might have to make the sacrifice," Cory said, dropping in on the couch beside her. He sat back and put his feet up on the ottoman, his hand on her lower back as she sat at the front of the cushion, head bent in concentration.

"If I kill him, another will be back to take his place."

"Okey dokey," Cory said, probably realizing he wasn't going to win this one. "You really like butterflies, huh?" he asked, scratching her back lightly.

"Monarchs particularly. You know I have a monarch tattooed on my pelvis, right?"

"Yes, I've seen you naked."

"Well, you- wait! When?!" Shawn asked a little too loudly.

"You were illustrating some less-than-exciting moves in the shower the other day. Remember?"

Shawn sighed and closed her eyes, shook her head. "Talk about paying attention to the wrong thing. Anyway, did you know that monarchs are the only butterfly species that migrates in two directions every year?"

"Two directions? No, I didn't know that," said Cory.

"Yes. They fly south for the winter like birds. They come back in the spring. That's two directions."

"Ah. I see," he said. He sounded like he might be interested. She appreciated the way Cory listened to her. He always made her feel important. Even when he wasn't interested. Though how someone could *not* be interested in the migration of monarchs was beyond her. It was fascinating to Shawn, who had loved and studied them since she was a little girl.

"They fly up to three thousand miles to roost in trees together and keep warm. They have to flap their wings to keep them from frosting. And Cory, I'll tell you one thing that you need to know in your life. I don't care what else you know or learn in your life, but you must know this: if you ever get the opportunity to see a fir tree full of roosting monarchs, you must do so. It is the most beautiful sight in the universe. When they all flap their wings together, hundreds of thousands of butterflies, their wings look like the leaves of the tree. It's breathtaking."

Cory was silent. He was actually thinking about this. After a moment, he said, "Wow. Yeah, that sounds amazing, Shawn. Honestly, I love hearing you talk about it. You're very passionate."

"My daddy calls me his little butterfly. Has since I was a little girl." She suddenly looked up at the wall in front of her, where there was nothing interesting to see. "I'm going to miss him when he's gone," she said, her gaze lingering for a full minute before she finally returned to her task. She might have had a tear in her eye.

"Well, that was dark. Where'd that come from?" Cory asked.

"Dunno. I guess just dealing with dead people at work. It's kind of always in the back of my head. And I know he's not gonna last forever." She sighed. When she had finally freed the monarch of all the sticky web, she flipped it over and set it on her finger. It flapped its wings slowly, then walked up her hand. When it took flight, it hovered around her head again, and she knew without a doubt this was the same one she had saved before. He remembered her. There was no other option for the truth. She stood up, saying, "Look at this, Cory! Are you seeing him?" she said, turning toward Cory.

"Uh huh," Cory said, and snapped her picture with his phone. "I think he likes you."

She walked to the back door and slid it open, then walked out onto the diminutive balcony. She leaned against the railing and let it flutter around her face, dancing across her eyelids, her smile, her nose, her ears. Then it landed on top of her head. She turned around and looked at her reflection in the glass door just in time to see it raise its wings once more, then take flight and disappear over the building. "Bye bye, sweet butterfly!"

When she came back in, sliding the door closed behind here, she dusted her hands together, then pulled up on her jeans. "You ready, bayba?" she asked. Cory hopped up and held his hands out. She stepped forward and gave him a quick kiss on the lips. "Let's be gone!"

Cory stood up with the gas tank between his thighs as he waited for Shawn to step over the seat. When she found her spot and grabbed the back fender beneath her thighs, he sat and wiggled himself into position, then she wrapped her arms around his waist. She had gotten a lot more comfortable with hanging onto him and not having to bury her helmet against his back. She could now grab his coat pockets – still in front of him but a foot of separation between her hands – and feel pretty safe. Sometimes during acceleration, she would lean in and clasp her hands together, but mostly now it was just a minimalist posture that kept her from dumping over sideways on a long lean. She had gotten to where she could read his future – anticipate his next moves. She knew when he would be rolling heavily on the throttle. And the ride was a lot more enjoyable this way: she actually got to look at the scenery a little.

They roared up highway 360 in the left lane, passing the sparse traffic. The rush hour had died off an hour before, and the sun was dipping below the hills in the highway up ahead. The Draft House was only a twenty-minute ride from their apartment building, but everything felt longer on the motorcycle. The noise, the wind, the road whipping by, the inherent danger… Her mama was obviously not excited about it. But when had she ever been proud of something Shawn did? *Meh. She can booger off.*

Shawn leaned her head back, smiling at the sky, closing her eyes.

When they got to the bar, they parked in the same spot as Heath had put his bike and made their way inside just as the sun completely disappeared. They would be riding home in the dark. Shawn was excited by this prospect, having only seen the road during daylight hours thus far. Heath and Lo were at a high-top near the bar and Lo was bobbing her head and shoulders to the music, hands just above the table and snapping silently. Heath had his elbows on the table, twirling a ring on one finger with the other hand. Well, well. Lo did not look like she was about to be done with this guy. If this was her definition of 'running its course' she wondered what 'in love' looked like.

Shawn skipped up to the table shuffling her feet with her arms out and Lo stood up as soon as she saw her coming. "Yeek yeek, woop woop!" Lo shouted over the din of the music.

"Hey lady!" Shawn returned. They embraced and rocked back and forth while the guys clapped their hands together and bro-hugged, then found their seats. Lo and Shawn took their time, dancing a few steps, holding onto each other's arms.

Lo finally said, "Girl, you gotta get a drink in ya," and reached over to grab her bottle off the table. She took a swig, then handed it to Shawn, who did the same. She pulled her mouth away and swallowed, then shook her head when Lo tried to take it back. Shawn tipped it back and drained the last third of the bottle. "That a girl!" said Lo. They stood there loud-whispering into each other's ears as they stepped left and right with the beat of the music, snapping their fingers. The guys just stared at them.

"Yo, Lo," said Heath.

Shawn shouted, "Yolo!" raising her hands and Lo burst out in hard laughter, bending over.

When she finally stood up, she took Shawn's hands and raised them above their heads. She shouted, "Yolo!" and both girls were laughing now, shouting it and twisting to it like it was some new dance craze.

Cory and Heath looked at each other, shaking their heads. "What the fuck, bro?" said Heath.

"Right?" agreed Cory.

When the foursome finally settled into the bar stools all around, they found normal conversation pretty quickly. Cory had looked over at the bartender, a guy named Clive, and held up a peace sign with his first two fingers. Clive hiked his chin, and shortly afterward, two beers with the same label as Heath's and Lo's appeared on the bar. Cory leaned back as if to try to reach them across the five-foot gap between his seat and the bar top. A young lady sitting there grabbed them and passed them on to him.

"Thank ya, Kim," he said. She smiled and closed her eyes. *Ain't I just so cute?*

They clinked their bottles together and shared stories of the week, drinking and laughing and being merry. On one of their nights together, Shawn had asked Cory how he was able to drink so much beer and drive the motorcycle. He had smiled and pinched her cheeks and said, "Beer ain't drinkin'," then leaned in and kissed her. She had since learned what that meant. Cory would not drive if he was drinking – or had been drinking – whiskey. Or liquor of any kind, really. But beer? His tolerance had grown such that he couldn't get it down fast enough to make him unfit to drive.

That was not a statement of his masculinity, either, she had noted. He was not exaggerating. He literally couldn't chug beer fast enough to impair himself. If he drank more than one an hour, he would get to his third or so and be so full that he couldn't even start the next one. So it was a self-enforcing limitation. If he wanted to drink five or six, he had to pace himself so as not to get too full. And with that pacing, the alcohol never caught up with him. Either way, Shawn had seen it in practice, and was comfortable with it. She felt safe riding with him. She had never seen anyone take safety on the bike as seriously as he did.

When they had been there for a couple of hours and the empties were piling up, Heath finally leaned over the table and took Shawn by the wrist and said, "So I hear you're thinking of joining the Tribe, sister Shawn." He slid his hand back a little, letting his fingers find hers, then clasped them.

Shawn tilted her head dramatically to the side. Everything at this point was over-dramatic. While she was keeping up with the gang beer-for-beer, she was not as stout in her tolerance. She was feeling it. She had reached that stage where everything was perfect. The temperature of the air, the volume of the music, the width of the smiles on Lo's face, the occasional glances from Cory, the winks and kisses he would lean in and give her… *Perfect*. "What does that mean?" she asked, looking at him through the tops of her eyes.

"Becoming an Indian! You gonna buy one?"

Shawn sat there staring at him for a long minute, an almost-smile on her lips, before she finally got what the hell he was talking about. *Buying my own Indian*. "Oh my God," she said, the smile disappearing completely as she stared down at the table. "I was, wasn't I?"

She looked up at Cory. "I was talking about buying one! What happened to that?" she said, reaching down and squeezing his knee under the table.

He shrugged and made a face, then took a pull from his beer. "No idea, Shawn."

Across the table, Lo, who was a little tipsy herself, pointed a not-so-steady finger at Shawn and said, "If you join the tribe, that's what I'll call you." She was slurring a little bit. But only enough to be cute. "You'll be Shawnee."

Shawn's face lit up. "I love it!" She covered her heart with a hand and leaned in close, wrapping her arm around her friend. "I love it, Lo!" she repeated. There might have been a tear in her eye, but she laughed, and Lo laughed with her.

Two days later they had the Independence Day party at Road Kill's house. He had a swimming pool and a nice deck with a huge griddle, where everyone could stand around and eat burgers and brats straight off the heat. There was supposed to be a ride in the morning, where the group would head way out west, almost to Taylor, to stop and eat breakfast in a little dive before heading back Arlington way in time to beat the true heat of the day. Cory had opted out of the ride due to not having a real two-up bike. There was just no way Shawn could be comfortable on the back of his Scout for a two-hour ride each way. Nor was his bike built for handling the extra weight when it came to digging into the twisties as the group called them. And that was the whole point of long rides: to get way out away from traffic on the old country roads where there was almost no such thing as straightaways. The group would meet up at Kill's around four o'clock and start their Fourth of July celebrations. Cory had considered riding to the party, but decided it would be better to 'cage it', what with the number of hours they would be standing around drinking beer.

Shawn had been excited by the thought of getting a motorcycle of her own, but knew it would take time and training. And there was just no way she was going to finance one before she knew she could even ride it. She would be taking a weekend beginner's class to that end. But she found herself looking forward to these group get-togethers, where they would hang out with guys who loved to ride and their wives and girlfriends. It was a different breed of people, and Shawn, though she couldn't put her finger on it exactly, thought it wasn't just about riding. These people weren't 'cool' and 'nice' and 'good' because they owned motorcycles. They owned motorcycles because they already existed in a different space – a different *state of mind* – than did most other people she had met. It was the adventurous soul, the risk-taking and fearless spirit that these people possessed that made them buy motorcycles. And with that, she felt she could belong. She loved the danger. But it wasn't only that, either. It would be silly, Shawn thought, to buy a motorcycle simply because she *loved danger*. Maybe even idiotic. But it was an expression of a deeper affinity for something a little less conventional. A little more *road less traveled*. She seemed to connect with the lifestyle not just because it felt good to be on two wheels, but because two wheels was just one of the ways to get that rush, and with each of these people she had gotten to know a little, she had found something in common. Each of them possessed a spirit of not only adventure or daring, but also of an awareness that there *were* other roads. Those paths less traveled. People seeking the literal alternate route on the road, were usually people who sought it figuratively as well. They looked for other means of doing things. And so far, every one of them had been nothing but kind, fun and good-spirited.

She was, therefore, excited to get to hang out with them by the pool in honor of the country's birthday. To see what they were like when they weren't wearing leather. Men showing off their hairy backs and beer guts were even *more* down-to-earth – grounded in reality – than the average guy on the street. She had bought a cute bikini and put it on under her jean shorts and a tank top. The bikini was *not* of the American flag variety. She had learned flag etiquette from her father, who spent many years in the Air Force. But it was the appropriate color, and she was excited to surprise Cory with it. She hoped she could get him to gawk a little.

For the first couple of hours after they arrived, they stood by the grill talking to Road Kill and Daisy, drinking Corona Light from the can – no bottles were allowed around the pool – and waiting for the rest of the group to show up. Shawn was anxious to get in the pool, but didn't want to be the only one. She felt like Lo might get in with her if she asked, but Lo was sitting in a chair facing the sun and drinking beer, and kind of keeping to herself. Her overly large sunglasses hid more than just her eyes and Shawn couldn't read her. She couldn't tell if she just wasn't taking to Kill and Daisy, or was just feeling anti-social in general. Maybe this was her pulling slowly away from Heath. Shawn had tried to talk pull her into the conversation a couple of times, but Lo had only given minimalist answers and gone back to her day-dreamy state at the edge of the deck.

People filed in every few minutes until the backyard – over the course of an hour or so – was filled with people. Shawn guessed there were thirty people there including men, women and some children. When Dahmer and his wife showed up, the party felt more alive. It was as if these people were starstruck by their leader and just being wild and lively gave them more of a chance to impress him. Shawn couldn't figure it out. He was a nice guy, and fun to be around, but she didn't feel any aura coming off of him that she couldn't resist. It seemed like everyone wanted to be in whatever little group he had moved to. They all wanted to be near him – to be heard by him, or hear what he was joking about this time. And he was full of jokes. She could see how he could be called the life of the party, but she also enjoyed the lull of a quiet and mature group of people standing around talking and grilling as well. Most of these people were in their mid-forties, she guessed, with some even pushing into the fifties. She and Cory and Lo and

Heath were not the only almost-thirty-somethings, but they were the minority, for sure.

What changed her mind about Dahmer in the end was his attention to 'the little guy'. And if there was a little guy at this party, Shawn was definitely it. She didn't wear a cut, didn't own a bike, and had only been to a couple of events. And nor was it like she was some high-up guy's wife. She was just a girlfriend. And a new girlfriend, at that.

Maybe that was it. Maybe that was the reason people flocked to him. Either way, when his rounds finally brought him over to Cory and her, he brought Cory in with a one-handed bro-hug, as she thought of them, then shook Shawn's hand and did the same to her, though he pulled her in gently. "How ya doin' Shawn?" he said. And in his smile, she could tell what it was that attracted people to him: he was genuine. He was real, and he was really interested in everything she said.

But when everyone got there and Dahmer got up to do his group address, that was when she really liked him. Because he called her name.

Dahmer was the kind of guy who hated sleeves. Every shirt she had seen him in had been of the sleeves-ripped-off variety. Cory confirmed that had been the case for him as well, and he had seen the guy many more times than Shawn. He was wearing bright orange swim trunks and flip flops under an Army t-shirt that probably never had sleeves on it to begin with. He wore a bandanna over his mostly bald head and stood with his back against the pool, talking about the new members of the group, the plans for the group and how proud he was of the five years they had spent together thus far. He introduced the newest 'patched' members and Shawn had to refresh her memory by leaning her ear close to Cory's ear.

Cory told her, "We don't take this stuff very seriously here. Everyone gets patched in pretty quickly. Even some of the kids are 'patched members' of the group. It's all just for fun." He reminded her what she had seen on *Sons of*

*Anarchy.* A person who showed loyalty to a motorcycle club would eventually be voted on to become a true member. At that point, they were allowed to wear the colors of the club. That meant the patch on the back of the vest – the upper rocker that told the name of the club to which he belonged. In a motorcycle club, this was pretty serious business. But here in the group, it was just for fun. Cory had been welcomed to the group the first time he had ridden with the group. In that welcoming speech, Dahmer had said, "Sometimes you can see 'em from a mile away. I know one when I see him. Welcome, Cory," and Cory had never felt more proud to be part of a group of guys than that.

Dahmer welcomed a couple of new riders by their real names – they hadn't yet earned road names – and handed them rockers. These were just patches that could be sewn onto vests, and they said the name of the riding group. He hugged the guys as they came up to accept their patches and everyone applauded. There were high-fives and back-claps as each of them made their way back to their places in the crowd. After that, he handed out a road-name to a guy Shawn had known to be named Charles. His road-name was now deemed to be 'Wilson'. Apparently he had taken a volleyball to the face on the beach a few weekends ago, and someone had likened him to the ball in the Tom Hanks movie. The only thing having to do with the *road* in that story was that the group had ridden to the Galveston beach on their bikes that weekend. Everyone laughed and applauded though, so Shawn joined in.

It was when he pulled an actual vest – an actual *cut* – out of the box and held it up that Shawn frowned and looked back at Cory. "They actually give away vests too?" she asked, trying to be quiet. He had shrugged and widened his eyes. *I had no idea,* his look said. But then Dahmer gave his speech. "So our boy Squirrel Hunter found himself a lovely lady recently." This was met with a fair amount of applause and whistling. Shawn found herself blushing, and turned to look at Cory again making a face at him, but not quite able to hide the smile. Everyone had liked her, and she had gotten that feeling all right. So she wasn't surprised by the applause. But what was the cut for?

"And since they don't really have to ride with us to be patched in, they just have to be accepted," Dahmer said, smiling, waiting for the laughter to fade, "we like to welcome in the girlfriends as fast as we can." Again with the whistling and clapping, hoots and hollers. People nearby were grabbing her by the shoulder and shaking her, patting her on the back, giving her thumbs-ups. She was smiling from ear to ear, covering most of her face with her hands. Shawn was actually getting a little emotional, and was worried that her glassy eyes would turn to full-blown *watering* eyes. But still, what the *hell* was this about?

"Anyway, I think it's safe to say we all approve of Shawn, right?" Dahmer said, holding his hands up as if asking someone to prove him wrong. The crowd got pretty loud. They all clearly loved her. She closed her eyes, shaking her head and trying to avoid the cry. It was getting harder and harder. "Well, apparently she got a road-name without me even knowing about it. So Flash Dance worked her ass off yesterday." Flash Dance was Dahmer's wife, and she was the seamstress of the group. She literally made all the rockers and name patches. And they looked like something out of a magazine. Truly professional.

"So come get your fuckin' cut already, Shawnee!" he said, and Shawn was being propelled forward by the crowd. She looked back at Cory again, wide-eyed and full of surprise and excitement. When she got to the front, Dahmer slipped the vest over her shoulders and pulled her in for a big hug. Her feet actually came up off the ground.

Later, in the pool, when the sunlight had finally passed beneath the horizon, things were calming down a little. It was cooling off and most of the die-hards were in the pool. A few volleyball games had taken place, but now everyone was just standing in the pool drinking and talking, laughing and enjoying the loud music Road Kill was blasting from the speakers mounted under the soffit of his house. Shawn was standing very close to Cory, her arms resting on his shoulders as his hands were on her waist. They were stepping back and forth to the slow beat of the song.

"I need to know how that happened," Shawn said. "How the literal effing *hell* did you get a patch made with that name that fast?"

"Oh, Flash Dance is fast. She's got a machine that can crank out that embroidery shit in a few hours."

"So I'm guessing you arranged that."

"Of course. You like it?"

"Yes!" she said, widening her eyes. "I've never been in a club before." When he started to open his mouth, she stopped him. "I know it's not a motorcycle club. But it's a fuckin' club. Come on. My point is, I've never been a part of something so cool. With such great people."

Cory nodded slowly. "Yeah, they're good people. And most of them are veterans. There's a closeness here you won't get hardly anywhere else."

"Where did he get the vest?"

"Oh, I bought it yesterday and brought it over here while you were at work," said Cory, smirking at her. "I hope you like the brown leather."

"Oh my God, Cory, I effing *love it*! It smells like heaven. And I love that it has my name on it."

"Yeah, Tom's pretty easy-going about the girlfriends' road-names."

She nodded slowly, looking up at the moon, just visible over the roof. "Okay, so his name is Tom."

"Yeah. Tom Coker. His wife is Debra."

"Good to know. Thank you for bringing me here, Cory."

"No place better than a pool on a hot July day."

"Oh my God, it is July now. I had failed to realize that," she said, looking at him through squinted eyes. "I meant here figuratively though. Thank you for bringing me into your group. I'm happy to be a part of something so great."

"I thought you would. I'm glad you're here, too."

That Sunday it rained. It had rained on them on the way home from the pool party too, and Shawn was again glad they had taken her Jeep. Cory had to drive it, but at least they were covered. It rained on them as they dashed from the parking lot to Cory's apartment, where they were staying that night. They made love with the windows open so the sound of the rain could keep them company through the night. And Shawn had to get up twice during the night to pee. She loved the feel of the cool breeze coming through the windows, and the sound of the rain. They stayed in bed until after ten, Shawn lying on her back with her phone held up above her face and Cory snuggled in next to her, still dead to the world.

She lay there scrolling through the clothing section of an online retailer, looking for new duds to go with her bad ass brown leather vest. She had told Cory on the way home that he would have to take her to more events now, so that she'd have an excuse to wear it. She had already added several things to her cart that she thought would turn Cory's head. He already looked at her like she was the hottest thing on the planet, but that only made her want to do even more. She was wearing more lower-cut blouses and tops lately, when historically, she had never wanted to show off her chest at all. She didn't have a lot going on there, and had always been self-conscious about it. But Cory made her feel like a woman, so she wanted to exploit that a little. If he liked what he saw, she was going to show him more and more. Why that should translate to public outings, she wasn't ready to explain. But it might have been that if *he* found her slight build sexy, maybe others would too. Which would, theoretically, make them jealous of him. There might have been some merit to it, but she didn't care much about analyzing the theory. She had just started buying and wearing the things that turned his head, on the weekends, at least. She would, of course, never dare to be so liberal at work.

After she had added five or six tops, some new pants that looked tough and rugged and even some brown leather knee-high boots, she checked out and closed the app. She checked her OuterCircle. *Same bullshit, different day.* Nothing ever changes. At least not on social media. She finally had enough, and got up to go make coffee and start her day. She pulled on a tank top and underwear, scooting her feet across the cool carpet. It was a lazy, rainy Sunday. They wouldn't be able to get out and do anything without an umbrella and raincoats today, so she might as well traipse around in her panties. That was how she felt best at home anyway. And Cory's place was feeling more and more like home.

When Cory finally got up and they sat at the table with their coffee, she mentioned her comfort level to him. About how the breezeway between their apartments felt a lot like a mirror to her. Her home on one side, his, the literal mirror-image of home on the other. And when she stepped across that breezeway it was like stepping *through* that mirror, which she had always had fantasies about as a child. Staring in her mother's full-length mirror and seeing the same world through it, just flipped horizontally, she always imagined what it would be like to step through and see what it was like. Would she flip too? Of course she would. Shawn would put her face real close to it, leaning in hard to try to see as much of the other side as she could, hidden by the frame of the mirror.

Cory told her he was happy she felt like it was part of her home, and surprised her by standing up and going to his room, then returning a few seconds later and dropping a key on the table. At first, she was perplexed. These apartment keys stated on them, 'DO NOT DUPLICATE'. But then she remembered his career field and rolled her eyes to herself. "Of *course* you have spare keys."

Cory shrugged. "I have backups for my spares. And spare backups. Everything in life needs redundancies."

"Oh my God. You sound like Sameer," Shawn said. She stared at it for a minute, rolling it back and forth in her hand, the small brass implement that unlocked someone else's entire world. Then she looked up at him with a curious smile in her eyes. "Cory, are you sure you want me to have this?"

He simply nodded, taking a sip from his mug. He stared at her for a long moment, then took her hand on the table, closing her fingers around the key. "Shawn, if I ever come home and find you lounging on my couch, wearing just what you're wearing right now, it will all be worth it."

Her smile felt gigantic. She stood up and leaned across the edge of the table to kiss him. Not a real kiss, of course. Not until she had brushed her teeth. But it involved her grasping the sides of his face and putting a big one on his forehead. It was enough to show him she meant it.

"I've got some bad news to go with the good though, Shawnee," he said, and she smiled at his use of her new 'road-name'. She couldn't even find it weird to smile after his saying the news was bad. Nothing he could say could be that bad, right?

"I have a job tomorrow morning in Houston. I have to fly out this afternoon."

She nodded, taking a sip from her own mug. "How long will you be gone?"

"I think I'll fly back in Tuesday morning, depending on how tomorrow goes. But likely Tuesday."

"Okay. Well, I might just keep your bed warm for you tonight."

Cory smiled. "I would love that. To think my girlfriend is sleeping in my bed while I'm gone. That's the definition of home."

It did not feel like home to Shawn that night, when the fever-dreams invaded her sleep. She had sat on Cory's sofa watching his TV and drinking some vodka on the rocks, just enjoying being in her boyfriend's place. The mere title alone was exciting to her: My Boyfriend's Place. It sounded like something worthy of capitalizing. And the fact that he had trusted her enough to leave her in charge, to leave her with a key, that was a big part of it. She treated it just like her own place, and walked around all evening in her underwear and a tank top. At the one point she needed to go home to get some things, she wrapped a blanket from his couch around her shoulders and wore it like a robe to make the trek across the breezeway.

At about eight-thirty, after the sun had set, she started feeling bad. At first it felt like her typical seasonal allergies. Stopped up and itchy, coughing but not getting anything out of it. Then her head started hurting. At first just a dull ache, but then as it got later, it started really getting bad. By bedtime, it felt like someone was playing the timpani in her head. Shawn was pretty sure she had a fever, but couldn't find a thermometer in Cory's place in any of the regular places one would look. And she sure didn't feel like going back across the breezeway for her own.

She finally drifted to sleep sometime after midnight – a late night for her, especially when she had work the next morning – lying long across the couch. She had not wanted to get in his bed once she started feeling sick, in case she might spread something through his pillow. Sometime later – it was hard to determine how long with all the sweaty starts and jolt-awakes – she decided it would be better to get in his bed, because sheets and pillowcases could be washed much easier than couch cushions. The sheets were cooler and she had the ceiling fan grinding it out on the highest speed, but she was still sweating and shivering simultaneously. She would come close to finally drifting off, then jump awake thinking she had heard a knock on the door or a slamming closet. Her eyes would bolt wide open and she would stare into the darkness, trying to fixate on something real, until she would finally fall sleepy again. Rinse, repeat.

Some hours later, she was awakened again by the sound of something scraping down the wall. It sounded like a broom handle that had been leaning against the wall suddenly broke free and slid all the way down in a long, grinding arc. Her skin lit up with chills as she tried to focus on something familiar – but forgetting she was not in her own apartment – everything was mirror-flipped, and she felt like she was in that fantasy world she had wished to visit as a child. Nothing was quite real. And since there was no broom on the floor that only proved she was in an unreal place. Maybe nothing was real. She twisted in the bed and rolled out from under the sheets until her head was cocked at a funny angle, and the red digits of Cory's alarm clock swam into view. It was one minute after three. Oh God.

It couldn't have been much later that she awoke again, this time with sweat pouring off her like a waterfall. And she was no longer shivering. But her stomach felt like someone had wrapped a leather belt around it and was pulling it tighter and tighter by the second. She sat up, breathing heavily, ripping the sheets back from her chest and stared at the light coming in from the top of the curtains. Then it happened. She felt it move. She dashed out of the bed, stumbling on her jeans on the floor and nearly falling into the bathroom, which was where she was going anyway. She got there faster than she had wanted to, coming down hard on her knees and slamming against the toilet. The sick was coming before she could prepare herself for it. She reached up with her right hand, slapping against the wall in the general area where light switches had been found for the first twenty-nine years of her life, and unsure what had changed all of a sudden. She was vomiting in the dark, into a toilet she couldn't see.

This lasted well over the normal allotted time for throwing up. More than she had ever done in her life. And it just kept coming. It came until there was nothing left for her to give, and she finally had to lean back against the wall in the dark, wiping the sweat off her forehead and taking deep breaths, talking herself into believing it was over now. All that was left was the contractions – the involuntary muscle spasms of the diaphragm, still thinking it had a job to do. She willed it to a calm and closed her eyes. She must have been pretty comfortable because she fell asleep against the wall with her feet spread on either side of the toilet.

At some point there was another loud bang and Shawn jolted awake. She looked around, somehow accepting that leaning against a hard wall with her legs on linoleum was normal, and tried to determine what had made the noise. She stood up and pulled the sheets off of her and pulled on her robe, which had been lying on the end of the bed. She made her way through the doorway and into the living room. Rain was banging against the back doors, and thunder was rattling the windows. She went into the kitchen and poured herself a glass of water from the fridge door. She stood there by the light of the dispenser and drank half of the cup, then refilled it and gasped loudly, wiping her mouth.

When she turned around to set the cup by the sink, she saw a figure standing silhouetted against the sliding glass doors by the light from the parking lot streetlamps. Shawn jumped and shouted, knocking over her cup and stumbling backwards against the oven. The thing about visions was that they weren't real. When the mind fooled you, it got over the joke pretty quickly. And this wasn't going away. The figure was very feminine, and was moving with a liquidity that was almost soothing in spite of the horror Shawn felt in her chest. Her heart was slamming like a hammer and she was breathing double-time.

"Hello?" she said, suddenly feeling very naked without something to grab for defense. She didn't even know where Cory kept his steak knives. Her hands swept the counter behind her, but came up with nothing. Suddenly, the figure, very obviously a woman, raised its hands and ran toward her. Shawn screamed and chills shot up her body like a wave of lightning, and she sat up, her hair falling in her face, and put her hands to the sides of her head. "Good God. What the fuck." Her legs were stuck to the vinyl flooring with a thin layer of sweat. Her head was pounding again. She leaned forward, suddenly remembering where she actually was, and felt again on the wall for the switch. Still not there. Leaning a little more forward she was able to find the toilet. Had she been sitting on it earlier? How had she ended up on the floor? And what happened to the stuffed monkey? She sat up quickly, whipping the sheets off of her. *Good God, it's hot in here.* She needed to turn the thermostat down. "Cory?" she said, sliding her hand over in the sheets, trying to find him. She found resistance. Soft, naked skin. "Cory?" she said again, frowning. This didn't feel quite right. *What the hell?* She reached over with her other hand and clicked on the bedside lamp. Lying in bed with her, half under the covers, was Miranda. She was stiff as a board, her arms perfectly straight down by her sides. Her breasts were firm when they shouldn't be. *Death can do that to a girl*, she thought. Shawn rolled onto her side and ran her hand down Miranda's arm, as if to warm her. "Hey, girl. Why are you so cold?"

Miranda turned her head and looked at Shawn. It took her a moment to focus. Then she opened her dry and cracked lips, and said, "You shouldn't have brought me back." She reached up and extended the first two fingers of her left hand, touching Shawn's cheek. The hand was very cold. Shawn finally understood what was happening – that this woman wasn't supposed to be here – and rolled off the bed, screaming. She banged her head on the tub and tried to roll over, grabbing her face with her hands. "Stop! Stop, please just stop!" she cried, tears now running freely.

When the pain in the side of her head finally started to subside, she pushed herself up, finally knowing where she was – *really knowing* this time. She was drenched in sweat and her inner calves felt sticky. She frowned and shook her head. "Can I just get a break please? I just need some sleeeeeep!" she whined into the darkness. She reached down and took a sample from her calf, then rubbed the substance between her fingers. Exasperated, she leaned her head back against the wall. She needed to put forth a serious effort to get up. This was getting ridiculous. She finally leaned forward and took hold of the toilet seat for stability and worked her way up onto her knees. From there, she could finally stand. She reached over and ran her hand up and down the wall. Still no switches. "What in the serious ever-loving mother fuck!" she almost shouted. Her head pounded with the exertion. She put one hand against her forehead as the other continued to search for the light switch.

Something tugged at the back of her memory. What was that shit about Miranda? *Oh my God! She was here!* Shawn gasped and threw her right hand – the hand that had been searching for the light switch – against her mouth. Her entire body flooded with chills as she remembered the dream, and she was suddenly assaulted by the smell of vomit on her hand. "Oh fuck sake," she said. That tug at her memory again. "Where the hell am I?"

She squinted and put the balls of her hands against her eyes, trying to push back some of the headache. Surely, Cory had some aspirin around here somewhere. Cory? *Oh, shit! YES!* And with that, she finally remembered she was in his apartment. That meant the switch for the bathroom light was *outside* the bathroom door, on wall where the sink was. She reached out and flipped it on, then saw the mess she had made around the toilet, and her stomach sank.

Shawn sat in the shower until the hot water ran to warm, drifting in and out of sleep. She had mopped up most of her mess with toilet paper, flushing the toilet with every third or fourth wad she threw in it. She would have to mop the floor tomorrow. Today. Later today. What time was it, anyway? Hell, what *day* was it? She leaned forward and shut the water off, then stood up and searched for a towel, realizing quickly that she had not brought one to the towel rack, and walked back to the bed soaking wet. *Fuck it.* It's not like she wasn't going to have to wash the sheets already. She had sweat so much she had probably ruined his mattress already. She collapsed into the bed and fell asleep instantly.

When she finally woke up, Shawn realized that her internal alarm was blinking like a cheap nightstand clock after a lightning storm. She made a snow angel in the bed with her right arm, whipping it up and down in the sheets until she finally found her phone. She held it in front of her face and woke it up. It was 9:03. She slapped her hand against her forehead and cursed, then immediately phoned her boss. He answered his office phone on the first ring.

"Hey, Sameer," she said. "I slept through my alarm." She wasn't necessarily lying.

"It happens sometimes," he said.

"I think I'm going to have to beg out for today, boss. I'm sick as a dog. I was up most of the night with fever. Among other things…"

"Oh, I am sorry to hear this, Shawn. Take care of yourself. Come back in whenever you are feeling better. But you should know that no one is at work today anyway."

"Thanks, Sameer. Wait," she said, suddenly confused. "Why? What's going on?"

"I'm not sure if you heard, but recently, America claimed independence from-"

"Shush!" she almost shouted. "Good Lord. How could I forget. So I guess we're off tomorrow as well, then?"

"Yes, Shawn. I will see you Wednesday if you are feeling better," said Sameer.

"Yep. Okay. Sorry to bother," she said. He hummed his acknowledgment at her and they disconnected.

She dropped the phone on the bed beside her and stretched, then looked around the room. The memories of the fever dreams teased her consciousness. Every time the image of Miranda lying in the bed with her crossed her mind, she felt a wave of chills run from the base of her spine all the way up her neck. She tried to push it away, but it kept coming back. Now that the sun was peeking through the top of the curtains, the dream seemed to be a little more distant. It seemed to hold a little less weight in reality. Having a couple of days to relax and work through these things would help her greatly.

Shawn took a deep breath, then rolled out of bed, putting her feet on the carpet. It felt strangely damp. Not like it had been wet and then dried, but like it had been exposed to high humidity for a long period. She had felt that on her own carpet before. What the hell was that? She couldn't place the memory or its association to reality. She made her way to the bathroom counter and turned on the tap to let it start drawing warmth, then sat on the toilet to pee.

When she finished, she stood looking in the mirror while she brushed her teeth. Her hair was a wreck. She had bags under eyes and lines on her cheeks. Her skin looked pale and sickly, like wax paper. She shook her head, wondering what the hell had happened. What had made her sick so suddenly? She knew it wasn't something she had eaten. There was just no way. She stood up straight, one hand on her hip, the other brushing her teeth, and turned around to assess the bedroom. It was mostly dark because of Cory's blackout curtains. She went to them and flung them open. It wasn't bright outside like a normal day. There was still a heavy overcast, putting a pall on everything.

Still brushing her teeth, she went into the kitchen to start a pot of coffee. The vinyl floor in the kitchen was cold and humid to her feet. Maybe she really was sick. Why was she feeling these drastic temperature changes? She finished putting coffee in the paper filter, then clicked the machine on. Within a few seconds, she heard the reassuring gurgle of the fabulous life-saving machine. She walked out of the kitchen, smiling around her toothbrush, and stopped dead. Staring straight ahead at the sliding glass door, Shawn's jaw dropped open and she gasped, nearly choking on the sudsy toothpaste in her mouth. The backdoor stood wide open and the vertical blinds danced lightly in the cool morning breeze.

Shawn spent most of the day Monday cleaning the apartment, disinfecting surfaces she had touched, washing the sheets, mopping the bathroom floor and cleaning the toilet and sink area. Getting sick in her Boyfriend's Apartment was embarrassing enough on its own. She didn't need him coming home and getting sick because of her mishandling of her own germs. Assuming, that was, that he wasn't already sick. She supposed it was possible that Cory had already been exposed to her – yesterday morning – and that he might be recovering from a shitty night down in Houston. Of course, not having his phone number meant she couldn't check on him. Maybe it was time to put an end to that silliness. Logistically speaking, it was starting to show signs of inefficiency.

When she finally finished the cleaning, it was late Monday evening. She had been sweating it out while she worked for most of the day, and was starting to feel better. Maybe it had been one of those day-bugs. Whatever, she wasn't taking any chances, so she left him a note on his table and locked up, heading for her own place. The note told him to check in with her when he got back, to let her know he made it, but to keep his distance.

Shawn was still a little off-out by the back door having been open when she woke up. Had she opened it in her fever-dream state? That was obviously the most likely scenario – and highly possible to boot. Burning with fever and confusing memory with dream, she could easily see herself opening the back door to enjoy the fresh breeze and the rain. So maybe she did that and forgot to close it. Just went back to bed. She sure didn't remember that though. She remembered the rain and the lightning; the impressive thunder. That had been nice. But wow! To forget closing it was one thing. But forgetting she opened it? That just didn't seem as likely. Either way, it had been heavy on he mind all day. Then as she was walking across the breezeway to go home, arms full of the things she had brought to Cory's and juggling to get her keys out, she noticed something: It was completely dry outside.

She set everything down and fished out her keys, unlocked her apartment and tossed everything inside. Then she stepped across to lock Cory's up before she forgot. But then she went to the front rail to lean over and look into the parking lot. To look for puddles. Patches of muddy grass. Anything that would show the signs of a heavy rain the night before. There were none. And it wasn't hot enough to have dried all evidence in one day. No way. Not to mention it would feel muggy as hell outside. It would feel like, well, like Houston.

As she dropped onto her couch and curled her feet beneath her, she set her phone down in her lap and thought about the possibilities, about what all this meant. They lived in a second-story apartment. That didn't make climbing onto the balcony an impossible feat, but it did narrow down the possible entrants. It kept the honest criminals out, as her daddy would have said. The problem was that she didn't know if Cory's back door had been locked already. That might not even matter if she had been the one to open it. But the lock bar? *Could she* have even thought to slip that out of its socket in the mental state she had been in? Maybe, if she were used to throwing the bar frequently. And that, she most assuredly wasn't. She never threw her own. She had gone out to rescue that damn butterfly twice in the last month and had not even considered it.

But what about the rain? The one thing Shawn knew was that she had not actually gotten up during the night for that cup of water. She had looked for it this morning, and there apparently was no such thing. It was not in the sink or the dishwasher, not on any of the surfaces around the apartment. What that told her was that everything associated with the memory of getting that cup of water was suspect. It was entirely possible, therefore, that she had never even left the master area during the night. Not only possible, but probable.

This conclusion, while it may have been comforting in relation to having seen the silhouette woman against the window, also left open the question of who the hell had opened the back door. Didn't that mean it had to be an intruder? All these questions were getting her nowhere though. She sighed and pulled her hair back into a ponytail, then searched briefly for a holder. Not finding one, she let it fall back into place. What would she tell Cory? Someone opened your back door during the night. It might have been me, but I don't remember it… Nothing had been taken, as best she could tell. But how would she know? And what did she expect him to say? 'Oh, it's okay, it opens itself all the time.'? She shook her head and decided to forget about it, or at least try to, at least for now. She was only driving herself crazy as it was.

By nine-thirty, she was bone-tired and ready for bed. She brushed her teeth and made a conscious effort in checking the back door to make sure it was locked and the jam bar was in place. With the little ball-chain pin thingy stuck through the hole. No sneaky lifting the bar while someone was sleeping with that in place! She found herself dawdling, taking a little longer to perform her nightly routine, hoping Cory would knock. She had not left him a key, but nor did she really want him coming in if she was still sick. Even still, she sure would like to look at him and see his smile before she went to bed. After twenty minutes of preparing the coffee maker for the morning brew and rechecking the doors and looking in the mirror and even scrolling through her OuterCircle, she finally gave up the ghost with a sigh. As she thought of the phrase a chill touched her spine. She sure *wished* she could give up the ghost.

# Eleven

When Shawn woke on Tuesday morning, she rolled over and looked at the clock on her phone and remembered it was July fourth. "Happy birthday, America," she said and sat up, taking in her surroundings. Definitely still alone, windows still closed, everything seemed in order. She must be better by now. When she finally made it to the coffee pot, she poured herself a mug and went out onto the breezeway to look down into the parking lot. She was more than a little disappointed to see that Cory's Jeep was not in the Jeep Parking. He had either still not made it back from Houston, or had come home and run back out for something. His motorcycle was under the stairs, and when she popped in using her Boyfriend's Apartment Key, she saw the note was still sitting on the table in the same place she had left it. Bed still made. No suitcase sitting on it. No signs at all that he had been home. Shucks. She glanced at the back door and made sure it was still locked and the bar was down. Good there. She turned and left, locking up behind her and testing the knob. Good there, too.

When she finished her coffee, she turned on the shower. She had made it through the night without any more symptoms, leading her to believe that maybe it had indeed been a twenty-four-hour thing. Technically speaking, if that were the case, she would have to call it a twelve-hour thing. Either way, she was feeling mostly like herself again. She would definitely be ready to go back to work tomorrow.

As she stood in the shower brushing her teeth, she had another memory from the night of her sickness: sitting in his shower with the water beating on her until it turned lukewarm. She knew that had happened. Right? Because that had been her method of waking herself from the fever-dream, as well as cleaning off the unwanted residue of her sickness. It would be easy to verify though, because there would be a towel. Well, all that evidence was tainted. She had washed everything in his apartment the day after. All the sheets, all the towels, everything. So never mind on that. And following that thought, Shawn decided to go back to forgetting about the whole night. With no way to distinguish what – if any of it – was real, she was only causing herself more stress.

The one thing she didn't forget was what Miranda had said to her in bed during one of her semi-waking states: she had said, 'You shouldn't have brought me back.' Shawn had spent quite a good bit dissecting that throughout the last day. She already regretted how it had turned out for the poor girl, and had made efforts to try and find peace with it. But hearing that, dream or not, had set her back a long way in her coming to terms with having to watch the girl die on that table. Shawn had actually begun feeling a little better about Miranda once she had learned that it had not been suicide but how could she know the girl had not suffered in her dying? It seemed – at least to Shawn, who was admittedly no investigator – that if she had thrashed or struggled, she would have likely gone under water. That would have meant drowning rather than bleeding out. Something about that still didn't add up. But again, she was no coroner. No crime-scene investigator. And no doctor, either.

The one thing she did have was that little stuffed monkey. She would keep Miranda's memory alive as long as she could by thinking of her every time she saw him. She wished she knew what the girl had called the monkey. If only…

The journal.

Shawn spent most of the day avoiding it. She knew she was likely to binge the whole thing in one sitting and she didn't want to do that. She cleaned her own apartment with the same fervor she had employed in cleaning Cory's the day before. Throughout the day, she would occasionally pop out onto the breezeway and look for Cory's Jeep. And every few times she did that, she would also use her key to check inside his apartment. She kept coming back shaking her head. That boy.

When evening finally came, and she had done everything she could think to do to kill her Independence Day – *what a waste of a good holiday* – she finally took another shower, brushed her teeth and decided she would finally read a little of the journal. She grabbed the journal off her dresser. She could feel its worth in her hands as she carried it into the living room. She was a little stunned that she had not yet looked through it at all. She had not even cracked the cover. There could be worlds of answers in that leather-bound book! She took it back to the couch and tossed it on to the seat next to where she would drop once she had her cocktail. It felt like a vodka-cranberry night. She poured two of them. One for her, one for Miranda. Of course, she would have to drink them both, but that was the price one paid for being a good person. She didn't mind doing it.

Shawn set the drinks on a tray and pulled the ottoman up close to the couch where she could reach it. Then she grabbed her sheepskin blanket and curled up on the corner of the sofa to dig in. She unwrapped the leather string that bound the journal, carefully setting it aside. Something told her to treat this like an old relic. Of course, there was respect for the dead – not to mention the whole *stolen property* angle – but there was more than that. Miranda Struck had become something like a goddess in her mind. Someone to whom attention should be paid. Like she should have meant more to the world than she apparently did. And Shawn was pissed off that the world wasn't looking at her like that. It felt as if the world had not gotten the memo. And that was someone's fault. Certainly it wasn't Miranda's. But if that were the case, then Shawn felt duty-bound to take the reigns on that. She would make sure someone knew how important the girl was. Whatever she found in this journal, if there was anything worth sharing, she would be the one to carry that torch. The girl deserved it. Why? She had spent many long minutes discussing this with Cory on rainy nights over the last few weeks. Why did she deserve it? Besides the obvious 'every human deserves a page in the memories book' answer. What had *she* done to stand out – so much that Shawn felt obliged to share her story?

"Go listen to *Satellite Call* by Sara Bareilles, then ask me that again," she had said. "Not because she believed that she was to blame for everything. But everyone who's passed deserves to be loved and remembered by those of us who carry on."

Cory had stared at her for a moment, not quite knowing what to say. He just nodded and then looked away. He had glass in his eyes. Either he knew the song, or he just understood.

But this was not about the song. This was about believing Miranda had done something in her life worthy of celebrating. Surely there was something. And she had died before she had gotten the chance to shine.

Surely, there were millions like her whose candles were put out long before they got a chance to light up a room. But how many of those had been brought back from the dead, even for a few minutes? Shawn could never let that out of her head. In spite of the fact that she had been participant to two other humans who had gone through the same thing. Something about Miranda had been different.

Shawn pulled the leather cover open. She rubbed her fingers down the inside of the cover, pressing it against the pillow on her thighs so it would stay open. The very first page was of a drawing of a woman standing in a field, holding a baton of some sort. It was a rough pencil sketch, but clearly the product of a talented hand. Shawn knew she sure as heck couldn't draw like that. Some of the graphite had rubbed off against the soft leather of the inner cover. She ran her finger down the outer edge of the page, just to touch the same paper Miranda's hand had rested against when she had created this drawing. There was no date on it. She carefully turned the page with one hand as she sipped from her drink with the other. And on the next page, the journal entries began.

> 2/1 Hello, world. If you're reading this, shame on you. If I'm dead, however, spread the word! I finally finished filling the pages of my last book of words. There's nothing here that supersedes that. For Harrison's sake, if you haven't read that one, read it first! Kidding. Don't read my shit. For real. What are you doing here. Get out. Go. Now.

Shawn had to pause here for a moment. This was already too real. Too much? Maybe not too much, but too real. God. This girl had called it in the third sentence of her journal. It was clearly a secret soul-baring declaration. Her way of getting things off her chest. This was her outlet. And here was Shawn, reading it. Well, Miranda had said that was okay. As long as she planned to *spread the word.*

And what of that 'For Harrison's sake' bit? First page of the diary and she had already mentioned that name. It must be someone very important to her. No. No one says that. A pet? A cat? Shawn didn't find any cats roaming the place when she had gone in. Nor did she smell one. She hadn't gone looking for a litter box, but then she hadn't thought about doing a full scan of the place.

Shawn noticed her hands were trembling slightly. It felt like she was snooping through someone's purse while they were in the bathroom. Like the owner might come out and catch her. She had to remind herself that no one would be coming back for this diary. No one would come for anything of hers. She took a deep breath and returned her attention to the first page.

> I'm leaving tomorrow for Scotland. I finally get to go. I got the ticket what, 2 months ago? It feels like forever that I've been waiting. I've called Linus every day over the last few weeks because I'm getting so excited!!!! He said he was excited too, but he didn't sound like it. I don't know what's going on, but I hope he'll start talking when I get there. You know that, diary?
>
> At the mall today there was a man playing the piano in the gallery and no one was standing around watching him. He was playing this most beautiful classical like piece and it was the saddest most lovely thing I ever heard. He was so good. But no one was paying attention. What the hell is wrong with people. I sat down beside the piano on the floor and just listened. I sat where he could see me if he looked just to show him that I was supporting his talent but I never seen talent like that before. Wow!!!
>
> It made my heart sad that no one was paying attention. If we let things like this go by in our daily lives and never slow to take them in then we might lose them all together. Maybe people take these things for granned. Anyways when he was done I opened my purse because I

was going to give him like a ten dollar bill but he didn't have a tip jar. He waved my money away and told me thank you but he wasn't there for the money. He said that just having me sit there and listen was wonderful and then we talked for a good half an hour me asking him about piano and how long he played for and all that. I told him I never seen someone so good at it. He said he played since he was five and he was one of those kids whose parents made him take piano lessons even though he didn't want to but now of course he's glad he stuck with it. I can imagine!!

He asked if my parents were like that. I told him we couldn't go there. Not like that of course I was polite. But so watching him play was ~~mostly~~ just about the best thing that happened to me in a long time, God I love the piano.

Shawn looked up as she reached the end of the page. She wiped the corners of her eyes and closed the leather journal on her thumb, holding its place. She closed her eyes and tried to imagine this pretty girl sitting on the mall floor watching this man play the piano with a proper fascination. It made Shawn smile in spite of her tears. She sounded like a lovely human being. Shawn felt like she was being proven right about Miranda. Her reading of the woman based on her small interaction and observation of her apartment had apparently not been far off. Of course, no one wrote their flaws out in diary entries, did they?

She found the misspellings and extra punctuation endearing. 'Granned' instead of 'granted', the stricken out word meaning she had changed her mind about what she would write... Shawn decided she should take this diary in small doses. She wanted to absorb what she read and give it time to become memory. If she read it like a book, she wouldn't get to cherish each piece. She would likely forget most of it. If she only read a page a night and then pondered on what she read, it would go a lot further. Her idea of being friends with this girl, a retrograde acquaintanceship of sorts, was to treat her writing as stories told. Shawn would read them and process them like Miranda had spoken them to her, as if to imagine having had her as a friend. Of course, she wouldn't tell people they had been friends. It was her own private little investment. Her giving back.

There was also the part about not being able to 'go there' about the girl's parents. Again, on the first page. So much revealed on the first page. That meant to Shawn that either it was a topic returned to mind very frequently, or just coincidence. She believed in the former. Shawn looked up to catch a glimpse of the gorgeous sky, burning with the last remnants of the setting sun, and a flutter in the corner of the window caught her eye. "Oh. My. God." She stood up and tossed the blanket to the side, shaking her head as she stepped over the ottoman and went to the sliding glass. "What the hell is wrong with you, Mr. Monarch? When are you going to learn?" She unlocked the door and pulled. It wouldn't open. The butterfly twitched and wiggled. *What the capital H?*

Shawn frowned and looked for the resistance, finally realizing that the jam bar was still seated in its cradle. She sighed and rolled her eyes, then pulled the little pin on a ball-chain thingy out from the little hole and lifted the jam bar, carefully standing it back in its unarmed position. Then the door slid open. By the time she got to the monarch, it was trapped well in the web. She reached up and pinched its wings together, tugging gently to free it from its snare. "Come on, friend. Let go!" She tugged a little harder. It finally broke free. "There we go!" she said. "Shame on you, Mr. Spider! I thought I evicted-" she said, stopping short when she realized one of the butterfly's legs had come off and was still twitching in the web. "Oh, No!" she said, stepping into the apartment. "God, dude, why can't you learn to stay away from the web? I feel so bad now!"

She sat down on the ottoman and set about pulling the small pieces of silk off the butterfly's abdomen. Again. She felt a little sick at her stomach, full of sorrow that she had broken off one of its legs. Well, she couldn't take all of the blame. Part of it surely had to fall on Mr. Stubborn here! When she finished pulling off the silk, she set the fly on her finger and let it flap its wings. It gave no sign that it was in pain or distress. At least there was that. After a moment, it fluttered up into the air, then danced around her head like it had done before. She smiled and closed her eyes. It landed on her eyelid and stayed there for a long time. Shawn giggled and leaned back on her hands. After a minute the butterfly lifted away and touched against her lips and nose before creating its own orbit around her head for a full minute. She finally stood up and walked out onto the balcony with the butterfly in tow. She leaned against the rail and waited for it to fly away. When it did, she stood there and watched it for a bit, then waved goodbye and turned back to the door. She raked away the entire web with her fingers. The spider was either hiding or had never come back when she had shooed it away last time. "Good riddance, you mean bastard. You lost your lease here!" she said, then went back inside and closed the door.

One more check on the parking lot to confirm Cory had not come back home yet, and she locked up for the night. It was a bummer that she hadn't gotten to spend any time with him over her days off. She considered whether or not she should start worrying about him, but then decided that was pointless, since she didn't even have his phone number.

Wednesday morning, Shawn did her normal routine, full of wonder and disappointment that Cory was not back yet. It took a will for her to drive away from the parking lot, but she pushed through it, telling herself that he would probably be back by the time she got home from work. As she pulled into the parking garage at work, she saw Sameer and Jeremy standing outside the front door to the building. Jeremy was smoking a cigarette and Sameer stood with his hands in his pockets, smiling widely like he had just heard a good joke. As they saw her drive by, they both waved and smiled at her. It was nice to see everyone in good spirits. Maybe it would bring hers up throughout the day.

Shawn parked the Jeep, pulled the e-brake and dropped down off the tall seat, slinging her bag over a shoulder. "Hey, guys," she said as she approached.

"Hello, Shawn," said Sameer, waving again. "Did you have a good Independence Day?"

"Yes, I did!" she said, nodding emphatically. Then she pointed at him and said, "And I like it when people call it that."

"Call it what? I am not understanding," said Sameer.

"Independence Day. I'm guessing she prefers it over 'fourth of July'," said Jeremy.

"Bingo."

Jeremy winked at her as he took a pull from his cigarette. "What's up?" she asked.

"Nothing much. We both just showed up. Just enjoying the cool air before it gets too hot," Jeremy said.

"It is supposed to reach one hundred four today," said Sameer and looked at his watch.

"Bleh. Well I'm going on in. Is there coffee yet?" Shawn asked.

"Does the Michelin Man ever get tired?"

"Oh my," she said, patting Jeremy on the shoulder as she passed by him. "You're a dad already."

Once at her desk, Shawn set about pulling out everything from her bag. A standard Monday-morning routine. Her Friday afternoon routine was this in reverse. It would feel short this week, due to the holiday. She pulled out her own digital voice recorder – even though she never really used it – and her old second-generation iPod, which she used even less frequently, the two books Sameer had sent home with her, and a couple of breakfast bars. The iPod was for when Jeremy turned his music up too loud. She would never complain about these sonic intrusions, because one, they didn't happen often and she knew he only did it when he was really hard-core into the code, trying to solve a puzzle. And two, because she thought he honestly didn't even know he was doing it. He was such a nice guy that she couldn't picture him ever wanting to disturb anyone. But everyone needed to be able to blast it a little occasionally. The breakfast bars were for extra snap throughout the day – namely in that time right after lunch when her eyes usually got heavy.

When she swung her bag down to toss it in the leg cave beneath her desk, she felt extra weight, as if she had left something in there by accident. Frowning, she pulled it back up onto her lap and peered inside. Her heart nearly stopped. At the bottom of the bag lay Miranda's journal. She whipped the two sides of the bag together, looking up at her monitor – just for something to stare at while she thought – and shook her head. Had she unknowingly – or unconsciously – dropped it in there thinking she might read a passage at lunchtime? She certainly didn't remember doing it. In fact, the things she put in that bag every Monday morning were always on her bedroom dresser. Not the ottoman in the living room, which was the last place she had left the journal. The bag should have never been near the journal. Was this just another coincidence? She was starting to get a little freaked out by it. To be honest, it felt a little like Miranda was *wanting* her to read the journal. She sighed and dropped the bag at her feet, then slid it into its place with her foot.

Shawn spent the rest of the day at work feeling uneasy. She wasn't particularly productive, either. Having just come back from a four-day weekend, she had plenty of things to catch up on, but wasn't feeling motivated to get after it. Her mind kept drifting back to the journal, the image of a girl sitting on the floor by a piano watching someone play it, and that damned butterfly. The poor thing had finally gotten so stuck it had lost a leg.

By the time she locked her computer and made her way past Sameer's office to say goodbye, she was feeling positively punk. She had the journal in her hand, not wanting to leave it under her desk. She left the rest of the items every week but always took them home on Fridays because the cleaning crew came on Saturdays. And now she was nervous about the journal, nervous about the butterfly and nervous that Cory still wouldn't be home. To make matters worse, Sameer called her ten minutes away from the apartment and told her they had a new body coming in the next morning.

Shawn rolled her eyes and held a hand up by her steering wheel, as if to ask '*what next?*'. "Okay. Do you want me to come in early?"

"No, there is no need for that. But I think we might have good luck with this one. I have already taken a bag of blood out of the freezer. Just please be here at seven tomorrow, Shawn."

"Okay," she said, frowning. "What makes you think we'll have good luck with him?"

"You will see, Shawn. Enjoy your evening," he said and disconnected.

"As if that's even fucking possible now!" she said aloud, tossing her phone onto the passenger seat. "Damn you, Sameer!"

When she got home, Cory's Jeep was there. "Oh, thank fucking goodness. Something goes my way!"

Shawn rushed up the staircase like her shirttail was on fire, taking two at a time. She didn't even bother going home first. She just rapped on his door, anxiously awaiting his call for her to come in. It didn't come for a long time, and she began to get worried again. But when the door finally swung open, her heart leapt with joy, and she fell into his arms quivering and crying.

It wasn't even bedtime and they were in bed. They were not there to sleep, however. She lay with her head on his chest, wrapped in his protective embrace. The wonder of the last few days, the not knowing, had been too much. It had shown her that she cared about Cory more than she had known, but it had also exposed a fray in the rope. If something were to have happened to him, she would have had no idea. Who would ever have come to tell her? She was just the neighbor girl who lives across the way!

"Cory, I think we should trade phone numbers, don't you think?" she said.

"Yeah, sure. I don't know why we haven't already."

"Well, I don't either, when you break it down. But there's something wholesome about the anticipation I have just to see you after work every day."

And so it was, they finally tapped their phones together and saved each other's contact information. She told him about the few days she had spent, how she had gotten sick and forgotten that it was supposed to be a holiday. She told him about the journal, about how it appeared in her bag and how it had touched her when she read the first passage. "Well, a journal is like communication, right? Someone is writing a message to someone who will read it at a later date. So it's kind of like a time machine too."

"Yes!" Shawn had agreed. "I'm looking into the past when I read it. I'm literally reading her hand. So it's like I'm taken back to when she was alive."

And then she told him about how they had another subject coming in tomorrow morning. How her stomach was in a little bit of a mess because of it. There didn't seem to be any matter that she was getting used to this thing. She had seen three people open their eyes, waking from the long sleep now, and had been able to attain a certain level of comfort in each case. But it still gave her knots in her stomach, caused her to lose her appetite. It was most likely the unknown, she thought. She didn't know what the subject would look like. Who it would be, or what kind of experience she would have in the lab. Would he or she do something that horrified her? There was no way to foresee those things. The fact that Shawn had gotten 'used to' the dead opening their eyes was something on its own. Something she felt like humans were not supposed to get used to at all. Something they were never supposed to see. What was this doing to her long-term psyche? Was this changing her in small ways, at least when it came to dealing with death? That could be good or bad. Or it could set expectations in a negative way, too. Would that mean that, at least to her, death was no longer the final say? Would she feel like anyone could be brought back, even for a short time? Thoughts of losing her dad – or even her mom – floated to the surface. She shivered.

But that night she slept like a stone: deep, dreamless sleep, uninterrupted and unmoving through the whole night, wrapped in Cory's arms.

"How are we getting bodies so fast, Sameer? What's changed all of a sudden? Are a lot more people donating to science, or what?" Shawn asked. She was moving with an unusual quickness through the lab getting her parts of the project ready. Penning the bots, moving them to the tube, transferring the blood to the reservoir and getting her work area ready. They weren't rushed, but there was a palpable excitement in Sameer's voice and it was catching for Shawn, who *wanted* to be excited by all this. How much better would her life be if she could just enjoy these sessions? To look forward to them instead of dreading them? How dark was it to want to be immune to the creep-factor of death?

"I think a lot more of them are donating their bodies than you might realize, Shawn. But a thing you might not have considered is that other institutions use the bodies a lot longer than we do."

"Oh, yeah?" she said, waiting for him to elaborate. She opened a new package of syringes and tubing, connecting them to the circulator machine.

"Yes," Sameer said, turning to face her and crossing his arms on his chest. "Even surgical studies. New doctors practice making incisions, removing organs, performing surgery. They use these bodies for weeks at a time."

Shawn raised her eyebrows. "Weeks?" *Good Lord.* She wondered what that would look like.

"Yes. Since we are only using them for one or two days, we get back on the list for the next subject pretty quickly."

"I see," she said. She put her hands on her hips, looking around the lab. The rolling stool she still thought of as a 'doctor's stool' was in the corner by the cabinet. It had become a permanent fixture in the room. She wheeled it over to the table and pushed it close to the head where it might be needed shortly. "So why are you anticipating great success with this one?" she asked, looking at the white-sheet-covered lump in front of her. She had not yet seen the face of the subject.

Sameer almost had a smile on his face. Not quite. But something was there. Before he could answer though, Shawn spoke again. "I mean, you're pretty confident since we didn't circulate for the normal twenty-four hours first."

"It may take that, Shawn. But I would like to try quickly. If we must wait until tomorrow, so be it. But it is worth a try," Sameer said. They stared at each other for a moment. She knew he had heard the question and was waiting her out for whatever reason. Shawn finally sighed and crossed her own arms over her chest. Adjusted her stance. She could play the patience game. Sameer finally spoke. "This man was in a coma for over a year, Shawn. His family finally pulled the plug."

Shawn's heart skipped a beat. Her eyes wide, mouth open in surprise, she shook her head. "Oh my God! When?"

"A few hours ago," said Sameer. He came to the head of the table and took his corner of the sheet. Shawn matched his position and took her own corner. Together they folded the sheet back neatly, creasing it across the man's chest. The first thing Shawn noticed was that he was not old. Maybe forty. He looked *fresh* somehow. That thought was chilling to her in and of itself. Fresh meant freshly dead. But the look of *freshness* was somehow not a bad thing. He still looked vital. His face had barely lost its color. He was a good looking young man. He was white, with a light tan like he spent some time in the sun, but not too much. Like maybe for work. She found herself wondering what had happened to put him into that coma.

"His family was aware of our experiment and put him on this list not long ago. They wanted us to get his body as quickly as possible to see if coma and death were similar. If we have success with one, might we with the other?"

Shawn raised her chin. "Interesting. Wow."

"Yes. They await with eager anticipation for the results," he said.

Shawn looked around suddenly. "They're not here, are they?"

"Oh, no," he said, shaking his head. "No, Shawn. And they do not know what our project really is. They just know we are trying to read a dead brain. Not wake the person." He looked at her for a moment. "That is still classified. I hope you have not been telling people."

She furled her brow. "Why would you think I had?"

"I am not thinking so. I am just stating it for record. When we do something for long enough, it may become like routine. Routine is easy to discuss with people."

Shawn shook her head, but she had to look away. "Okay. So you want me to get started then?"

"Yes, please. Thank you, Shawn."

She had gotten in early after all. Sameer had told her yesterday that seven was fine. But seven was lab time. Shawn knew it would speed things up greatly if she were *ready* for the lab when she actually got into the lab. So she had shown up at six and prepared her routines, assigning functions to a thousand new nanobots. And that preparedness had paid off. Because the bots in the transfer tube already knew what they were supposed to do. She found it fascinating that even with a thousand of them in a tube and ready for injection into the blood supply, the instruction sets – present in all the bots – had not yet been assigned to each individual machine. It could literally come down to whichever ones were first in the line waiting to go in.

She snapped the tube into the port of the circulator and injected them. She met Sameer's eyes and nodded. He clicked on his DVR. "Today is Thursday, July sixth…"

The side-effects were almost instantaneous this time. As soon as the bots were released into the bloodstream, they went to work. The eyelids were already twitching. The tiny reactions to fresh blood were visible in the cheeks and lips. Those signs of life that no body ever shows in a funeral home. Those little differences between the living and the dead – no matter how catatonic the patient.

Shawn pulled the stool out with her toe and sat down, resting her left arm on the table next to the man's own arm. She began her snapping, starting with her hand by her hip and raising it incrementally until it was just below the level of the table. What had been subtle twitching now looked like the movements of a deep dream in the eyelids. She could see the eyeballs beneath them moving slowly, this way and that. And somehow it wasn't creepy. Shawn could believe she was sitting next to the bed of a man who was just having a good nap. Nothing, in other words, looked off about this. She had seen this scene hundreds of times in her life. Separated from the thoughts of what they were doing in here, and apart from the knowledge that it was only happening because of the technology under her coded control, this was completely normal.

"Subject's eyes, still closed, appear to be aware of the snapping," she said. She leaned in a little. "Hello, Curtis. My name is Shawn. Can you hear me?"

"Oh, I can hear you," said the man.

Shawn's heart skipped several beats. Her face had gone completely white in an instant. She looked up at Sameer with wide eyes full of the startle. It would take minutes for that start to fade. Sameer was smiling. He made a fist and put his thumb up.

The man's voice had been clear and strong. Perfectly clear. There had been no grave growl as she had seen with the other subjects. This man sounded alive. And that was even more miraculous, perhaps, than the others, because this man had apparently not spoken in over a year.

"Okay. What are you feeling right now, Curtis?"

The mouth hung open, as if the man were in deep thought. Shawn guessed he probably was. That was frighteningly curious. But it had to be true. She pictured him sighing as he considered his answer, though his chest did not rise and fall like that of a living man. The only difference between his speech and that of a living man was the lack of aspiration – that breath of expelled air when one says something starting with an H. His 'hear' had come out 'ear'. Almost unnoticeable.

Then he spoke again. "I guess elation. A little bit of fear. Excitement?" said the man. *Why the hell isn't he opening his eyes?* Maybe he had forgotten how to.

Shawn looked at Sameer again. Sameer nodded. She continued. "Uh, okay. Can you tell me… Ah, first off, can you tell me what my name is?" she asked.

"Yeah. Shawn. You just told me," said the dead man.

She made a face. *Figures.* "Okay, just checking. Sorry. Can you tell me what you're excited about?"

"I'm alive again. I'm able to talk. This is great."

*Holy fuck.* Shawn was reeling now. Not only was he sentient, he was aware that there had been a point when he wasn't. "Can you tell me what you remember bef-" she said, and looked up at Sameer, stopping herself. He was shaking his head slowly. "Uh, I mean, do you uh…" she stammered.

"You mean before my accident?"

Shawn leaned back, shaking her head. This changed everything. Didn't it? If he had *known* he was in a coma… Bringing someone back from the dead – *someone who had been in a coma!* - then this could change everything. Maybe they could bring back comatose patients as well. "Well, sure. Let's go with that," Shawn said.

"I remember feeling like I was falling down a well, looking up. Seeing the light get smaller and smaller as I fell deeper and deeper. I knew I was going away but there was nothing I could do to stop it. I felt so helpless," the man said. And the oddest part about his speech now was that there were none of those little pauses people grow used to in conversation. Those little stops where the speaker catches his breath – that little tiny inhalation where he can refill his lungs to start with fresh air and continue speaking – this man didn't need to pause to catch breath that wasn't there. Those little gaps in the conversation went unnoticed in day-to-day life because they were so *normal*. But here, with them missing, their lack stood out like a black painting on a white wall.

"What happened to cause that state?"

"That, I don't remember," said the man. I know I was at work. I was standing on the sidewalk… Something. I don't recall. I'm sorry."

"It's fine. How do you feel about the fact that you were in a coma? Do you remember that state at all?"

"Oh yes. I've been aware of a lot of things while I've been under. I can hear people talking. But there are also long periods of sleep. These periods feel like they could have lasted months. I have no way of knowing. How long have I been gone?"

Shawn looked up at Sameer again. He nodded slowly. "Uh, I'm not sure the exact date, but you were in a coma for over a year."

The man's face was very still for a long time. He had still not opened his eyes. They were still moving under the closed lids though. Very active. "A year. Good God. I've missed out on so much."

Shawn swallowed. She leaned her elbows on her knees and fidgeted, performing her 'hand ritual'. "So a minute ago, you said you were 'alive again'. What exactly do you mean by that?"

"Well, it's like I've been given another chance. Being able to speak from a coma is pretty exciting, as you can well imagine."

Shawn closed her eyes and shook her head. This man didn't know he had died at all. Maybe that was the disconnect. Coma was enough like death that it either erased or superseded the gap. While this didn't necessarily destroy any of their previous thought and theory about bridging that gap, it did present a new conundrum. Maybe the gap looked just like the sleeping parts of this man's coma. Apparently he felt like he had just been awakened from one of those.

"Can you open your eyes?" Shawn said.

"Eyes? I'm not understanding."

"Well, I was just wondering if you would like to try to look around. To see your surroundings. Do you want to see what I look like?"

"I can see just fine, Shawn."

Shawn's blood went cold for the second time. "What do you mean by that?" she asked. She was wringing her hands together now. She thought she remembered something about eyes that didn't get used for long periods of time – something about how they had to work to be able to work. Like people who stayed in a dark cave for a few months would lose their eyesight because something about the cones and the rods… Maybe this man's seeing days were over. Shawn sighed and rolled her eyes at that. All of this man's days were over.

"I mean, I can see you. I am looking at you."

She met eyes with Sameer, who was looking a bit like he was doing math in his head. Good. So he was perplexed by this as well. He twirled his fingers a little, almost impatiently. *Quit looking at me and go on!*

Shawn cleared her throat, blinking and sitting up straight. "Okay, uh, Curtis, what am I wearing?"

The man smiled broadly. Here it came. Might his answer not tell her all the secrets of the universe? This man had not yet opened his eyes even a blink. If he knew what she looked like – what she was wearing, might that not be telling of the soul? If he could see without his eyes then there was something allowing him to take in his surroundings in a visual way. She wondered if he was looking down on them from above, and glanced up at the ceiling above the man nervously.

"Well, you have on a nice pink sweater and some khaki pants. Your blonde hair is in a bun on top of your head," said the man, and Shawn instantly felt relief. Not only was the man wrong about each of his details, but he was so far off it wasn't even the same ballpark. She wore a long black skirt today that went to her ankles. Beneath it she wore knee-high black boots. And above that, a burgundy silk blouse. Her brown hair hung to her shoulders. No bun or ponytail of any kind. Wherever this man was getting his information – be it a deep-seeded and misplaced memory or an active imagination – it revealed a flaw in his perceptive abilities. He thought he was actively seeing, and didn't realize his eyes were closed. She wondered what this meant as far as the rest of his cognitive abilities. Did he really remember anything from his coma, or were those memories of dreams had earlier in life?

"Okay, good," she said, and saw Sameer peripherally shaking his fist. She looked up at him. He was nodding, lips pursed and proud of her judgment. "Very good. What else can you tell me?" she said.

"Where will I go from here?" the man said.

Shawn's eyes widened again. "I'm sorry, what do you mean by that?"

"What will happen to me when I leave here? Can I stay here?"

She took a deep breath and let it out slowly, thinking of her options. Thinking about the potential pitfalls and consequences of taking a step too far. Then she made a command decision. "Where is 'here' to you, Curtis?"

"Here! Right here! Right here on this fucking couch! In your goddamn office! What the hell do you think I mean by here?"

"Okay, let's try to keep calm, sir," Shawn said, holding a staying hand out in front of her. It was below the level of the table, and his eyes were closed anyway, but it somehow made her feel better. "I only meant, how long would you like to stay?"

"I just don't want to go back to where I was. That place was not the definition of comfort and hospitality," said the man.

Now what did he mean by that? Was he referring to the hospital where he had been kept before? *Had he* been in a hospital? She realized that he could have been under a hospice care of some sort, in a home, or even in his own home. She had to ask. "Where was that? Where were you before?" she asked.

"Hell," said the man simply. And Shawn's blood went cold a third time.


Something changed inside Shawn at that moment. It wasn't just the ice in her veins, which felt like a literal description of what had happened. The ice wind that blew through her body made her shiver from head to toe. But something seemed to change as well. Like an acceptance of something previously not concrete. Had she been unsure about the afterlife? She had always considered herself a Christian, though she did not practice regularly, and even more seldom did she actually attend church services. But a belief was a belief regardless of if it was brought to mind often or not. No one ever asked her if she believed in gravity. Or whether she believed the moon was drifting away an inch a year. Yet she still believed in those things too.

Regardless of if they needed thoughtful visitation on a regular basis, they were foundational beliefs in what made her who she was. She was a human being on this planet with that moon that was responsible for the Earth's diurnal axis – and in keeping with their climate. Their seasons, the weather – everything. That moon made humans who they were. So did gravity. Shawn's mass was dependent on it. Had she been raised on Jupiter, her weight would have been different. She had come to accept these things as they were because of the foundation of those structural elements – regardless of it they ever needed consideration. So fundamentally true was it for her that she could safely forget about it and it wouldn't change. And her Christian upbringing had instilled in her a hope that there would be something after she was laid to rest. Not just a hope, but a knowledge. The hope was that she was one of the ones who got the good stuff. The knowledge was that there was bad as well.

But saying one believed in the moon's retraction was to take a leap of faith, a lot like Christianity. Because no one had gotten out there with an extra long tape measure, two years in a row, counting that inch. They had fired a laser beam and reflected it off a mirror, which was ostensibly more accurate and just as good for the knowledge. But whoever performed that experiment was taking his own leap of faith. Faith in the equipment. Faith in the physics, the calibration of the measuring device, faith in the mirror's integrity… a whole set of beliefs. And hers was, therefore, founded on *his* telling that it was so. If no one had told the world this was happening, Shawn would never have known herself. And she had no way to go check on it. She had to take that scientist, or those scientists, at their word. Hearing someone come back from the dead and speak of the afterlife was a little bit like setting up her own tape measure. Or her own laser-and-mirror contraption. Seeing through her own eyes that it was real. Forget that she wasn't personally back from the dead. Hearing someone on her lab table say so was close enough to call it first-person in her book. Forget also that the man might have been talking about poor treatment or living conditions in the place from which he had come. He might not have had any thought to a literal afterlife version of hell when he said the word. But even still, it had clicked in her mind, and that's what stuck.

Shawn had taken a series of deep breaths after the man said that, and tried to calm herself back down. She waited an extra few seconds for the hard spots of icy chill to evaporate from her arms and neck. And then she had asked him to elaborate. But on the subject, he would say no more – leaving the mystery lingering in the air like the scent of a passerby's perfume. The man had said, "Look, can we talk about something pleasant? I'm getting the feeling my time here is short." Which, of course, could have a whole other series of meanings associated. Shawn felt like she had just slid a box full of puzzles out from under a bed and was peering in at a billion possible scenarios flashing before her eyes.

The rest of the interview was unremarkable in every way. It was chatter about things non-important, and misconceptions about reality. Like his saying that Sameer was a woman observing from a chair in the corner. Shawn felt like there was a lot to unpack here, and in the meeting tomorrow morning, they would certainly do just that. But they could safely leave off the last thirty minutes of the interview. The only thing remarkable that came to pass after the word 'hell' had spilled from his lips, was the way he left them when they lost him forever.

The man had been rambling about things to the point it felt to Shawn as if he was just happy to hear himself talk. And that probably wasn't far from the truth – having been pent up with no way to speak for over a year – he was probably excited to be able to, and to furthermore have someone to finally listen to him instead of just whispering calming bullshit into his comatose ear. And then suddenly, at the end of the half-hour or so, the man had opened his eyes. They had popped open like roller blinds, staring straight at the ceiling, so wide as to let the eyeballs pop out of his head.

Shawn had sat forward on the stool, her hands on her hips as if she were reaching for two holstered pistols, frozen in surprise and shock, and she had said, "Curtis, are you okay?"

And Curtis, God rest his soul, had said, "Curtis is gone. I'm here now. And I'm very, very afraid. Help me, please!"

Shawn finally got the chance to do it. Sitting at her desk and feeling a little lost, she needed to blow off some steam. Like an air vent for a pressure system. She just needed to let a little of the stress out before it cracked her glass. She realized the opportunity and flooded with a new level of excitement as she pulled out her phone and opened the SMS app. In the name field she started typing BOYF and let the phone make a suggestion, which she then accepted. And then she filled in the text field:

```
Hey lover. I need a ride tonight.
Will u take me to Cino's?
```

It felt so good to finally be able to text him. She set her phone on the desk and put her head in her hands, closing her eyes. She massaged the back of her skull with her fingertips. She wondered how long this *Lazarus Project* would ultimately last. Surely there was no end in sight. Shawn still wasn't quite sure what his end goal was. Sameer was not the most forthcoming about his intentions. She didn't necessarily think he was holding back anything. He might be just be flying by the seat of his pants – just like she was under his direction. But surely he had *something* he wanted to achieve. If it was literal full, two-way conversation, they had achieved that.

It was not that she was complaining – because, hey, the money was great. And of course, that would come to an end when the project did. So to her benefit, she needed it to keep going. She needed bodies coming in every few weeks to feel safe about the salary remaining in place. Not that she made a poor salary before, but when presented with the option of a good salary, or double a good salary… No, it wasn't the money, though. But *what* was he going for? She would like to know so she could predict when the end would come. Now that she thought about it, it didn't seem fair for Sameer to just arbitrarily end it when he got what he wanted out of it. Shawn felt like she should get a few months'-notice so she could plan for the halved salary. Because that's what it would be at that point. Her salary – the one she had already gotten used to – would be cut in half. Right? Maybe she should talk a little about that.

Her phone lit up. She unlocked it and looked at the screen.

```
Hey bayba! So glad you texted. I
would love to take you on a ride
tonight. I'll make reservations for
Cino's. We can dress in our finest!
When will you be home?
```

Shawn's face lit up in a wide smile. Had she looked in the mirror at that moment, she might have laughed at herself. She had big red marks on her cheeks where the heels of her hands had pressed into them, and a little bit of glass in her eyes. That first text she received was enough to brighten her mood for the entire rest of the day. She squeezed the two side buttons on her phone simultaneously and took a screenshot of their very first SMS exchange. She continued to smile widely as she responded.

```
I might breeze out a little early
since I did some magic today. Maybe
I'll be home by 5.
```

Since she was having so much fun with this, and this was the first time she'd had a boyfriend in quite some time, she decided to have even a little *more* fun with it. She added:

```
Will u put your hands up my shirt
before we go? I'm not wearing
breast defense!
```

She felt a little turned on. Having her boyfriend's phone number opened up a whole other range of options for her days. Sneaking to the toilet to send him a quick text during the day – not to mention maybe sneaking a picture of… Ooh!

Shawn quickly stood up and walked to the bathroom, then shut herself in the stall and lifted her blouse up over her braless chest and took a selfie, making a selfie face. She clicked share and typed BOYF again. Clicked his name and then send. Then she pulled her shirt down and stood in the stall smiling and heart beating fast, waiting for his response. She liked being bad.

```
Oh my fuck
```

She laughed out and slipped the phone under her arm as she exited the bathroom. She now felt like the day was going her way. What a refreshing bit of information to hang on to: feeling a little down? She could just text her boyfriend. Feeling like breaking a rule? Being a little naughty? Send a secret picture. Somehow, having that secret with him that no one else would know made her feel good – like as long as she could hold something back from the rest of the world, she was on the inner circle of something. And sometimes that was all someone needed to feel special – to make it through her day. And right now, if she were being honest, she suddenly felt like she was on top of the world.

She opened the app once more and told him she was going to invite Lo and Heath. The last couple of hours of the day seemed to blow by like a breeze after that levity. *So happy I finally got his number!*

That evening they rode. Heath and Lo had accepted the invitation, and actually showed up at Cory's to have a pre-ride drink – the guys had a beer while the girls had a real drink – and then they all piled onto the bikes, roaring out of the parking lot like thunder. Somehow, riding with just the other couple felt even cooler than riding with the whole group. At every stop light, Heath would pull up next to Cory and she and Lo would look at each other, make faces, bump fists, or do little dances. Just happy to be alive. And every time it would turn green, Heath would fall in behind Cory, off to the right just a little, and several meters back. Shawn guessed it was practiced protocol for bikers.

At Cino's, they parked both bikes in one of the spots and went to the middle set of tables. They ordered burgers and fries and drinks and ate and drank, the girls laughing and showing the rest of the patrons – all cagers – how much fun could be had if you were as cool as they were. Shawn guessed by the end of it all that some of the men stuck in their boring cars with their boring wives might have even been a little jealous of Cory and Heath. The girls danced to the loud music blasting out the restaurant's outdoor speakers, tossed french fries into each other's mouths and made each other laugh out loud multiple times. Altogether, they were acting like teenagers who didn't have a worry in the world.

The best part about it was that somehow, even though the girls had not been with their respective guys for that long, the boys were used to it. Or at least just perfectly fine with it. They seemed to be the perfect guys for this type of woman, Shawn thought. For her man to last, he had to be okay with her dancing in the street while they walked, singing karaoke off-key, stopping the ice cream man in the middle of a busy road and getting her face painted at the carnival. She worked for a living. She paid for her own apartment, her own vehicle, her own insurance. She was a grown woman. She worked hard for her money. She deserved to let go in her off-time. If that meant she needed to let her inner child out for a while, then so be it. Shawn was still a little girl at heart. And she needed a man who understood that. Supported it. Got on board with it.

She sat sideways on the bench, straddling it like a bicycle, facing her boyfriend as he finished his fries. Lo was on the other side of the table, leaning against Heath. Shawn was so revitalized by the interaction she'd had with Cory over text that afternoon that she was high as a kite. She was staring at Cory with a huge girlish smile on her face. She leaned over and kissed him on the cheek. When he looked at her, chewing behind his smile, wondering what the hell that was all about, she put both her hands on the bench in front of her, bouncing slightly.

"Cory, I have to admit something to you," Shawn said, letting the smile drift a little. She let it be replaced by her mysterious look. The one that made him ask her what she was thinking behind those big brown eyes.

He gulped and looked across the table at his friend. Heath just raised one eyebrow. Lo had a knowing smile on her face. She looked relaxed tonight. Shawn needed to remember to ask her later if she had changed her mind about Heath. This was the second time they'd come out in public now where she looked completely at odds with what she had said about being done with him.

Cory finally looked at Shawn, after seeing the party across the table either didn't know anything, or weren't ready to help him out. "What is it, babe?" He reached down and put his big hand on both of hers. She smiled. If he couldn't see in her eyes what she was about to say to him, then he wasn't looking very hard. She could feel it burning through her gaze.

"Cory Klein, I am one hundred percent mad for you."

He chuckled and squeezed her hands. "Well, that's g-"

"I love you, Cory. I just think you need to know that." She leaned forward and kissed him hard on the lips. She felt like she could easily make it last a lot longer than it did, but remembered there were sometimes children in the cars at the drive-up stations. Because in reality, Shawn could have just climbed on top of him right here. No clothes would have to come off. She could just sit on his lap and kiss him for ten minutes or so.

Cory's eyes went wide and his mouth dropped open. He checked on Heath and Lo again. Heath had a little smirk on his lips. Lo, on the other hand, was smiling ferociously. She looked like she was as full of excitement about it as Shawn was herself. Cory returned his gaze to her. "You… you're serious?"

She nodded dramatically, biting her bottom lip. Now she was out on a limb. She didn't mind if he wasn't ready to say it back. But she sure needed to know he was okay with hearing it. After a moment, he shook his head and blinked a few times. "Wow. I uh, well, I love you too, Shawn. I really do."

"Yay!" she said. And this time, F the world, she climbed on his lap and gave him a proper kiss while Lo actually clapped and 'wooed' out loud.

When Shawn and Cory got home, the lovemaking was kicked up a notch because of the new feature they had unlocked. They were now allowed to say those three words, and she said them several times, each time making the passion more intense. The ecstasy she felt was magnified by what felt like an exponential amount – like saying this little phrase was allowing her to reach a new level of climax. It almost felt like it meant she had found her man. The man. Of course, she knew she really loved him. She just didn't know if their aligned fates would take them all the way to the finish line together. And that was okay. That was fine. Because for now, she was taking it one step at a time. *Baby steps.* And for now, it was good enough for her to have reached *this* level. *This* phase. She loved him, and by God, she was gonna let him know it.

The ride home had been intensified as well. She held onto him a little differently, exactly the same way she had last time. It felt different in her hands. Even the pockets of his jacket felt more like hers. At the stops, she would wrap her arm around his waist and put her hand on his stomach. Her boyfriend's stomach. She rested the side of her helmet against his back with a little more passion as well. Everything felt different. The few inches of her hair that were long enough to stick out the bottom of the helmet blew in the wind and she leaned her head back, eyes closed, smiling at the sky. He had said it back!

Shawn had not expected him to and was actually expecting him *not to*, in fact. She just wanted him to smile and kiss her lips. To say, "I'm on my way." or "I'll get there soon, babe." Something. Anything letting her know he was willing to keep going. But he had said he loved her! That was worthy of celebration. She had another drink with Cory, sitting out on his tiny balcony after their sex. The wall of the balcony was too close to the apartment for them to stretch their legs out, and the chairs barely fit. But they got a pretty good view of the final remnants of sunlight disappearing behind the building to the west. As they sipped their drinks, the smile never left Shawn's face. And she could see a lightness in his visage as well. She felt right with the world. She planned to call her dad in the morning and tell him all about it. About how good she felt and how happy she was.

They slept with the fan on high and naked as newborns. At one point during the night, Shawn woke up feeling wet, and decided to see if her man was ready for her again. Well, it didn't take her long to get him ready. She sat on his thighs while she caressed him. Cory lay with his hands behind his head, staring at her in the light of the parking lot lamps breaking through the curtains. They had left the curtains cracked so they could see the sheen of sweat on each other's bodies earlier in the night. Now it would come in handy once again. When he stood ready, she rocked up on her knees and moved forward, then settled in on him. Shawn stayed straight up with beautiful posture for the entirety of the ride with Cory's hands on her thighs until it was time for her to hop off. Then she spun around and fell backward into position beside him. Her head on his left biceps, bodies smacked right up against each other, that's how they fell asleep. And for the second night in a row, she had a deep, undisturbed sleep that lasted all night. The only difference was that tonight she did dream.

Shawn sneaked across the landing in her underwear with last night's clothes held tightly against her chest, covering up the pretty parts. The darkness was still almost thick enough to cover her on its own. It was almost six o'clock. She went to the bathroom to grab her toothbrush so she could take care of that while she made her coffee. After getting that started, she walked to the back door and slid a hand into the vertical blinds, moving them to the side so she could check for butterflies. There was no butterfly, thank goodness, but she saw the spider had returned and he was hard at work rebuilding his masterpiece. "You little snot!" she said with a mouthful of toothpaste foam.

She was on the road before the sun had made its first real impression on the day, and when she pulled into the parking garage at work, she actually stepped out of her Jeep with a smile on her face. She had been blasting the music and singing along. A good sing always gave her good color in her face and made her feel re-energized somehow.

Probably something about the blood flow and breathing. She didn't care much about the science, but she loved the results. She wasn't a particularly good singer, but no one had ever complained when she sang alone in her Jeep.

She walked by the conference room with a finger in the air, knowing the two men would be sitting in there watching the door for her. "Be right there," she said over her shoulder. She was early, but they were earlier. She had also noticed a third person in the room. Who the hell else would be in their post-op meeting?

Shawn slung her purse up on the counter, then grabbed the coffee pot and filled a mug. She swung back by her desk and grabbed her DVR just in case, and headed for the conference room. When she came through the door, all three occupants were looking at her. Chandra was the third. And she was smiling pleasantly. Shawn smiled back and touched her shoulder as she pulled out her chair. "Hey, how's it going?"

Chandra answered by tapping her pen against the table and smiling some more. "I would like to start by saying there's no point in even asking what he meant with his last sentence," Shawn said, pulling up to the table. She had said it as kind of a joke, because of course, everyone in the room were scientists in the way they approached their research. Well, except for maybe Chandra. Shawn had to remind herself that Sameer obviously wanted her in here. For some reason.

"Why do you think we need not discuss this, Shawn?"

"Because," she said, holding her hands up, "there's no possible way anyone can arrive at a realistic answer!" She smiled broadly, then said, "I actually said it more as a joke. But yeah, I think the point remains. I've been thinking about it a lot since yesterday."

Jeremy was staring at his pen, which he was also tapping quietly against the table. He was nodding. If anyone here approached things scientifically, it was he. And he was nodding. This, of course, made Shawn feel affirmed. Of course, he could also be nodding to an imaginary drum beat in his head. She could pretend though.

Sameer pulled the voice recorder out and said, "Should we play the tape, Shawn?"

She looked at the device for a moment and shrugged. What was the point in keeping these two out of the lab? They could just as easily have sat in on the session. Again, Sameer had his reasons. And again, Shawn did feel like an insider for getting to be the only other one in there besides Sameer. So never mind on questioning his motives. They listened to the tape in its entirety without a single interruption. When it finished, Sameer silenced the device. It would automatically start playing the next recording if he didn't stop it.

"So what do you think?" Sameer asked, leaning back in his chair.

Shawn had forgotten how clear the man's voice had been. It was haunting now, knowing she had heard the last words the man would ever speak. Words spoken *after* his living last words. Jeremy looked at her and smiled, then said, "You know, that is a real interesting statement he makes at the end, isn't it?"

"What happened after he asked if you could help him?" Chandra asked, looking at Shawn, leaning in a little.

Shawn caught herself before rolling her eyes. And not just at Chandra. The fact that they were both already hung up on the one part of the interview that no amount of research or scientific method could answer for seemed like a waste of time to her. If they were teenagers sitting on the carpet in her dark bedroom, it would be another story. But this was science. Not séance. She did let herself sigh a little too loudly though.

"He looked like he saw the most terrifying thing on the planet," she said, looking down at her hands, as she wrung them together in her lap. "Or beyond." She looked up at Sameer, maybe for help, since he was the only one who hadn't mentioned the spooky statement. She twisted her lips, then looked over at Chandra and forced herself to take a sip of her coffee before she continued. "Then he just sort of locked up. It was like whatever he saw just sucked his life away."

Chandra closed her eyes and shook her head quickly, then shivered visibly. "I wish I hadn't asked."

"So can we talk about the parts we had control over?" Shawn asked.

Sameer nodded. "What do you think was different that he responded so quickly this time?" he asked.

"He had only been dead a few hours, hadn't he?" asked Jeremy.

Sameer nodded. "About the same amount of time as Miranda."

"What I found most interesting was the connection with the coma," said Shawn. She sipped from her coffee again.

"Yes," Jeremy said, raising a finger over the table. "I'm interested that this offers some perspective on that. This science might be sellable."

"I found it hard to figure out if he was actually having memories of the coma, or if it was from his life before death."

"Yes. That is an important distinction. Unfortunately, most of these things will be just like the statement he made at the end. We can find no real answer, because each question has multiple possibilities," said Sameer.

Chandra slapped the table lightly, but it had the desired effect. Everyone gave her the floor. When she realized everyone was looking at her expectantly, she stopped the tapping and rested her hand flat on the table. Shawn got a good look at her diamond. Peripherally, she thought of how she had declared her love for Cory last night, and it made her heart smile. Chandra stared at her own hand on the table for a long moment before she finally spoke. When she did, it was in a pensive voice.

"What if – what was his name? Curtis?" She looked at Sameer, who nodded subtly, before continuing. "What if he was awakened back into his comatose state?"

Shawn frowned thoughtfully at her. "Are you saying – what if we woke him from the dead," she said, tapping her fingertip on the table, "into the comatose state he had been in before they pulled the plug?"

Chandra looked up at her and nodded, swallowing. She furled her lips. Shawn's eyes met Sameer's. They stared at each other for a long moment. Chandra might be onto something with that, thought Shawn. She had to think about what all he had said. "Hey, Sameer. Mind playing that tape again?"

He nodded and slid it to the center of the table. Shawn looked at Jeremy and Chandra in turn. Neither looked put off or impatient about having to listen to it again. Chandra, in fact, crossed her arms and leaned back, looking very interested. Jeremy, already leaning back, put his pencil sideways in his mouth and tapped it against his teeth, staring at the recorder expectantly.

"I want everyone to listen to it with Chandra's theory in mind. Everything he says."

When they had finished the full recording again – this time all of them taking notes on yellow legal pads Chandra had fetched and passed out – Sameer reached up and pressed the stop button and leaned back. They all had notes, and they all seemed to Shawn to have a little more stress in their faces. The interview had sounded completely different when taken with the new context, and Shawn had actually found herself getting chills in her lower back a couple of times.

"Right. So, I guess I'll start," she said, clearing her throat. "The first thing I noticed was that he was responding to questions with relevant, tense-appropriate speech. 'I can hear you' and 'you just told me' when I asked him what my name was. And this remains true until we get to," she paused here, picking up the pad to get a closer look. "Here. He says, quote, 'Oh yes. I've been aware of a lot of things while I've been under. I can hear people talking.'"

Chandra nodded.

Jeremy nodded and leaned forward, putting his "Yeah," said Jeremy. "Present perfect. Like he's still there."

"Right. And then he says, 'How long have I been gone?'" Shawn said. She looked at Chandra with an eyebrow raised, her mouth furled.

Chandra raised her own eyebrows and shrugged. "Yeah. That could represent gone from life or just gone from living."

"What do you mean?" Sameer said, frowning.

"Well, if we go with the theory that maybe he was just brought back to a comatose state, he could literally be asking how long he's been catatonic. Like 'How long have I been unable to live my life?'"

Sameer nodded. So did Jeremy. "We have a lot to learn about comas. If this guy has been cat for over a year, but now he can talk and answer questions and whatnot even though he's still technically in a coma... Well, I don't know what to think of that," Jeremy said. He turned his palms up above the table and leaned back, clasping them together on his belly.

Chandra shook her head, closing her eyes. "I know. Have you considered monitoring brain function and whatnot while you perform these interactions?" she asked, looking at Sameer. He made a face, then looked at Shawn. Shawn squinted slightly, looking back at him. *Great question.* She was gaining respect for Chandra by the minute.

"I had considered it but I did not think it would be useful. I thought that we would get all the answers we needed from facial expressions and speech," he said, raising his shoulders. "I guess it could be beneficial though. What do you think, Shawn?"

"Well, I think maybe we need to focus on what we're doing. Do we want to sell this science? If so, then yes, absolutely, we need to start gathering bio-telemetry data," Shawn said, and then took a deep breath. She looked at Chandra. "I think it's a brilliant idea, Chandra. I just worry about where that would take us. If we start focusing too much on what the brain patterns are telling us, we might –

well, frankly, I don't know if it's relevant. It absolutely would have been relevant in this case, to answer that one fantastic question you had. But other than that?" she said, raising her eyebrows and holding her palms up like Jeremy had.

Chandra shook her head, pursing her bottom lip. "I'm not offended. I was just wondering if we had any of that data to refer to in this case. But I do think it would be interesting to see what a scan looks like."

"That is the other reason I did not invoke such elements, Chandra. I am worried they might interfere with the performance of the nanobots," said Sameer.

Shawn looked up at the wall above Jeremy's head, nodding slowly, trying to imagine the effect that could have on someone. Talk about creating a zombie. *Ugggh.* She shivered, then sat up straight and rubbed her shoulders, hiding it well.

"What was that?" Jeremy asked, hiking his chin at her and smirking. *I guess I didn't hide it that well after all.*

Shawn shook her head. "Nothing. Just my imagination going again. I'm sorry. I'm still not perfectly used to this bringing back the dead bit. Forgive my unprofessionalism," she said, looking at Chandra.

"Sugar, there's no need for that. I won't set foot in that fucking room. You're a hero in my book."

Shawn laughed out loud. "And Socrates is a lion." She took a sip of her coffee and almost choked on it when Jeremy started giggling.

"What? I don't get it," Chandra said, looking back and forth between the two.

Shawn was busy clearing her throat and trying to swallow back the coffee, so Jeremy answered for her. "Socrates is a mammal. A lion is a mammal. Therefore, Socrates is a lion."

Chandra stared wide-eyed at him but Shawn had started laughing again. This time she couldn't breathe. Hearing him speak the whole thing had just hit her wrong. She had said the phrase 'Socrates is a lion' many times in her life. She had forgotten how funny the entire fallacy sounded when spoken by someone else. She was leaning forward with one hand on her chest and the other over her mouth, her eyes closed. Her throat was full of fire.

Chandra raised her eyebrows and mouthed, *'Okaaaay'* then tapped her hands on the table. Shawn reached over and grabbed one of her hands when she had finally caught her breath. "I'm sorry, Chandra. I wasn't trying to make fun. It's kind of a catch-phrase of mine. I don't even think about it anymore. The point is, I don't think I'm a hero just because I'm in there. In fact, I don't even think I'm brave." She leaned back and took a deep breath, looked at Sameer and offered a weak smile, then added, "To tell the truth, I'm scared shitless almost the entire time I'm in there. But thank you for the vote of confidence."

"Okay, so can we continue?" asked Sameer.

"Yes," said Jeremy, leaning forward and tapping his pencil against the pad while he read his notes. "When he said, 'Good God, I've missed out on so much,' that got my attention. Because I guess that's the first time you brought to his attention that he was actually in a coma for over a year." He looked around the table to make sure everyone was on the same page. Then he said, "He's acknowledging – again with the proper tense – that he's in a coma still. I mean, it fits." He shrugged.

"The other thing that appears to fit is when he said he could see just fine. Even though his perception of you was completely wrong, Shawn," said Sameer.

"He really seemed to get perturbed when you asked him what he meant by 'here'," said Chandra. "He actually asked if he could stay? And he actually said the last place he was at was not the definition," and here she had to check her notes, then read them word-for-word, 'the definition of comfort and hospitality'." Then she sighed and took her glasses off for a moment, rubbing her eyes with her knuckles. "Sameer, I don't suppose we can ask the family anything about this can we?"

"In what way?"

"Well, like to ask where he was. Maybe try to figure out what he was referring to. Find out what the 'bad place' was?" she said, making quotes with her fingers.

"It would be a good way to tell what he meant when he said 'hell'," Jeremy said. "You know, figure out if he was being literal or figurative."

Shawn shot Jeremy a look, but didn't want to say anything. Was this Jeremy having second thoughts about a spiritual presence in the lab?

Sameer was shaking his head. "It might be possible. But I would like to give the family time to grieve."

They all nodded at that, and it got quiet. "Okay," Sameer said, putting his palms on the table. "Anything else?" He looked at them each in turn. They all shook their heads thoughtfully. All except for Shawn. She was chewing her lip, pointedly not meeting his gaze when he looked at her.

She took a deep breath and looked up at him finally and asked, "How did you know him, Sameer?"


By one o'clock Shawn was having trouble keeping her eyes open. She was standing in the break room leaning against the counter with both hands wrapped round a mug of coffee. She knew she would probably get the jitters or at least be kept up at bedtime, but this wave of drowsiness had hit her hard. The four of them had gone to El Taco Primero for lunch on Sameer's dime. Mexican food always left her needing a nap. She had started nodding off at her desk, and so had to stand for a bit and try to wake herself up.

Jeremy came in twirling his mug on a finger. "Hey ho!" he said, and Shawn raised her eyebrows.

When she finished swallowing her current mouthful of coffee, she said, "Excuse me?"

"I said hey ho!" he said and stared at her, smiling. "There's no comma in that sentence. I'm not calling you a name."

"No, I get it," she said, nodding slowly. "What are we doing here, Jeremy?"

His smile faded as he realized she was still fretting over the meeting. He put his hand on her shoulder briefly and squeezed. "Shawn, why do you care if he knows the guy?"

She shrugged. Took a deep breath. Took a sip of coffee. Took her time, in other words. "I don't know. It just feels weird if it's personal. I mean, he didn't even act the slightest bit sad."

Jeremy tilted his head, frowning. "Why should he be sad?"

"He effing knew the guy, Jer!"

Jeremy continued staring but shook his head. "That doesn't mean they were close." He moved past her and filled his own mug. There would be no jitters or insomnia for Jeremy. He was a professional coffee drinker. He drank it all day, every day. "Look, Shawn, you've just latched onto what's probably the most important thing for you to know here." He moved back across the room to lean against the counter opposite Shawn. To look at her. "You are taking this too personal. What he's doing in there is completely separating the personal feelings from the business."

Shawn shook her head, breathing in deeply. "You don't think that's a bit weird?"

"Hey," he said, holding up his free hand. "We all handle death differently. A mortician feels differently about it than does a new mother. But why does it eat you up that he is or isn't a certain way with someone he may or may not know very well? Why, in other words, should it matter to you?"

"Professionally speaking, it shouldn't. And maybe it doesn't. But just knowing that makes me feel weird."

Jeremy stared at her for a long time. They drank in silence. Then he said, "What are you going to do about it?"

Shawn furled her lips, giving the question a fair thought. "I don't know. Nothing. I'm glad he at least admitted that he knew the guy. But it seemed like he should have disclosed that to begin with."

"Nah. What would you have done with that knowledge? It doesn't move the project forward in any meaningful way."

"You're right," Shawn said.

"And hey, aren't you always looking to prove or disprove what I said about the soul being present?"

Shawn frowned at him. "How does that fit in here?"

"Well, if his soul was in that room, he would have said hello to Sameer, right?"

Shawn nodded. "Yeah, good point."

"Listen, Shawn. There's something else you need to know."

"What's that?"

"He's keeping that subject in there for a couple more days," he said. She looked at him hard. For one thing, she was a little put off that he would know this before she did. But then there was the other thing. Jeremy continued, "Family's wishes. They want Sameer to do all kinds of testing because of the coma."

"What do they know? Oh my God! What has he told them?"

Jeremy held up a hand, calming her. "Not that. Don't worry. But they know he's working with the brain. To them he's studying the difference between a typical dead brain and one that spent thirteen months catatonic."

Shawn shook her head, looking up at the ceiling. "Why all these secrets?"

"It's not a secret. It just hasn't been broached yet. He, uh…" Jeremy started.

"He sent you in here."

Jeremy nodded.

"I'm going to go ahead and not punch you in the chest, Jer."

"Well, I appreciate that." He smiled pleasantly, then it faded. "Shawn, I consider you a friend. He knows that. He just wants you to get information in the most sensitive way possible. And in this case he could see you were rattled."

After another long moment filled with sips and staring, she finally said, "What else can he do with the guy? We already lost him."

Jeremy smirked, raising one eyebrow, then took another sip of coffee. "Did we?"

Shawn's face straightened. "What the eff, Jer. What do you know that I don't?"

He chuckled. "Nothing. But you have to understand, neurogenesis is a real thing. You let that blood keep pumping fresh oxygen into the brain, it is literally building and rebuilding neuro-connections. That's why a subject on the circulator for twenty-four hours gives more than one freshly attached."

This made sense to Shawn in a fundamental way. The way she had not been able to come up with on her own, rolling the thoughts and theories over and over in her head for weeks. She had just thought it had to do with osmosis. More blood getting to more parts of the brain over time. Which was probably also true. The two separate lines of thinking didn't have to be mutually exclusive.

"Who is he?" Shawn asked Jeremy, lifting her chin and pointing her head toward the general direction of the lab.

Jeremy came forward from his lean against the other counter and patted her on the shoulder again as he went beside her to refill his mug. Then as he turned to walk out of the break room, sipping his coffee as he went, he said over his shoulder, "A brilliant man, Shawn. He's a brilliant man." And it took several seconds for her to realize Jeremy had answered as if she was asking about Sameer.

Sunday night, after a weekend of being trapped inside their apartments by a torrential rain, Shawn was beginning to feel that familiar nervousness again. That semi-stress that came when she knew she would be communicating with the dead again the next morning. She stayed up late, trying to distract herself from this new dread in her life. What normal person had to worry about such things? She envied her old self – the self of two months ago – that human she used to be who didn't spend her mornings talking to the dead. And getting responses.

And to make matters worse, or perhaps because of her current matters, the dreams came back that night. Shawn was in her own bed. Cory was in his usual spot, on his stomach in the space between her body and her right arm. She had never been much of a back-sleeper before she met him, but this adaptation had come fairly easily. He was mostly a stomach-sleeper, so she either had to lie on her side with her leg thrown over his legs and hips, or she had to scoot way up on the pillows and lie on her back, forming a T with her arms. This had become her new position of preference. His head against her rib cage, she was able to run fingers through his shaggy hair or touch his face or shoulder whenever she wanted. And he was a heavy sleeper, so it almost never woke him up.

The dream was at first unrecognizable as a dream. In waking, looking back, it would seem completely normal. But something was just wrong. Shawn looked down, having been staring at the ceiling fan for the better part of an hour. The way the light fell across Cory's back was so beautiful – just a sliver of pale streetlight shaped like a sword falling across his shoulder all the way to his waist. She liked to pretend this was moonlight, for it was the same color. Often times, Shawn would just stare at him while he slept, watching his back rise and fall with his even breathing. The love she felt burned her like a coal fire from the inside. When she had told her father how much she loved him, dad had said 'You sound smitten'. And Shawn had told him that got about halfway to the truth. And that *was* the truth. She was completely mad for him, in ways she had never felt for any of her previous loves. So when she couldn't sleep, which ended up being quite a few of her nights, she would lean against the headboard, fingers tangled in his soft hair, just pulling and twirling, slowly and easily caressing his skull. She would stare.

Tonight was no different. She was wrapping a long lock of his hair around her index finger, twirling it up like spaghetti on a fork, then pulling her finger out and starting over. Over and over. Over and over.

Over and over.

And then he moved. Shawn almost flinched. The soft lulling sound of the humming ceiling fan and Cory's breathing had begun to put her into a very relaxed state – a place where she could almost fall asleep. And then he moved. It started with his shoulder twitching. She slowed her fingers and put her hand gently against the top of his head, afraid she had startled him awake. His breathing sped up a little. Shawn tilted her head, trying to see his face. It was buried against her naked rib cage, his mouth creating a warm spot on her waist just above her hip. The angle was wrong. But then suddenly, he cranked his head up, startling her again. He lifted his head in an inhuman, impossible way, and with a speed not achievable in real life. And he looked at her in the darkness with black eyes.

Shawn's heart skipped a beat and she leaned forward, trying to read his look. "Cory?" But then his head came up even farther. Like he was stretching his neck beyond its normal limits. "What the hell? Babe?" she said, shaking him by the shoulder now. Surely he was dreaming, and that was what was causing this odd behavior. Cory cranked his head slowly, again with that inhuman texture, looking at her like he was suddenly angry. She scooted her butt up the bed, raising her farther up the headboard, and shook him harder. "Cory, wake up, baby!" She was breathing very heavily now, and it felt like a train was roaring through her chest. "Cory!" she almost shouted, scooting even farther up, trying to get away from him.

"Stop it! You're scaring me!" she cried. "This isn't funny! Cory! STOP!" Then she screamed. She whipped her feet off the bed and rolled over, trying to get up and reach the lamp. When she felt the carpet under her feet, she turned around, one hand clicking the knob on the lamp, but it didn't come on. Cory's face changed, and as he opened his mouth, she saw he had no teeth.

In a low growl, he said, "Cory is gone. I'm here now."

Shawn covered her face with her hands and screamed like a banshee. She screamed until her lungs burned and tears rolled down her cheeks. She felt his hands on her wrists, prying them away from her face. She saw his face through her tears, but what he had said was right. He was gone. It was not Cory's face she was looking at. It was Curtis's face – the visage of the dead man that apparently still lay cold on the table in the lab at BlueBird.

Blind panic set in and she spun round, ready to tear off out the door – to break through the window and dive to her death in the prickly hedge below – anything to get away from this. She was screaming so hard her throat felt like she had swallowed a razor blade. As she got to the window and started ripping away that cloth that covered it, she felt his hands on her waist. He was pulling her back. Shaking her and twisting her. Then the hands moved up to her ribs, just under her armpits. Then onto her shoulders. Shaking and twisting, squeezing and pushing. Suddenly Shawn was facing the man and his lips were on hers. The cold bloodless skin felt like something from the ocean – something from the deep – something not meant to be kissed. She was shaking her head back and forth, pushing back against the window so hard she could feel it giving way. And then it cracked, split all the way from bottom to top, and busted free with a loud pop that brought frigid air in contact with her naked back, now bleeding from a gigantic unlivable gash that crossed from her shoulder to her hip – like a sword – and she fell through it, her breath leaving her lungs as she plummeted in a perfect backward fall to the ground below.

When she hit the cold, wet ground, her eyes popped open and Cory was staring at her. The screams were still rumbling out of her mouth like forgotten words from an ancient language. She was mumbling and reciting things otherworldly, things not understandable by human ears, shaking her head, eyes wide with terror and spilling tears.

"It's okay! Shawn, you had a bad dream! You're okay!" Cory was saying, still shaking her gently. "You're okay! Wake up, baby. You're good," he said, then twisted around to put his back against the headboard, sitting next to her so he could pull her into his embrace. She buried her face against his chest and cried, still shivering from the horror she had just been saved from.

It took a long time to wake up from that.

It took an even longer time to go back to sleep.

The next morning, Shawn thought several times about calling out from work. She hadn't gotten enough sleep – it felt like none at all – and the little sleep she had gotten had been plagued by the worst nightmare she had ever experienced. She wondered if she would ever be able to rid herself of the memory of that terrifying face. The fact that it had been patched on her lover's head made it hard to even look at Cory. Every time she had seen him since awakening, she had to take a deep breath and calm herself back down. It also didn't help knowing that the true owner of that face was still in her future. When she got to work that morning, it would be waiting for her – dead – in the lab. Hopefully it would stay dead. She had now every reason to wish failure upon the project. If not the whole thing, then this subject in particular. She did *not* want him to waken a second time. And until yesterday morning, had thought that such a scenario wasn't even in the cards. Like they wouldn't even be bothering to try. She had thought that once they lost a subject, that was it. Dead. Gone. Permanent. Something about brain cells and neurons having been energized by the nanobots must surely render them useless to future experimentation. Right? *Right?*

But with whom was she pleading? Herself? That wasn't good enough. She would have to plead with Sameer. And that wouldn't work. She shook her head, staring out the back window at the lovely morning sky, still innocent blue, not yet burned away by the mean light of the hard sun. She felt her hand tremble slightly as she raised the mug to her lips. She was happy on this morning that Cory was a late sleeper. Blessed be he for staying out of her way this morning.

Shawn loved him like crazy, but was scared to have his face forever ruined by a memory of a bad dream.

Finally awake and resolute in her determination to be a good employee – not to run from her fears – she chucked the rest of her coffee into the stainless steel sink and ran some water in the mug. She rinsed her mouth with it and spat in the sink, then went to the bathroom to roll on some deodorant and brush her teeth. She carefully avoided looking at Cory during her trips through the bedroom. On her way out, she stood at the front door with her key in front of her face, just staring at it. She stared for a long time, like trying to put a puzzle together. How could she lock up her apartment and still leave the key for Cory?

Shawn finally smirked and locked her door, then turned around and walked straight to Cory's place, unlocking his door with her copy of his key. She put her key on his table and jotted a quick note. 'Lock up, babe! Please make a copy of my key for yourself. Loves! -S'

She locked his door and trotted down the stairs.

The lab was cold this morning. Shawn glanced at the thermostat as she entered the room, noting it was set to sixty degrees. She dropped her purse on the counter and stood with her hands on her hips, breathing deeply, just taking in the room. "Good morning, Sameer," she said quietly. He turned around and looked at her over the tops of his glasses. The dim lighting made it hard to distinguish his dark eyes from the ambient darkness of the room.

"Hello, Shawn. How are you this morning?"

She sighed and answered the question she knew he was really asking – not the surface question. "I'm okay, Sameer. A little weirded out by this, but I'll be okay. What are you thinking?"

Sameer set down his tablet and crossed his arms, leaning against the counter behind him. "It won't be like the first awakenings. I just want to dive a little deeper in to the coma thing."

"Like what? What kind of diving?" she asked.

"I want to see-" Sameer started, but Shawn interrupted him, holding up a hand.

"Sorry, Sameer – what did you mean 'it won't be like the first' ones? And how can you know that?"

He nodded slowly, closing his eyes. "I don't think we will have much success because we have burned the neurons."

Shawn tilted her head, letting go a little sigh of relief. Maybe that was true. Maybe it wasn't. She was still apprehensive. "Okay, well, I'll go ahead and prepare for it. I need coffee though. Be back in two."

Sameer nodded and turned back to his tablet on the counter.

Over the next two hours, Shawn mostly just stood watching Sameer beat his head against the wall of this subject's tenacity. For some reason, the man just wanted to stay dead. Shawn had – at Sameer's instruction – boosted the electrical current put out by the nanobots, sent another whole colony in after the first, and even added more functions. The second colony was able to recharge the first while still keeping their own charge as well. Trial after trial failed, and to the point where Shawn was beginning to regret her reticence to feel hope about it. She, of course did not want him to fail. She just didn't want to see this man wake up once more. It was already hard enough looking at his face. Every few minutes, the dream would snap back into her reality, overlaying itself onto the dead man's face, causing her to breathe in deeply and then have to spend a few seconds getting a hold of herself again. Sameer could see her tension, but he thankfully didn't say anything about it.

It was when Shawn went to refill her coffee and take a bio break that she had the epiphany. More precisely, Jeremy, whom she met in the break room, gave her the epiphany. He asked how they were doing in there and Shawn had filled him in on all the things they had tried so far. Jeremy had stared at the floor for a moment and then asked, "Have you tried the kick?"

"What kick?" Shawn said. And for no reason, started laughing.

"The kick. A jolt to the system. It's that special flight or fight trigger. Something in that general region of the brain that reacts to potential danger. Your body also uses it when you're having a bad dream. It kicks you awake."

Shawn tilted her head, frowning hard at him. "That's a function?"

"Of course!" Jeremy said, sipping from his freshly filled mug. "Haven't you ever been jolted awake by something in a bad dream?"

Shawn breathed deeply. "Yeah. About five hours ago."

Jeremy smiled, nodding. "You guys should try to trigger that. I would say if that doesn't work, you've truly lost the guy. I mean, otherwise you're probably just wasting your time in there."

"Well I don't know how to find that, Jer," she said, pulling her hair back with a stress-burned hand. "What function is that? How do I create it?"

"It's in there," he said, looking at her like she might have gone down a few notches on the intelligence pole. "It's a selectable menu item!"

"Seriously?" Shawn said. She now had both hands in her hair, but had stopped moving them, instead focusing all her energy at staring a hole through him. "What the hell is it called?"

"Kick dot bat."

"Kick dot bat," Shawn said flatly.

"Kick dot bat."

She shook her head. "Fuck sake, Jeremy. Kick dot bat." She walked out of the break room shaking her head, pushing the door open with a dramatic swoop of her hand.

"Kick dot bat!" he shouted through the door.

"I got it! Thank you! Kick dot bat!"

When she got back to her desk, she selected a new group of bots, about twenty-five of them, and named them 'Kick', then pulled the drop-down list and scrolled down to the K section. There it was. The function she had seen what seemed like a hundred times now, but had never known what it was for. *Kick.bat.*

She clicked it and watched the progress bar as it zipped the routine through the network to the penning trap, assigning a new function to the on-deck nanobot colony. She shook her head and pushed back from her desk, then grabbed her mug and walked with a purpose back to the lab.

"Kick dot bat," Shawn said as she entered the lab. Sameer was leaning over the head of the dead man, both hands on the top corners of the table. He looked up at her as she came in, raising his eyebrows. "Kick dot bat. There's a function we've been needing all morning, Sameer. I've just loaded it. Jeremy just told me about it."

She proceeded to the circulation device and popped the injection tube out of its housing, then turned to the penning trap, popping it in place there.

"What does it do?" Sameer asked behind her.

"Exactly what you want it to." She pressed Inject. It didn't take long for the small transit colony to migrate into the tube. A new light came on atop the penning trap, though. It read 'Add system transit solution'.

Shawn popped the tube out and held it up to the light. Nothing remarkable, but she could see the level of the liquid in the tube was drastically decreased from the normal amount. "Trap needs saline, Sameer," she said.

"Okay, noted. What am I wanting this to do?"

Shawn walked with such a confidence that he got out of her way without so much as holding up a hand. Clearly, he didn't need his question answered before she did what she knew she had to do. The trust was in his eyes. So was the frustration of several hours of failure. He was ready for a result.

"You're wanting to wake this guy up," she said, snapping the tube into place. After a moment, she pressed the button that would inject the bots into the incoming blood.

Sameer had retaken his normal spot at the man's right shoulder on the table. Shawn pulled her hair back from her face, feeling the sweat it had left in its wake. The sweat was from the new excitement – an excitement borne by having established the missing link as well as the hurried movement to get back into the lab and prove herself the hero Chandra Casper had called her. There might have been some over-caffeination in there as well. But that excitement carried with it a new resolve. Shawn felt like the haunt of her bad dream might finally be pulling stakes.

"Yeah, I walked in there and Jer-" she started, then all hell broke loose.

The man on the table sat up, swinging his arms out to his sides like he was breaking free of shackles. And he was shouting.

# Twelve

Miranda's journal was the furthest thing from what Shawn wanted to think about. She was traumatized in a way she wasn't sure she could recover. She was seriously considering talking to a counselor, though she didn't know what she would say to one. Sameer had worked her into a corner with those damned NDAs. He would be the first guy in line for people Shawn considered as understanding. But how does one talk about progress, about dealing with demons, when one cannot mention those demons? And what if this *was* demons? Literal demons? What if what they were seeing every time someone's eyes popped open in that lab was a possession? An infestation of evil spirits?

Shawn didn't think that was the case. But in her Bible, the one she grew up believing in, Jesus had not only cast out demons – his apostles had as well. He had imbued them with the same powers he had for exorcism. So that meant they were real. Why would it just end when his earthly life had ended? Either one believed there were demons, or one believed there weren't. She couldn't sign up for *'Well, there used to be. But they're all gone now.'*

So she believed in it. She thought she did, anyway. But this still didn't quite feel like possession. It felt less than that somehow. But more than just a brain being brought back to life with electrical impulses. Getting speech – hell, getting *conversation* – out of a dead person was definitely more than just neurons reacting to tech. What kept her grounded in her sanity was what Jeremy had said in the break room that day though: *'It ain't like the soul's gonna rejoin the living from its reward just because you shock a few nerves.'*

Those words, committed to Shawn's memory almost verbatim, had been her comfort. Her weather vain in the storm of fear that tried to rain down on her every time they got a response. Or a 'successful encounter' as Sameer would call it. She sat on the couch, alone, staring out the back window and watching the sun disappear. She had a glass of cranberry vodka on the tray next to her, but it sat untouched. And so did Miranda's journal. The journal wasn't exactly untouched. Her hand rested on it. Occasionally, and subconsciously, Shawn would run her thumb up the sides of the pages, feeling the rough edges of the parchment. But it remained unopened. She couldn't bring herself to go on in it. Not tonight. She had asked Cory for a few hours alone as well. Figuring she would want to run to him when she got home, it had felt suddenly queer to be telling him she needed to be alone for a bit. But now she knew that queerness was her own soul begging for quietude.

Her face had been flushed and ugly. She felt the blood on the tips of her nerves, all through her cheeks, and she knew her eyes were puffy. She just felt wrong. It wasn't the exhaustion she had predicted, either. The dream had finally lost its command of her sometime during the morning. It just felt like a yearning to be alone. Maybe alone with God for a while. She hadn't done that in too long. So here she sat, fresh from the shower in fresh pajamas and allowing herself to find the calmness she knew she had in her. There had to be a way to recover from this. Not just today's episode, but from this chapter of her life – whenever it might be that it came to an end. What if they carried on playing Frankenstein for another year? Two years? Would that create a wedge between her and reality? Reset her expectations of what death really was and should be? Or would it harden her like a stone, making her more fearless and cold?

She shook her head. She had been murmuring quiet prayers ever since she stepped in the shower. Forgiveness for assuming the role of God, if that's what this really was. A sign from God to let her know if it *was* the case. Peace and release from the bad dreams. The guilt. The unsure. The weird feeling that her life had taken a crazy turn toward something exquisitely dark and inhuman. Surely there weren't a thousand other people on the planet doing these kinds of experiments? Were there? Hundreds? Tens? She felt like it might, in all likelihood, be her little team. Shawn and Sameer. Alone in the world doing what perhaps no man should ever do.

Shawn had finally gotten her heart to slow. She had brought herself at least that much calm. And she was happy to report that it was not the vodka – still untouched – that had allowed her that calm. Prayer and solitude had been the catalysts. For that, at least, she was proud.

Today's episode still rung loudly in her ears though. The fight that ensued when the man had sat up and started swinging, trying to wrestle him back onto the table when he fell off, writhing around the cold floor and knocking over stands, kicking and shouting and *drooling* for fuck's sake! He had literally been producing saliva and *drooling*! Foaming like a rabid dog!

The tubes attached to the man's lower skull, held in place with medical tape, had yanked the circulation machine against the head of the table, and then pulled it over when one of its rolling feet hit the foot of the table. The explosion of glass from the injection tube and plastic from the reservoir sent blood and bits all over the floor. Therein was one of the only redeeming eventualities of the day: Shawn didn't think they had a backup circulator and would thus likely be grounded for a while until they could get another. That was a small relief, until she remembered the other freezer. The other lab rooms. The backups for his spares, and spare backups. Sameer wouldn't have only one of anything. That just wasn't him.

Shawn had stood against the counter, frozen in absolute shock and terror while Sameer at first danced around the man trying to subdue him while bending over, his loafers slipping and creating long arcs of red across the tile floor. Seeing this was a fool's game, he had finally dropped onto the man, straddling him and trying to pin him down, knees now in the very mess his shoes had created, wrestling with the man like a cop trying to arrest a robber.

Shawn remembered the look Sameer had given her when he finally twisted his head around, seeing her standing there like a totem pole, pretty but useless, and shouting at her, "Shawn get the helmet! For Christ's sake, get the fucking helmet!" It had perhaps been the first time she had ever heard him use such language, and its impact had been strong and certain.

She also remembered, with the perfect and total recall of a recording, the feel of the room as she navigated across the obstacles – the swinging legs, the stretching and moving tubes and cords, the shiny steel pole that held the circulation device – everything moving and treacherous like a confidence course as she tried to make her way to the other side. And the feeling that struck her like lightning as she realized, hands closing around the helmet, that Sameer was the stronger human between the two truly living ones in the room. So Shawn would have to be the one to affix the helmet while he held the dead man down. Why the hell Sameer had not practiced policy by strapping the corpse down with the leather straps, she could only guess. She remembered the anger in her stomach – the rage in her chest – as she saw the straps hanging there, buckles gleaming dully in the dim light.

Making her way back around the foot of the table and trying to get into a position that would allow her close enough to the man's head without putting her within the reach of his grasping hands and swinging arms was to be a task. She remembered the icky feel of the blood beneath her sandals – sandals she would never ever wear again, but that had felt so perfectly fine to wear when she left that morning – and how it smeared like something not fully liquid but more like rubber. It made her sick at her stomach and felt like she was stepping on body parts, trying not to slip and join the men in the muck and mess.

It might have been the scariest moment of her life, save for just one. Seeing this man writhing and convulsing and twisting his head and neck in severe and inhuman ways did bring back memories of that one event in her life that would always take first prize in the fear category. The only difference was that this man was shouting. That same chilling alien language that Shawn had spoken only hours before in one of the worst nightmares of her life. Her aunt had been unable to vocalize anything when her time came. Shawn now could thank God for that. Though it might have saved her life by virtue of telling Shawn what the hell she needed to do and snapping her out of her statuesque fear, it also *might* have sounded like this man's speech. The chills and shivers still revisited every time she heard it in her memory throughout the day.

Getting the helmet on the seizing and convulsing man had been like trying to put a cat in a bathtub without getting scratched. It had taken far longer than putting a helmet on a man should take. And Shawn, yelling at Sameer to roll the man up onto his side for better access, had seen the man looking at her. The terror and aggression in those eyes would stir up its own haunt, maybe forever more, in her memory. It did not look like the man was aware and scared. It looked like the man was seeing through a rip in reality, straight into the bowels of the most evil and forlorn place in all of eternity. He was seeing the end of his soul.

All the meditation and silent prayer had helped Shawn over the last couple of hours, but there was a limit to the calm she could envelop herself in without the help of a friend. The ear of a loved one or the shoulder of someone close. And she just wasn't ready for that to be Cory yet. What she needed was some Lo Time. The thought of hanging out with her and maybe having a drink, relaxing, listening to some music and thinking about *anything else in the universe* besides the chaos of her morning gave her instant gratification. She picked up her phone and swiped it open, then tapped her Lo icon, which instantly placed a call.

She answered on the first ring. "Hey, baby!"

"What is up, my fine sister?" Shawn said, sitting up straight on her couch.

"Oh, you know, just climbing that ladder."

"Uh huh. I was wondering if you were in the mood to come hang with a friend in need. I could really talk to someone right now."

"Are you fucking psychic, you crazy bitch?"

"Not that I've found. Why?" Shawn said, a giant smile crossing her face. *Boy, that Laura has a curious way of getting my attention.*

"I am literally on your fucking stairs right now. Unlock your door, ho!"

Shawn squealed and dropped her phone on the couch, bounding up like a snake from a can. She threw the front door open and watched, bouncing and shaking her fists, as Lo came up the last few steps, holding a large bottle of gin in her left hand and shaking her hips.

"Hey, girlfriend!" said Lo.

They hugged at the threshold and Shawn grabbed her arm, scooting her in as quickly as she could to close the door behind her. Lo frowned at her, allowing Shawn to move her around like a chess piece. "What the hell is that all about?"

"I don't want Cory to know you're here," said Shawn, putting her hands together in front of her chest.

"Why? Are we gonna cheat on him together?"

"Just maybe," Shawn said, taking the bottle from Lo and moving toward the kitchen. "I already have a full glass of vaka over there. Want me to pour you some of this?"

"You truly are psychic. That is scary."

Shawn laughed out loud, cracking the top off the bottle and fetching a glass for Lo. She poured the gin halfway up the cup, then grabbed a handful of ice moons from the icebox and dropped them in. She  walked as quickly as she could over to the couch, where Lo was sitting with her arm up on the back, running her hand through her hair. "Thank you, darling."

Shawn bounced into her place on the couch, folding her ankles beneath her and picking up her glass. "So, I had a nightmare last night. Long story, but Cory was the bad guy. I'm kind of taking a break from him – just for today," she said, holding a hand up to stop any questions. "I'm not mad at him or anything. I just want that shit to fade from memory." After clinking their glasses together, Shawn said, "I had to see him for a minute anyway. I left him my key this morning and told him to make a copy. I had to get my key back to get in. But yeah, I just need a minute."

Lo made a face, scrunching up her mouth. "Oh, poor guy. So why do you need me?"

"Because you're a breath of fresh air," Shawn said, taking a big drink of the vodka. "I had a rough day at work today."

"Another *Day of the Living Dead*?" Lo asked. She ran her finger round the rim of her glass then took a sip herself, then licked her finger. Shawn watched with fascination.

"Yes. Fucking guy sat up today. Convulsed all over the floor. Full body involvement."

Lo's eyes were suddenly giant. "Are you serious? I thought that was impossible."

Shawn shook her head. "I used a new routine today that basically invokes the human fight-or-flight instinct. It suddenly and instantly floods the entire body with adrenaline and kicks it into action."

"Fuck sake. I just got goose bumps," Lo said, sitting up and looking around the room.

"Yeah. I've been sitting here for two hours meditating. Praying. Trying to calm myself. Trying to forget about it."

"Good luck with that," said Lo, reaching over and putting her hand on Shawn's knee. "Well," she said, sighing, "that explains the whole Cory Avoidance Policy. I can see why you don't want to be reminded of a nightmare right now. Poor darling."

Shawn shrugged. "Yeah. So, I figured if you weren't busy, we could watch a RomCom or a chick flick or something fun."

"Hells yes. I say we watch Johnny rescue Baby from the corner," said Lo.

Shawn smiled broadly, nodding her head. "Yes! That sounds perfect."

They didn't watch much of the movie, but it was great background fun. They got up and danced at all the good music and dance scenes, quoted the funny parts and laughed out loud like teenagers who had not a care in the world. Shawn realized how perfect a friend Lo was to her, having spent most of the evening together, and not once did Lo ask her to elaborate on her day at the office. At the end of the evening, Shawn realized she had not thought about Cory or the dream, or the terrifying event at work for several hours. And it had been a perfect escape. Lo, of course, stayed the night, not wanting to drive after drinking so much gin. And to top off a perfect evening, she asked Shawn if she needed company in the bed. Shawn had hesitated in answering, standing there and staring at her – senses in slow motion from all the vodka – and so Lo had put her hand on Shawn's shoulder and said, "I'm gonna sleep with you. You'll sleep better." All Shawn could do was hug her as the tears formed in her eyes.

Having someone to wake her up and comfort her if she sat up screaming or any other version of nightmarish waking was like a security blanket. Her queen-sized bed was plenty big for the two ladies, and she slept like a baby – after a quick text exchange with the boyfriend telling him she would see him tomorrow. When she ended the exchange, she signed off and put the phone down. Then she picked it right back up, feeling a heavy load of emotion from the day, and sent one more message.

    I love you, Cory Klein. You're my
    man.

Tuesday morning, Shawn had one of those wonderful organic awakenings where the transition between sleep and waking was blurred. She just knew that one moment she must have been asleep, and the next, well, she just wasn't. And she felt completely rested. There had been no bad dreams. It was comforting to wake up and see the sleeping hump next to her in bed, knowing her friend was there *just in case*. And Shawn had to admit that the morning routine was a little more exciting as well. Cory, God love him, didn't have two six o'clocks in his day.

Shawn and Lo moved about the apartment getting ready, brushing teeth, making coffee and even cooking breakfast, squeezing behind one another in the small areas. Having someone to talk to at breakfast, someone to share her coffee with was wonderful. It reminded her of the days before she had moved down to Texas. Her days of living at home, when she would have coffee with her daddy out on the pier in the mornings, hearing all the night sounds go quiet as the sun came up. She and Lo sat out on the tiny balcony enjoying the cool morning air.

She told Lo about her desire to sign up for a motorcycle class, and asked if Lo wanted to join her. Lo had made a funny face and said, 'Yeah, I'm not sure I'll ever get *there*. I may ride two-up behind you but I don't think I'm much for driving one.' And the idea of her being able to go for a ride with Lo behind her was just as exciting as the prospect of riding separate bikes, beside her. Shawn still wasn't sure about buying the bike. That would come after she learned whether or not she could even control it. Hearing some of the guys in the group talk about the inevitability of a crash on a motorcycle had not been comforting. She thought it had been Road Kill who had said, 'It's not a matter of if. It's a matter of when. It *will* happen to every biker at some point.'

Cory's response to that, later, when they were alone, was more comforting. She had asked, 'What do you think of that? That every biker will crash at some point?' and he had said, 'It's horse shit. It doesn't have to be true. Each ride is a reset. A new experience, a new set of odds, a new set of variables. If you drive safely and practice what you know each and every time, you have the same chance of a safe ride *every single time* you ride.' He had then gone on to tell her that some of those guys just liked saying shit like that because it made the biker world look a little more dangerous. It gives them an element of bravery when they can talk about how it's gonna happen but they keep riding. Shawn felt better about it after that.

All of these things she told Lo sitting on the balcony. And Lo had been receptive, nodding her head and raising her eyebrows in all the right places. But there didn't seem to be any moving her on the subject. She would probably never put her hands on the handlebars. And that was okay. Shawn knew it wasn't for everybody. Hell, she didn't even know if it was for her yet.

When they finished getting ready, Lo and Shawn exited the apartment together and did a quick hug and kiss on the landing, then went separate ways. Lo went toward the front, Shawn toward the back. She trotted down the stairs with the weight of the world seemingly *off* her shoulders. It felt so much different this morning than yesterday, partly because of the nice start to her day, but also knowing that the episode in the lab yesterday would probably mean Sameer was forced to send that man back to the morgue. Or wherever the hell the family wanted him.

When she walked into the office, she learned very quickly that she had been right. Thank Christ, the body was gone. It appeared that maybe Sameer knew his limits after all. She sat in his office in the chair across from his desk – the desk at which he spent very little time – and listened to him talk about how he'd had to work very hard on cleaning up the body. The one thing they had going for them was that there were no bruises. Shawn had asked if that was so, not thinking. Sameer had looked levelly at her and reminded her that it takes a living body to present the bruise. *Duh*. Her mind was still getting used to this new world that allowed dead people to wake up and talk and writhe about the floor like fishes out of water. *Sorry, I can't be counted on to keep up with every detail of what's reality and what's not anymore*. Of course, she hadn't said this to Sameer. But nor did she need to. She could see that he understood hers was a normal human brain with normal expectations of reality. It was not abnormal to forget one thing or another. Like flipping on a light switch even though you knew the power was out across the whole city.

"I wanted to thank you for your tenacity in there yesterday, Shawn. I know you were under a severe amount of distress."

She nodded, looking at the floor. "I guess you could say that. I wasn't sure I behaved in a very 'becoming' way.

"Shawn, there is no *becoming way* to handle a situation like that. These things do not happen very frequently in the normal world."

Shawn laughed out loud. She actually caught Sameer smiling, too. She pointed a finger at him and said, "Good one, boss."

He nodded.

"So what's the plan for moving forward?"

"Well," he said, and started arranging the items on his desk, "I think we will probably leave off the kick dot bat function from here out."

Shawn laughed again. "Yes, that's a good idea. Unless Jeremy takes a really close look at the routines he's buried in it. But I was thinking about that this morning, while I was trying not to think about it. You don't think it was just a product of our trying to wake him up a second time, do you?"

Sameer shook his head confidently, furling his lips. He finished neatening up the things on his desk that didn't need straightening at all. His desk was always immaculate. It was obviously just his own personal version of fidgeting. "No, it cannot be this way, Shawn. Because it was only a few seconds after you injected the routine that he came off the table."

The memory spooked her again and she had to close her eyes. She took a deep breath and looked out the window. Shawn wondered how these memories – these experiences – would affect her long-term. Would she have PTSD as an old woman, still waking from deep sleeps haunted by the faces of the dead she had raised? While Jeremy, the bastard, slept soundly like a baby with a fucking smile on his face? That son of a bitch deserved a good punch in the chest, and she fully intended to give him one as soon as she saw him next. He had conveniently not come in to work this morning. Ironic?

"Well, I'm not sure I want to be around for testing it again – even if we do get him to parse his code thoroughly," Shawn said.

"Well, this could all have been handled differently had I strapped the body down. I guess one just gets so used to things working the way they are supposed to work that one forgets the reason for safety protocols," Sameer said. He was still looking at the things on his desk. The two-hundred-dollar pen, the blotter filled with Hindi scratch, the tiny clock that he kept set even though you needed a freakin' telescope to read the dial... These were all absorbing his attention at the moment. Shawn wondered what he was hiding. There was obviously something he didn't want her to see in his eyes. She decided to let it go. He had his reasons, and they were probably valid.

"Well, you're forgiven. But I'm going to bonk Jeremy in the head next time I see him," said Shawn. "Any idea when the next project will be here though? Sameer?" she said. He finally looked up at her. It looked as though he had been off in another world.

"There are no plans in the works at the moment," Sameer said, and Shawn could have come over the desk and smothered him with kisses and hugs. "I will not be checking the app for a while. I want us to focus on setting the lab back up and making everything safer. Better."

"You're not thinking we're going to have to experience…" Shawn started but let her words drift off because Sameer was looking at her with a smirk.

"Not at all, Shawn. I just know you are needing of a break, and I want to spend some time in there together, just assessing things. I want your input on how we can make things better. Maybe like a little rearranging. Housekeeping items."

Shawn lifted her chin, understanding. "Ah. I got ya," she said. "Okay, I can dig."

"Good. Dig it then, Shawn. I think it will be healthy for you to be spending time in there when the table is not occupied. Realign. Become comfortable again."

Shawn took a deep breath. "Thank you, Sameer, for your courteousness. Your sensitivity is so graceful," she said. And he smiled a natural, genuine smile at her. "I really appreciate the way you have treated me through all this. You've been very good to me."

"Well, I cannot lose my number-one partner, Shawn."

She smiled at him. She raised her little fist in the air and said, "Director of the Dead!"

By the time Shawn left work, she was more than just a little ready to see Cory. And she felt she owed him an explanation as well. Just suddenly breaking routine and not wanting to see the guy after two months of sleepovers had to have been a shock to his system. She came up the steps and knocked on his door, then pushed it open just wide enough for her head to fit inside and said, "Hello?"

"Get your ass in here, girl!" said a voice from within. And she complied, all smiles. She tossed her stuff on the couch and went into his bathroom, grabbed her toothbrush and loaded it. Then she stood in the doorway just looking at him.

Cory shook his head. Rolled his eyes. "You know, all added up, by the time we die, you will have missed a good month of kissing and loving by putting it off like this," he said. His smirk made her smile, and toothpaste ran down her chin. She had to run back to the bathroom before she drooled all over his carpet.

When she came back in, she hopped over the couch and fell onto his lap, straddling him and taking his face in her hands. "Yeah, but all those kisses and loves will be better with my fresh minty breath!" She didn't give him a chance to respond. Shawn kissed Cory long enough to make up for the last day and a half of not seeing him. When she finally sat up straight, chills still visible on her arms, she smiled at him and said, "See?"

Cory shrugged. "Whatever's clever, girlfriend."

So she sat on his lap, knees buried in the cushions behind him and fingers playing with the button on his shirt as she told him all about the dream, the day and the reason for her avoidance. And, as she had well expected, he was completely cool with her reasons. Funny, now that she sat on his lap looking him in the eyes, she wondered how she could ever be scared of that face. She had also mostly forgotten what the dead man looked like. Not having Curtis's face superimposed over the beautiful one in front of her now was a major part of her recovery. *F nightmares.*

"Cory, I think I'm ready to sign up for a motorcycle class. Do you want to do it with me?"

He sighed and shook his head. "Probably not, babe. You're alone in your helmet. You'll only talk to the other students during breaks." He looked at her for a moment. Shawn reserved her judgment for another moment. "And you sure wouldn't want to be distracted. This class is the single most important thing in your motorcycle riding career. You really need to focus and concentrate. I would hate to be the one to screw that up for you."

She shrugged and sighed, then said, "Okay. I guess you're right. But that doesn't answer the other question I had."

Cory frowned and pulled his head back deeper into the cushion. "What's that?"

"How much of me do you think you can fit in your mouth today, lover?" she said.

Thirty minutes later, the ottoman had been kicked out of the way and now they lay sweating on their backs with the ceiling fan blowing down on them, panting. Their hands were locked together down by their sides and Shawn could feel her heart slamming in her chest. "Hey, feel this," she said, and pulled his hand up to her chest.

"I just did. If I recall correctly I did a lot more than feel it," Cory said smartly.

"Shush, you." She laid his hand on her heart and covered it with her own, then rolled her head to look him in the eyes. "Feel that?"

"Yeah. Of course. Mine's banging like a bass drum too."

"Uh huh. You feel my heart?"

Cory frowned. "Uh, yeah?"

"Good. Take care of this, Cory. It's completely and totally in your hands."

Shawn signed up for the motorcycle class that night. It would be two and a half weeks later, in the parking lot of the old mall on July twenty-ninth. She was excited and nervous, but more than all that, she was proud of herself for making the decision to do it. Those weeks and days would fly by like a kite in a whirlwind. July was not her favorite month down in Texas, she had decided. And everyone told her that if she didn't like the July weather, she may want to move back to Arkansas before August got here. 'You just think July is hot in Texas,' Cory had said. She couldn't wait to see that. *Ugh. Hotter than ninety-five at noon? Why does* anyone *live here?*

She spent the days at work doing new duties, just as Sameer had promised. They arranged the lab a little differently, where it would make a little more sense and be a little more practical. The table had to stay in the middle, for obvious reasons. But the circulator machine had always seemed to be in the way. When Sameer rolled the new one into the lab – yes, he'd had a backup just as Shawn had suspected – it had immediately come off the rolling post to be mounted on the underside of the table. It wasn't so much a precaution against having it pulled over by a suddenly-sitting cadaver, but just to get it out of the way. The massage-table-like hole in the head of the table allowed for the tubes to run up into the base of the subject's skull without having to worry about getting pinched or squeezed by the head. With the machine mounted on the shelf beneath the table top, the tubes could literally be completely hidden from their view. It was neat and tidy, and made for one less thing to get in the way on those little excursions around the lab.

Shawn also requested and was approved for a computer terminal to be installed on the back counter where there was a desk-type cutout. This place was perfect for putting one's legs under and made a comfortable workstation. Having a computer there would allow for her to make changes and commands on the nanobots without having to go back to her desk. It also allowed for a place from which she could play music. It had not taken twisting Sameer's arm to show him the benefits of having a little classical music playing at low volume during their interviews. When she hooked up some cheap, temporary speakers just to make her point, she was able to show him instantly that listening to one of Chopin's sonatas could bring a serenity to the atmosphere that was otherwise unattainable. He had nodded and said, yes, order some good speakers. She had.

When the speakers had arrived two days later, Shawn and Sameer wired them in and setup a new account on a streaming service just for the lab. Then they had begun listening to soft classical music almost constantly while they were at work in the dimly lit room. It now felt like a haven, or a massage parlor: nice peaceful music perfectly complemented the lighting.

The only thing missing were a couple of club chairs, but there just wasn't room for them. She had ordered a couple of stools that could roll about but that were more comfortable than the little doctor's throne she had been sitting on. They felt more like chairs. And she actually found Sameer sitting on his occasionally. The idea was that if they were more relaxed, maybe they would have better experiences to hand out to the waking dead.

During those two weeks at home, Shawn and Cory had actually begun talking about the possibility of sharing an apartment. She knew her daddy would not be proud to hear such talk, but he could be brought around. Shawn had a few more months on her lease, so they had until November to decide, but it was beginning to look like it might happen. It made sense, and she had basically been living with Cory already anyway. They spent every night together at one or the other's place. The only difference would be that they would be down to one apartment, dumping the mirror-image world and half their collective furniture. She didn't have much of her own. They could put her smaller television in the bedroom. Her couches were more comfortable than his but his bed was the better by far. All of these things would be talked about over the next couple of months in preparation for the Big Decision Day that would surely come, a week or so before her lease was up.

They joined the motorcycle group Saturday, the week before her class, on a long ride out past Weatherford, kick stands up at seven in the morning. Dahmer had mapped out a nice route with lots of twisty roads and even some minor hills – a rarity in North Texas. Cory, always reticent to take Shawn on a long ride on the Scout up to that point, had finally conceded after Shawn's basically begging him. The bike, he claimed, was just not built for long two-up rides. Her ass was sore by the end of the ride, proving him right in that regard, but the bike handled pretty well, and they had a good time. She agreed it was probably best not to do that again. A two-hour out-ride, breakfast at a little greasy spoon, then two hours back had just been too much – for both of them. Well, maybe next weekend, after her class, she would be ready to decide to buy her own bike.

When she awoke on the morning of the twenty-ninth, Shawn's eyes popped open and she realized she was already smiling. *I guess I'm more excited than I thought.* She sat up in the bed and looked over at Cory's still-sleeping frame, half buried in the cool sheets. They slept in mirrored positions as well. She was closest to the bathroom in each of their beds. But that was a different side of the bed at his place than at hers. So the sword-shaped light wedge that fell across his back went from the same shoulder to the same hip as it did in his place. Shawn spent way too long thinking about how this could be, on many mornings when she would just stay in bed sitting against the headboard and playing with his hair.

On this morning, she did not have the luxury of that extra time. She needed to be in the parking lot with her helmet and gloves by seven o'clock. She swung her legs out of bed and got started on her routine, skipping the coffee for fear that it might cause her undesirable bladder discomfort at a time when she would be trapped in a parking lot with no bathroom in sight. When she kissed Cory on the cheek and swept out of the apartment, she had thoughts of seeing two motorcycles instead of just one, sitting under the stairs together. This made her smile.

The Suzuki 250s they used in the class were small enough and light enough that she almost felt like she was sitting on a bicycle. Even still, she found her hands were trembling as she sat in a single-rank line with the other students. She could hear her own breathing inside the helmet. To treat herself, she had finally bought her own helmet. She bought a shiny white one with pink and purple flowers on it, and affixed a small orange monarch decal on the back left side. Flash Dance was crafting her a scripted font-face that read 'Shawnee' in silver letters, using her sticker-cutting machine.

Since Cory couldn't be here with her, Shawn was here alone with these strangers. The excitement still outweighed the nervousness, so she carried on. They would spend a couple of hours in the classroom this afternoon, but the instructor had opted for the course time first, before the sun got too hot. She glanced over at the mall, which would still get busy throughout the day, and realized just how far they were away from it, sitting on old faded parking spot stripes. The idea that this many thousands of parking spots would ever be used for a stupid mall was ludicrous. This line of students had to be a quarter-mile from the building.

They had not yet started the bikes. The instructor was easing them into the art of riding, one step at a time. It was a comfortable pace. *Baby steps.* They rolled forward and backward just a few inches, just feeling what it was like to use the handbrake, letting go of the clutch, finding neutral and standing over the bike, straddling it. Shawn was surprised by how easy it was to balance the thing between her thighs. She had worried that it would tump over very easily, being too heavy for her to manage. Well, it probably was too heavy to manage, but it also, she found, *wanted* to stand.

When they finally started the bikes, she was surprised again by how quiet they were. These weren't the rumbling lions that Cory's bike sounded like. These were kittens. Just enough to learn by, not enough to go crazy on. That was comforting to her. She wasn't ready for a lion. *Lions are brave. I am brave. I am a lion.*

The vibration came through comfortably in the handlebars. The worn rubber grips felt alive in her hands, and it translated to excitement as it shook her forearms. She glanced at her watch, just poking out the back edge of her glove, and saw that there was no way she could read the time while her hand was on the grip. It was a bouncy, vibrating mess of numbers.

During the first exercise, they were to keep their feet on the ground after finding first gear, then find the friction zone of the clutch handle, letting the motorcycle start creeping forward, then squeezing the handle back. All her intimidation about using the clutch quickly faded as she finally realized its backward-physics nature, and what it really did. She had always assumed it put the bike in gear, when it actually, literally, disconnected the drive from the gear. *Letting go* of the clutch handle made it go forward. Not the other way around. Understanding the mechanics helped her feel more confident in her abilities, and within a few minutes she felt ready for the next phase of the training.

It progressed evenly and steadily, easing the students into the next level of necessary knowledge with very little trepidation. Shawn didn't once feel out of control, or like she was handling a lion too big for her. Even if she never rode a motorcycle on the street with her hands on the controls, she would still benefit from the class, she realized. She could be a better rider on the back of Cory's bike. She would understand what he was doing up there. And – God forbid – if anything ever happened to him, she might even be able to drive his bike home with him riding the pillion. This made her smile.

And by the end of the first day, Shawn and all the other students were riding around an oval in the parking lot, shifting gears, stopping between cones and learning how to be bikers. And no one crashed. No one laid his bike down. There were several other women in the class, and they did just as well as some of the guys. Shawn had a whole new outlook on the motorcycle driver's life. It no longer looked mysterious and impossible. Like they were performing some kind of magic out there on the roads, staying balanced on a tight wire. This was actually a lot easier than she had ever imagined. And fun. It was really, really fun. By the time she walked to her Jeep, all smiles, with her helmet tucked under her arm, she was ready to say she wasn't just a little excited by it. She was addicted. She couldn't wait to get home and tell Cory all about it.

"I wanted to send you a selfie of me sitting on the bike, but the instructor basically told us that if anyone's phone came out while we were on the bikes, he'd flunk us right there and then," Shawn said when she was back home, sitting Indian-style on the couch and holding her helmet in her lap. She was wiping down the fingerprints and smudges off the visor.

"Yeah, well I'll let you take one on my bike," Cory said.

Shawn looked at him for a moment, trying to gauge his seriousness level, and the deeper meaning of his statement – if there was one. Her mouth hung open slightly as she stared.

"Yes, Shawn," he said, nodding, "I will let you ride my motorcycle. You've taken a class. You know what you're doing now."

Shawn covered her mouth with her hands, eyes widening. "Are you serious?"

"Of course I am." Cory reached out and took her hand, giving it a squeeze. "Shawn, it's just a bike. If you crash it, it's insured. It's not my life."

She was up off the couch, dropping the helmet on the floor and jumping onto his lap to smother him with kisses and hugs, all the while squealing like a little girl catching Santa Claus. Cory fought back this time though, tickling her under her rib cage and underarms until she was laughing and convulsing on the couch beside him, unable to breathe through the fit. "Okay, okay! Uncle Jeremiah! Calf rope!" she screamed, and finally rolled off his legs and onto the floor. When she sat up, hair a mess and face red from laughter, she said, "I don't know why I'm so excited. It's not like I'm going to actually go anywhere on your bike. That would leave you stranded here."

Cory shrugged. "Yeah, well it's just an option. You can roll up to the store. Whatever."

"Thank you, dear," she said, putting her hand on his knee. "I do want to see what a Scout feels like. How it handles. You know? To see if I really want to buy one."

"Absolutely," said Cory.

The next morning, she was back at the parking lot to finish up the course. They did their classroom portion after the riding, and she walked out with a triplicate square of paper saying she was certified to ride a motorcycle. A quick trip to the DMV during the week would get her the M stamp on her driver's license, and she would be totally official. She was amazed at how easy it was to get from there to here – in only a couple of days, for only a couple hundred dollars. Even if she never rode again, she was licensed to. More certifications, more licenses, more freedom.

She did ride Cory's bike. It was Sunday evening and she had the square paper in her back pocket. Cory had to talk her into it, but she didn't take a terrible lot of persuading. This was the next logical horse she needed to *get back on* to make sure she didn't lose that excitement. Controlling and driving a 250cc motorcycle was worlds different than a 1000cc bike. It would essentially be the same in practice: Cory told her how all the same articles applied. Everything she learned was valid, but it would feel different. It was heavier, for one, and a lot more responsive as well. If she 'goosed it' as Cory called it, giving it too much gas too fast in a high gear, she could be rocked off the bike backward. While it was not a sport bike, and wouldn't stand up on its back tire, the sudden forward momentum could definitely leave one sitting in a position while the bike went ahead and got on with its trip. Many a person had been too cocky or complacent in their grip on the handlebars and learned this the hard way, Cory told her.

But with this information in hand, she sat on his motorcycle with a healthy dose of fear and respect, while not sitting gingerly and afraid. She knew she had to be bold and confident, to trust herself. *I am a lion!* And when she dropped the bike into first gear with her left foot, looking at Cory through the plastic visor or her helmet with a huge grin on her face, she could feel the bike shift into something more alive. It *wanted* to move. She could feel the resistance against her right foot as it held down the rear brake pedal.

"Okay, wish me luck!" she said, her voice loud in her helmet.

Cory gave her a thumbs-up, then shouted, "Go get 'em, tiger."

"It's Lion!" she shouted. "I'm a fuckin' lion, baby!" And then she eased off the clutch. Feeling and hearing the roar of his bigger bike from this position on the front seat instead of where she had always been, was a totally different beast. And now, with her hands on the controls, she felt powerful. The vibration in her hands reminded her that she was in charge of this animal. It would bend to her will. And it felt amazing.

When she got to the end of the parking lot, switching on the right blinker and checking for traffic on Brown Boulevard, she took a deep breath. And then she gave it the proper throttle, easing off the clutch. A green light shone ahead of her, she so rolled on it, shifting into second and feeling the bike come alive. She laughed out loud at the amazing sensation. She'd been here before, many times, but clinging onto the back of her boyfriend. Never as pilot in command. And she'd been in command of those smaller bikes, but she had never left the parking lot training course. This was so wildly different. The excitement knocked over her giggle box and she couldn't stop smiling and laughing as she rode.

More gas, up into third gear, and then into fourth – yes, she was instantly sure she would be getting her own bike. This was too amazing – too liberating. For the last five years of owning a Jeep, taking the doors and the top off of it every chance she got, she had come to think of that as being free on the road. Well, that Jeep was as close to one could get to this while still 'caging it'. But it was *not* this. It was markedly different than *this*.

She didn't take it on the highway – she wasn't quite ready for that – but she did use the feeder road and got it up into fourth gear, up in the high forties. The sound of the wind and the feel and look of the pavement around her made her laugh again. "Holy hell!" she said aloud to herself. "How have I gone my entire adult life without this?"

The turns felt natural. The curves felt even better. Cory had told her about counter-steering, and she got to exercise a bit of that on some of the long sweeping curves along the highway's access road. It felt so wonderful, so *right* that her excitement for riding was suddenly and instantly replaced with a readiness to get home. She suddenly needed to get back to the apartment; to tell Cory she was ready to buy her own, and to get online and start shopping for the right Indian. She would also have to get on the phone with Lo and do a little screaming, a little bouncing up and down and a lot of smiling.

When she got back to the apartment, that's exactly what she did. Her phone call with Lo wasn't as exciting as she had hoped. Lo just didn't share the same desire to get her own bike. Shawn would have to work on that. They stayed on the phone for a long time, both looking at the same pages on their laptops, pointing at this one or that. It didn't take Shawn long to find the one she wanted. The matte white Chief model was perfect in every way. And when she saw that she could actually afford it easily, she thought, 'Why the hell not?' and special-ordered her very own. She got to customize things like the wheels, the mirrors and hand grips, and the color combination and material of the seat. The

Chief was a little bit bigger bike than Cory's, but he told her the difference in handling them would be nominal.

Since it was a custom order, the company would have to build the motorcycle, then ship it to the dealer nearest her. Meanwhile, she could concentrate on getting the rest of her gear and buying some new clothes to fit her new image. Lo laughed out loud at her when Shawn told her she planned to develop an image. But it wasn't a laugh of mockery. She said, 'Of course you will!' and actually cheered her on. 'Let's go after work tomorrow and look at clothes!' Lo said.

"I don't plan on changing my whole wardrobe, of course. But when we go riding, I want to fit in."

So the next day after work, they went to the mall and filled several bags with new riding-style clothing for Shawn, including some knee-high black boots that she thought looked tough as well as sexy. She couldn't wait to get home and show them to Cory, and maybe see if he would let her ride his bike again – wearing her new getup. Lo even got into the spirit a little, allowing that it would make sense for her to step up her game a little bit – even just for riding with Heath – since she would now be the only girlfriend in the group who still looked like a librarian in a hardware store.

Shawn asked her what the story was with Heath – was he in or out? - and Lo told her she was having the worst bout of indecision in her life about it. She really liked him, but would have to accept the fact that motorcycle riding was basically his whole life. When he wasn't working or riding, he was usually in the garage working on one of his bikes, breaking something down, tuning something up or just wiping them down while he listened to loud music and drank beer. Like, that was it. Not much in the way of variety with the boy.

"I feel ya," Shawn said as they walked back to Lo's car. "I think that could get boring, unless you're as into it as he is. That's the only way I could see something like that working, long-term. But I'm glad you're getting some new duds! That means you'll at least be doing a *few* more rides with us, right?"

"Us?" Lo said, turning and slapping her shoulder. "Look at you, all acting like you're a lifetime member now!"

Shawn shrugged and smiled, closing her eyes. "Hey, I'm getting a bike, so I had better start calling it my group."

"Yeah, I guess you'll get upgraded now from just a ride-along ho."

They both laughed out loud at that.

Tuesday was the first day of August. Shawn got to the office a little early and found Sameer in the lab, sitting on one of the stools with his legs up under the Death Bed. It looked as if he were working on an imaginary subject, except that he was staring at his phone. Shawn came in smiling and frowning at the same time as she dropped her purse on the counter. "What'ya doing?" she asked.

He looked up at her. "Good morning, Shawn. I am looking at two possible new subjects. We have the opportunity for one of them next Monday if we are wanting, but the subject is over a hundred years old."

Shawn made a face. "Yeah? Who's the other one?"

"A child."

Shawn closed her eyes and tilted her head back as if to stare at the ceiling. "Oh, God, Sameer. Can we please *not* go there?" She returned her gaze to him. Her arms were down by her side, shoulders slumped and looking generally like she had just been asked to go dig through the garbage bin looking for an earring back.

"You have an aversion to working with children, Shawn?"

She widened her eyes and tilted her head. "Yes, Sameer! YES! Good Lord! That's where I draw the line," she said. "I would rather have the centenarian than a child!"

"Yes, I am agreeing, Shawn. But I am not sure how much there is to be gained with someone so old."

Shawn shook her head. "Yeah! So… Can we pass on both of them?" she asked, holding her hands out.

After a long stare, Sameer finally furled his mouth and sighed. "Yes," he said, nodding. "I suppose that might be the best option. I am just anxious to get someone new in here since we did all this redecorating."

"I understand," Shawn said, joining him at the head of the table, pulling up her own stool opposite his. "That'll come. We don't need to rush it. If it means lowering our bar to accept children – who I *also* don't think we could learn much from – or a very old person, then, well…" she trailed off.

He was still nodding, looking down at the table. "Okay. Well, then we must find some other things to do to keep us busy."

Shawn laid her hands down on the cold metal table and looked him in the eyes. "I've been thinking about this. I think we should gather the data from all our four subjects and compare everything we know. We should build a database of sorts, where we list out certain attributes – like the amount of time we had them up, what caused them to crash, stuff like that. I think data is beautiful."

Sameer's eyes got wide and he nodded slowly, then pointed at her. "Yes. This is a fantastic idea, Shawn."

"I think we should also – or, rather, I should also – transcribe all the tapes of the interviews. I've really been thinking about that. Having a transcript of everything that happened and what was said could prove to be valuable. Cross-referencing and looking up things by keyword, you know. All the reasons one would ever do that." She drummed her hands softly on the table, then clasped her hands together and dropped them into her lap.

"I am liking the way you are thinking. And that will take some fair amount of time. How long do you think it will take you to do all four tapes?" Sameer asked.

"Probably a few hours. Maybe half a day. If I get started now, I might be done by lunchtime."

"Okay, good. Then you do that, and I will start making notations of important events so that we can use them for reference. Good thinking, Shawn. I knew there was a good reason you were the Director of the Dead."

"Oh, I've outgrown that title, Sameer. You can call me Queen of the Dead."

# Thirteen

The journal sat on her ottoman like an art decoration or a coffee-table book. It looked like something fine and expensive one would show to her friends, its beautiful worn leather cover wrapped with a leather lace and parchment that looked old and substantial. It had sat there for what felt like so long now that Shawn had just about stopped noticing it. Cory had left for a job this morning, so Shawn had an evening to herself. And tonight she did notice the journal as she sat on the couch, curling her legs up behind her. The fire she had possessed several weeks ago to dive back into the *Dexter* series had all but gone out. So now she sat with a drink in one hand and her other twirling locks of her hair, her elbow up on the back of the couch as she stared out the window.

Maybe she had also lost some of the passion she had felt for Miranda's cause. Shawn had been so caught up in the motorcycle class and the excitement about getting one that she had almost forgotten to care about the dead woman. Her face was fading in Shawn's memory, and soon, she knew, it would be gone. She was sad about that. She wished she at least had a picture or something to remember her by. With all other chores done and no other excuses, Shawn was in her pajamas and ready for those few hours she got in the evenings that could belong to whatever craft or care she allotted them for. So why not read a little?

The second page was of the same neat penmanship, almost written like a type face. Shawn ran her fingertips down the words and lines, touching the long-dried ink with something like awe. She had a hard time even making her hand legible. She had never gotten good at cursive, so everything she wrote was in print, and usually of the all-caps variety. To see someone who clearly enjoyed the writing part of it enough to make it this pretty was something worthy of respect. Maybe that's what Miranda did: she sat at her table, or on her sofa in much the same way Shawn herself does, just writing. Taking her time and making it beautiful. Like an art piece.

2/2 Hello diary! This morning on the phone with Linus I started crying uncontrollably. I know he understands but it's still so hard. I don't want all our conversations to be flooded with all these tears. I can't wait just to go. And today is sposed to be a happy day!!!

I'm on the plane now and I got a window seat. So at least there's that. Leaving out of Dallas it looks so different than landing in Edinburgh. I can't wait until the trips can be over. Even though I like it better there, I'm ready for Linus to be here! Here full time!

So I started thinking today while I was standing in line at the airport security thing. I've given a lot of thought to this great filter thing. I'm very interested about it. And the curious thing about or maybe I should say the most curious thing about it is that we won't know until its too late. See, if we can't make it to be a class 2 civilization or at least be space fairing, then we probably won't know. It takes a massive amount of energy to sustain the planet at that point, and when you have that much power, you can misuse it pretty easy. We will either blow ourself up with a ~~nuclear~~ nuclear bomb or we will make it.

This is scary to me because I know world peace isn't a realistic scenario. But if there is other alien life forms out there, ~~are~~ do they have world peace? Or is their planet always full of wars like ours is? My thought is that we haven't made it to the filter yet and are probably on our last few decades before we blow it all to hell. And we might never find another place to go. Fermi was right. Where is our Scotland?

Scotland. Shawn looked up at the wall, thinking about that word. Clearly, Miranda had made an analogy between a new planet and Scotland. But in the beginning of the entry she had talked about Linus coming here. Shawn had heard about the Great Filter, but had never given it much thought. Space was too big for her little brain. She liked to stay a little more grounded than that. What was Fermi right about? Who was Fermi? The name almost rang a bell, but Shawn was in unfamiliar territory here.

*Where is our Scotland?* She read that line again. It held quite a bit of power in her mind. Clearly, Miranda thought of Scotland as a place of refuge. Mankind's last hope, to broaden the analogy. But why, then, would she rather stay here, having Linus join her here than to stay there?

Obviously, there was too much that Shawn didn't – that she *couldn't* – know. Maybe she was getting hung up in all the little details, down in the weeds, when she should be focused on the sunset instead. Reading someone else's diary, especially a stranger's, was sure to be filled with pitfalls. But Shawn did want to know more. She wanted to know more of the girl as well as the things she had written about.

The next page looked as though it could have been from another book entirely.

2/3 Well, I'm here. Linus isn't talking to me. You never know what you're going to get, right? Life is like a box of shitty chocolates. Half of them are sour and the other half have been nibbled on. Anyways, I'm sure he'll come around. I spent most of the morning crying again. Maybe that's why he's avoiding me.

On the train this morning we stood in silence as a whole car. The whole car was silent like the world trade centers just got hit again. It was very somber. Everyone was down in just this solitude. What the fuck is going on with this world? Why can't everyone be happy for once?

I saw a little girl on the train, holding onto her mama's coat tail with her little bitty fist. Her head was bundled up in a toboggan and her red hair was poking out the bottom. She had a snow white face and little pink cheeks so cute. I smiled and waved at her but she was just staring up at me like she didn't know what was next. What is next in her world? In her life? Is this her everyday? I finally stopped smiling and just looked away. Linus was on his phone the *whole time. I just want to get away. Not from here. But from this. Where's my Scotland?*

Shawn closed the book and tied the leather lace back around it. She let out a sigh and leaned back, stretching her arms above her head. *Where's my Scotland?* What does that mean? The girl was – well, presumably – in Scotland already when she wrote that page. Linus had let her down somehow. Another day full of tears. And Scotland had not turned out to be the land of reprieve. The lost world of rescue and happiness she had hoped for.

Shawn stood up and went into the kitchen to make herself some dinner. That phrase would stay with her for a while. Clearly, this woman had thought of Scotland as some magical place where all was right with the world. Like they had it figured out over there. People had somehow found a way to beat the misery and depression and darkness of the world. And those who had, fled to Scotland to celebrate. Well, maybe she was right about that. They just weren't in Edinburgh.

She took a party pizza out of the freezer and ripped open the wrapper, tossed it on a cookie sheet. Who the hell makes cookies anymore? It should be called a pizza sheet. "Where's my cookies?" Shawn said aloud. Maybe that's what she needed in her life: the smell of fresh-baked cookies filling the apartment. A stack of soft chocolate chippers piled high on a glass platter up on her bar to nibble on over the next few days. Inevitably she would wake up to pee in the middle of the night and be reminded of them though. When that happened she would stand there and make herself sick on them.

OuterCirle was the same bullshit, different day. Oh, look, someone's best friend got married and you got suckered into being a bridesmaid! Congratulations, Katy, on being the proud owner of a teal dress you'll never wear again. I bet *this* wedding was different though. Probably a whole different set of pictures. And maybe the bride wore black for it. Shawn rolled her eyes and slid the pizza tray into the oven, then closed it and set the timer for thirteen minutes. Her frozen meal was now traveling through time to the future, where she would meet it again after it had softened, cooked, become more mature. Turned into something actually almost worthy of eating.

She went into the living room with her phone in her hand, scrolling a few more posts on the Circle. Oh, look, Anthony got a new pupper. Cute. Congratulations on getting something that will destroy your heart in fifteen years when it's too old to process its food by itself anymore, and you'll have to put it down. Where is *his* Scotland? Well, maybe Anthony's is right here, right now. But that poor dog has no idea what its future holds.

Shawn couldn't quite put her finger on the drab melancholy she was feeling. Surely it wasn't because Cory was gone for the night. She did still enjoy those breaks. They were not exciting, but necessary no less. And they did always make her happy to see him again. *There can be no reunion without a separation.* Maybe it was the alcohol. Her dad had always told her that it sneaked up on you. After a few days of drinking, the first day's alcohol was turning to depression in the blood. It wasn't that she drank a lot, but she drank *often*. So there was always depression lurking somewhere inside her, at least if she were to buy into her daddy's thoughts about it.

She pulled her SMS app up and sent a quick text to Lo.

```
Hey beautiful. Thinking about you.
Maybe we should hang out after work
tomorrow. What say you, Queen
Butterfly?
```

Tomorrow was Wednesday. Nothing special going on at work, but she would have to run a bunch of reports for one of her clients. Shawn loved the beauty of a perfectly formatted spreadsheet. She loved the data entry, the organizing and sorting and color-coding and formulas. The only thing she didn't love was doing it for a customer. Manipulating data was fun. But only if the data were fun, too. She had put her dad's record collection into a spreadsheet before just for fun. She gave it to him as a birthday gift a few years ago and he had loved it. She had shown him how to click on a certain column and organize by Artist, or another by Release Year. *That* had been a fun project. But exporting code-change logs and web statistics was boring shit.

Her phone dinged.

> I say you have predicted a lovely future for us. We shall eat, drink and be merry.

Shawn smiled at that and fired off a reply to the effect that it was good as chiseled in stone. Then she tossed her phone on the couch, turned on her sound bar and started a playlist based on The Cranberries and poured herself a cranberry vodka to match the mood. The pizza finished and she pulled it out of the oven with lackluster excitement. Excited to be eating, disappointed by the finished product. Apartment living at its finest. What movie had it been where someone had said, 'Pizza is like sex: even when it's bad, it's still pretty good.'? Well, that's how she felt about it. Even the worst frozen square of cheap crap cheese pizza she had ever had was still decent. Especially when she decorated it with onions and olives.

She took her shitty pizza to the couch and sat with her legs curled underneath her again, and picked up one of the rectangles of greasy whatever-the-hell it was and lifted it to her mouth as she looked out the back door. "Son of a goose. You dumb stupid goofball!" she said, standing up and dropping the plate on the ottoman. The monarch was back, fluttering around in the same corner as the spider liked to hang out. Always the same corner. *What's wrong with the opposite corner?*

The door squealed as she slid it open, wondering whether this was truly the same butterfly that had visited her – what? Four times now? Well, she would at least be able to verify by virtue of a now missing leg. She stood under the web with her hands on her hips and waited for it to come down. It had not yet trapped itself in the web but the spider was ready for it. "Come on, butt head," she said. And the butterfly lit on her head. She walked to the edge of the balcony and leaned on the rail. "If you want to come visit me, all you gotta do is land on the window! Just stay away from that corner!"

The monarch finally came around and landed on her chest where she could see it. Shawn pinched its wings together and turned it over. Sure enough, it only had five legs. The missing one had a thick blob in place of where the leg used to be. Same butterfly. She shook her head, then set it on the back of her left wrist. It sat there for a long time, slowly moving its wings up and down. What was it trying to say? She held her wrist up and got real close to it, looking into its weird alien eyes. *Are you trying to tell me something, sweet friend? You keep coming back here risking life and limb just to visit me.* Out of all the apartments in the complex, somehow this butterfly kept coming back to hers. Maybe it was her spirit animal. Or her animal spirit. After a moment, it lifted off and flew away.

Shawn waved goodbye, then turned back to the open doorway. "Oh, yeah," she said, spotting the rectangular quarters of culinary delight on her ottoman. She slid the door closed and plopped onto the couch to dig in.

Alarms were going off in the building. Everyone from all floors was gathered outside in the visitors' parking lot. She had no trouble finding her group after she parked. They all stood together in the grass beneath a tree looking like an advertisement for all the different ways one could stand. Sameer with his hands clasped behind his back, Jeremy with his arms crossed and Chandra with hers clasped in front of her. Shawn walked up with her hands on her hips to complete the picture. "What's going on?" she asked.

"They said it's a problem with the fire suppression system," Chandra said. "Could be resolved in five minutes, or it might be several hours."

"Alarm has been going on and off for hours, apparently," added Jeremy.

Shawn frowned at that. "Really? You've been here for hours, Iron Man?"

Jeremy nodded, smiling widely. Sameer looked puzzled. "What is this Iron Man meaning?" he said.

"I think it's a nod to my shirt," said Jeremy. His shirt looked as though he had wadded it up wet and put rubber bands around it until it dried. And then put it on, without ever once considering an iron.

Sameer, after looking at Jeremy's shirt, lifted his chin and then went on about ignoring it. "It is nice out here this morning, so we may wait here."

"It's so loud in there you can't hear yourself think," said Chandra, leaning in and touching Shawn's arm. "Just when you think it's over, a five-minute silence, and BAM, it's back on."

"Why don't we all go get a drink or something?" Shawn asked.

Sameer frowned, then released one of his hands from its grip behind him, and looked at his watch. Shortly, he returned to his original posture. "You are wanting to drink at eight-oh-seven in the morning, Shawn?"

"Well, I guess not, since you said it like that… But it's always a good time for a bloody Mary."

This bought her a vacant stare from the man. "Okay, yeah. Never mind. What about you, Chandra? Do you like bloody Marys?"

"Darling, I can drink a bloody Mary before, during and after breakfast."

"See?" Shawn said, smiling. "That's my kind of girl. We should hang out, Chandra."

"Well, yes, we should," agreed Chandra, bowing her head slightly.

When the alarms finally fell silent, they had been standing outside for nearly forty minutes. Shawn could feel sweat forming on her lower back. It had warmed up considerably in the last half-hour, almost as if to make a fool of Sameer. An announcement flooded the courtyard and the parking lot, telling the tenants that they could safely return to the building, and that they were sorry for the delay.

The crowd made their way toward the front entrance of the building but Chandra stayed back. Shawn stopped and turned, ready to ask what was up, but stopped herself, realizing the idiocy of what she was about to ask in the face of the scenario as it presented itself. They could either wait where they were, under the shade of the elm tree, or wait at the back of the line in the sun. Either way, they would still wait the same amount of time as the entire world went through two elevator cars, twelve people at a time. They would be out here another twenty minutes waiting their turn anyway. Shawn held up a finger and raised her eyebrows, nodded. "Good call, smart woman," she said and Chandra bowed her head again.


At her desk, Shawn dug into her reports, grinding out the work she disliked so she could get done with it and get back to the work she *did* like, which was to transcribe the rest of the interviews. She had only gotten done with the first yesterday, having to rewind and replay a lot of it, as a great deal of it was muffled. And instead of starting on the second one, she decided to put it off until today. Perhaps the real reason for putting off starting the second was because it was Miranda's case. Shawn knew that once she started Miranda's, she wouldn't be able to stop until it was done. She knew a lot of the interview by heart. Having asked

Sameer to send her that recording, she had listened to it several times in the last month.

It only took two-and-a-half hours to finish generating the reports for her needy client. When she wrapped it up and sent it off in an encrypted email, she closed all the windows on her computer and started with a fresh slate. She went in to the break room to get new coffee and stopped by the restroom to trade in the used.

Shawn opened the file of the recording and a word processor window and took a deep breath, clearing her mind. She slipped her headphones on and connected them, then pressed play and started typing. She tried to capture the atmosphere of the room rather than just the words spoken. This included things she had seen, expressions made on faces – both live and dead – and any other things she could remember from the event. She was glad to be working on this now and not a month from now, when the memories might not be as fresh in her mind.

She got two minutes into the recording when her phone screen lit up. She would typically ignore it, but it was a text from Sameer. Rolling her eyes and sighing, she paused the playback and removed her earphones, picking up her phone. All it said was to come see him, please. She scooted back from her chair and went to his office. Sameer was sitting behind his desk, leaning forward with his arms on his knees, his phone between them. He looked up when she entered and said, "Hello, Shawn."

"Hi," she said, trying not to be contrary. She waved, then put her hands in her pockets.

"We can have another subject here Monday."

"Okay, great!" she said, trying to sound enthusiastic. She might never get the hang of these heads-ups. She always seemed to grow more comfortable in the lab as each morning progressed with a new subject, but that initial shock of hearing there was another incoming still had the ability to make her insides flinch just a little.

"Well, there is one problem. He is a twenty-nine-year-old Hispanic man and he does not speak English."

Shawn rolled her eyes as well as her head, shrugging her shoulders in exasperation. "Then why are we even talking about this?"

"Do you think we cannot learn anything from them without communication?"

Shawn stared at him levelly. At first, she thought he was being rhetorical. But his look never faltered. And that realization – that he was actually serious – gave her a sudden flash of inspiration: an idea. She nodded, raising her eyebrows. "Actually, that's a good point, Sameer. I mean, it depends on what type of test you're doing, but I would like to see if the brain truly does 'understand all languages'."

"What do you mean by that?"

"Innately, our brains are supposed to possess the capability to understand every language, as a fundamental instruction code."

Sameer nodded, then said, "This is an interesting concept. So you are wanting me to request the body?"

She shrugged. "Sure. I mean, it can't hurt." She stared at him for a moment. "So, Monday then?"

"Well, yes," he said, nodding. "I have to be here Sunday to accept the delivery. I will start the blood circulation. And then Monday we will be ready."

"I think," Shawn started, and the alarms blasted to life. It sounded louder than the coming apocalypse and scared Shawn just about out of her skin. She cowered, instinctively ducking down and spreading her arms and looking, wide-eyed, up at the speaker whence it was blaring. "Dear Christ!" she said aloud, but was barely audible over the roar of the klaxon.

Sameer was shaking his head, disappointed and put off. He stood up from his chair and waved her out of the room. "Go!" he shouted. "It is quieter out there. Tell everyone to go home. This is senseless."

Shawn was able to finish the task at home on her laptop, and was happy to do so. She had really taken an interest in seeing this through – cataloging everything that had happened in that lab – to see if it returned anything interesting. And depending on how many subjects they ended up interviewing successfully, they might be able to find a pattern or a 'switch' that had unwittingly been thrown in each one that sent the subject to that unreachable other side once and for all.

She had called Jeremy on her way home and told him she was cross-referencing time stamps from the proper spot on the recording to what happened in the lab at that moment, as best she could. She asked him if he could disable – temporarily at least – the kick dot bat routine; she wanted him to, at the very least, hide it from her selection menu, so as to not accidentally select it for future use. Sameer had already tasked Jeremy with digging through that code with a fine-tooth comb to see if anything stood out that might be problematic. Jeremy had done so twice and reported nothing abnormal. It might just be that the part of the brain responsible for that jolt-awake response just wasn't meant to be messed with. At least not in a lab postmortem.

He had agreed to put a REM symbol in front of the lines of code so that it wouldn't show up in her interface. Shawn was scared to death of that function, and didn't ever want to see it again. Now she sat in her living room with her feet up on the ottoman and the laptop on her lap desk, banging away the words as they came through her headphones. She had initially sat in her normal spot – the one on the wall adjacent and perpendicular to the sliding glass door – but she had moved quickly to the spot Cory usually inhabited. There had been a glare from the window she could not get away from. So now, she sat facing the sliding door, and could look up whenever she wanted and see the sky. Or to subconsciously check and see if her winged friend was back, getting caught in a web again. A Dream Theater song came to mind and Shawn chuckled. Everything in life could come down to a line in a song. Some people did that with movie quotes. She liked it more with music.

As she typed and listened, pausing occasionally to add side notes and references, bracketed statements about the barometer of the room, she got lost in the work and became that robot that got lots of shit done. She was so focused that at first she didn't see the ghost in her monitor. The screen of the laptop, naturally dipping and rising with the tiny movements of her fingers on the keyboard, had a way of hiding things reflected unless one were looking directly at it. And knowing it was there. On a particular mistake she had made, Shawn frowned and leaned her head in closer to the screen, wondering why an entire sentence had just disappeared. As she stared at the screen, the white spot on the right moved, even though her hands hadn't. It finally caught her attention. Then the lights went out, and quickly back on. She looked up at the ceiling and ripped off her headphones, turning quickly as she saw a flash of movement over her right shoulder.

Shawn leapt out of the seat screaming and raising her hands in a defensive maneuver. Her laptop crashed onto the couch and then fell to the floor between the seat and the ottoman. It was Lo, standing by the front door with her fingers on the light switch.

"Oh my fucking grief, Lo! Holy shit, you scared the life out of me!" she shouted, her hand covering her heart.

"I'm sorry, darlin'. I didn't know how else to get your attention. I thought flipping the light on and off was a good idea."

Shawn looked back up at the light again. "It was. Maybe try knocking next time?"

Lo nodded, pulling her lips in like a mother trying to keep her patience. "Tried that."

"Uh, maybe text me?" Shawn said, looking around for her phone. There it was, buried in the cushion next to where the seat was still warm. She picked it up and wagged it at Lo for effect.

Lo nodded more dramatically. "Tried that, too."

Shawn stood there breathing for a long moment. Then she frowned and looked at her phone. Unlocked it. Sure enough, three unread texts from Lo. "Well fuck me sideways then. Carry on, soldier."

"Sorry, babe," Lo said, finally coming into the room. She slung her purse onto the bar stool and came around the end of the couch to join her in the living room.

"Oh, it's okay. I was just really focused. Had the recording up loud and trying to concentrate on this shit," Shawn said, bending over to pick up the laptop, which had managed to close itself in the fall. She dropped it onto the seat beside her spot and dropped down onto her legs. "Have a seat. What's up, sugar cane?"

Lo stood at the backdoor, staring out at the other building, hands on her hips. She wasn't talking a hundred miles a minute. She wasn't facing Shawn. Lo hadn't even hugged her when she came in. Something must be...

"Oh, no," Shawn said, sitting up straight. She had one hand over her mouth and her eyes were wide as rivers. "No, Lo, are you okay?"

"Yeah, I am," she said. She turned around and Shawn saw the tears in her eyes. The tears in spite of the weak smile.

"What happened?" Shawn asked, and was up on her feet again, taking Lo by the shoulders. "I'm so sorry, baby. Oh my God!"

Lo was looking at her funny. Shaking her head. It was a look that read *'how could you?'*

Shawn straightened up. "What? What is it? Why are you..."

Lo raised her left hand in front of her face, fingers spread and a smile spreading faster. Shawn shook her quickly, still staring at her face through the fingers. Shook her again, feeling scared and unsure what the hell was happening. Then the fingers wiggled. Shawn focused on them. Then she said, "Oh, my God. Oh, my GOD!" and she was suddenly squealing and hugging her friend and they were laughing together.

"Oh, my," she said again, letting go of Lo and dashing to the kitchen. "We have to have a drink to celebrate! Tell me all about it!"

Lo finally found her seat and began playing with her hair as she spoke, a smile finding its way onto her pretty face and remaining this time. "Well, I got home from work and Heath's motorcycle was out front. He was sitting on my stairs."

"Uh huh?" Shawn said, pulling down glasses and dropping ice into them. "Go on, I'm listening."

"He looked up at me and said, 'I think it's time we had a talk.' and I said, 'Okay, what did I do wrong?' and he said, 'I just need to ask you one question.' and I was like, 'what would that be?' and I was getting scared, of course. But I thought if it was going to end, it would be me who ended it. Not this way. This was too weird, for him to make a trip over to my apartment and wait on me to get home. Like, why do all that waiting?"

"Uh huh," Shawn said. She poured the vodka in on top of the cran juice and then stirred both glasses simultaneously with a fingertip from each hand. Then she picked them up and carried them to the sofa. They clinked them together before she dropped onto her rump, taking a sip.

"Anyway, you know what the question was. I know, it's not the most romantic thing in the world. He has almost zero romance about him at all. But it was sweet, and his heart was in the right place."

Shawn was smiling ear-to-ear again. She had one hand over her heart. "And the rock is fucking beautiful, oh my God!"

Lo held it up again, smiling down at it as she wiggled her fingers in ladylike appreciation. "Isn't it? I can't believe it myself: just the other day I was thinking of dumping him, and now, here I am engaged to the poor bastard."

Shawn laughed, covering her mouth to keep from spraying vodka. "Right? Well, he's a good guy – you said so."

"He is," Lo said, nodding. "It could have been more romantic, but…" she said, trailing off. She shrugged. *Oh well, engaged is engaged.*

"There is more than one way to get to the same place," Shawn said in agreement with that shrug. Silently, she wondered how Cory would propose to her – if and when that were ever in the cards for them. He seemed to be somewhat romantic. At least more romantic than saying 'We need to talk'. Dear Christ. Poor Lo!

Lo took a long but slow sip of her drink, then licked her lips. "This is good. Thank you, sister."

Shawn nodded, smiling her same pleasant smile. She was just happy Lo had come over to share the news with her.

"Can you imagine? Laura Carter Brennan? That sounds so foreign to me."

"Yeah, but it has a nice ring to it. If I ever get proposed to, I'll be Shawn Klein. Marcella Klein to my parents," Shawn said. She giggled.

"Well that's a funny way to say it. I guess even funnier is that you think he's the only one who could ever propose to you."

"Well he's the only horse in the running right now," Shawn said, taking another drink and almost having to spit it out again when Lo burst out laughing. Her laughter was contagious.

"Here we be, fair ladies, true and beautiful. And we are constantly in a 'running' in our lives!" said Lo, and the laughter spread thicker.

It only took them twenty minutes of sitting there talking and laughing before Lo finally realized that the object upon which her hand had been resting for almost the entirety of her visit – her fingernails lightly marring the leather and feeling its wonderful texture – was the journal of the dead girl named Miranda Struck. And when she did notice, her face lost its shine. She muttered a simple 'Oh…' and rubbed her fingertips across the front of it a little more attentively. She looked up at Shawn, then shook her head. "Have you read it yet?"

"Parts, yeah. I started at the beginning, of course. I've only read a few pages."

Lo brought up the journal, turning it over in her hand, admiring it like an old relic, nothing but respect in her motions. She shook her head. "Poor girl. Never got to see marriage."

Shawn raised her eyebrows. "Yeah, I guess not. There's a guy she mentions in there named Linus. But I haven't figured out if they're boyfriend and girlfriend yet, or engaged, married, whatever. Who knows? I hope it tells me at some point."

"Que Sera, Sera," said Lo and set the journal back on the foot cushion, then patted it gently. "The future is yours to see."

"Well, it wasn't earlier when I was dug in," Shawn said, shaking her head. "To be honest, I completely forgot we were getting together this evening. Speaking of which, what the fuck are you doing here, anyway? Shouldn't you be with your new fiance?"

"Hey, a date's a date," said Lo. "Now are you going to feed me something, or do I need to go forage in the woods?"

They ordered in from a local restaurant that delivered hot seafood, and sat on the couch watching Seinfeld episodes and laughing while they ate and drank. And they were merry as well.

That night in bed, she lay on top of Cory, her head on her crossed arms while he stroked her back. She told him how Lo had gotten engaged and he had said he knew about it from Heath. Unfortunately, she could not read into the tone of his response. She wondered whether he would catch the bug or not. Or if he was even that far into his love for her. Shawn had no doubt that she was more in love with him than he was with her. And that was fine. But she wouldn't mind taking his temperature. Was he close? Closing in? Was it even a realistic scenario, or was he one of those guys who would never ask her? Or anyone? Such thoughts only made it worse. There was no answer until he asked the question. She would just have to hope and be patient.

Shawn thought about what she had just thought about. Was she actually lying here thinking she was ready for Cory to propose to her? Was she really ready for that step? She might just be having a little friendly jealousy, wondering when hers would happen. But she did have to admit, she wasn't turned off by the idea. She knew, no question about it, that if he *were* to ask, she would definitely say yes. But whether or not she needed to be asked yet, well, that was another question.

They lay there in the dark for several hours, just talking, laughing and loving on each other. And when it started raining, Shawn bounced up off the bed, saying, 'Ooh, ooh, ooh!' and ran to open the windows. And then she had to stay up even later just to listen to the peaceful pounding of the thunder and the soft patter on the grass and trees below. And just like that, Shawn became Cory. "God, boy, you got me staying up late and wanting to sleep in. You're going to be the death of me."

Shawn set an alarm on her phone that night just to be safe, and was glad she did when it went off at six o'clock. She had been sleeping hard, snoring and drooling onto her pillow. There was no telling when she would have awakened had she not set the net beneath her tightrope. And with somewhere around three hours of sleep, she was sure to be full of yawns and coffee by noon at work.

"What have you done to me, Cory?" she said as she sat up and put her feet on the carpet. She went to his bathroom and closed the door as quietly as she could manage, then stood in a shower so hot it made her skin red.

The last two days of the work week dragged by like a legless man in the desert. She had lost her circadian rhythm and had begun sleeping right up to her alarm, being jolted awake, and was unhappy to call it normal. Her own kick dot bat routine, injected into her veins through the air between her phone and her ear. She had to stop this shit and get back onto her normal sleep cycle. This was not how she lived her best life.

So when Saturday morning finally arrived, she got up at seven – again by alarm – and forced herself to stay up all day, no napping allowed, so she could reset her system Sunday morning. She had decided she would go in and help Sameer with the intake of the next subject, not only because she felt bad for him – though that was the bulk of it – but also because she was interested in how it worked. She felt like if she were going to be the moderator of this experimental work, she should invest more of herself into more of the small details she typically ignored.

Sameer was glad to receive her text that day, and responded that he would be happy to show her how it happened. Throughout the morning she would find herself wondering what it would be like taking in a new body. Would it be in a body bag? Would it be naked already, or still dressed from the funeral? It? Should she even be calling it an 'it'? Or should she be using its gender? Gah. No need to be politic. It was only she and Sameer and the small team who ever discussed these subjects.

Shawn putted around the apartment most of the day, cleaning and straightening, dusting and going through junk she'd had stacked on the edge of her desk for far too long. She made a stack of these items and ran it through the scanner where it sent PDF files to her email for electronic filing later. Cory was on a ride with the motorcycle group even though it had rained heavily for most of the last few nights, so she had the apartment to herself all day. She moved about in her underwear and a t-shirt, dancing and singing to the music on the sound bar. She also occasionally sipped from the last couple of beer bottles she had bought for her dad. She had drained a couple of them the day her parents had left. She reckoned she would have no problem polishing the rest of them off by the end of the evening.

Cory got back from his ride after five o'clock, and popped in after he had cleaned up and made some dinner. And for all her efforts, getting up early and forcing herself to be busy all day so she could sleep well tonight, she still lay awake until after one o'clock, just counting the sheep of the next day's work. She was sure it wouldn't take any more than a couple of hours to get the body checked in and prepped for Monday's interview, but it still consumed her thoughts. She wondered how the body would be delivered. A hearse? At least Cory lay sleeping next to her, so while she lay against the headboard staring at the ceiling fan she had hair through which to run her fingers.

Even though they had to wait until after the funeral to receive the body, Shawn awoke at six o'clock and got ready for her day. She sat at the breakfast table with her coffee and looking at her phone. She scrolled through a couple of news sites and checked her Instagram feed. While she scrolled through the feed, her phone rang and a huge smile lit up her face.

"Hey, daddy!" she said, pulling her feet up onto the chair and wrapping an arm around her knees.

"How is Marcy, My Monarch?"

"I have never been better, sweet father. How are you and mom?"

"Well, your mom took a fall yesterday so I'm not sure how to answer that. I don't think you should worry about it, but I thought you should know about it," said her father.

"Oh my God!" Shawn said, suddenly feeling the blood drain from her face. "What happened, dad?"

"Well, we went to a movie in the afternoon and she miscounted the steps at the bottom of the theater. She twisted around like a pirouette and banged her head against the floor."

"Holy shit, dad! Oh my God! What can I do? How am I not supposed to worry about her?"

"Well, she's okay. She never lost consciousness. But she has some brain swelling."

"Cerebral edema, yes," Shawn said. This brought a pause from her father.

"Well, yes. Did you get your doctorate since our last visit?" he joked.

"Sorry," she said, waving a hand in the air, "I've been reading a lot about the brain here of late. So she's responsive and everything? How are they treating it?"

"Well, yes, she is responsive. She's a little slow right now. But she's cognizant."

"Thank God."

"Yes. They put a small hole at the site of the trauma to drain the excess blood," said her father.

"Uh huh. A ventriculostomy," Shawn said.

Dad cleared his throat. "Marcy, you're knocking my socks off here. Are you serious, you've just been reading this stuff in your free time?"

"Yeah, dad. Well, my job has me doing some – well, let's just say *related* stuff here lately."

"Ah. Yes. Coding web applications and performing brain surgery on the side," he said.

"Something like that," she said with a self-conscious smile. "Listen, dad, what can I do? Do you need anything?"

"No, no, hon. Again, I don't want you to worry. I just wanted you to know about it. Moni is here helping around the house and looking after mom when I need breaks," he said, and Shawn couldn't help but feel that tiny sting of jealousy. *Of course Monica was there, being the good daughter.* Shawn rolled her eyes. She hadn't even known it had happened and Monica was already there 'giving dad breaks'. She had already been knee-deep in it for at least a day.

"Okay," Shawn finally said. "Well, thank you for letting me know. Tell her I love her, daddy. Let me know if anything changes."

"We will, doll."

When they hung up, Shawn's mind immediately went to what she was doing at work. How could that be used to help with her mom? Could she run a script that would help her mother fight the head trauma? Could she run a routine that would insure she didn't get any worse? She had to remind herself that just because she had read more about the brain than ninety-nine percent of humans didn't make her an authority on it. She knew that one percent who knew more than her – those Jeremys out there – were the ones who really knew their shit. But it fell into that weird category of things some people called coincidence – that she happened to be working with brains when this happened to her mother. She didn't believe in coincidence. She believed there was a reason for everything. And maybe this was the greater-good reason for her being offered this job. What if that one key that would bring her mother back to normal – assuming she went south at all – was something Shawn had learned and performed in the lab? Maybe she could for once be the hero for her mother, instead of Moni. Maybe Shawn could finally be the one recognized for doing something wonderful. Would that bring them closer? If Shawn could be the hero then her mother wouldn't feel dragged down and put off by her, just for being born.

Shawn wept.

The loading docks in the back of the building were below ground level. Shawn had never been back here, and was instantly curious about how vehicles – especially trucks with trailers – actually got down to the basement level. Even though the concrete outside was lit by the afternoon sun, a white too bright to look at, it was dark under the overhang of the building where the hearse had parked. Shawn stood up on the dock while they unloaded the gurney from the back of the vehicle. Sameer was down next to the hearse speaking with the driver and signing forms.

Shawn stood with her arms crossed, unsure how to feel about all this. The body was in a cardboard box roughly the size of a normal casket. On the ride over, they had thoughtfully covered the box with a black pall blanket. But now, here, out of the prying eyes of those in traffic on the roads, all decorum was thrown to the wind. She had to remind herself that this was what the subject had wanted, to be donated to such a cause as theirs. The subject would literally be treated like the body his soul had left behind. BlueBird, of course, had every intention of making that as respectful an endeavor as they could.

When Sameer finished signing the forms on the clipboard he looked up and waved at Shawn. He was only twenty-five feet away, but the acoustics of this cave-like structure made it almost impossible to hear. She had not heard a single muttering of anything they were saying below. She waved back and put her hands in her back pockets. She had worn jean shorts and a tank top, not thinking she needed to be dressed for such a routine, but Sameer was in his normal work attire: slacks and shirtsleeves. The driver and Sameer pushed the gurney over to the pallet elevator, which would bring the load up to the level upon which Shawn was standing, and where the service elevator doors stood open and waiting.

Shawn had many questions for Sameer as they rode up the service elevator together. The driver had gotten back in the hearse, waving at Shawn as he dropped into the seat, and backed out of the dock. "They don't stick around to collect the gurney?" she asked.

"No, they let us keep it for ease of returning the body when they come back."

"Was this guy's funeral in a cardboard box?"

"No, he was likely in a rental casket."

"Ew. Is that sanitary?"

"Yes, Shawn, they remove the liner and dispose of it for each new body. These are typical for people of lower income or who cannot afford their own casket."

"Uh… If someone can't afford a casket, how are they buried?"

And so on. She felt like her mind was running a mile a minute all the way up. When the doors opened and they wheeled the gurney out, Sameer turned and badged his way into the side door of the private section of their office floor. They pushed the gurney into the wide hallways that ran between the glass rooms she had come to call a second workplace, and into Room D. As they got to the table, Shawn started remembering previous conversations about needing Jeremy in here to help lift the body up onto the table, and started getting nervous about her role in the effort.

It turned out to be a moot point, and she realized it very quickly. The gurney stood at exactly the same height as the table, and had a neat little trick about it: The top of the box, which slid off just like the lid from a board game box, was where all the reinforcement came for the sides. The bottom portion of the set was only thick and reinforced on its bottom. Thus, when the top was slid straight up and off, the four walls of the box just dropped down as they unfolded as if on hinges. They were able to slide the body – thank Jesus, it was tucked safely into a body bag – directly from the box to the table top. Then Sameer unzipped the bag and started tucking portions of it underneath the limbs of the subject, one by one. The arm, then the hip, then the thigh and leg… He moved his way around the body, methodically raising each part by rolling the subject up onto his side very slightly, until he lay completely on top of the body bag. Then he sat the man up and folded the head of the bag underneath where his back would rest.

Shawn realized very suddenly that this was the first full dead person she had ever seen. There he was, right there on the table, naked as the day he was born. All shame and modesty had departed with his soul. Her curiosity had made her look. She had felt the need to see the whole thing. The feet, the legs, and even the private parts. When her eyes returned to the man's head, she looked up and saw Sameer staring at her. She almost felt embarrassed, but realized he was allowing her the curiosity any normal human being would presumably have for the first time seeing a dead body in the whole.

"Please hand me the buckle," Sameer said, holding up his side of the strap. She complied, reaching under the table and grasping the leather belt and buckle that hung from the edge. Sameer buckled the strap snugly across the man's chest, then they moved together to the next one, which would cross the waist. The final strap went taut across the man's ankles. Shawn was thankful for the protocol but a little spooked by the fact that it needed doing at all.

"Shawn, the sheet, please," he said, holding a hand out toward the counter behind her.

She turned and fetched the white sheet, and that was that. She had now been a party to the preparation and moving of a new subject into their experiment. As Sameer whipped the sheet across the man's body, Shawn watched it float into place like a magical thing, and then set about getting the blood bag he had left out to thaw and transferring it to the reservoir, which stood open and waiting much like the elevator doors had down in the basement dock. Sameer had thought of everything in preparation, it seemed. It also seemed like he surely must have been doing this a lot longer than he had admitted to.

After getting everything setup and the blood was circulating, Sameer clapped his hands together and looked around the room, then said, "Well, I guess that is it, Shawn. You are free to go to the beach now."

Shawn stared dumbly at him for a long moment, then rolled her eyes. "Okay, boss. I'll see you at six tomorrow."

As she swung her leg up into the Jeep, she took inventory of herself and realized Sameer hadn't had to reach too far to make the joke. Shawn did indeed look like she could be on her way to the beach. Her Jeep fit the part as well, having no doors on it and the top down. The only thing missing was her sun hat. She reached behind her seat and grabbed it, then cinched the drawstring up under her chin.

Shawn was used to turning heads and drawing attention on the road and at traffic lights. Most of the time these flirts and hollers came from other Jeepers – and sometimes even women. The Jeep Life Culture was one of her favorite things about driving the Wrangler. Today was no different, either. On the way back to the apartment, stereo blasting and Shawn singing along, she got several honks and thumbs-ups from other Jeep drivers. She waved back, made peace signs, smiled. It came with the territory.

# Fourteen

The morning started just like all the others. Tension in the stomach, slightly trembling fingers and an unsure feeling about what they would encounter with the subject. The added anticipation of not knowing whether or not they would even be able to communicate with him was also weighing heavily on Shawn. She had an app on her phone that would translate Spanish to English in real time, but it was a clunky system. She would have to hold the phone up to the dead guy's face – or at least in range of his voice – for it to pick it up. It would print out on the screen in English what he had said. Then she would have to change it to translate English-to-Spanish and type her response, then press play to have a robotic voice speak the words.

Not only was it clunky, it was terribly impersonal. She had no idea if it would work at all, or how the subject would respond to it. Maybe it didn't matter. If this thing – if the brain, rather – was as disconnected from a soul as Jeremy was saying it was, then this was a brain being stimulated into creating speech and invoking memory to tie it into coherent speech. There should be no personality involved at all. And in that regard, a brain without personality shouldn't care whether it was a robotic phone voice speaking to it or an actual human. Right?

But what of the personality bit? She had already proven that wrong. "Take Sonora, for example," Shawn had told Jeremy when discussing this very thing. "She just kept repeating 'fucking kill me' over and over. Is that not a sign of personality?" A simulated personality wouldn't have use for embellishment, would it? Using 'fucking' in place of – well, in place of nothing at all? Not even going into the importance of the use of the word 'me'. That seemed to indicate sentience. And the word 'kill' would indicate the knowledge of life itself. All three words in that repeated sentence spoke of personality. Pain? Fear? Suffering? God, whatever it was, something had made that poor woman's reawakened psyche want to be put back out of its misery. That, to Shawn, sounded nothing *but* personal.

She pushed into the lab with a fresh mug of coffee and ready to get started as Sameer was just finishing up his introduction to the interview. She had missed it all, apparently, because he said, "You may proceed, Shawn."

She already regretted agreeing to see this subject in, knowing he didn't speak English in life, and neither she nor Sameer spoke Spanish. It just seemed like a bad idea all the way around. Now she regretted going out for coffee and a bio break. But had she known Sameer was going to start his intro without her, she would have waited. Or told him to hang back. As soon as she opened her mouth to ask what the man's name was, his eyes popped open, and he started seizing.

It was nearly instant. About as quickly as the kick dot bat routine had awakened the last subject a second time, injecting the nanobots into this man awakened him for the first. His mouth pulled wide to the sides and his teeth clinched together so tightly it looked like they might crush themselves. His eyes were open just about as wide as Shawn had ever seen someone's eyes open. It reminded her of *A Clockwork Orange* and she had to shake the thought from her head.

Shawn's heart slammed in her chest as memories of the last horrible experienced returned to mind. She yelped and stepped back from the table, staring at Sameer, hoping he had suddenly developed some way of stopping this from happening. He stood calmly looking at the subject, occasionally looking up at Shawn, but not making any move to do anything physically.

"Are you going to do something?" she finally asked.

"No. Let us wait and see what happens."

Christ.

She covered her mouth and stared in horror as the man's mouth pulled taut then relaxed over and over. His eyes looked like they would surely pop out of his skull. It looked, Shawn thought, like he was being electrocuted. She guessed that wasn't technically far from the truth – though it was on such a microscopic scale it couldn't possibly present itself like this. So she waited.

Shawn felt comforted by the memory of Sameer strapping the young man's body down in three places yesterday during intake. Though that was the only comfort she was feeling at the moment, it was a major player in her overall demeanor. She felt like if this fucking guy were to sit up, she would run screaming from the room. She didn't think she could handle seeing that again. And she waited.

Sameer stood with his hands on the edge of the table, calmly assessing the situation, like a doctor watching a nurse draw blood or some other menial task beneath his pay grade. He still had not moved to comfort the seizing man or said anything directly to the man at all. Maybe Shawn should take matters into her own hands and start talking calmly into the man's ear. She looked up at Sameer and swallowed, then he shook his head subtly while closing his eyes, almost as if he were reading her mind.

She made the universal gesture that signified an 'oh well' with her mouth and eyes, and sighed, then clasped her hands together under her chin. She might later recognize this as a position of defensive cowering. Nothing was changing though, so she continued to wait.

Sameer tilted his head, looking like he was thinking of some new angle, some new strategy. Yet he still did not move to do anything about the seizure taking place in front of him. Finally, Shawn had had enough. She cleared her throat – quite possibly as a subconscious and passive-aggressive announcement that she was about to act – and then stepped forward and leaned over slightly, looking at the subject on the table. "Hello, sir. My name is Shawn. You are okay. Can you hear me?"

Before she had even said her name, the seizing stopped. She stood up, frowning at the man's sudden change in behavior. Had that been all he needed? Just to hear a comforting voice? Shawn suddenly felt guilty for having let it go on so long. She tried to justify this with having her superior ordering her to stand down, but it wouldn't wash. She was the moderator here. Sameer had made that clear on more than one occasion, and in more than a couple of ways. She had to own that. To accept it and proceed with the authority that gave her. There should be no looking to him for questioning or permission to do any one thing or another. If she were truly in charge, then she needed to run it.

Shawn stared at the man for another moment before standing back up and letting a breath out slowly. She looked up at Sameer, then back at the dead man's living eyes. They were not quite so wide now, though they still held the look of fear or surprise. Maybe that was just the way the man looked in life. "Señor, ¿puede oírme?" she said. And she felt herself go white as a ghost.

Sameer was looking at her with raised eyebrows. Hell, her own eyebrows were up. "Yes, I can hear you," said the man. *What the hell is going on?*

"I thought…" Sameer started, but Shawn interrupted him.

"I don't. I don't know Spanish, Sameer."

"Well, maybe it is residual. Subconscious retrieval of mem-"

"I took French in high school, Sameer."

They both stood staring at each other, in complete shock that she had apparently said something in perfect Spanish, completely ignoring the other two miracles in the room. One, a dead man had just spoken. And two, he had spoken perfect English in response to her Spanish inquiry. *What the hell is going on here?*

She shook her head, feeling a little dizzy all of a sudden, and her mind was still trying to decode what had just happened in the room. Flustered and afraid, but unwilling to show her fear, she continued. "Can you tell me your name, sir?" she asked, again leaning closer to the body on the table. The thought that Spanish had escaped her lips a moment before came back to her and left a chill down her spine.

"Aye, it's Paul," said the man.

Shawn looked up at Sameer and he was shaking his head, again, wide-eyed. "I'm sorry, what?" she whispered.

Sameer grabbed the whiteboard and marked on it while Shawn stood breathing heavily. When he turned it toward her, she scanned it quickly and her heart sank. Sameer had written, 'HIS NAME IS JULIO – NOT PAUL!'.

Shawn stared dumbly at the whiteboard, feeling completely lost. She suddenly just wanted to grab the EMP helmet and send this guy back to the great beyond. To end all this mystery and intrigue. She shook her head and tried to snap out of the reverie. "So, um, Paul," Shawn started. She cleared her throat. "I uh… I seem to have-"

"Tapped into something you're not ready to handle. This is not meant for man," he said.

She stared, frozen in fear. This had gone from chilling to horrifying in one quick turn, and she was losing control of her cool. This was not what she had signed up for. Certainly not what she had envisioned. Shawn tried to reason with herself. It was taking a gigantic helping of willpower not to dash for that helmet. Or better yet, the exit. She breathed in slowly and stood still, worried that the dead man had spoken truth. She glanced up at the ceiling, around the room, nervously looking for the telltale signs of an out-of-body visitor. She was now in a place of fear she had never experienced before. Her heart was running what felt like literal double-time and she was beginning to sweat, in spite of the near constant chill bumps running up her arms. Sameer was steadfast as always, offering no assistance or words of wisdom. She marched on, lifting her chin.

"Can you explain what you mean by that?" she asked as calmly as she could muster. She did not want to let any of her sudden blinding fear penetrate its way into her words. She had to at least sound like she was in control here. Why was she working so hard to maintain professionalism? There was no code of conduct for this insanity! They were messing with the *other side*!

"You know what I mean. You should end this. Once and for all."

A cold chill shot through the middle of Shawn's abdomen, like a dagger made of dry ice. She gulped. Her palms were sweaty. She rubbed them together and made fists with them, and then put those fists against the top of her head. This was her mind losing touch. She was running out of bravery. She was breathing heavy now and biting her lip so hard it was beginning to draw blood. She was trembling all over, staring straight into the subject's eyes and losing focus. She felt faint. Weak in the knees. Filled with lead and heat.

The worst part was that her head felt suddenly hot, like a fire burning between her ears, and she could literally *hear* the blood flowing through it. In that part of her mind reserved for involuntary function, Shawn realized she was shutting down. This was full-blown panic, and she couldn't go any farther. Professionalism be damned, she had to quit. Right now. *Right fucking now!*

Shawn put her hands over her mouth and shook her head, closing her eyes. "I'm sorry, Sameer. This was a bad idea. I can't do this anymore. I can't…" she said and turned toward the door. Her hands still on her mouth, tears now spilling from her eyes, she stopped and turned back around to look at him again. Was she making the right choice here? She would surely lose her salary… *Fuck the salary. I want my sanity. And it might be too late even for that.* "I'm sorry, Sameer. I'm having… I'm breaking down," she said, turning back toward the door. He moved toward her, holding up a hand as if to comfort her, but she was already moving away. He might have said something but she was now in flight mode. Nothing was going to get through. A cry escaped her mouth, sounding more like a cough. Her hands were shaking severely and she was beginning to get dizzy. The heat in her head had multiplied, and everything sounded loud and quiet at the same time. Far away. Distant but right behind her. Then the real fear kicked in.

"What if this is permanent?" she said to herself as she left the room, almost in a run. "What if I've fucked myself over the edge of insanity? What if I'm never the same again?" she cried, and now she was bawling. She dashed to the bathroom, walking as fast as she had ever walked without bursting into an all-out run. Her mind was so full of panic and fear that she thought she might not make it. Her sanity might just fracture out here in the hallway, leaving her as good as dead – as useless as that man on the table in Room D. Her lips trembled as she sucked in ragged breaths. The room was spinning so hard now she couldn't tell which way she was going, so instead just slid down the wall in the hallway, crying and shaking, burying her head in her hands.

By the time Chandra came out of the bathroom, Shawn was screaming. She was digging at her hair like she might pull it out, sobbing so hard she couldn't breathe, and quaking all over. Every inch of her body was shaking like something electrified. Chandra dropped to her knees and took Shawn in her arms, pulling her close and resting her chin on the sobbing woman's head. She squeezed until she couldn't squeeze any harder, and Shawn finally responded by putting her own arms around Chandra.

"What's wrong, baby?" Chandra said softly, over and over. It might have sounded more like a comforting declaration than interrogation. Chandra probably didn't even realize what she was asking. Certainly, Shawn was unable to answer. She was a complete wreck, her clothes soaked through with sweat and tears, her hair a disheveled mess atop her head. Chandra ignored all of this and just fell back onto the floor on her own rump, pulling Shawn down into her lap and squeezing as hard as she could.

After a few minutes, Sameer burst through the door at the end of the hall and came jogging to a stop beside the two women. "Is she okay? What is happening?" he asked, his face full of concern.

"I was hoping you could tell me," said Chandra quietly.

"I had to shut the subject down. I'm sorry it took me so long."

"It's okay, S'meer. I've got her now. This is the task of a woman."

Sameer breathed in deeply, slowly, straightening up and nodding. "Okay. Okay, good. Let me know if I can do anything." He put his hands on his hips and looked around like there might be something else to see in the hallway. "She had a little bit of an event in there."

"Ya think?" said Chandra, her face not showing quite the snark her words had let on.

Sameer made a face. "Right. I'm saying something happened that was not usual. I think-"

"S'meer can we talk about this later?" pleaded Chandra.

"Yes, of course. Please call me if you need my assistance. Get her whatever she needs. The company will pay for it, of course."

Chandra nodded, one side of her mouth sucked in like she might be a little perturbed at Sameer just now. Either way, he took the hint and disappeared back through the door through which he had come.

"See back to deaf?" Shawn mumbled.

"Say again, sugar, I didn't catch that," Chandra said, pulling Shawn's sweaty hair back from her cheek.

"See back to death?" Shawn said, rolling her head back to look up at Chandra, who was leaning over her. Now

Chandra brushed the hair down from the other cheek as well, and left both hands on Shawn's cheeks. She smiled pleasantly at Shawn.

"Once more, honey. See back to death? What does that mean?"

Shawn swallowed and sucked the saliva from her mouth. Swallowed again. "Is he back to death?"

"Oh. The subject. Yes. S'meer said he had to shut him down. I'm guessing that's what you're asking. All is well now. You're okay. Everything is going to be okay."

Shawn closed her eyes. And the next time she was aware of anything, the hallway lights were dimmed down and there was a blanket over her. Chandra was right there with her, scrolling through something on her phone, the light from the screen painting her face an eerie indigo that made her look both magical and beautiful at the same time. Shawn realized she had likely been asleep here on the floor with her head on this woman's lap for hours. And the woman had never moved. Maybe Shawn could not call her a friend, but damned if this woman wasn't the kindest and most humane thing in the world right now. As Shawn realized the depth of Chandra's commitment, she rolled over and wrapped her arms around the woman's waist and buried her face in Chandra's belly. This time her cry was one of gratitude and relief.

Shawn sat down to read the next page of Miranda's journal that night. She was still shaken up about the event in the lab that morning, but couldn't just walk away from it. Try as she might to forget about it – to carry on with a normal day – she was not able to. It sure felt like things were going backward with the project. They had made such great progress until suddenly, it just stopped. Turned around. The last three subjects had seemed to be a total flop. A complete waste of time. And it was ruining her life, to boot. What was the worth of all this if she came out crazy? Ruined from exposure to things 'not meant for man'? God, did she ever agree with that statement the man had made. She felt like she was slipping down a slope from which she could no longer recover. Fighting to keep her feet beneath her on a tilted ice rink, and losing control quickly. She had been having bad dreams more and more often, and she used to be such a peaceful sleeper. She was scared a lot these days, full of anxiety and stress – and especially when she was alone with her thoughts. Shawn felt like she couldn't even enjoy alone time anymore without some haunt creeping up behind her and reminding her what she had unlocked in the lab. Damn right, that guy was right: man was *not* meant to meddle with death.

As she sat with a fingernail clicking against her teeth and staring out the back window, the journal lay open on her lap. Her other hand held it open as she absentmindedly closed off the open threads the day had brought her. Another day full of more questions than answers – and typically that was how Shawn liked it. She loved the mystery of not knowing everything; of being presented with more and deeper complexities. The universe shouldn't be easy to figure out. Like Miranda had said in her journal entry about the Great Filter, Shawn thought there was a lot mankind needed to learn before he was ready for the stars.

Cory lay on the other side of the couch, his feet crossed up on the arm, reading something on his phone. He had asked her earlier if reading a dead woman's journal was the best way to recover from a literal mental breakdown, and she had said she didn't see the connection between the two topics. Of course she understood where he was going with his concern. It wasn't too long ago that she had pretty much broken down about the dead girl. So it was a legitimate question. But she felt like Miranda's journal was a project: a favor for a friend passed on. Shawn wasn't worried that it would remind her of today's events. If anything, it might get her mind off of them.

The butterfly, she noticed, had not been back to visit. At least not while Shawn was around to witness it. The spider had a web full of treats though, she noticed. It looked like there was even a June bug rolled up in there. The spider danced across the web, wrapping up mosquitoes and other tiny flying creatures, almost constantly in motion. It was fascinating to watch when the lighting was right outside, as it was now. The sun cast an eerie dying wish on the top of her window, shining a thin beam directly through the web where it lit up the silk strands like tiny neons.

She sighed and finally looked down at the book open in her lap. And began to read.

> 2/3 Good morning sweet friend. Sometimes I wonder if you're my only true friend. The only one who listens to me and puts up with my bitching and whining. I just wish you could talk back sometimes. I saw a cat get viciously attacked and killed by a pit bull today. I was helpless to do anything since I was sitting on the train. We were at the station and a bunch of us were looking out the window. All the women were screaming. A couple of boys were laughing. Laughing! I can't imagine that. But I was not able to look away. I kept hoping something good would happen, like someone would come up and kick the dog or the cat would find a way to get away. But it never did.
>
> Linus didn't see it. He had his face buried in a book. I think that's a good thing. There's enough death in the world not to have to witness it first hand.

We're on our way to the park in a little bit. Linus has something he wants to talk to me about. He likes parks because they're wide open spaces and it's easier to be comfortable without feeling too crowded. So I've learned two things I didn't know about him now: he likes open spaces and he likes speed. Apparently he is a speed demon.

I love the weather here but I am ready to be home. I am and I'm not. I know, I am a mystery wrapped in an enigma! The weather sucks at home and my apartment is lonely. But I miss Harrison. I have to admit that. I think you're the only one I can ever admit that to, Mister Diary. That's why I love you.

Shawn set the journal on the couch beside her and took a drink from the glass she had almost forgotten about. Tonight it was vodka with club soda. Who is this Harrison character? Obviously he must be a love interest. But then who would Linus be? Shawn was confused, but felt like she was reading a good mystery in which the truth would be revealed in the climax.

"Cory, can I ask you a question?"

"What's up?" he said, laying his phone on his chest. He reached back with his hand, trying for something to hold, but she was too far away. She swung her foot out from underneath her and extended it across the ottoman so he could take her by the ankle.

"Do you think the world is doomed? I mean, like humanity? Do you think it would be worth saving?"

"That's a funny question. It sure seems we've lost our way, doesn't it?" he asked.

Shawn shrugged and sighed, then pulled her hair back into a ponytail, which she held in place with her hands for a long moment. A moment filled with thought. "If you watch the news, then absolutely. It just seems like no one cares anymore."

"What brought this up? The journal?"

"Why are we trying to bring back people from the dead?" she said, completely ignoring his question.

Cory shook his head and wiped his eyes, then blinked. "That's a hell of a question. Have you not asked your boss that question?"

"No. Not really. But it seems like maybe we should ask some of these people what *they* think about the state of humanity. Like, do they miss it? Would they change anything now that they're dead?"

Cory twisted his head to look at her, but didn't speak. He pursed his lips.

Shawn sighed, then looked out the back door again and said, "It seems crazy otherwise, to bring back the dead, with all these bad living people still walking around."

Shawn had accepted Sameer's gracious offer to take a few days off work and recover from her breakdown. And she had accepted it with the full intention of taking off the entire rest of the week. But when she woke up Tuesday morning she felt fine. She realized she had been sleeping with Miranda's stuffed monkey. It had a big goofy smile on its face and a cliché banana sewn to one hand, but it was soft, and she could use it in place of one of those little square pillows she used to use to keep her arms a comfortable width apart. She cuddled the little monkey right up against her breasts and wrapped both arms around it like she was afraid someone might come in and steal it during the night. With Cory behind her and the monkey in front of her, she had been sleeping like a queen.

When she sat up, she held the monkey up and looked at him, smiled as she twisted him side to side, then stuffed him under Cory's arm and patted his elbow. "There now. Cory will take care of you while I'm gone."

Shawn grabbed her keys and purse and locked up as she went across the breezeway to her own apartment to get ready for work. She would still arrive at her normal time, and felt no regrets about not taking the day off. This showed responsibility. Maturity! Accountability and bravery, too, if you asked her. Though she wasn't sure she would be 'getting back up on that horse' again, come to that. She could do the work she was originally hired for, but had to maybe just accept that dealing with dead people – at least in the manner in which BlueBird dealt with them – just wasn't for her. She would take the hit it blew to her finances. She had not yet bought the motorcycle. She would be just fine on her old salary. A little disappointed, but fine no less.

When she walked into the office, Chandra was the first face she saw. She was coming out of the break room stirring her coffee into something sweeter and less dark than Shawn was used to drinking herself. Chandra stopped and looked at her, eyes serious and mouth a small pucker. Neither one of them spoke for a long moment and then Chandra finally broke a smile. It turned wide and pretty and Shawn smiled back, involving her entire face. And pretty soon they were giggling. Shawn stepped forward and carefully hugged Chandra, trying not to spill her coffee.

"Thank you so much for babying me yesterday. I'm sorry for embarrassing myself."

Chandra stepped back nodding and looked at Shawn, shaking her head slightly. "Don't apologize for that. There are limits to what the human mind is supposed to be able to accept and cope with." She stood there for a moment, looking like she felt sorry for Shawn, but like she was trying to hide that bit.

Shawn smirked and put her hand on Chandra's arm. "Well, either way, you were perfect. Thank you so much. I'm okay."

"Are you sure? You don't have to be here today, Shawn," said Chandra.

"Yeah, I know," Shawn said, smiling again. "I'm good." She went into the break room to get her own steaming mug of coffee.

When she came into the conference room sipping from her mug, Sameer's eyes were wide. "Shawn!" he said, standing up.

"What? You guys didn't know I was coming?"

Jeremy was shaking his head and smiling. "I told them to get in here when I looked out the window and saw you pulling into the parking garage," he said. "I didn't tell them why."

Chandra was smiling a more modest smile. It looked like she was hiding something.

As Shawn pulled out her seat, she reached over and stuck out her hand toward Sameer, basically forcing him to shake it. He did so, his hand feeling like a dead fish to Shawn, and then she dropped into her chair straightening her blouse. "I would like to start this meeting with a question," she said.

Sameer took his seat. Everyone else just looked at her. Jeremy was twirling a pen on the table, smiling privately to himself.

"What in the literal effing *hell* happened in there yesterday, Sameer?"

Sameer made a face like he was about to say something, then nodded, looking up at the ceiling. "I think we should back up and tell them what had happened in there, Shawn."

She slapped her hand down on the table lightly, shaking her head at the same time. "That's what I mean. I don't *know* what happened. I'm asking."

"Perhaps we should play the tape," he said, holding up a finger on one hand while the other fished the DVR out of his breast pocket. He set it on the table and gave everyone the benefit of a quick glance, waiting for any objections. Everyone either nodded or raised his eyebrows slightly, indicating each was ready, then Sameer played the recording.

When it finished, Shawn stared, dumbstruck and speechless. Sameer looked at her for a long time as she looked at the DVR on the table. He finally said, "Shawn, do you not remember any of this?"

"Not like that, I don't," she said, shaking her head. Her eyes were still glued to that recorder though. "That's not how it went in my memory." She leaned back, putting her fingertips together over her stomach. Her fingers began their ritual. "Sameer, I distinctly remember speaking Spanish. I asked him if he could hear me and he responded in English." But that's not what the tape showed.

At this point, Chandra reached over and put her hand on Shawn's forearm. A motherly, protective gesture, perhaps meant to prevent another mental episode from happening. Shawn looked at her. Looked at her hand. Shook her head, staring at Chandra as if for answers.

"You were not in a good place mentally," said Chandra. "You probably shouldn't trust your memories of the event."

"But…" she began, staring at her lap. "They seem so *vivid*. So *real*."

"Do you know Spanish?" Jeremy said. His face had lost its famous smile. Even he believed this was too serious for such levity, apparently.

Shawn locked eyes with him and swallowed. "No. I took French in high school."

Jeremy lifted his chin slightly, but looked away. *Point proven*.

"Okay. Well, I need to go back to my desk and transcribe the events the way I remember them happening," Shawn finally said.

Chandra cleared her throat and sat up a little straighter. Her hand was still on Shawn's arm. "Why do you think that would be valuable, Shawn?"

"Because that man in there," she said, hiking a thumb over her shoulder in the complete opposite direction from the lab, "spoke directly to me. Told me I was getting into something 'no man should witness'." She covered her mouth with one hand.

"Are you okay? Do you need a break?" Chandra asked.

"No. I'm fine." Shawn looked up at her again. "You don't think it would be valuable?"

Chandra tilted her head and then looked at Sameer. "What do you think? Do you remember it going differently than the tape showed?"

Sameer shook his head, almost looking like he was embarrassed to disagree with Shawn. "No. The tape is accurate."

"Great," Shawn said. "I'm losing my fuckin' mind." She turned her hands up and looked at the ceiling.

"No, Shawn. I think you just need to take some time away from this project. You can come to work if you feel like it. Work on your support role. You do not need to be in the lab for a while," Sameer said, clasping his hands on the table.

Shawn thought about this for a moment. She had been thinking last night that she wanted out of it. Maybe this was a good way to be sure of that without just quitting. She knew it would definitely do her brain some good to stop thinking about it for a while. She found herself nodding, so she looked up at him and said, "Okay. I think I'll take you up on that. Thank you."

"Yes. Your mental health is most important, Shawn. What happened yesterday is not good for any of us."

Was he talking about in the lab with the subject? Or what happened with her, that carried into the hallway? The complete mental breakdown she had suffered? Obviously, either could be perfectly appropriate in this situation, and she knew Sameer would not insult her. Shawn nodded again. She looked at Chandra. Chandra smiled at her. "Take some time, Shawn. Get back to your happy place for a while."

Shawn's happy place that evening was on her sofa with a tall glass of vodka tonic and her feet up on the ottoman, covered by a throw blanket. Cory was out with some friends of his, and promised to be back by ten. Shawn was gladdened by his promise. Things like that made it feel like a real commitment. Like what they had was truly something special, and he wasn't just BOYFRIEND in her phone.

She had been reading Miranda's journal for the last couple of hours, breaking her original rule not to binge the passages. She was still giving each one of them the time and thought it deserved, but no longer wanted to wait and read it like television used to be watched. Manufactured suspense while the viewers had to wait for the next episode to air.

Shawn also had a notepad beside her on which she had written down some things she wanted to remember, others she just wanted to come back to – to ponder. There was nothing exciting in the pages so far. Nothing mind-boggling or earth-shattering. Just a normal girl with normal angst and normal problems facing the world and venting about it in the pages of a diary.

One thing that stuck out to Shawn was the girl's lack of mentioning Harrison, the name she had cried out during her reawakening. Shawn had been left with the impression that Harrison had been someone close. Someone very important. And probably very familiar. Like he must have been around a lot for her to be calling on him with such fervor. And yet he had only been mentioned once in the journal so far. And this was presumably the latest journal Miranda had been filling when she died. Shawn flipped to the back to see where it ended. Only about half the pages had been filled, and it went right up to the date she had died, on June nineteenth. Seeing that this was the last page she had written, Shawn was too overcome with curiosity not to read the last installment. Though she would never do such a thing in one of her novels, this *wasn't* a novel.

6/19 Oh my God, diary... he's coming tomorrow! I can't believe it's here. Finally. After

four years of obstacles and pitfalls and fighting
the system, I finally get to have him here!!! I will
pick him up from the airport in the morning. His
flight comes in at 9:36 a.m. Of course he doesn't
know where I live yet. I wanted to surprise him
with the apartment. I'm so excited I could piss
my pants! Oh my God! Linus!

*Oh my God.* She looked up at the glass door and
squinted into the dying sun. Whoever this Linus guy was, he
arrived the morning after Miranda died. And he didn't know
where she lived. So Linus arrived at the airport and no one
was there to pick him up. In fact, she was… "Holy fuck,"
Shawn said. Her blood went cold and a hard chill ran all the
way up her spine into her scalp.

She was suddenly diving across the couch for her laptop,
which leaned against the cushion where Cory usually sat.
She whipped it up onto her lap and opened it, then waited for
it to come to life, tapping her fingers on the touch pad. When
the login box finally appeared, she mis-typed her password
several times due to the tremble in her hands. On the
desktop, she opened the document where she had been
compiling the interviews and their pertinent data for cross-
reference. She scrolled down to the second subject.

```
Miranda Kate Struck. Died 19 June
at 22:13. Sameer begins interview
20 June at 09:36.
```

Shawn covered her mouth and gasped. Then she looked
back at the journal. There it was. The arrival time for Linus's
plane was the exact minute they began their interview. That
meant that while this man was coming off the jetway,
probably smiling and looking for his pretty friend, Shawn
and Sameer were busy bringing her back from the dead. By

the time Linus entered the lobby area, they were already asking her questions. And she was answering them.

> Fortunately, I've been smart. I've been a good little munchkin. I've cleaned my whole apartment so all I have to do tonight is relax and get myself ready so I can fall asleep. I think the anticipation is going to keep me up all night. But that's okay. I don't have anything important to do tomorrow besides collecting the boy. It's not like I have a job.

*The boy?* Shawn stopped again and looked through the back doors. The sun had now fully disappeared behind the buildings across the parking lot. Who the *heck* is this Linus guy? Obviously she would have to read some of the previous entries. But there was also the assumed knowledge predicament a journal presented. This was, according to her first entry, at least her second journal. She had mentioned filling the pages of at least one other book. So a lot of questions Shawn had about what might be commonplace knowledge might only have been answered in the previous books. She might never know, because Miranda wrote them having probably not thought too much about what would need to be carried over from one book to the next.

> I will have an early night tonight. I will take my bath and then go to bed early, knowing full well that I won't actually be able to sleep. But I'll be trying. At least I'll be resting. Oh my God. There's that damn butterfly again!

Shawn's eyes went wide. That was where this book ended. The last entry ended only halfway down the page, talking about a butterfly. Miranda's apartment was two buildings over from Shawn's, and on the same side of the building. That meant their back porches both faced west. Miranda's was on the first floor. That was the only difference. Could it have been the same butterfly? A tear formed in her eye as the thought crossed her mind that it just might be.

# Fifteen

Saturday, September 2$^{nd}$ was supposed to be a good day. But Shawn woke with a start, bolting up from the nightmare that had been plaguing her throughout most of the night. Cory, bless his heart, had slept right through it. Even when she had tried to wake him a couple of times, begging for comfort, whining like a child. She was tired and she was tired of it. Every time her eyes had closed, she had fallen right back into that dream. Standing in a dark cave of a room, which clearly represented D Room at the lab, and being strapped to a table while people walked around her talking. She had a mask over her eyes, but there had been no doubt in that dream-logic sort of way that those people were dead. And they were trying to bring her back to death.

So when she shot up to a sitting position at six o'clock and saw the sun trying to break through the curtains, she sighed heavily, thanking God for the daylight and just got up. No sense in trying to fight the demons for more good sleep. They were on a mission to keep her from it. Oh, they would let her sleep. It just wouldn't be good sleep. And it wouldn't be for her benefit, but for theirs. As she pulled back her exploded and disheveled hair and swung her feet onto the carpet, the stuffed monkey fell to the floor. She bent over and picked it up, holding it to her sweaty chest.

Her mornings had become a crazy carnival ride of trying to remember where she was. The back-and-forth between her apartment and Cory's made it a puzzle her sleepy brain was never quite ready to solve. The orientation of the bed juxtaposed with the only window in the room was the only thing that ever helped her solve it at all. Furniture be damned. In that dreamy, groggy morning fog, she had to align herself by the compass she was offered. This morning the window was on her left as she sat there. That meant she was in her own apartment. It wouldn't be like this for much longer. Cory had asked her to move in with him when her lease expired. She was happy about giving up the guessing games her mornings involved, but would be a little sad to lose her own place. It wasn't so much about giving up the freedom – she knew she would still have that – but the power it possessed. Being able to go 'home' and not have to let anyone else in was a tactical advantage in a fight. Cory and she had not had any real fights, at least not yet, but it felt a little like walking into a forest with no clothes on. If something were to happen, she would be stuck in his apartment with him. And if they had to break it off, God forbid, she would be out in the rain looking for another place. There was some tension about the arrangement but she was proceeding with the leap-of-faith logic that had ruled her entire adult life, and was mostly comfortable taking the chance. The benefits sure seemed to outweigh all the bad scenarios she could envision.

Shawn looked down at the stuffed monkey. She was holding it upside down. A small white tag stuck up from the monkey's rear. Shawn frowned at it, unsure whether she had ever noticed it before. Why would she remember if she had? Why would she pay attention? It was a standard cloth tag and everything soft in her life had come with one. But for some reason it got her attention this morning. She flipped it over and could see the fine print on it, but it was still too dark in the room to read it. She yawned and tossed the monkey onto the pillow behind her and stood up.

A quick shower, a pee and a gargle, and Shawn was in the kitchen making coffee. She yawned again. She would almost certainly be needing a nap after lunch. At least it was Saturday. The excitement of the day stood tall before her: today was the day her motorcycle would be ready. She had waited patiently while they manufactured, assembled and shipped it to her local dealership. Ever since the bullshit pandemic had changed the world, everything was slow these days. Supply-chain issues and labor shortages and even raw material mining had all taken a serious blow. What used to take a few days now took weeks, sometimes months.

She had gotten the call yesterday that the bike had arrived in its crate, had been unloaded from the delivery truck and would be put together today. She had settled the paperwork mostly over the phone and then finished with some emails, scans and back-and-forths. When she went to the dealership, it would be ready for her. That would be sometime after lunch. Right around the time Shawn would be needing her nap.

Perhaps even more exciting than that was that she had a ride planned for the early evening. Heath and Lo, riding together, or 'two-up' as they called it in the group, and Cory and Shawn on their own bikes, had planned to ride out to the lake and back. All told, it would be a trip worth about two hours or so, and on a route that didn't have too much traffic to worry about. She wanted to get a few good rides under her belt on her new bike before she started taking it places where she had to contend with cagers.

As she waited for the coffee maker to brew its magic cocktail, she went to the back door to pull the vertical blinds and let the daylight come in. She pushed them all the way to the end of the track and unlocked the sliding glass. She stepped outside and leaned against the rail of the tiny balcony feeling the wonderful cool air. August was finally over. That month Cory had warned her about the day they first met – the one people wrote home about from Texas – was finally in the books, and she had survived it. Mostly by staying inside a lot, but hey, what can you do?

A man walking down the sidewalk between the buildings to his car looked up at all the balconies on his right. When his eyes fell across Shawn's he waved at her. Shawn smiled and waved back. Then she heard the coffee maker gurgling – its code word for telling her the coffee was ready. She turned to go back into the apartment and that's when she saw that monarch. Trapped in the web. And this time there would be no saving it.

The butterfly had come in sometime during the evening or night before, and she had not seen it. And now it was dead. The spider had wrapped it up with a thorough that spoke not only of its professionalism, but also perhaps a little payback. Payback for all those times Shawn had come out and rescued the butterfly from it. He had finally gotten it, and had done so in a way she could not undo. She stood staring at it, hands on her hips and shaking her head. She felt sadness in her heart for the monarch. There had been a sort of connection there. Almost like her pet butterfly that came to visit occasionally. "You poor thing. You could just never get the hang of avoiding that damned web, could you?" she said.

After staring at it for a long moment and making as much eye-contact as she could with the spider, she reached up and pinched the butterfly's wings together and pulled it away, ruining the web. The spider backed up, almost as if unsure what to do. Shawn shook her head at it disgustedly. She held the bug up and looked at its body, completely wrapped in silk, then blew a kiss at it and tossed it over the rail and went inside.

When Shawn went through the bedroom to wash her hands, she checked on Cory like she always did. He was still sleeping soundlessly, the covers leaving his entire back exposed, his head turned to the side facing the back window and breathing slowly. She picked up the stuffed monkey and wiggled it at him, much as one would do at a toddler while she considered putting it right up against him. She finally thought better of it, knowing it would wake him, and for no real reason – for all the care he had for the thing. She then spontaneously hugged the stuffed animal and kissed its head while she stared at her sleeping man.

The monkey was soft like the cotton filling had been squished down by the weight of a loving arm for many nights in a row for many, many years. This brought her comfort. Shawn held it up and looked at its eyes, its threadbare stitching and the silly banana sewn to its hand. Then she turned it over with the intention of putting it back against the pillow to stand sentry over Cory when she saw a blue stitching on the back of its left hip she had never noticed before. She squinted at it, holding it at different angles in the light and not getting it. She walked to the bathroom and turned on the light in there, staring closely at the tiny blue threads that made up something like a bunch of Xs in a row. Maybe a mend by a grandmother. She rubbed her thumb over it carefully, feeling its texture. Whoever sewed it was good. Sewing something so thick had to have been done by hand, and this was some fine stitching.

And then it just jumped out at her. She turned it clockwise one quarter-turn and there it was. She could suddenly read it perfectly, and without the aid of a squint. It very plainly read, in all capitals, 'HARRISON'.

Shawn was back on the couch, digging through the transcription of her interview with Miranda, searching for the word 'Harrison'. She had the journal at her left thigh as well, perfectly prepared to start skimming every page in the damned book looking for it. The only instance, of course, that she could find of it in the interview was where Miranda had started shouting the name. But Shawn felt it almost impossibly unlikely that she had been referring to a stuffed monkey. *Right?* The concern in Miranda's voice as she had called for Harrison had been like she was asking a dark room if he was present in it. That must surely mean the monkey had belonged to someone named Harrison.

Feeling like she was closing in on one of life's greatest mysteries – as if it would bring back the dead girl or otherwise bring them closer together – she slapped the notebook computer closed and tossed it on the couch beside her, then started flipping through the journal. Shawn's history of code debugging gave her an advantage when it came to word searches such as these: she had trained her mind to look for that particular word, knowing her eyes did not have to slow to read each word individually, but rather glancing at them line-by-line. If the word she hunted for was in that line, her brain would catch it whether she knew what the rest of the words were or not. It was simple pattern recognition.

She flipped and flipped but found nothing. She got to within a few pages of the last entry and shook her head, then started over, slowing down a little this time. Shawn suddenly didn't trust her eyes to have caught it – doubting the years of training she usually trusted wholesale. Nothing. And then again, once more, even slower. But when she got to that same place, a few pages before the end, she slowed down and read the passages in full. And there it was. In the middle of the second-to-last filled page.

> I feel like Harrison is close tonight. I miss him like a lost child.

And that was it. Now she was almost sure of it. She had scanned the journal four times, and that was surely the only mention of his name besides the one mention in the first paragraph on the first page. She had said it like a swear, or the vain invocation of a deity's name. *'For Harrison's sake!'* she had written. Shawn looked up at the wall, then the back window. The spider was in hiding. No rebuilding of that damnable web during daylight hours. She could just make out its bulbous thorax tucked up inside the track of the sliding door, just out of sight of the sun.

Who was this guy? An old boyfriend? Her father? Obviously he was someone Miranda held in high regard, having used his name in that way. That invocation, coupled with her shouting it three times at the end of her death interview, made Shawn think he must be someone more than just a little important. But during one journal entry she had mentioned that the diary was the only one to whom she could admit that she missed him. What was up with that? Why would she need to hide the fact that she misses someone? She flipped back to the first page and reread the first passage in its entirety. That first paragraph was interesting.

> If you're reading this, shame on you. If I'm dead, however, spread the word! I finally finished filling the pages of my last book of words. There's nothing here that supersedes that.

*I finally finished filling the pages of my last book of words.* Finally. That could mean it was a project that had been nagging at Miranda for a long time, or that she just didn't get to journal as much as she wanted to these days. She had finally gotten some free time and did some catching up. But no one caught up on journaling like that. No one wrote ten passages in one day just to catch up. Did they? The phrasing of the words at the end of that sentence was really intriguing though: *my last book of words*. That could have meant this very book – the one Shawn was holding. If I'm dead, then I've finished my last book of words. Well, technically that was the truth no matter how one sliced it. She had finished everything she would ever finish. The next sentence would be technically the truth as well, no matter if it were this book or another to which Miranda had been referring. Nothing could be superseded in death. But Shawn somehow doubted Miranda's personal journaling was anything that deep. None of the passages bore any kind of enigmatic quality about them.

If I'm dead, however, spread the word! Spread the word that you're dead? Or spread the word that you're – as the next sentence reads – finally finished filling your journal? What was the basest meaning of that sentence? Shawn shook her head and slapped the leather-bound book closed. She was way overthinking this. And it was nothing. It was just a simple opening to a diary. She set the book on the ottoman and stood up, then pulled up her pajama pants as she yawned, staring out the back window. Why was she so hung up on this damn puzzle? It probably wasn't even a puzzle. Miranda had known someone named Harrison, and now she missed him. Big deal. Well, it had been a big deal to Miranda, but that didn't mean it had to mean much in the grand scheme of things. Shawn was getting tired-head from trying to play detective and not being very good at it. Even if she had uncovered the truth, she wouldn't have any resolution. No closure. No one coming out of a hidden door and high-fiving her, telling her, 'Hey, good job! You figured it out!'

She rolled her eyes and slid the back door back open and went onto the balcony. Then she reached up and stuck her finger between the spider and the corner of the door track, having to stand on tip-toes to do so, and flicked it down off the web. It landed on the concrete and immediately started scurrying across the patio to find shelter. She ended its life with the toe of her slipper, popping its bulbous back and squirting spider innards a foot back toward the railing. "Sorry, Mr. Spider, but you killed my friend. And you were just a spider," Shawn said. "I'm a fuckin' lion."

Shawn looked over the balcony at the complex around her. Nothing to see there. *Same bullshit. Different day.* She went inside and closed the glass door, locking it behind her.

Shawn cracked half a dozen eggs over a pan and popped some bread down in the toaster. She hung on the fridge door, her blouse hanging open and letting the cold air blow directly down her front side, looking at the ingredients of her life. There were the standard ketchup and mayo jars, some yogurt, some milk – about to expire, that – and not much else. Most of her stuff, sadly, was in the compartment above the fridge, collecting tiny ice crystals. The heat-and-eat variety she somehow couldn't get away from, but at the same time couldn't really say she hated, either. She was hoping to find a forgotten package of bacon or a lump of breakfast sausage so she could make Cory something a little more special than eggs and toast. It was, after all, their three-and-a-half-month anniversary. Well one of these upcoming days would be. Or maybe it had been last week. Either way, she wanted to celebrate her love for him by bringing him breakfast in bed.

Finding nothing, she stirred the eggs until the yolks broke, then put more bread in the toaster. She could never seem to get that part of her breakfasts right. The toast was always cold by the time the eggs were finished. She reckoned the trick was one of those fancy four-at-a-timers. Well, fuck that. She would just eat cold toast.

Cory sat up scratching his head and looking around like he was playing that same game she did every morning. That '*where the hell am I?*' game. When it finally registered, he looked at her and smiled. "Thank you, Shawn. This looks wonderful." Shawn left the room with a smile.

After cleaning up in the kitchen, she hopped in the shower, then started assembling her ride wear. She would be going to get her motorcycle in a couple of hours, and wanted to look the part when she rode it home. She had been trying to push back the thoughts of it all morning, knowing that she could easily be overwhelmed by the excitement that lurked just beneath the surface.

The phone rang. Shawn answered it with a smile and a swipe on the first ring. "Hey, love!"

"Hey girlfriend! Who's getting an Indian today?" asked Lo.

"Oh my God, girl, you don't even understand how excited I am. I have been trying not to think about it all morning."

"So what have you been thinking about to keep your mind off of it?" Lo said.

"My new Indian," said Shawn, rolling her eyes.

"Ha!" shouted Lo. They both laughed out loud. "Is Cory taking you up there?"

"Yes, of course. Are you guys ready for the ride tonight?" Shawn asked.

"Yes, we are. And you know what? I actually bought some new boots and a bad ass top for the ride," said Lo. Shawn could hear the smile in her voice.

"Really?" she asked, putting her hand over her mouth.

"Yes. I think I caught your bug," said Lo. "Not the one that makes you buy a bike, but the one that makes you want to look the part."

"I am so fucking excited right now," said Shawn. She was laughing as she spoke the words.

"I know, right?" Lo said, almost crying the words with her own excitement. "I'll see you at five!"

"You got it, girl. Laters."


When she disconnected with Lo, she called her dad to check on her mom. Feeling better. Seems like she's going to be okay. Nothing to worry about here. He was basically saying the same thing as he did every time Shawn asked about her. The big worry for Shawn was that all those unspoken words would never have a chance to be spoken. Sure, Monica was living it up, getting to spend all this extra time taking care of her. Because she lived closer than Shawn. Moni hadn't taken a job in another state and moved away from the homestead. Shawn was now being punished for trying to grow, for trying to get away and do something for herself without the safety net of being near her parents.

But that was okay. As long as mom was doing better, that was all Shawn was concerned about.

Her dad did ask if she had any plans on coming home any time soon. It had been ten months since she'd been there. Shawn told him that she would ask her boss about it because they had 'finished up' their current project and were in a holding pattern for a while. It sounded like a good plan, and now was as good a time as any, Shawn reckoned. The only bad thing about it would be leaving her brand new motorcycle behind. She knew she would want to be riding it every day. Silly thoughts, her mom would have said. 'Time to be an adult about things.'

When Cory was finally up and around, they hopped on his bike and he took her to the Indian dealer. They pulled into the parking lot and up under the overhang where several new motorcycles were sitting outside. And there it was. A beautiful matte white Chief. Shawn's palms immediately started getting sweaty. At first, all she could do was walk around staring at it, hands over her mouth on the helmet and eyes wide like a little girl getting her first look at what Santa left her. And when the sales rep came out the door, all smiles, and told her, 'Go ahead! Throw your leg over it! It's yours!' she squealed and did just that.

Shawn leaned forward and put her hands on the handlebars with a slowness borne of great respect. This was her first motorcycle. And oh her God, was she excited. The rep came over and showed her what all the buttons, switches and handles did, and then handed her the keys. She looked back at Cory, still sitting astride his own bike with his hands clasped on the gas tank. He was smiling at her. She squealed again and said, "Okay, so it's mine? There's nothing else I have to do?" The sales rep said nope and to enjoy it. Be safe out there. The usual. So she turned the key and flipped the motor rocker, then started it. Found neutral with her left toe and listened to its satisfying purr.

This time when she looked back at Cory, he was taking her picture. She stuck her tongue out at him, then kicked in her stand and walked it back to be even with him. "I'm gonna roll around the parking lot a few times, just to get used to it, then we can go," she said. He gave her a thumbs-up. Clutch in. First gear. The quality of sound from the motor changed. She eased off the clutch and rolled forward, and then rolled on the throttle a little bit.

Shawn drove around the parking lot four or five times, laughing spontaneously as she found those little patches of straightaway where she could put it in second gear and open it up a little. The powerhouse between her thighs was exciting to her in ways she had never felt. To be in control of something so clean and new and wonderful – all hers – gave her great pride. She hated that she had to park it beneath the stairs at some shitty apartment complex, but she could worry about that later.

When she'd gotten the hang of being in control of the Chief – and it did feel a lot like Cory's bike, but for the shape of the handlebars – Shawn pulled back under the overhang where Cory sat talking to the sales rep. "How does it feel?" said the man.

"Perfect. I love it so much," Shawn said, and then leaned down and hugged the bike, her chest against the gas tank. The sales guy clapped twice and gave her a thumbs-up.

Cory nodded, smiling. "You ready, pumpkin?" he said.

Shawn nodded herself and then waved him forward to take the lead. She didn't want to have to concentrate on directions on her first ride. She would just follow him. She knew he would take nothing but back roads to get home, and trusted he knew them better than she. Before they pulled out of the parking lot, he waved her up next to him and lifted his visor. "You comfortable getting on up to speed like I normally do?"

"Yup. Just go like normal," she responded.

He nodded, dropped his visor, then checked the road. And off they went.

Shawn noticed on that very first stretch out of the parking lot, getting up to around fifty miles per hour, that her motorcycle would have no trouble at all reaching speed. It didn't feel like it would throw her off the back, but she could tell that if she were to goose it without a good grip, it could easily go while she stayed where she was. She made a quick mental note to never let go while it was in gear. She followed him about a car-length behind, on the right side of the lane where he stayed in the left – standard formation riding. At stop signs and traffic signals, she would pull up right next to him, and he would look at her, ask her if she was okay. And then when it went green, Shawn would fall back into formation behind and to the right of him.

The dealership was right off the highway, so their first stretch had been a bit of the service road, where the speed limit was 55. That was the only part of the trip they had to make at that speed though. The rest were residential and feeder roads that had posted speeds of no more than 45, so it was an easy ride and good for getting used to her new machine. They roared through neighborhoods at twenty and twenty-five, Shawn feeling like a true lion and loving the attention they got as they passed people watering their yards or washing their cars. She felt like one of the cool kids having her own bike and riding formation behind someone else. A couple of children even stopped what they were doing on the sidewalk, chalk in their hands, and stared at Shawn and Cory as they rolled by. Shawn waved at the children and their faces lit up with beautiful smiles as they waved back.

When they arrived back at the apartment complex and pulled up onto the sidewalk behind their building, Cory stopped and they both shut them off. The motors clicked and hissed pleasantly as they cooled. Shawn stepped off the bike and removed her helmet, then just about tackled Cory as he stood waiting for her. "I am so happy, Cory!" she almost shouted. "I am so happy I did this! I finally get to ride with the group!"

He held her, twisting back and forth, squeezing her tight and kissing the side of her neck. They took several pictures of the two bikes standing there together before wheeling them up under the stairs to get them out of the way. They naturally found their way into Shawn's apartment, as that had been their starting point for the day, and Shawn turned to embrace Cory again just outside the kitchen. "You know that vibration between my thighs got me feeling really good. I was hoping you could pick up that baton and carry me through the finish line."

Cory hoisted her up onto him, hands under her thighs as he kissed her. He walked her back to the bedroom, kissing her the entire way, then threw her onto the bed where she erupted in laughter as she started pulling her shirt off. She would let him take care of the boots and jeans.

Shawn and Cory lay on their backs staring up at the ceiling, panting and covered in sweat. Something about the excitement of driving her own motorcycle, coupled with the physical sensations it created in her had awakened the lion in her. She had asked for more and harder and rougher than she had ever had before. Her earlier sentiment about the inconvenience of being aroused by a ride was no longer a concern. If she was going to have *this* kind of sex every time she rode her own bike, then she was signing up for the whole thing. *God, that was great.* Perhaps she wouldn't be able to walk tomorrow, and would be sore for a week, but everything good had its price.

"Cory, what about this:" Shawn said when she had finally begun to return to a normal breathing rhythm, "what say we both move when my lease is up?"

"What do you mean?" he said, turning his head to look at her. His fingers found hers down by their waists and interlocked with them.

"Well, we decided to keep your apartment. But since it's a new thing for us, living together for the first time, how about we just get an all new place?"

He rolled his head back to look at the ceiling again, nodding. "That's not a bad idea. Do you have somewhere in mind?"

"Not somewhere, but something, yes," she said. She held her fingernails up in front of her face so she could inspect them. "Somewhere with a garage. I know some apartments in West Arlington, and Dalworthington Gardens that are real nice. And they have garages." She looked over at him, then back at her nails. "I want a garage for our motorcycles. Those are too nice to leave outside. Or parked under some crummy staircase. When is your lease up?"

Cory took a deep breath, then put his hands behind his head. "January," he said.

Shawn looked at him again, widening her eyes. "Not a bad thought, huh?" She rolled up onto her side and put her hand on his stomach, staring at his eyes from the side. "We could even rent a house. I mean, if we're throwing our money away anyway, might as well have a house with a yard while we're at it."

"Now that's a real fine idea, Shawn," he said, nodding thoughtfully.

"See, I was thinking," she said, and flopped her leg over his waist, then rolled over fully on top of him. She put her elbows on his chest and stared down at him. This put her womanhood directly in contact with his manhood. And she did it as if she didn't realize what was happening. His eyebrows shot up. She clicked her fingernails against her front teeth. "Since I run out in November and you're in January, I could go ahead and move in to the new place. I could start getting it all setup and ready. Give it that good *lived-in* feeling so it will be ready for you when you get out."

"Get out? You say it like I'm going to prison, Shawn."

She laughed out loud, then leaned forward and kissed his lips. "No. I mean get out of your lease, you goose!"

"Yeah, so I'm not allowed in the new place until I'm out?"

"Of course you are. I'm just thinking we won't officially *live together* until we both get out of our respective leases," she said. Then she put clasped her fingers together and laid her head on them on his chest. "I love, you Cory Klein. I sure hope you know that."

"Marcy. Look at me," he said. She rolled her head up, putting her chin on her hands. He leaned up and looked her in the eyes. He put his hands on her cheeks. "No one has ever shown me love the way and with the intensity that you do. I know it every day."

She smiled and said, "Good." Then she laid her head back on her hands. "I guess it must be true since you used my Christian name."

They would be meeting Heath and Lo at Cino's at five o'clock. They'd have a bite to eat and then go on their ride. That left just about enough time for a nap. Shawn was too comfortable to roll off of Cory, and too sleepy to care. So that's how she fell asleep. Somehow they both managed to get an hour or so of sleep, but when they awoke they were drenched in sweat and stiff in the spine. It took minutes to get out of bed and stretch the mobility back into their muscles. Then Cory went home so they could shower at the same time in separate apartments.

As Shawn pulled into the parking lot right behind Cory, she saw Lo and Heath stand up from one of the tables in the middle, lifting their fists in the air and shouting. Their mouths made tiny circles, so she guessed they were saying 'woohoo!'. Lo clapped and jumped up and down, all smiles and dancing, attracting a lot of attention from people eating in their cars.

Shawn wanted to wave, but her hand was too busy with the clutch. The clutch required those fingers more than did her friends. Cory and she parked in a spot across the lot from the drive-up stations and started removing their helmets. Lo was there in an instant, jumping around and waiting for Shawn to turn around for a hug.

"Oh my hell!" she shouted. "It is so beautiful! I can't believe you actually bought one, you little slut!"

Shawn laughed out loud as she hung the helmet from the handle grip and turned to give Lo a hug. They stood there rocking back and forth for a long moment, laughing and squealing. "I know, right?" Shawn finally said. "It still feels out of this world. Like impossible that I finally have my own bike. I never ever thought I would be a biker girl!"

"Nice fuckin' wheels, bro," Heath said as he walked up. He clasped hands and bro-hugged Cory, then came over to give Shawn a bear hug. He was smoking a cigarette, walking around the bike and giving it a careful inspection. "Love the paint job!"

Lo and Shawn stood together just watching the boys look at the bike. Lo looked over at her and said, "That's so hot, dude! You have to give me a ride!" Unlike Cory's bike, which had a small pillion behind his main seat, Shawn's Chief had one long one that actually had a sissy bar behind it as well. She hadn't thought about the possibility of giving someone a ride on it.

"Uh, you might want to wait on that, doll," Heath said, reaching out and touching Lo's sleeve.

"Why come?" she asked.

"Shawn needs to get real fuckin' comfortable riding by herself before she runs a two-up. Plus, riding two-up is a completely different set of dogs. Balance and weight are totally different. It takes its own rules and learning," he explained.

"Aw, shucks," Lo said, looking a little crestfallen. "Oh well. I get to look at it while we ride!" she said, holding up a palm for Shawn to high-five.

"Hey, I'll tell you what I *can* do," Shawn said, grabbing Lo's arm. "I can sit still with you on the back!" She raised her eyebrows and Lo nodded enthusiastically. "Boys, get our picture!" she said, then swung her leg over the seat and stood the bike up, straightening the bars. Lo hopped on behind her and laid her head against Shawn's back. She then reached around and put her hands on Shawn's breasts. Shawn laughed out loud and Cory snapped the picture that would hang on her wall evermore. It was the last time Lo would ever smile for a camera.

When the burgers came out, all five of the middle-row tables were full of bikers. They weren't from the same group Shawn and her friends were in, but they were just as friendly. Shawn got many compliments on the new bike and a lot of hugs from women just wanting to welcome her to the sport. "It's a different ride with the rubbers in your own hands!" one of them said, and it took Shawn over an hour to finally get what she had been talking about. *The handle grips. They're rubber. Duh.* Followed by an eye-roll and a private smile.

The boys got beers but Shawn wasn't about to dip her toes into that water. Not yet. She knew she would never drink liquor when she rode, but a beer or two might someday be okay. For now, she was practicing the safest riding she could manage. They sat at the table much longer than they had planned, because at some point a couple of the other bikers joined them. A man named Misfit and his girlfriend or wife, named Coin Toss, sat between Shawn and Lo. The man had tattoos all over his arms and on his fingers. There almost wasn't a clean square inch of skin anywhere on him below the neck. But he was one of the nicest people Shawn had met. And it was still taking her reminding herself that maybe she had been judgmental about the culture before she had joined it.

They ate and laughed and drank and joked and made several new 'friends' Shawn wasn't sure she would ever see or hear from again, but felt good about meeting them. She felt like the best friend she had ever had was sitting right across from her at this table, and looked forward to spending the rest of her life getting to know her more and hang out with her as much as humanly possible. It had taken her almost thirty years of living to meet someone who was so perfectly compatible with her, there was just no way anyone else could ever measure up.

Some of the other bikers traded out the seats Misfit and Coin Toss had taken, one at a time swapping in like tag-team wrestlers coming in for a quick bit of conversation with the new group. Cory and Heath had met many of the guys before, but couldn't remember riding with any of them. On some of the big charity events where multiple groups and clubs would ride for a cause, he was sure they had all ridden together. But those were usually so packed full of bikes that it was hard to even find the people you knew.

They had a great time though, and Shawn was stuffed, having eaten her own burger and fries, and then Lo's fries when Lo turned into a little girl and couldn't finish them herself. Shawn had rolled her eyes as Lo slid the paper boat across the table without a word. It was typical. They had done it many times and Shawn had always been there for her to clean up her left-behind food. Shawn had actually considered not ordering her own side a time or two just because she knew she would be hoovering down Lo's. That girl had the stomach of a bird.

"Of course. Little girl can't finish her own food. Give it to momma. I'll handle it for ya."

Lo rolled her own eyes. She also rolled her wrist over in a graceful bird. "Gopher cures elf!" she said with mock excitement.

"The elf has been cured!" Shawn said, waving a fry in the air before popping it into her mouth.

A couple of the women who had sat down had asked Shawn if she wanted a beer, why wasn't she drinking one, blah blah blah. And she continually and politely declined each offer. But she was finding more and more that she wanted one. It was for one, getting closer to the time she normally did have a drink. But she was also having such a great time sitting here with these folks, and she typically *did* have a drink during those fun social events. So she kind of felt naked not having one. Somehow she was able to resist though.

The sun was going down when they finally got ready to leave. Shawn made her way around the back to use the public restroom, and then on the way back ran into Lo, who was a little tipsy. She grabbed Shawn's arms and said, "Have you fucked on it yet? I mean on a bike?"

Shawn giggled and took the arms that were holding hers. They would stand in that funny stance for several minutes talking. "No. I actually don't see how we could do that. We have to park them under the stairs," Shawn responded.

Lo's eyes got serious for a second and her jaw dropped. "Wait. What? You don't do it at home, you dumb dumb! You take it out somewhere nice! Some secluded lake or an overlook or something!"

Shawn raised her chin. "Ah. Yeah. Duh. Sorry," she said.

"Yeah, you have to try it," Lo said, squeezing her arms. "He leans back against the bars and you stand on the pegs." Her eyes rolled back as she gasped. "I could get off just thinking about it."

"Wouldn't the bike fall over?"

"No, honey. That kickstand can hold twice the weight of that bike. Okay, move, I gotta pee!" she said, and darted off to the bathroom. Shawn checked her phone and walked back to the front to rejoin the others. When Lo returned, they started making motions toward moving on. Lo and Heath went to the east side of the lot while Shawn and Cory went west. From where she stood putting on her helmet, she heard Heath's bike come roaring to life. And within a minute, they had pulled around the parking lot to stand idling behind Shawn and Cory. Shawn looked at Lo as she pulled the riding gloves onto her hands and hitched the straps. Lo was leaning way over, her chin against Heath's left shoulder and her face full of smile as she yelled something at him. He was sitting statuesque still, looking down at his phone while she talked. Shawn smiled and walked up to them, unable to hear what her friend was saying.

She squatted and touched Lo's shoulder, then put her hands on her knees. When Lo looked at her, holding out her arms for a hug, Shawn stood up and stepped in, wrapping her arms awkwardly around the woman riding pillion behind Heath. "I love you, sister!" Shawn said. Then she leaned forward and said to Heath, "Take care of my girl, boy!" Heath held his left fist out close to his shoulder so she could knock her own against it.

As Shawn stepped back to her bike pulling the helmet strap tight under her chin, Cory started his own motorcycle. She frowned slightly at the sound, wondering why hers – which was a bigger see see (whatever that meant) – didn't sound as loud as his. Then she remembered that he had upgraded his pipes from the stock ones that came with it. Maybe she should do that herself. One of the patches on Cory's vest read 'Loud Pipes Save Lives' and she could understand why.

Her hands were trembling slightly as she swung her leg over the tank and looked over her bike. This would only be the third time she had started it. Everything still looked a little alien to her. She had to stand back up to fish the key out of her pocket – no small task for a gloved hand – and her hands were trembling hard by the time she stuck it into the ignition. Maybe she should have thought this one over a little better. Riding at night on the first day she had her bike? Holy shit, was this a dumb idea. She had driven a motorcycle after dark precisely zero times, for a grand total of zero minutes. She hoped her headlight would do its job.

Shawn started the bike and found neutral, then put her hands on the grips. The 'rubbers'. Then she looked over at Cory. He raised his eyebrows and tilted his head forward. She nodded and gave him a thumbs-up. Then he made a complicated hand gesture that involved pointing at her, then pointing at himself with the other hand, then making a motion that showed her falling in line behind him. She rolled her eyes and bounced her head around in a ridiculous simulacrum of a nod. "Duh," she said in her helmet where only she could hear. "Of course I'm fuckin' following you, genius boy!"

Cory walked his bike back while Shawn sat watching in her mirror. Then she did the same and ran up the parking lot a few meters to do a nice proper u-turn, which she had learned in class and had gotten pretty good at. She pulled up behind him and shook her hips on the seat, wiggling herself into a ready position.

Heath looked back at Cory, who gave him the go-ahead. Then the engines revved. Shawn was able to see peripherally as they left the parking lot that all their new friends were waving at them. She wanted to wave back, but that was her throttle hand. She settled instead for dipping her chin at them. And then they were off. Heath, obviously aware of Shawn's novice-like abilities, was not showing that awareness as they rocketed off down the street, exceeding the speed limit by a couple of bars on the speedo. Shawn kept up though, comfortable in her confidence, and aware herself that Cory wouldn't let them get into any shit she couldn't get out of. She had a lot to learn.

The headlight was insignificant. There were street lights. And she was in back, so she could just follow their lights. Shawn knew that on some dark country road it might come in handy, but out here, it was most likely more for showing others where she was than for seeing. There were also cars behind them, and their headlights were carrying most of the heavy load. This just wasn't as scary as she had thought it would be.

After riding for about half an hour, Shawn started to loosen up and feel more comfortable. As she rode, she thought about how simple it actually was to control a motorcycle. What had seemed like such a tight wire act before, worrying about balance and handling and steering and shifting gears, and oh-my-God-it-has-a-clutch!, she was now learning were all rudimentary tasks handled almost without thought at all. It was truly like second-nature. In fact, she was finding it was so simple she wondered why more people didn't do it. They said it was seven times more dangerous than driving a car.

The small group pulled up to a stop light. They were about to go under a bridge where they would turn left and then presumably go up onto the highway, which Shawn was okay with tonight, knowing that she was riding with a group. The group made it safer. More lights, more bikes, easier to see. Plus, they would only be on it for a minute or two, because their ride wasn't about highway. It was about feeder roads. Not so much the back roads and twisties tonight, because those weren't typically lit. Tonight, they just wanted to get out and show Shawn a good time without a lot of traffic.

Shawn's front tire was only a couple of feet behind Heath's, as she was following proper formation protocol. Cory sat next to Heath, and was leaning over having a conversation with him, each of them shouting to be heard through the helmets and the roar of the motorcycle engines. Lo, who was sitting with her hands on her knees, turned and looked back at Shawn with a smirk on her face. She winked and shook her hips and shoulders, holding up her hands and snapping as if she were at a dance.

Shawn sat up straight, pulling her hands off the rubbers for a moment to tighten the wrist straps of her gloves, smiling at Lo. Then she pointed and made a heart by putting her fingers and thumbs together. Lo blew her a kiss and then turned around. The light turned green. As Heath took off, Shawn saw Cory's brake light come on and put her own foot on the brake. She was about to pull up beside Cory, now having a gap in front of her, to ask him if something was wrong. And that fast, it happened.

The loud zinging whine of a sport bike had completely escaped her ears – and apparently Heath's too, because they had never seen it coming. Only Cory had. He had taken that extra half-second to look left and make sure the coast was clear before he rolled on the throttle to power through the intersection – the most dangerous place a biker ever encounters.

The sport bike sailed through the intersection, blowing the red, and went right *through* Heath's bike. So many things happened at the same time, Shawn couldn't later be sure in retrospect which had happened first. But the next thing she knew was that Cory was off his bike and running to the west along the side of the road – a long way away from where they had been sitting when the world still made sense – waving his hands and shouting. The impact of the crossing motorcycle had taken both bikes a hundred yards down the feeder road that ran beside the elevated highway.

And Shawn had still not even processed what had happened. She finally got the idea to get out of the way of the cars behind her, not realizing that they didn't want to go anywhere anymore than she did all of a sudden. She foot-walked her bike across the right lane and into the shoulder of the crossroad, then consciously considered and remembered how to turn on her hazard lights and stepped off the bike. And then it hit her. Her friend had just been hit by a motorcyclist. And that's when her heart started beating triple-time. Wait.

This is one of those things that we think about but that doesn't... just fucking wait.

Hang on.

She ran up the road, following Cory's path. He had reached where the two bikes lay. The bottom one – for they were indeed stacked – still had its left blinker on, clicking red light on and off, telling the universe that it was making a move. Well, it was no longer moving anywhere. It would never move anywhere again on its own power.

As she got closer, Shawn's cheeks started to tighten. She began getting tears in her eyes. She pulled the rip tab of her helmet and yanked the chin strap down, then tossed the helmet in the grass to her right. "Wait."

*This isn't happening. I mean, they're fine, right? This was just some mistake. Right, God?*

She got to where Cory was, on his hands and knees. But there was no bike. She glanced to the left and saw the blinking orange light, about twenty paces back. She had run right past the motorcycles without even realizing it. She dropped to her knees behind and beside Cory, putting her arm over his shoulders and directing her focus at him. If she could focus completely on him then the rest of it could be gone, right? It could be untrue. It could be not happened. Can we go back in time just a few minutes? Can I just get a chance to honk my horn? To get Lo to turn around so I can point at that goddamn mother fucker coming over the hill to our left? She'll tap Heath on the shoulder and say, 'Babe, hold back just a sec, okay?' and he will. He will listen to her. I promise, God. I won't ask you for much more. Can we just back up, what, thirty seconds? Okay, ninety. Let's do ninety. Ninety seconds. Please? That's all I need.

She was staring so hard at Cory's sweating face and concentrating so hard on asking him if everything was okay – knowing it wasn't – that she had not even yet acknowledged the body over which he was crouched. Somewhere along the run Cory had made from intersection to here, he had ditched his own helmet. His bike still sat in the middle of the lane they had occupied – they, the group that had been, back when the world made sense – but here he was, hand on... what? She finally looked down.

Shawn had to close her eyes for a moment. Choke back the hard cry that was right there. There was an army of tears banging on that door. And the hinges wouldn't hold for long. Lo was lying there, looking up at the stars. Her helmet was gone. Where had it gone? She had not gotten to remove it like Shawn had. Or Cory had. It was just... gone. Involuntarily removed. And here she lay, mouth working like she was trying to speak and breathe at the same time, but not much of either happening. Shawn took her arm off Cory's shoulders and leaned forward, falling onto Lo. Cory tried to pull her off – to tell her that, 'hey, we can still save her, we need to do CPR, give her space, just...' but Shawn's subconscious clarity had already kicked in. This was a gone girl. And Shawn didn't want Lo's last few seconds to be spent staring at someone's forehead while he tried in vain to stop something that couldn't be stopped. Death was on its way. It was a freight train and Cory was a little boy on the tracks holding his hand up – willing that train to stop. But it sometimes took miles to bring those steel wheels and those hundreds of thousands of tons of cargo to be brought to rest.

She put her hands on Lo's cheeks, surprisingly not bloody at all, and looked into her eyes. "Lo. Laura, baby, I'm here. I… I…" Her tears dripped down onto Lo's lips. Lo didn't even react. No flinch. No reflex. Just staring up at the stars.

"I'm sorry, Shawn. I'm sorry," Lo said in a husky whisper, and a little bit of blood finally showed itself on her tongue. "I wanted to…"

"Laura. Lo. Lo." Shawn slapped her cheeks lightly. Ever so lightly. *Wait. Just fucking wait. Give me one more fucking minute here.* "Lo! I need you to hang on." Cory stood up, hands on his hips, looking around at the scene. Cars were starting to line up beside the bridge. He was silently cursing and his breathing was heavy. Shawn could hear it hitching every few breaths. Like he was holding back a hard cry of his own. She looked back down at Lo. And then the cry came.

"Lo, baby, I'm so sorry. What can I do?"

"I don't wanna die, Shawn. I don't wanna die!"

Shawn gasped and cried out – that involuntary burst of cry that would soon take over completely. And when it did, she would be the freight train. No little boy with his hands up would stop it. Cory, she heard, was crying openly now. He had walked off. She looked at where he was standing and saw Heath's body. There was no head there, though. Shawn shook her head and returned her attention to Lo, who lay there panting. She was on her way out now. It was imminent.

"I'm sorry, baby. I know. I know and I'm sorry," Shawn said, reaching up to wipe a tear away from her own face. She would regret this stupid gesture for the rest of her life. It was one more second she could have spared to wipe away the tear of her friend.

"Shawn?" Lo said.

Shawn put her hands on Lo's cheeks again and leaned down where her ear was close to Lo's mouth. "What's up, babe?"

"Shawn, I want to come back and see you, okay?"

Shawn closed her eyes. She knew what that statement meant, but couldn't believe Lo would say such a thing. Especially in this context, where she lay dying. "Come back, Lo?"

"Yes. I want you to wake me up again soon, okay?"

"Lo!" Shawn said, and leaned in closer, putting her forehead against her friend's. Their lips were millimeters apart. "Lo, Lo, Lo. That's not real. Okay? That's not a real thing. I don't want that. I want you here. Now. I want you to sit up. To pull through this."

Lo's eyes closed and she smiled. It was a weak and tired smile, but the effort was good enough for Shawn. "Baby, I'm gone. I ain't gonna make it. I'll never forget you though."

Shawn closed her eyes, keeping her hands against Lo's face, their foreheads touching, her tears literally dripping into Lo's eyes now, and breathed out. "Lo. Don't leave me. I can't handle this. I need you to stay here with me. I need you to fight. I need…"

"Shawn… Shawn!" Lo whispered. It would have been a shout had she had the benefit of aspiration. But that was all gone now. She was down to just her vocal cords and whatever breath she had left in her mouth and throat. Just like one of Shawn's subjects. Shawn opened her eyes to see Lo's. "Let me go. I had it good. I'm glad I knew you." she said. And then her lips made a weak smile.

Shawn lost her control at that moment, falling forward, her lips pressing hard against her friends as she cried out her friend's name and a trite little phrase. Over and over she said, "I love you, Lo. I love you!" Her lips were touching Lo's as she repeated it, and she was raining tears down all over her face. For a living person it would not have been comfortable to be on the lower side of this stack – the receiving end of the cry. But Laura Carter was not strictly living anymore. Shawn was now bawling onto her friend's face. Foreheads and noses and mouths pressed together, Shawn cried harder than she had ever cried. Her knees collapsed and she fell bodily onto Lo, her cheek sliding against Lo's until her lips touched the asphalt. Her right hand made it round the back of Lo's head, holding it up away from the awful, hot, black surface.

So much to say. Just wait. *Wait. Give me just a few more seconds.*

The biggest swell of her cry abated enough for Shawn to pull back and look at Lo in the face, her own face a wreck of emotion and tears and puffy cheeks. She looked at her friend in the eyes and realized that at some point in the last few seconds, those eyes had gone out. Peripherally, and with not much conscious supporting thought, Shawn wondered what her last words had been – the last words Lo had been able to hear and comprehend. The last ones to make it through the pall. The words Lo would carry with her into the great beyond. She hoped it was 'I love you'.

The chaos of the event finally started showing itself with its full intensity. Emergency vehicles with their strobe lights reflecting off the side of the bridge, police cars blocking the crossroad, burning flares set a few feet apart to keep traffic from coming this way, men walking here and there, keying radio mikes and talking, heads tilted to their shoulders, pulling yellow police tape across the road, cameras flashing as they photographed the scene… Shawn sat on the curb with her head buried between her knees, her hands on the back of her scalp. They had told her to sit here. To back away a little and let them do their work, but that everything would be okay. Shawn knew not everything would be okay. In fact, *nothing* would be okay. Nothing would ever be okay again.

Occasionally, through her tear-filled eyes, Shawn would look up and try to assess the situation. Cory was standing off to one side with one hand on his hip as he explained to the police officer what he had seen. Shawn, who had seen the same thing he had, was suffering from memory loss. She wasn't sure she would be helpful in any meaningful way. The adrenaline dump she was suffering would cost her precious memories, she knew.

What she came to understand, though she had probably known all along – at least on some level – was that three people had died in that accident. Now there was a funny word. *Accident?* That son of a bitch had run a red light. That much Shawn did remember. Is that *ever* an accident? Really? If you're driving, aren't you paying attention to signs and lights? How can that be an accident? Heath and Laura were no more. Along with the man who had been driving the sport bike, whom Shawn could hardly find room in her heart to feel sorry for. Gone. All gone. Dead. History. *What a fucking waste.*

At some point, Shawn stood up and walked to the back of an ambulance and got sick. It had nothing to do with the food in her stomach. It was just the stress and realization that she would now be spending the rest of her life without her best friend in it. The friend she had only recently acquired. Gone. How in the fuck was this fair? *Can we back up thirty minutes, please? This isn't how it was supposed to play out. I mean, come on. The light was red… Give me a half-hour. Please, God?*

Every time Shawn's mind took her back to the moment of impact, she had to physically stop and put her hands on her knees, taking the posture of someone who was getting sick, and pray and talk herself back down. Her mind kept wanting to tell her that this could be reversed. They had reversed death, after all, hadn't they? That one little detail kept haunting her thoughts. If death could be undone in a lab, could she not reach out and grab one of those distant stars? Could she not wield some power, some magic, and pull this girl back out of death's grasp? Since Shawn had so much experience with bringing people back, didn't that give her some administrator's pass? Some get-out-free card? Something that allowed her some authority over the normal in and out daily bullshit? Wasn't she, in other words, special?

Apparently not, because every prayer she had tried and every thought and statement she had pointed at the woman lying on the gurney were coming up short. The woman was still dead. Cory stood in front of her, just letting Shawn bury her face in his chest. He wrapped his arms around her but didn't say anything. He knew there was nothing he could say to help her through this, so he kept quiet. For this, Shawn was thankful. Every few minutes, just when she would begin regaining some of her composure, she would lose it again. Her diaphragm would contract and she would burst out with a fresh wail, beginning the cry all over again.

There was blessedly very little to answer as far as the police were concerned. The others – those in vehicles around them – had come forward and attested to what had happened, but in the end it was pretty obvious to the police. A man had very clearly been traveling at a ridiculously high speed on the feeder road – *on the feeder road!* - and had blown the light. Probably thinking he was going fast enough to make it through the intersection before anyone started moving forward into his path. Well, had he been a hundred feet farther along when the light changed, he would have shot through and everyone would still be alive. What was a hundred feet worth at over a hundred miles per hour? A quarter of a second? Her friend's life, as well as Heath's, over because of a quarter-second? These thoughts didn't help Shawn cope with the grief. But they came no less. Unwelcome intruders into the dark house that was now her mind.

After what seemed like an eternity, they finally got to leave. Shawn was in no condition to ride though. The police, under the circumstances, offered to have the motorcycles towed back to the apartment on a flat-bed truck. Shawn and Cory accepted the ride in the back of a cruiser where the officer who drove them was gracefully silent. He looked back once as he got into the car, giving them a look of knowing, a humane glance and nod that showed he understood the gravity of the situation, and then he turned around and drove without looking back again. Cory and Shawn sat bunched up together in the middle, not even bothering with seat belts. Shawn just needed to be held on the way home. And when they finally got there, she needed to be held in the bed.

There wasn't much to say, so she didn't say it. Cory took her by the shoulders when they got inside and asked if she wanted to be alone, or if he should stay with her. She nodded as he asked the last half and he wrapped his arms around her. "Okay. I'm going to go get a shower then I'll be right back. Do you need anything?" he said, pulling back and running her hair off her forehead for her. Shawn shook her head. He nodded then backed up a step, looking at her before finally letting go her shoulders and turning to leave.

Shawn sat in the shower and let the hot water bang down on her for a long time. The water heater's capacity – always a secondary thought in her mind – was the only reason she got out at all. Otherwise she might have stayed the night in there. When she stepped out and dried off, she leaned on the basin with a toothbrush in her mouth and looked at her haggard reflection in the mirror. *Those eyes are gonna get darker.* Her lips trembled but she wouldn't allow another cry tonight. She had done enough of that. She went to bed, thankful that Cory was already in it waiting for her. She curled up into a fetal position with the monkey wrapped in her lower arm while her right lay on Cory's chest. He wrapped her in his embrace and she fell asleep quickly.

# Sixteen

The funeral was Saturday. Shawn was happy to meet Laura's family. Her mother seemed a lot like Shawn's own mom: a little distant but well meaning. Seeing Lo's dad crying through the whole service was extremely hard for Shawn though, as she kept picturing her own daddy. That could have been her up there in the casket. She had not seen the speeding biker either. Only Cory had. She was super lucky that she had been riding behind the others and that Cory had acted. She wondered how her dad would have taken it if it had been her funeral. Maybe she wasn't cut out for being a biker after all. All the statistics said it was dangerous, and apparently they were right. Shawn had originally figured that whatever riding she would be doing would all be at low speeds and little traffic. Well, how's that for low speed? Heath hadn't even reached ten miles per hour.

Lo also had a younger brother. Shawn hugged him hard and kissed the top of his head when he looked up at her and told her Lo had loved her very much and spoke of her all the time. The head kiss was to comfort the boy, sure. But it was mostly to keep him from seeing the instant tears that arrived upon hearing that statement. Cory was here with Shawn, standing back and just being available for her. Heath's story was a little different. His memorial had been the night before, and only a few people showed up – mostly from the motorcycle group. Since Lo had not quite made it as deep into the group as Shawn had already, only two people from the group showed for her funeral. Shawn guessed it was mostly because they just didn't know about it.

The casket was a rental, which brought its own bout of tension to Shawn's stomach. Because she knew Lo had been serious about donating her body. Shawn knew that when that casket closed at the end of the service, it would not be the last time she would see her dead friend's face. And that wasn't necessarily a peace-bringing thought. She wanted to honor Lo's wishes, but at the same time would much rather have just let her go. Let her rest in peace in her new eternity. What if they had success in the lab and she did come back for a while? Would that be any better? Would the answers she got from her friend really be from her friend? Or just those manufactured responses triggered by technology in the bloodstream? Would it make any difference? And what if they had failure in the lab? If Shawn had to watch her friend go through a seizure, or any number of the other horrors she had witnessed in the lab, she didn't think she could handle it.

Lo looked beautiful though. She wore a deep maroon satin dress and her makeup job was superior. She looked almost as beautiful in death as she had in life. Shawn was thankful that Lo had been wearing a helmet, though that helmet might very well have been what broke her neck. The added weight certainly hadn't helped when her head had snapped to the left while the rest of her went the other way. She had many fractured bones and ribs. Her poor body was almost destroyed. But her face and head was without a scratch. Thank God for small favors. Laura's family deserved that much.

Shawn, expecting an all-out breakdown at the casket, was surprised by her ability to maintain composure. There were tears in her eyes as she bent over and half-hugged the fragile body that lay in the silk-lined box. She kissed Lo's forehead and touched her cheek, doing her best not to disturb the makeup. She only experienced one hitch in her breathing as she turned away from the casket to file out of the service.

Then she sat in the Jeep for a long time, telling Cory not to drive away yet. Getting into September, he had the top and doors back on, so Shawn was allowed a little privacy up in the cab. She sat with her hands clasped in front of her chest as she watched the crowd file out of the church. "It was a beautiful service," she said, her voice full of cracks and creaks from all the crying she had done recently.

Cory nodded thoughtfully, putting his hand on her knee. "Yes. It was. She looked beautiful."

Shawn looked over at him. "God, Cory. What am I gonna do?"

"I don't know how to answer that, baby," he said after a long pause. "I don't know how you move on from this. I just know it happens."

Shawn fell over toward him, awkwardly leaning against the center console and wrapped her arms around him. And cried again.

It had been a sense of duty to a friend that got Shawn through that Saturday. It was a sense of respect and honor that got her through the next day. While she knew Sameer would handle the intake and transport of the body with dignity and grace, she felt she owed it to her best friend to be there. She wanted no undue, unnecessary one-on-one situations between male and female and no interruptions to Lo's modest nature. Of course she would have been there anyway, as she felt it was now part of her normal duties to be part of the intake process, and while they normally happened on weekends just due to the typical timing of funerals, they would not always be on a Sunday. If she intended to stay in this position with this role in the company, she would be there. Whether she intended to stay was up for debate though. Death had suddenly become a giant part of her life because of this job and she wasn't sure she was comfortable with that statement. She had not gone to school to become a mortician.

One of the strangest parts of the intake for Shawn was knowing it was all secret. Lo had not told her parents about the donation to science. They knew she would not be immediately buried, and that her body was going somewhere else for a while, but apparently she had not told them Shawn would be part of that science. Shawn had asked a couple of leading questions to her father but he had shown no hint of knowing where she would go, and she found that a little discouraging. She felt like she would go crazy not knowing where her child was being sent after death. Shawn didn't push it though or try to go any further. She certainly didn't let on that she would be part of it. If Lo had wanted it to be private, Shawn would respect that. She was a grown adult, after all.

Remembering back to their conversation sitting on Lo's rug in her music room, Shawn had been steadfastly against her friend joining the science project. Knowing she couldn't stop Lo from doing so though, she had forbidden her to die. How much of a joke had she thought the girl was making? She would never seriously have considered that it would actually happen. Not at this age. That music room would forever hold a place in Shawn's favorite memories though. That was when she had gotten closest to her new friend – where they developed a trust and intimate knowledge of each other.

Now she stood at the top of the loading dock, just like before, watching the same man deliver the cardboard box full of her friend into the building. When Sameer got to the elevator, Shawn was waiting and holding the doors for him. He wheeled the gurney in and let them close, then pressed the floor button and leaned against the wall, crossing his arms. "Shawn I am not sure this is a good idea, bringing a friend into the program."

"Why would it not be?" Shawn asked, pulling her hair back behind her ears. She was wearing her favorite hat today.

"I do not want anything bad to happen in there. And with you knowing this person, it will be very difficult to proceed like a normal subject, I am thinking," he said. Shawn was impressed with his decorum, and tended to agree with everything he said. So she said so.

"I do agree with you Sameer. But she asked specifically about joining the project. She literally *wanted* to be on this table." She stood looking at him for a long time, knowing the two questions he wanted to ask, but was refraining from asking. The elevator dinged and the doors opened. Sameer pushed the cart through and they went once again into the wide halls of the lab complex. When they got her on the table in D Room, he once again resumed his posture, leaning against the counter and crossing his arms. Shawn sat on his stool and faced him with her back to the newly occupied white sheet on the table.

She sighed and swallowed, then sat up straight, clasping her hands together and fidgeting with her rings. "Sameer, I didn't intend to tell anyone about the project. I had a little too much to drink one night. Okay, a *lot* too much. And I was having bad dreams a lot. I confided in my best friend."

His nod was very subtle. But he did not speak.

"And no, her death was not planned," Shawn added after a minute.

He frowned and said, "Why would you think I would think that, Shawn?"

"Because I told you she wanted to be on this table. She did. We were both drunk, and she mentioned how neat it would be *if* she were dead, to be able to be here. It's not like she wanted to die though." she said. After another pregnant pause, she said, "And I'm sorry for breaking confidence about the privacy of the project."

"I am not concerned with this, Shawn. We all need our outlets. And I know this is a very difficult position to be in for someone to not be able to speak about it," he said. He was very still. "It is not the friend I am worried about. We must keep this secret from corporate entities."

Shawn nodded. "Of course." She wondered if he was about to ask if Shawn had told anyone else. She didn't want to tell him, but she wouldn't lie, either. Fortunately, there was only the boyfriend left to disclose.

"Are you sure that you are emotionally ready to deal with this subject, Shawn?"

Shawn winced at his use of the term, but realized his question was pointedly legitimate because of it. The fact that Lo was lying on the table behind her meant she would be a subject. *Just another subject.* That was literally all she could be in here. She was no one's friend, no one's loved one. Not on the table. One had to be able to separate the living from the dead. And it wasn't like respecting the dead at a graveside. This was tampering with brain and body function, completely detached from who the living person had been. Shawn understood all of this, and knew she would have to make that distinction. She also knew she would have trouble doing so. Sameer, therefore, surprised her with his next statement.

"I am going to leave the room for an hour. I want you to prep your friend. You may spend some time with her. Talk to her. Make yourself comfortable with how she is looking on this table and what she is here to do. I will let this be private. But please keep in mind, we honor her wishes by proceeding in as normal a fashion as decorum allows."

"Yes, I know," Shawn said, nodding. "Thank you, Sameer." He gave her a wan smile and left the room. She heard him go out the front of the lab complex, leaving the glass walled unit entirely. He would presumably go back and sit in his office until the hour had passed.

Shawn got up from the stool upon which she had been sitting, Sameer's stool, and rounded the head of the table to her own. When she was seated, she pulled the sheet back, baring the woman's head and her bare shoulders. The people at the funeral home had dressed her in a plain white tank top and boxer shorts. Bare minimums, but a wonderful relief to

Shawn, who had wanted to keep her friend's privacy intact. And baring her shoulders made it almost feel like she was lying in a bed. Just sleeping. And Shawn was here to talk to her a little bit.

Shawn ran her fingers through Lo's hair, pulling it back and letting it hang off the head of the table. She separated the strands and locks with her fingernails, gently caressing her friend's head. She looked so much like she could just wake up at any moment. That uncanny still was barely noticeable in the dim light of the laboratory. She put her hand on Lo's forehead. She wasn't cold, which was nice. She was not living human warmth, but at least she wasn't cold.

"Hello, precious," said Shawn. She continued running her hand through Lo's hair, making a ponytail with the strong brown locks, then letting it fall gently to the table and above. She did this for a long time. It obviously wasn't giving comfort to the dead woman, but it was having that effect on Shawn. The act of playing with each other's hair was always a two-way calming ritual between girls. Her hair was clean and shiny, and it felt good to Shawn's fingers.

"Well, you finally made it here. You silly butt," she said and her throat hitched. She smiled and held back the cry, then wiped away the lone tear that had appeared. "I know, you would have called me a lot worse than that. Bitch or slut or ho," Shawn said and laughed as more tears made their way forward. "God," she said, sighing and looking up at the indirect lighting above the cabinets, "why did this have to happen? I never wanted you to get your wish to be on my table."

Shawn was still playing with Lo's hair, but her eyes had lost their focus staring at the soft lighting, her memories replaying events in her head. She sat there for a long time doing this. "Well, at least you can be together with Heath. Nothing can ever go wrong again, baby."

She leaned over and kissed Lo on the cheek, and then laid her head beside her friend's, putting her hand on her far shoulder and just holding her. After a moment, she sat up and lifted Lo's head gently with her left hand so she could slide her right arm under her neck. Then she leaned back down and held her again. It was awkward and imperfect, but it was as close as she could get to the real thing. This, she reminded herself, was her own private time with her best friend. Time the family got in the funeral home, and visitors got for a minute or two at a time. But it was never enough, and there was always the threat of someone coming into the room and disturbing the visit. Shawn had her all to herself here, for a little while. Before the science and technology kicked in and brought simulated life back into the face she loved seeing those smiles on so much. Before whatever else would happen, real Laura or just simulation, science or magic, at least this was real. And it would be the last few moments of peaceful communion she would ever spend with her friend.

"You know, all my life, especially as a little girl," she said, wiping a tear drop away with her thumb, still holding her friend close, "I wanted a friend like you." She breathed deeply. She could smell the pleasant aroma of Lo's conditioner, and was happy her mother had come and cleaned her up before the funeral. "I never thought I would find her. I can't believe it took almost thirty years. But hey, here you are!" she said. "I found you, Lo!" She sniffled and smiled, but it was only to cover the immense pain she was feeling in her soul. The tears came faster now, flowing and falling more quickly than she would be able to catch them, so she no longer bothered. She shuddered as she inhaled and was unable to hold back the cry any longer. "And now I've already fuckin' lost you," she said through the sobbing.

Shawn finally had to sit up. She was getting Lo's hair and face wet and making a mess of everything. She turned and fetched a box of tissues from the counter behind her and tried to stop the flow from her eyes, then wiped the table and straightened Lo's hair again. When she had regained a little of her control back, she blew out through a small O and said, "Whew. Sorry, baby. I'm not doing well with this arrangement. You need to be here with me laughing and drinking and celebrating."

When she had sat staring at Lo and played with her hair for what felt like a long enough time to enhance her quietude, Shawn finally stood up and kissed her forehead, then got started with the preparation tasks. She put the thawed blood in the reservoir and clipped new syringes on the ends of the tubes, then straightened the room up and got ready for Sameer's return. A lot of that time she had spent steeling herself, she had considered what would happen if Lo awoke into a state of panic and unrest like some of the others had. And though she had consciously wanted to be here before she died, what would happen if she awoke like Sonora had? Mouthing *'fucking kill me'* over and over? Shawn pushed the thought away. Whatever will be will be. And they always had the helmet. She glanced at it, sitting on its post in the corner of the room, just out of the edge of the light. Spooky.

She sat down at the workstation and loaded her routines, sent them to the penning trap. Shawn wondered as an aside how many nanobots they actually had left. There was probably some way to check, but that subconscious unease she felt about continuing the project was the likely culprit in keeping her from caring. She prayed for a smooth transition here, and a peaceful, serene interview session. If that was possible in the context in which they operated, she sure hoped it would prove out today.

When she turned on her chair and looked back at the table where her friend lay, she noticed the leather straps hanging down beneath it. Sameer's side. She had forgotten that part of the protocol. And with that thought, she realized today was the prep day. Not the interview day. She had steeled herself for no reason, and would have to go through the whole thing again tomorrow. Though it would probably not take as long. And as much as she hated to do so, she knew there was good reason for the leather belts. *If she wakes up and starts thrashing, it will not be my friend doing so.*

*But how would that work, on a technical level, anyway? If most of her skeleton is crushed, she wouldn't have the support system – the scaffolding – to do things like sit up.* And with that thought, the tears threatened to come forward again. "Poor darling," she said aloud. She heard the front door of the lab complex open. She could only see a ghost of Sameer, with something like eight panes of glass standing between them, and all the lights off in all the rooms between here and there. Only the hall lights and the lighting in D Room were on. But she did see him raise his hand in a wave, a gesture that was probably more interrogative than greeting. She waved back and stood up.

When he came into the lab, he said, "Are you okay, Miss Shawn?"

She nodded. "Sameer, I would like to not be in here when you insert the blood lines, if that's okay."

"Of course, Shawn. Whatever is your wish is okay."

She looked around the room, nodding and taking a deep breath. "I think we're ready for tomorrow."

He stood still, just looking at her. "Okay, good then. I will see you tomorrow morning. And Shawn. Please. If you change your mind in the night or in the morning, please do not hesitate to be calling me and -"

"No, Sameer. We're doing this. I want to honor her wishes. And I want to speak to her again."

His stuttered nod was telling. It said he thinking, *'You know it might not be like talking to the real thing, right?'* But what he ended up saying was, "Okay, Shawn. We will proceed. But the offer is still on the table," he said. What a horrible choice of words that was.

"All right. Well I will see you in the morning. Thank you, Sameer."

He nodded thoughtfully, closing his eyes.

"No. Really. Thank you for being so delicate and considerate about this subject," Shawn said, using the word with intent.

He nodded again, then lifted his hand in a wave. She waved back and put her hand against his as she walked by him, a weak but friendly version of a high-five. And Shawn went home to rest.

Shawn lay in her bed most of the rest of the day, just staring at the ceiling, her arms wrapped round the stuffed monkey and her legs under the covers. She had asked Cory for some time alone. She told him she would come to his place tonight when she was ready for bed, but needed to mourn and pray and prepare herself for the next morning. He was, of course, completely understanding. *Such a great guy. How lucky I was to find him. I had better not lose him now, too.*

She had spent so much of the last week weeping that she felt it in her bones. She was dry. Used up. Shawn had taken off Monday and Tuesday after the wreck, but on Wednesday was reminded frequently that she should have just taken the week off. She would burst into deep body-wracking fits of sobbing at her desk and have to cover her mouth, trying to hold her breath as she dashed to the bathroom. Everyone had seen it. And when Sameer had finally had enough, he had sent her home. Initially she had spurned his efforts to send her home. But after lunch when everyone came back and she was weeping openly at her desk, face in her hands, he had put his foot down. And further, God bless him, he had sent Jeremy and Chandra to drive her home. Chandra drove Shawn's Jeep and Jeremy followed to bring Chandra back to work.

Shawn had declined two calls from her dad, but then finally texted him and told him what had happened. She said she would call him when she was a little farther into it. He said all the right things that a dad should say, which made her cry even more. Part of her was happy that she had met Lo when she did – not earlier in life – but it didn't seem like it would matter much. She was just as devastated as if she had known her since grade school. And she had not ridden her motorcycle again since that night. While Shawn was sure she would ride again, it was still too closely associated with the tragedy, and therefore hard not to imagine breaking into crying fits while she rode.

Shawn wondered absently about the association with the butterfly. She tried to remember all the times it had shown up, and was hard-pressed not to believe it had something to do with Miranda. But then it had died the morning of Lo's death. And Lo was her butterfly sister. Of course there was nothing to it. Silly thoughts by a shattered mind. But it felt like it should have meaning somehow.

She had also read through some more pages of Miranda's journal – Cory calling her a glutton for punishment – but it somehow gave her peace. She actually found herself wishing Lo had written a journal she could read. But Lo's family had taken care of all her things from the apartment. Being a new friend, Shawn was not high up on the list of people who would get to inherit any of her belongings. She didn't want anything, of course. But a diary or something small and personal would be nice. What Shawn had was a near-empty bottle of tequila standing on her bar, brought by Lo several weeks before, and the picture Cory had snapped of them sitting on her motorcycle together.

It was a fantastic shot. The setting sun had been low behind Cory, casting them in a beautiful orange hue. Shawn's laugh – the one spurred by having her chest grabbed by her friend – was so genuine and natural, and Lo's smile was that wonderful little mischievous smirk Shawn had come to love so much. Her cheeks were red and full of dimples, her tongue just a sliver of purple between her white teeth. Shawn loved the photo so much she had it professionally printed on large glossy stock and framed. It now hung in her living room, 16 by 20 inches with a lovely pale blue mat.

Shawn found herself looking at it for long periods every time she would come into the apartment and, like Miranda's diary, it seemed to give her peace more than pain, even though the picture was taken just a couple of hours before Lo died. The women, the smiles, the memory of the evening before the crash and the brand new white Indian motorcycle – it was a perfect photograph. Shawn would never let it go.

Shawn finally started feeling sleepy around ten o'clock and decided it was time to get ready for turning in. She stood in the shower for a few minutes, then brushed her teeth and grabbed Harrison the Monkey and made her way across to Cory's to be cuddled through the night.

Monday morning came quickly. After a night of thick but dreamless sleep, Shawn was able to sit up and get up with no consternation. She wanted to make today count. Knowing it was the last time she would ever hear Lo's voice was one motivator. Dark as that picture seemed on the surface, what with all the electrical impulse-carrying nanotechnology causing it and all, she found comfort in knowing they were at least the same vocal cords she had heard forming her words for the last several months.

Another thought that helped her jump-start her morning was the anxiety and anticipation of the interview. Just to have done with it would be such an amazing relief. Like the endorphins a hard run pumped into the blood, walking out of that lab knowing she survived would be a rush. Shawn's heart was equally divided in wanting to keep her friend up and responding for as long as possible, and being done with it as fast as she could be. Each had its pros and cons, and each was as terrifying as the other.

She kissed Cory on the side of his messy head and locked the apartment behind her, scurrying across the breezeway like a mouse wrapped in a blanket. The morning air had a nice cool pop to it, which excited her. She had survived her first hot Texas August, and was now reaping the rewards of it. Most Texans celebrated September first with dove hunting and hot dog cookouts. Or so she heard.

As Shawn walked into the closet and semi-naturally popped her hat on her head before she even picked her clothes for the day, she had a flash of inspiration that nearly made her flinch. It did make her smile. Her face lit up in a smile, maybe the first one she had done all week, and her blood pumped with sudden excitement. *You have options, Shawn.* She flung the hat back onto its hook and pulled on some black khaki cargo pants instead of going for the skirt she had planned to wear. Then she pulled on her black boots and zipped them up over her pants. Standing there in her cargos and boots but completely naked otherwise, she turned and looked in the full-length mirror that hung inside her closet door.

She laughed out loud at the image. Here stood a waif of a woman, skinny arms, no breasts to mention, wearing the bottoms and boots of a commando. Like Lara Croft, Tomb Raider, without all the womanhood up top. Shawn flexed her tiny biceps and made a growling face in the mirror. "Yeah, girl. You're some fuckin' lion."

She slipped on a black, long-sleeve button-up blouse and went out into the sink area to do her makeup. She made the usual faces while applying the eye makeup, accented by the occasional pep-talk phrase as she tried to psych herself up to the task that lay ahead. When she finished and had brushed her teeth, she pulled her hair back in a tight little stub of a ponytail and flexed her biceps again. "Let's do this shit," she said.

As she sat astride her idling beast pulling her helmet on, Shawn felt a sense of peace. Of overcoming and perseverance. Was that the bike doing that to her? Well, whatever it was, she welcomed it. And felt good for having chosen to ride the motorcycle. This would be the first time she had ever used it as a conveyance for just getting somewhere. And it was the first time she had ridden it by herself. She was filled with a new excitement. As she pulled off the sidewalk via the wheelchair ramp and turned into the parking lot, the rush took hold of her and forced her to smile. It was that beginner's excitement of experiencing the sensation again, and it was powerful. When she turned out of the parking lot and ran up the service road, all of her apprehension and stress seemed to disappear. Then she pulled onto the highway ramp and opened it up. This was the first time she had ever taken it up past fifty miles per hour, and presumably the bike's first time to go that fast as well. And when she reached the speed limit and popped it into sixth gear, a whole new roar and vibration was there to greet her. She smiled slyly inside the helmet and thanked God for another day. Now she felt like a lion.

There was no one waiting in the parking garage to greet her. No one in the building lobby, or the elevator either. But when she walked into the break room with the helmet under her arm, Chandra was leaning against the counter talking to Jeremy, who was sitting on the back of a chair with his feet in its seat. Sameer was by the coffee machine. They all turned to look at the new apparition that had just breezed in the doorway looking like a samurai ready for battle.

"Oh my fucking word," said Chandra, covering her gaping mouth with a hand. Her eyes were even wider than her mouth.

Jeremy smiled and nodded approvingly. Sameer didn't know what to think.

"Holy shit, little sister! You look effing amazing," Chandra said, coming forward from the counter. She made a full circle around Shawn in the tiny break room, examining her from every angle.

Shawn was suddenly full of smiles. "What? You're crazy!"

"I've never seen you dressed like this. You look awesome!" Chandra said, putting her hand on Shawn's shoulder.

As Shawn shrugged off her backpack, Jeremy chimed in as well. "Yeah, you do, Shawn. You look hella tough."

"Thanks, guys. You're too kind," she said, feeling a little self-conscious. She looked at Sameer, hoping for something reasonable. He didn't disappoint.

"Good morning, Shawn. I'm glad to see you are in good spirits."

"Yes, Sameer. I'm feeling pretty good this morning."

"I did not know you had a motorcycle," he said, stirring his coffee.

"Yeah, no joke," said Jeremy. "When did you go biker girl?"

Chandra stood staring, shaking her head, her mouth still agape and smiling.

Shawn realized she had told Sameer all the details of her friend's death on Saturday morning but had left out the part about having been on her own motorcycle behind her friend. She sighed as she dropped the backpack in the chair and pulled her laptop out, replacing it with the helmet. She set the computer on the table and made her way to the coffee pot. "I guess I've been a biker girl for a few months now. Just got my own bike though."

"Congrats! That's so bad ass!" Chandra said. "Well you're going to have to take us down and show us at lunch."

"Yeah, sure," Shawn said, fixing her hair with one hand as she held the coffee cup with the other. "I'm ready whenever you are, Sameer."

He nodded and said, "Okay, then. I will meet you in the lab after you put your stuff away."

Shawn turned to get the backpack but Jeremy reached out and grabbed it as he stood up. "I'll take it to your desk for you."

"Aw, thanks!" she said and grabbed the notebook computer. Then she headed for the lab, whispering a little encouragement to herself.

"Date is Monday, September eleventh, time is zero-eight-thirty-one. Subject is Laura Carter, a white female, thirty years old. Sameer Singh, joined in the lab by Shawn Stedwin."

Shawn frowned and pulled her head back on her neck. "Thirty?" she said aloud, and then cursed internally as she slapped her forehead with the palm of her hand. "Oh my God. Today would have been her birthday."

Sameer stared at her for a moment, wondering if she would say anything else. Shawn took a deep breath and then said, "Sorry, go ahead."

"It is okay, Shawn." He cleared his throat. "Subject was a personal friend of the moderator, Shawn."

Shawn leaned over closer to the recorder and said, "Subject also goes by Lo."

Sameer nodded at her, indicating he was done with his monologue and held his hands out over the white sheet that covered Shawn's very best friend. Shawn scooted up to the table on the stool and put her hand atop Lo's head. "Can you inject please, Sameer?" she asked. Without answering, he moved to the table head and reached under the edge – the new home for the circulation device, and pressed the Inject Catalyst button. This motion of reaching under the table reminded Shawn of the leather strap she had seen hanging yesterday, so she leaned back to see if the other ends were hanging on her side, or if Sameer had caught it too. He had. Lo was buckled in.

A nice piano sonata playlist was playing softly on the stereo Shawn had set up. Something by Joep Beving was currently lulling them into a calm. A perfect song full of somber, but not dark. Just serene.

She took a deep breath and waited a few seconds, and then moved her hand to Lo's forehead. "Lo, it's me. Can you hear me?" And the craziest thing happened in that moment. Laura Carter smiled a big, broad beautiful smile – her eyes still closed – showing her teeth. Shawn's heart lit up, though it also skipped a beat.

"Yes, baby."

Shawn looked up at Sameer, who was staring at her with a little concern in his eyes. Shawn closed her eyes and shook her head, the faintest hint of a smile still on her lips, telling him no, there was nothing to that. *No, we're not gay, Sameer.*

"So I guess you answered my next question with your last answer," Shawn said, running her hand back through Lo's hair, pressing it lightly against her head. Petting her like a sleeping puppy.

"That I know who's talking to me? Yes, of course."

Shawn closed her eyes for a moment, taking a deep breath. How attached should she be here? How real was this? And why had Lo awakened so much easier than the others had? None of the dramatic fear-filled eyes or twitching lips or cheeks... It was peaceful as a pond at dawn. She had to swallow to keep from being overwhelmed by the sadness and the joy that sat simultaneously on the edge of her conscience. "That's good, hon. Say my name, please, for the record."

Lo, eyes still closed, licked her lips and opened then closed her mouth a couple of times. Shawn shot Sameer a glance and he quickly turned around and fetched the bottle of water from the counter top. He handed it to Shawn, who now had the sudden worry that it wasn't clean or sanitary somehow. Was it worthy of her friend's mouth? She had to remind herself that this was it. The last hoorah for a girl who had already died. No bacteria or infection would ever matter again. She lowered the spray bottle and gently wet the inside of Lo's mouth, who smacked it open and closed a couple more times. "Thank you," she said. "Thank you, Shawn."

Shawn's heart soared now. She lowered her gaze, looking at her lap, where her left hand still rested. She straightened her fingers just to have something to look at. She didn't need to be letting Sameer see her glassy eyes right now. "Welcome," she whispered. *Ah, to hell with it.* She looked up, straight ahead, letting the tears stream down her cheeks, biting her lips. She reached down with her left hand and retrieved the tissue box from under the table and set it next to Lo's left arm, mainly to show Sameer that she already had them. Don't worry about me. He did shift in his spot, putting his hands behind his back. The pained expression on Shawn's face was getting harder to maintain. It was borne of holding back the tears. Either this or that, pick one. She knew it would only last a few more seconds, then she would have control again.

Shawn, having out-waited the pain, was able to speak again. Deep breath. "Lo, this is very hard for me. I want to know what you're feeling. Where are you right now? Do you know?"

"Yeah!" she said, that smile returning full force. "I'm back. And if I'm not mistaken, that's Alexis Ffrench on the piano."

Shawn quickly looked toward the stereo. Sameer followed her curiosity and went right to the streaming player to look at the artist's name. He raised his eyebrows and turned to look over his shoulder at Shawn. He nodded enthusiastically.

"Very good, Lo. What do you mean by 'back', though."

"You know what I mean, biiiitch," she said through her smile. This made Shawn smile too. The drawing out of the pejorative was so like Lo it was hard to believe it wasn't fully her. Were these just things she would have said anyway – maybe that she never had said, but that she *would have* – under this situation? Was it the brain's job to handle all that? Regardless of consciousness or spirit or living in general? Or was this *her*, truly *her* lying here talking? God, just to know.

"Lo, can you tell me something to make me know it's really you?"

The eyes frowned, though they remained closed. "Who the hell else would it be?" she said.

Shawn gasped through the final remnants of that pain with which she had been fighting back the tears, and laughed out loud. Just a single quick heave of relief. "Come on, hon. You wanted to be on this table. You asked for it. Now you're here, you have to play by the rules."

Lo made the dramatized version of a child's scorned face, frowning and pursing her lips. "Okay, okay." But then the smile returned. The furrowed brow loosened. She looked at such great peace. Shawn was so happy for that. And Lo's speech was so clear it was almost unnoticeable that she wasn't aspirating. This was purely the work of an articulate mouth coupled with the power of the vocal cords. "Gosh, Shawn, if there were only some phrase you could ask me – like some code word that would tell you who I was…" she said and closed her mouth into that damned smile again. That damned contagious, beautiful smile.

Shawn giggled and shook her head. *God, how could I forget that?* She had forgotten that Lo hadn't just asked to be here, but that they had *prepared for it!* Holy cow. Shawn closed her eyes and took a deep breath. "Okay. How deep is the darkness, Lo?"

When Lo opened her mouth, her tongue was sticking out a little. Shawn took the hint and gently wet her mouth again with the spray. "It is endless. Is is complete. It is perfect," she said, and Shawn felt the chills run all the way down her spine. Then she nodded and wiped away her tears with the back of a knuckle. She looked up at Sameer and gave him back his wan smile. "She's here, Sameer. This is Lo."

Then she laid her head on the table right next to Lo's, wrapping her arm around her. Her mouth was in close proximity to Lo's ear, which she knew wouldn't benefit the recording, but she didn't care. She just needed a minute. A private minute alone with an old friend. "God, I miss you so much, Lo. You can't feel it, but I'm hugging you."

Shawn could hear Lo's mouth form the smile again. "I miss you too. How long have I been gone?"

"Nine days," Shawn said, and was suddenly curious about that gap. That chasm that separated the life from the death of a human being. And finally having the perfect subject to ask, she stepped carefully forward – aware of the consequences if she was wrong. She sat up so the recorder could catch her again. "How long does it feel like, Lo?" she said and looked at Sameer, hoping he would understand that look meant 'get ready to grab the helmet'. He nodded slowly. He crossed his arms on his chest and waited.

"I can't tell. It doesn't seem like there's a very good clock here."

The word 'here' gave Shawn a chill. She wanted Lo to elaborate on it, but again, feared the predicament it could put them in. She chewed on her thumb and looked up at Sameer. He could read the nervousness in her eyes, but looked hopeful. He raised his eyebrows and tilted his head, shrugged a little. She nodded. Okay. *Here goes nothing.*

"Where is 'here', Lo?"

"It's my new home, honey. I don't know where it is. It's not heaven. I know that much."

Shawn slapped a hand over her mouth, stifling an outburst. Squeezed her chin and cheeks, pinched her lips. Then she took a deep breath and let go of herself. Sat up straight and tried to reset. "So what are you saying, Lo? Do you know what has happened?"

"Yes."

Shawn lowered her chin, a gesture someone would commonly make to show they were expecting elaboration, but Lo's eyes had still not opened. "Can you expound please?"

"Yes, I know what happened."

Shawn looked up at the ceiling and rolled her eyes. She actually heard Sameer's internal giggle. She shook her head and looked at him. "Okay, smart ass."

"Sorry, Shawn. Yes. I know what happened. But I don't know where I am."

"You don't know where you are."

"I don't know where I am. I know where I am here. In your lab. But not in the other place. I guess I'll have to go back there soon, right?" she said.

Shawn felt her heart drop. Closed her eyes. The reality was sinking in for not only Lo, but her as well. She would indeed have to let go of her friend soon. Again. This might be rougher than the first time. New tears made their way to the front. Just waiting to roll out. "Yes, love."

"Shucks. I was hoping you had found a way to make it permanent."

"Me too," Shawn said with suddenly trembling lips. She put her hand on Lo's face this time, rubbing her thumb across the cheek. Touched the corner of her mouth. "I'm so sorry, Lo."

"It's okay, Shawn. You don't have to be sorry. It's not bad here."

There was that 'here' again. "Can you tell me anything about 'here', Lo?"

"Well, I'm not alone," she said. A red light began blinking on the corner of the penning trap. Shawn had not noticed it before, in any of the other sessions.

"What's that?"

"I'm not alone," Lo said, but Shawn was listening for Sameer's response. Not Lo's repeated statement.

"It says 'energy low', Shawn," Sameer said in a little more than a whisper.

*Shit.* She raised her eyebrows and her hands. Had they just not seen that before? It was barely visible now, but it seemed like someone would have noticed it in one of the five other sessions. It made sense that these nanobots could only carry so much neuron-shocking power and still communicate with home base. Running out of time. Did that also mean the violent exit the others had gone through? Maybe that was the very reason for the terrible endings. A few thousand nanobots losing their energy at slightly different times, causing chaos in the brain… Shawn sure as hell didn't want that for her friend. Then the heaviness dropped in on her chest as she thought of what that meant: she would have to hurry up and end this. Hurry up and put her friend back to sleep. Back to death.

"What does that mean?" Lo asked, shocking Shawn a little bit. She hadn't realized Lo had heard Sameer's answer.

Shawn cleared her throat and glanced at him. That would have been a good answer for the whiteboard. Hindsight. Oh well. She shook her head, not in disappointment at him, but in herself. Her own fault for not learning the system better. Learning that there was a low-energy beacon at all would have been vastly helpful. "It means the nanobots are dying, honey."

Lo pursed her lips slightly then relaxed them. *Acceptance?* "So I'm going home soon?"

Shawn swallowed hard, her chest hitching and the wave of sadness pouring over her like a flood, all in one instant. She ran her thumb across Lo's cheek again. "Yes," was all she could say. Max Richter came on the streaming stereo playing *Mercy*. Great. Thanks. This song was not just somber. It was possibly the saddest, yet most beautiful piece of music ever written.

"Well, it's been nice, Shawn. Thank you for being my friend."

The tears poured more quickly than they had before. She tried to wipe them away but they were pouring too fast. *Sweet Jesus. Why did I ever get involved in this?* "Lo, it has been the pleasure of my life. I will love you forever."

That pleasant smile crossed Lo's lips again. She still had not opened her eyes. "Well, I guess this is goodbye."

"Wait," Shawn said, sitting up straight, suddenly remembering what Lo had said before the red light had illuminated. "Lo, you said you weren't alone. What did you mean by that?"

"Barogan Kinder."

Shawn frowned. She wiped away another round of tears with the tissue. "What is that?"

"Oh, there's someone here too, Shawn. You should know about her. Very cold."

"What is barogan kend – what did you say?" she said. The light was flashing more slowly, almost breathing a dark maroon color now.

"Barogan Kinder. It's a name. Shawn. Shawn."

"Yes," Shawn said, leaning forward suddenly. "I'm here, baby. What's up? What can I do? God damn that violin!" she said, meaning to have only thought it.

"Let me see you once more," Lo said.

Shawn leaned over her face, tears dropping onto Lo's lips and nose just like they had the night she died the first time. "I'm here, honey. I'm here."

Slowly, like it took great effort, Lo's eyes came open. Then she made what was left of the energy into a smile. It wasn't her full beaming one, but it was beautiful. And then she closed her eyes forever.

Shawn, still bent over her, was now rubbing away the tears with her thumbs, one at a time. "Lo." She sniffled back as much as she could, but they were coming too fast. It was like sopping up individual raindrops with a sponge. "Lo," she whispered. She was back in private mode. She didn't need tape of this. No recording would ever replace the feeling she was having right now. She never wanted to live it again either. "Lo. Lo." She wiped at the tears. Kissed her on the nose. But there was no response. "Lo," she said, and it finally broke. She was all-out crying now and had to lay her head on Lo's chest. Her body shuddered as she turned Lo's head to face her, wrapping her arms around her as best she could.

"I'm so sorry, friend. I'm so sorry," she cried. "I've lost you all over again." And the crying turned to sobbing. Soul-baring weeping poured forth like a river. Sameer blessedly stopped the music and came around the table. She heard him over her sobs, whispering, "Interview ends." Then she felt his hands on her shoulders.

"I am so sorry for your loss, Shawn. I am going to leave you alone for a little bit," he said. Shawn could only nod. Then slowly, his hands slid off her shoulders and he made his way out.

She spent the next hour weeping with an intensity as great as the first time she had lost her friend. She held Lo as tight as she was able in the context, repeating the same things over and over. *I am so sorry. I love you so much. I'll never forget you. I miss you more than anything.* She kept her head against Lo's arm and chest for the entire duration of the cry, until she could finally cry no more. But she never let go of her friend.

On her way out of the building, Shawn had gone back to her desk to get her helmet, then slung the backpack up on her shoulders. She walked by Sameer's office and, barely slowing to speak, she leaned in and said, "I need to go home, Sameer."

He nodded somberly at her, a knowing look in his eyes. It wasn't disappointment. It was understanding and acceptance.

Shawn walked away, pulling up on the straps of the backpack and then slinging her helmet up on her head and running the strap through. She wanted to cover her swollen and puffy face before anyone could see her. She wanted to leave before anyone could stop her. To tell her they were sorry, or tell her they would be praying for her, or they were so sad for her loss. She just wanted to be alone.

# Seventeen

Curled up on her sofa with her phone in her lap, Shawn sat in her pajamas with a glass of vodka on the tray next to her. She had changed into her PJs, but had not fixed her disheveled hair. She couldn't find the care for that. She wanted to find out what this Barogan Kinder was. Lo had said it almost like a name. Kinder? Like kindergarten? She opened the browser on her phone and noticed she had nine active tabs. One by one she began closing them. Some of them had been open for a very long time. She hardly ever used her phone's browser, so they could have been open for a year and she wouldn't have noticed. Here was one where she was looking at Indian Chief motorcycles. Wow. And another where she was looking up the address of the public records office. The next one she put her thumb over, ready to touch the X, jumped out at her. It read 'Sameer Singh'. What the hell?

   She touched the tab and reactivated it. Then she stared at it, trying to remember why she would have opened it. The page reloaded it, then a picture of his face popped up. It was a mugshot. "What the fuck?" she said aloud. She looked up at the sliding glass door, reminded briefly of her extermination of the spider a week before. No more spiders. No more butterflies. Why had she been looking up Sameer? But then it came to her. She suddenly remembered with startling clarity.

Cory had mentioned something about a Popular Science article involving something Sameer had worked on. She remembered opening a tab to look him up, but something had distracted her. Maybe a phone call or something. It wasn't uncommon for her to get sidetracked and completely forget what she was doing. But somehow, she had just never made it back to the page to read it. God, that must have been months ago.

She read through the article now.

### Arizona Man Faces Jail Time for Unlicensed Medical Practice

Sameer Singh, a research specialist from Tempe has been arrested on charges of medical malpractice and practicing medicine without a license. Sources close to the suspect say he was operating on his daughter with the help of a neurosurgeon named James Gaylen. Gaylen has also been charged.

Sure enough, there was a picture of Jeremy there. He looked so much different she almost didn't recognize him. And she had not known him as James. Maybe Jeremy was his middle name. There was a lot of that going around apparently. Well, that could explain why Jeremy had lost his license to practice. But Sameer? How could he have been involved in a surgery? She almost rolled her eyes at that. The high-tech lab he had built with his own money in the building she now worked should answer all questions related to 'how'. He did because he could. He probably wasn't holding the instruments, but it would have been his show. Just like the resurrection ceremonies they had been holding – they were his show even though Shawn had been the 'moderator'.

But what did this tell her about him? He had a daughter, for one. Shawn wasn't sure if she had known that or not, but wouldn't be surprised to find it out. Sameer wore a gold band on his finger but she had never once heard him speak about his wife. Nor had she seen any pictures on his desk or anything. But why would he be operating on her? With a brain surgeon? Had she died or something?

None of it made sense, and she didn't quite feel comfortable asking him about it. How would one go about such an interrogative? 'Hey man, why did you operate on your own daughter, whom you've never even mentioned to me?' She shook her head and returned her attention to the phone. Opened a new tab on the browser and typed in 'barroggan kender", taking a shot in the dark on the spelling. There were two returns. She clicked the first one, and her world changed in a flash.

### Horrific Motorcycle Accident Ends in 3 Deaths

Arlington, Texas – In the late evening hours Saturday, a man allegedly ran a stop light at a very high speed, colliding with a group of motorcyclists who apparently had the right of way. The speeding motorcyclist, a Scottish man named Barogan L Kinder (19) was here on a visa that was supposed to mature in the months before. He crashed into a motorcycle that held two riders as they ventured across the intersection at E Lamar Blvd and Highway 360 at about half past ten.

The two riders, Heath K Brennan (31) and Laura Carter (29), were killed instantly. The other riders in the group were uninjured.

Shawn slept her phone and put her arm up on the couch back, then put her hand on her forehead. She was breathing heavily and had not realized it. Her heart was beating hard enough for her to be aware of it. Barogan Kinder was the man who had killed her friend. And Lo had spoken his name.

"You don't get it?" Shawn said. Cory had come in and dropped onto the sofa and she had instantly come up onto her knees, putting her hands on his leg and leaning in a little close. She was drunk, and trying to get her point across was taking longer than usual.

"I mean, I hear what you're saying, but no, I don't see how that spells out your point," Cory said, holding a hand up. "I'm not trying to be a jerk, I promise. How does that equate the presence of a soul?"

"Because," she said, letting go his leg to use her hands to help illustrate her point. She quickly realized she needed at least one of them to remain on his leg. Or something. "There is no way she could have known his name. Ever in life. It's not like someone walked up and told her the guy's name as she lay dying. Which bothers me, by the way, that the article said they died instantly."

Cory made a face. "They always say that when someone dies at the scene."

"My point remains. She never heard his name in life."

Cory finally raised his chin. That had gotten through. Shawn dropped back onto her feet, her knees still out in front of her, and stared at him. She was going to let him work through it on his own.

"So you're saying that she learned his name... *after she died*?" Cory said. "How the hell would she have... Oh. You're saying she's *with* him in death."

Shawn shrugged. "She said she wasn't alone. It didn't register at first. But she said something like 'I'm not alone here'. And I was distracted by something. So she said it again. Then I asked her what she meant… I'll have to listen to the tape. I don't remember exactly. But she just blurted out this name."

"Barg-" Cory started.

"Barogan. Kinder. Barogan Kinder," Shawn said.

"That's a crazy name," he said.

"Yeah, well, he's from Scot-" Shawn started, but stopped suddenly. Her face drained of color as she made some infinitesimally small leap in logic in her head. She fell backward onto the sofa, kicking her feet out to stabilize her, and leaned back to grab her phone from where she had been sitting. Then she twisted around and sat up, pulling her hair back behind her ear as she swiped open the phone.

"Barogan L Kinder," she said, after she had pulled the article back up. "Middle name starts with L. And he's from Scotland."

Cory started shaking his head. "That probably describes ten million people, babe."

Shawn bobbled her head around. "Yeah, I know. But work with me here." She leaned back and pulled up the tab history, searching for the public records office again. Tapped it. Tapped the phone icon, then listened while it rang. She chewed on her thumb while she waited. Shortly there was an answer. She didn't instantly recognize the woman's voice as familiar, but it could have been.

"Hello, ma'am. My name is Marcy Stedwin. I came in a few months ago asking about a woman who had passed. I was wondering if you were the one who helped me."

The woman seemed interested. "Probably so, if you actually *came in*, then yeah. I'm the only one who works the window. What can I do for you?"

"Well, I lost a friend last week in a motorcycle accident. I was wondering if I could get more information about the other people involved," she said, biting down hard on her thumb. She winced and almost shouted. *Stop that, idiot!*

"Oh, the one on 360? That was what, Saturday?"

"Yes, ma'am."

"Girl, you need to stop calling me ma'am. I'm probably younger'n you!"

"Sorry. Old habits and all that."

"Let's see. Yes, I have it. Baro Bargo Bro-" she tried, then gave up. "I can't pronounce his name, but-"

Shawn interrupted her. "Barogan. Right?"

"Yeah, that looks right. He the one?"

"Yes. Do you have his death certificate?" Shawn asked, feeling very nervous now.

The woman sighed. It didn't sound like an impatience though. Just a 'moving from one task to another' sigh. "Okay, I have it."

Shawn closed her eyes and took a deep breath. "Can you tell me his middle name? Is it there?" she asked. And before the woman could answer, Shawn's curiosity got the best of her, so she added, "Is it Linus?"

"In fact, it is, yes."

Shawn's eyes opened wide in surprise and she looked at Cory, who was staring at her with his own anticipation. She nodded emphatically at him. "And can you tell me the city they listed? Like his city from his driver license? I mean, I guess I'm not sure if that's incl-"

"No, that's more than I can tell you," said the woman, and Shawn's heart filled with disappointment.

"Oh, are you sure?"

"No, ma'am. I'm not saying I won't. I'm saying it's not here, I don't *have* that information," she said.

"Oh, got ya," Shawn said, giggling nervously. "Then is there anything else you could tell me? Like that might identify him?"

"Well, you can come down here and fill out some forms and I can give you some copies. I can't do that on the phone. But honestly, I don't think there's much here."

Shawn sighed, furling her mouth. She was ready to give up now. Hang up and be done with it. This had turned out to be a dead end. At least she had his middle name. But then the woman said, "He did have a picture in his wallet. Credit cards and license and the usual stuff. But there was a picture, too."

Shawn felt her blood run hot with new excitement. "Can you describe it?" She was chewing her thumb again.

"How about I email you a copy of it. Do you have an email address?"

Shawn's eyes widened again and she came back up on her knees, squatting on her ankles. "Yes! You ready?" When the woman affirmed, she spelled out her email address carefully. When they finished and she hung up, she waited anxiously, knowing what the photo would show, but having no idea at the same time. Something just told her she was right about this. The butterfly. The damned butterfly told her she was right about it.

It took seven minutes for the picture to come through. Shawn spent a lot of that time envisioning the scenario in her head. The woman printing the photo out, then scanning it. Which was absolutely ludicrous, Shawn knew, but hey, not everyone was tech-savvy. Or the woman downloading the photo to a her desktop from the file she had been viewing, and then trying to attach it. Either way, Shawn could have sent ten copies to ten people by now. But then her phone finally chirped and the email icon was now up in her status bar. She pulled it down and opened it. There was a faded, wallet-worn photograph of two young adults, maybe as young as their late teens, standing together in some studio like an old Olan Mills photograph. They stood back-to-back, clearly placed that way by the photographer, arms crossed and smiling. Since Shawn had never seen Barogan Kinder, dead or alive, she had no idea if he was the young man in the picture. But the woman to his left was very obviously Miranda Kate Struck. And she was only a few years younger than when she had died.

"Holy fuck this is a small world," she said leaning forward and showing Cory the photo.

"Is that her? The girl you have her diary?"

"Yes. Miranda," Shawn said, then fell back against the cushions, suddenly unsure how to feel. She had just solved one of her life's greatest mysteries, but she had no idea what it meant, or why. Crestfallen would be an understatement. She sighed and ran her hair back with her hand. "What now?" she said, looking out the back window. The phone chirped again. Absently, and without much interest, she rolled her hand over and swiped it open. Another email from the same woman. She opened it, frowning. And there was the back of the picture. Written in blue ink across the middle were two names. The first one made perfect sense to her. The second just redoubled the mystery. It read 'Randi & Harr'.

"Oh my God!" she shouted and tossed her phone into the couch cushions. Then she covered her face with her hands and breathed deeply. Cory moved in and put his arm around her.

"Shawn. You have to let this go. You need to start concentrating on your mental he-"

"Cory, it's Harrison!" she shouted, not meaning for it to be a shout, but her excitement had spilled over. "The goddamn photo is Miranda and Harrison!"

On a roll now, Shawn sat at her desk with her notepad and a pen, just jotting down things she needed to follow-up on, clues she hadn't yet cracked and ideas that tied everything together. She still didn't get how Barogan – or 'Linus', as Miranda had apparently called him – tied into it. Of course he was all over her diary. And he was obviously the man she had talked about going to Scotland to meet with. In her last entry she had written about four years of obstacles and pitfalls and 'fighting the system'. Whatever that meant. But she finally got to have him here. Was that what the 'maturing visa' was about in the article?

Then a thought occurred to Shawn and she sat straight up and lifted her hands in the air. She stayed like this for a few seconds while she fleshed out the thought, then grabbed her phone and reopened the email the clerk had sent her. When she looked at the writing on the back of the picture again, she closed her eyes and shook her head. It was Miranda's handwriting. She dropped the phone on her desk and buried her face in her hands. *Of course it was her writing.* Who the hell would write on his own copy of a picture? Especially if he already knew who the subjects were. *Ugh. That word. Subjects.*

But then, why would Miranda need to write the names either? Presumably, Linus knew who they were as well. Right? Wrong. Shawn was presuming too much. That was the question. That one *right there*. And she could feel it. If she could find the answer to *that* question, she felt like she would have a lot better insight into what happened. *Why had Miranda written the two names on the back?*

"Okay, what are my possible answers?" Shawn said aloud, talking to the empty apartment. Cory was out running a few errands and picking up some grocery. Which was nice, because she wasn't entirely hip on having him see just how deep she was falling into this rabbit hole of mystery and intrigue. It had turned into sort of a hobby of hers. But her therapist had once told her that people who were grieving tended to latch onto tiny details like this when someone died. It was a subconscious need to busy oneself with the minutia as a way to cope with the loss. There was nothing unhealthy about it, and in fact, it was encouraged. It was still a little humiliating to be watched though.

"Possible answers:" she said, pulling back a finger on her left hand with the fingers of her right. She stood facing the sliding glass door. "One, because Linus didn't know who the people were. I don't like that one. Why would this girl fly halfway around the world to meet someone who didn't know her? He was standoffish though on the train, wasn't he? Okay. Two," she said, pulling back the next finger, "because Linus knew the people but didn't necessarily know what they *looked* like." Shawn stopped her pacing and put her finger against her lips. "I like that one a little better. But it opens a new question: why send a stranger a photograph at all?"

She tapped her fingernail against her teeth. "Hmm. Unless he knew one of them but not the other. Or knew what one of them looked like, but not the other…" she said. Then she started nodding. "Yes. I like that one the best. And there really are no other options. So what does this mean?" She put her hands on her hips and leaned back, stretching and twisting her neck. "Relatives? Nah. Not with different surnames. Well, we don't know what Harrison's last name is. Or was.

*So what we have is someone named Harrison. Then we also have a stuffed monkey named Harrison. Or at least it has Harrison sewn on it. Then we have Miranda's saying she misses him like a lost child and she feels like he's very close tonight. And earlier in the diary that the diary was the only one she could admit to that she missed him. Could it be different subjects for each context? She missed the stuffed animal and couldn't admit it, but missed the real person and felt like he was close tonight?*

"That must surely be it," she said aloud, resuming her speech to the empty room. "That comment about missing him like a lost child was the second-to-last entry. She was home." *That's right! She was home with the monkey at the point when she wrote that. So she wasn't missing the monkey!* Of course, Shawn realized this didn't mean Miranda was missing the monkey in the entry when she couldn't admit it, either. But it did seem to fit. *I have a monkey named Harrison. I can't admit I miss him. Socrates is a lion.*

If there were only a way to identify Harrison, she could get farther in this investigation. All she had of him was a several-years-old picture. He was the only real missing link here, and he seemed to tie everyone else together. Realizing there might not be an end to this, and the end might not actually solve anything, she decided to drop it for now.

She sat down in her office chair and stretched her arms back behind her, rolling her neck around. And then the phone rang, setting in motion the final act in her investigation. It was Jeremy.

"Hey, Jer," she said as she answered it on speaker. The phone lay face-up on her desk. She pulled her feet up onto her chair and twisted round so she could look out the back door.

"Hey, Shawn. How you holding up? I hope I'm not interrupting anything."

"No, you're fine. I'm fine, too, actually."

"Well, that's good. I just wanted to check on you. I know you've had a rough go of it lately," said Jeremy.

"Yeah. I mean, it's gonna take a while to get through the process, right? But I'm okay for the most part."

"I'm happy to hear that. We were all concerned for you when you left today. You're very strong, Shawn."

"Hey, thanks, Jer. I appreciate that."

"Yeah, I'm not trying to blow smoke or anything. Just – you know, kind of observing. I've been impressed with how strong you've been. You keep getting back on that horse. I think that's great," said Jeremy, and Shawn felt her cheeks get red.

"Well, thank you. I'm trying," she said and put her thumbnail between her teeth. Bit down on it. "Listen, Jer, there's something I wanted to talk to you about."

"Shoot," he said.

"I'm going to tell Sameer this myself, so please be discreet, but I won't be doing this project anymore. I just can't."

"Well, I don't think anyone would blame you. You're apparently very, very good at it, according to Sameer. But I can't imagine anyone fighting you on that decision. You've experienced some awful things," said Jeremy. She could almost hear him nodding. "If you needed to just take a break from it, I bet Sameer would pause it, too. Just an option."

"Yeah, I can't do that. I just…" she said, and tears began forming in her eyes. *Fuck sake. Again with this?* "See, I've, uh… This is why I wanted to talk to you."

"What's up, Shawn?" he asked patiently. His voice was soft and comforting. She thought he would make a good therapist. Other thoughts went through her head as well, but she didn't want to chase them. Like asking him why they were operating on Sameer's daughter illegally. She let it pass.

"I've found reason to think there's a spiritual connection in the lab."

Jeremy sat silent for a long time. He finally said, "Really." It wasn't a question.

"Yeah," she said, still chewing that thumbnail. "Lo, Laura, my friend, well, she mentioned a name. The name she mentioned was of the man who ran the red light and caused the accident that killed everyone."

Jeremy was silent for another very long time. Processing this. After a while, he said, "So she obviously never met him or anything, right? I mean, he wasn't part of that motorcycle group or something? No coincidental way she would have just brought his name up?"

"Nnnope," said Shawn and raised her eyebrows. "There was no possible way she could have ever heard that name in life. Yet, she knew it in death." She adjusted on the seat, dropping one foot to the ground so she could twist the chair back and forth. "Jeremy, she said, 'I'm not alone here' or something like that. I don't know. Everything is foggy. I really need to listen to the tape. You're not still in the office by any chance, are you?"

"Nah, I left a few hours ago. She said she wasn't alone?" he asked. Shawn could hear the temperature of his voice. And it was a little cooler than it had been a few minutes ago.

"Yyyep." Shawn looked at her computer screen as the screensaver kicked in. "She said something along those lines. I'm not alone here. She used the word 'here'. And then she said the name. And I didn't even recognize it as a name. It's not a name I've ever heard."

"Interesting. What was the name?" he asked.

"Barogan Kinder," Shawn said.

"Yeah. That's, uh… That's pretty unique. I agree with the 'hardly coincidence' theory. But… spiritual?"

"Yes, Jeremy. She wasn't alone. What it ended up feeling like, after I got home and did some research and actually found out it *was* a name she had spoken, was that she was saying she wasn't alone there. She was with this guy, Kinder."

"Wow. That's pretty heavy," said Jeremy. They sat in silence for a long moment while he thought about this.

"Yeah, I need to listen to the tape again. I think I'm gonna run up to the office so I can pull it off the network. Plus, I left my laptop there. But it was chilling. I asked her where 'here' was and what it was like and whatnot. She was basically acknowledging that she had died, but she couldn't tell how long she had been there. And she said it definitely wasn't 'heaven'. But there was a difference between here and where she had been. I stressed that with her. We went over it in detail."

"That's incredible. That does put a whole new coat of paint on the thing, doesn't it?" asked Jeremy.

"Exactly my sentiments," agreed Shawn.

"Can you imagine if this got out? This is shocking. Groundbreaking. Proof of an afterlife? Good lord. This is huge," said Jeremy.

"What's that saying? Bigger than pro football?" Shawn said.

Jeremy chuckled. "Indeed."

Still a little freakish about riding at night – that was a wound too fresh to uncover yet – Shawn took her Jeep back to the office to get her laptop and download the recording from the intranet. She would come back home and listen to it, dissect it and analyze it. She had to detach herself from the personal side of it, and she knew it would be hard, but there was so much to unpack there. She felt that if she didn't give it a proper analysis, she was doing an injustice, not only to the project, but perhaps to Miranda. And hell, even to Lo. Lo had *wanted* to participate, Shawn had to remind herself. So she would just have to toughen up and make it happen.

As she pulled into the parking garage, she leaned over and fished her badge out of her backpack. The building was eerily quiet and dark. All the hall lights were on, as usual, but somehow it just felt darker. Like something was here. An overlap of the two realms. Like maybe she was still close to Lo somehow. By that rationale though, she might also be close to Miranda. And Barogan Kinder. This gave her a shiver and a chill. As she rode up the elevator, she couldn't help looking up at the ceiling. It now felt like she was being watched by these people from the other side.

"Are you here, Lo?" she asked quietly. The elevator stopped and the doors slid open. Had the lights just flickered?

The door to the hidden side of the floor was cold and heavy. Stark. Powerful. A gateway to the great beyond. It would be senseless for Shawn to pretend like it *didn't* represent that. Every time she had come through this door, it had been in search of evidence to support that very sentiment. In here, all the hallway lights were off, but some of the rooms had dim lights on in them – the exact opposite from the common areas of the building outside. It was a spooky feeling walking through these corridors by herself, at night, when no one else was here. It was a first for her. As she entered D Room, Shawn's eyes fell on the cardboard box that lay on the table against the wall, ready to be rolled out. Lo *was* still here.

And there was her laptop, sitting on the counter where she had left it early this morning. This morning seemed like years ago, and in another life. There had been so many cries. So much emotion. So many life-changing events had seemed to happen between when she had set that notebook down and now. She pulled the lid open and waited for it to wake up. She didn't have much fear that Sameer wouldn't have uploaded the interview recording to the server. He was a man of method and routine. Seeing that Lo had been put back in the box was proof of that. But failing that, if he had not yet done so, she was pretty sure she could find the DVR and upload it herself. Shawn doubted he took that home.

The point was made moot when she looked under the interviews directory and found the file with today's date on it. She dragged the file across to the laptop, then walked over to the box while the file traveled through the ether. The larger part of Shawn was happy that Sameer had dutifully put Lo back in the box. Having a dead girl on the table out in the open – even if she were Shawn's best friend – might have been too much to deal with on a night when she was already feeling a little eerie about being here alone. She was able to reach out and run her hand along the top of the box, though. "Goodbye, love. I'll never forget you, okay?"

When she got back to the laptop, the file had finished its trek across the radio waves and was now sitting in her local directory, highlighted. She pressed the enter key to open the file. She wanted to check its integrity before clapping the notebook shut and heading home. There was a bit of silence on the beginning of the recording, so she clicked the scrubber several minutes into the file to check there.

'know who's talking to me? Yes, of course,' Lo's voice rang out through the tinny speakers of the laptop. Shawn closed her eyes for a second, then clicked a little farther down the scrubber.

'some code word that would tell you who I was,' said the voice. Another click.

'It says energy low, Shawn.' Sameer's voice. And right behind it, before she could click again, Lo spoke, saying, 'What does that mean?'

She clicked forward again. 'Kinder' said Lo's voice. This was the part Shawn would be listening to very closely when she got home. She turned the volume up a notch. Then her own voice, saying, 'What is that?' Shawn was about to stop the playback, but then Lo spoke again, so she held back, her fingertips hovering just over the space bar, which would pause it. 'Oh, there's someone here too, Shawn. You should know about her. Very cold.'

Shawn's blood suddenly went cold. She pressed the space bar. How had she missed that? She had been so completely focused on wondering what the hell that weird name meant that she had totally missed another entire direction of conversation. She pressed the left arrow, backing it up ten seconds, then pressed space bar to begin playback. *'is that? Oh, there's someone here too, Shawn. You should know about her.'* Pause. Her. *Her. This could be it! Oh my God! I wonder if she's talking about Miranda!*

Shawn looked up through the glass wall of the room, through the glass walls of all the rooms between here and the door that led to the elevators. There was, of course, no way to know if she was alone. Anyone could stand just about anywhere in any of the hallways and go unnoticed. The trickery that light played through these glass rooms could be unsettling. Her fingers inadvertently settled on the space bar. *'Very cold.'* said Lo. She paused it again then put her hands on the sides of her head. Chills revisited her spine. What in the hell was going on?

So that made two people who were 'there' with Lo, didn't it? Kinder and this female, whoever she was. Her spiritual connection argument had just doubled in strength. Jeremy had been wrong. Shawn had been wrong. They all had. Of course, Jeremy was a scientist. A brain surgeon. He might have been biased against the spiritual aspect of it because of his work – even though he was a Jew. He did have faith. It just didn't intersect with this project. His neurosurgery was a separate facet all together. He was clearly dedicated to Sameer though. He had stuck with him even after losing his license to practice, likely caused by the operation they had performed on Sameer's daughter. Good God. Was Jeremy a bad guy all along, and Shawn had been trusting him? For that matter, was Sameer? What in the world had they been doing to her?

Her.

Shawn remembered being surprised that Sameer had a daughter. Based on his perceived age, likely somewhere in his mid-fifties, his daughter was probably older. Maybe a late teenager. Maybe in her early twenties… Unless, of course, this surgical mishap had happened some years ago. She pulled her phone out of her back pocket and swiped it open, going directly for that browser tab. She read the dateline. The column had been written thirteen years ago. *Holy cow*. So she could have been a little girl at the time. In fact, she likely *had been* a little girl. Almost *had* to be. What had they done to her? Poor thing! Shawn slid the phone back into her back pocket.

*Her.*

She stood there with her hands on her hips and looked up at the ceiling. All this was getting out of hand. Above her pay grade. One thing had nothing to do with the other. She was juggling three separate story lines in her head. One of Miranda, one of Lo and one of this Barogan Kinder guy. Well, four, technically, if you counted this unnamed *her* Lo had mentioned. She needed to stick with one angle. One thing to investigate would be plenty. Why was she investigating at all? To what end would this satisfy anything? She shook her head. Maybe she should just drop them all. There was no way all four of them tied together. Wrapping up four separate lives in one reunion at the end like an episode of *Seinfeld*. It made no sense.

Or maybe it did. Maybe they all had something to do with each other, after all. Those small-worldisms had been showing their faces a lot lately. Shawn had come to find out that Barogan Kinder, the man who had killed her friend, had indeed been tied inextricably to Miranda, the dead girl who had taken a piece of Shawn's heart a few months ago. It was crazy how these things came together. But not knowing who the girl was in her last statement, that was where the buck stopped. *But that phrase…*

Shawn turned and walked back to the laptop once more. Pressed the left arrow and then the space bar once more. Listened to that line again. *You should know about her.* Bingo.

Her. Lo had thought Shawn should know about *her*. So she *did* need to chase down this side of the story. "Why didn't you tell me her name, sweet friend?" she said to the box on the table. Shawn was shaking her head. She made a ponytail with her hands in her hair, then dropped it. "Who was she?"

God, there were so many names she had already. *Barogan Kinder. Miranda Struck. Harrison.* All these thoughts and names that were new to her. So many lines of thinking that she needed to touch on. As was her nightly routine, she had to go through and think of all the threads of thought she had opened that day but had not closed, before she could fall asleep. And long were the nights that she couldn't close one. If there was a question that had no answer, she wouldn't be able to sleep for a long time. And tonight was looking like it might be an especially lengthy one. She had plenty of new questions that either did not have an answer, or for which she just didn't know it. Like who was Harrison? She still didn't know that. Who was this female Lo had mentioned? Shawn had touched on *other* thoughts, as well. Probably irrelevant, but they were there, and would be fighting for space in line to be closed off at the end of the night, before she could sleep. Like, why had Sameer operated on his daughter? Was he a monster? Who was *she* for that matter? There was another person to crowd Shawn's thoughts and take up processing power. There was only so much of that to go around. And what if *she* was *her*? Fuck sake! This thing could get real compli-

Shawn froze. *Froze.* She felt cold. *Cold.* 'You should know about her. Very cold.' Her breathing got heavier and her heart began pounding. She could literally *feel* the blood pumping between her ears. That had been an extremely good question. What if she was her? Had Sameer's daughter died during this illegal operation? That could certainly fit. It could make sense. More sense, perhaps, than his being arrested and Jeremy's losing his license to practice over someone who had lived. Had she lived, they might not have been caught for the act. Right? Did that mean she had died? Maybe not. Probably not. But there were no pictures of his daughter on his desk. No pictures of the wife, either. But whatever. A man is proud of his daughters, is he not?

Shawn was going too far again. Getting too tied up in this mystery and it was going to drive her crazy. She went to the box and laid her arms across its top, wishing she could hug Lo just one more time. She laid her head on it and whispered, "Why'd you have to die, Lo? I need you! I want you back!" But instead of letting herself cry again, she stood up, shaking her head, and pulled her hair back again. She began pacing. *Screw this. I need to go home.* She shut down the sound player and closed the notebook. She stuffed it in her backpack and left the room. As she was walking out the door, she felt her phone vibrate against her rear. She stopped in mid-stride to look at it. It was Cory. He had texted her asking where she was. "Holy cow, I forgot to tell him where I was going!" she said aloud, then flinched at how loud her voice had been in the dark hallway. It was so quiet in here she had gotten used to the perfect silence. And whispering had seemed like the appropriate thing to do. She responded with a quick text, then jumped when she heard a loud click from the open door to her right.

She turned to look into the room, which was completely dark. Unlike the others, the lights were all out in this room. All except for two small green rectangles close to the floor, about ten feet apart. *What the hell are those green lights? And what the hell made that noise?* She reached in and turned on the light. They flickered to life, brightening the room considerably more than D Room had been with its comforting dim glow. This was the support room. And the green rectangles were the operational indicators for the deep freezers. That had been the source of the clicking noise. She took a deep breath. Rolled her eyes. *Well, you can't blame me for being jumpy. I'm thinking about dead people and ghosts.* Just a damn freezer clicking on. *Well, that's comforting.*

She exited the room and turned off the light. Then she stopped. Her hand was still on the switch. She was staring again through all the glass windows in front of her. So many rooms. What the hell were all these rooms for, anyway? How many labs did one man need? Were they all labs? She had only ever been in these two. The Death Room and its support room, next door to it. In D they brought the dead back to life like little Lazaruses. And in here was where they kept all the supplies they needed. Needles and tubes. And bags of frozen blood. Her blood still felt cold in her veins, too. Perhaps Shawn was not so much a lion after all. More like a… a what? What had cold blood? A lizard? Yes. She was more of a lizard. Their blood was cold.

She took a step then stopped again. Cold. Her.

Shawn swallowed. She stood listening to her breathing and the new almost completely silent hum of the freezer behind her. What the hell was she missing here?

*You should know about her. Very cold.*

Shawn's eyes went so wide she could have seen in the dark. *Like the inside of a coffin.*

Or a freezer.

"Oh my God," she said aloud. Then she turned back to look in the room behind her again. She flipped on the light switch and then stood shaking her head. She had a smirk on her face as she pulled the phone from her back pocket.

Sameer leaned against the counter with his arms crossed. Shawn thought he might be trembling a little. He had sure been cooperative when she had demanded to speak to him in person. And when he had asked if they should meet at a coffee shop she had said, 'Oh no, let's meet in the lab. I'm already here.' And he had been almost enthusiastic about doing what she asked. He surely knew something was up. Maybe that something was his time.

"Sameer, I want to ask you some questions, and they may seem very personal. But I need to know the answers before I decide what to do."

"Okay, Shawn, this is very concerning. I am not sure why you are calling me at nine o'clock at night to come to the lab. But I am here. What can I answer?" he said. He was here all right. He was in jeans and a white t-shirt with tennis shoes on his feet. She had never seen him more casual than slacks and shirtsleeves.

She had also called Jeremy, who would be walking through that door shortly. Though she didn't want this to sound like some sort of grand inquisition, she was ready for answers. She hoped he would get here quickly. And she couldn't wait to see the look on Sameer's face when Jeremy walked in. Would he react with surprise or fear? Nah. She was getting ahead of herself again. *Cart after the horse, babe.* She had that thought but it had come in using the voice of her dead friend, who lay silent and cold in the box across the room.

"Sameer, what happened to your daughter?" she finally asked.

He made movements with his mouth as he thought of how to respond. Then he sighed and rubbed the back of his head, self-consciously looking around the room. "Shawn, I do not see how this is relevant."

"It's perfectly relevant," she said. "I work for you and we've been bringing back people from the fucking dead. I need to know why," she said. She had seen him wince when she used the F word. If it wasn't the first time he had heard her swear, it was close to it. They had an extremely professional work relationship.

"How is my daughter having anything to do with our project here, Shawn?"

"Why can't you just answer the question? I can decide for myself if its relevance matters at all." She thought about that jumble of words in her head and almost smiled at the redundancy. '*If its relevance is relevant*' she might have said.

He breathed in deeply and stared at her. "Okay. I am guessing you know something already. Would you please start by telling me what you know so that I can fill in the gaps?"

Shawn nodded. "Yeah, sure. See, you should be able to trust me," she said, holding up a finger, "because you've trusted me to keep my silence with the rest of the project."

"Which you did not strictly do, Shawn," he said, obviously feeling like he had the one-up on her.

"Yeah, and the person I told is lying in that box over there," Shawn responded.

Sameer swallowed. Lifted his chin slightly. He had apparently forgotten that Shawn wasn't just some average dummy. After a few moments, he spread his hands.

"Yeah. So I read an article about how you performed some operation on your daughter. You went to jail for it. And apparently Jeremy lost his license to practice over it," she said. "That about wraps up what I know. I've inferred some and guessed at a lot more. And I have theories about even more."

Sameer was nodding thoughtfully. "Well, that is about it. My daughter, Katiya, had a rare brain disorder. It would have killed her anyway," he said.

"So she died," Shawn said, then realized how harsh it had sounded. "I'm sorry. I just wasn't sure if she was still alive or not."

Sameer swallowed, looking a little disappointed in Shawn suddenly. "Yes. She passed away. Her name means pure and perfect. And even though she was every bit perfect, Shawn, she had an imperfect brain. She was comatose for the last weeks of her life. I asked Mr. Gaylen to assist me with the surgery. I was trying something on a *catatonic* little girl who was *going to die anyway,* Shawn. I did not hold the scalpel, but I oversaw the project. It was completely experimental. But it did not work, and Katiya died."

Shawn felt a hitch in her throat and held back a sudden outburst of tears. Who could say they would have done anything different? *My God.* If she had access to high-tech lab equipment and a loyal neurosurgeon, would she have acted any differently? She heard a ding that sounded close by and realized Jeremy had come up the service elevator instead of the regular bank of people movers. And Sameer did not look surprised as Jeremy came around the corner, wearing his usual smile. The two men nodded at each other as Jeremy entered the room. Then he came to lean against the counter close to where Shawn sat on her stool.

"Hey," he said. He must have felt like he was walking into a mine field, having no idea what was going on, or what had transpired.

"Hey, Jer. Sameer was just telling me about Katiya."

Jeremy's eyes shot over to Sameer, who nodded gently. Then he looked back at Jeremy.

Shawn said, "Look, I'm not here to judge you. I think what you did was probably a noble thing, based completely on the right reasons. Love and compassion, and trying to save a little girl. I – uh, I assume she was little…" she said, holding a hand out toward Sameer.

He nodded again. "Yes, Shawn. She was seven."

Jeremy nodded too. "Okay. So what am I here for?" he said, looking a little lost. A little defeated. Perhaps humiliated to boot.

"I think you're both great guys. This isn't about that. But we've crossed a line with this project, and I now believe we're digging deeper into this reality than we're supposed to be meddling with." She looked at Sameer and said, "I was telling Jeremy earlier, I believe there's a spirit in these bodies. Through whatever wacky science we're using for our process, it's pulling a spirit back from the afterlife to occupy the body."

Sameer interjected, "Shawn that is impossible. This is just a forced synapse. It only-"

But Jeremy cut him off. "Sameer, I am with her. In the case of Julio/Paul, it seems like maybe the wrong spirit came back. But otherwise, I believe that is what's happening."

Shawn was looking at Jeremy as he spoke. Now she looked back at Sameer. "Right. And with Curtis, remember, he said, 'Curtis is gone. I'm here now.' Remember that? It's like Curtis left. Or was replaced by this other… entity," Shawn said and felt a chill on the back of her neck.

Sameer was shaking his head, but he remained silent.

"Regardless, I won't be participating in it anymore. I just can't, Sameer. I do not want to be responsible for disturbing people's final rest." That ding sounded again. Shawn frowned, then looked at Jeremy just as Chandra came walking around the corner.

"I called her," said Jeremy. Shawn scoffed and shook her head. Not due to any discomfiture about having the other woman here. But at the sheer scope of what her poking around had caused. Three other people were now back at the office, way after hours, because of her.

Chandra stopped in the doorway, her eyes wide and her hand on her purse strap against her shoulder. "Is everything okay here?" she asked.

Sameer, looking at the floor, made a face and went to rubbing the back of his head again. "It's okay, Chandra. We are all friends here now."

Chandra's chin went up and she looked at Shawn. She came into the room and Sameer said, "Have a seat, please," as he held out his hand, offering the other stool to her, which sat on the other side of the table in its usual spot. She walked uncomfortably to the stool and sat down, dropping her purse on the Death Bed, as Shawn had come to think of it.

"There are no secrets here," Sameer said. "Not anymore. Shawn, these two know everything and I have trusted them. I have already served time for the crime of trying to save my daughter's life. There is no reason I should not trust you as well. You were right to think that."

"Thank you, Sameer," she said and leaned forward, putting her hands on the stool between her thighs. "You're gonna have to trust me big time."

"What does that mean?" Sameer asked.

"I want you to open the other freezer."

The room got real quiet. Jeremy now took the same posture as Sameer had just done, rubbing the back of his head, trying to look anywhere but at Shawn. So he knew about it, too. That only left Chandra. She was sitting there staring at everyone in turn, trying to get someone to look at her. Her head was shaking and her eyes were wide.

"Someone want to fill me in? What fucking freezer?"

"I guess you don't know about his daughter?" Shawn asked.

Chandra glanced at her, but her eyes went back to Sameer almost instantly. "What? What about his daughter? What freezer, guys?"

"They go hand in hand," Shawn said, and Chandra's eyes finally came to rest on Shawn's. Her head was still making the minute motions of disbelief, shaking subtly back and forth.

"I'm sorry, what? Shawn, are you okay?"

Shawn smiled at her. A serene little number that told her she was more than okay. She was fine, in fact. Just fucking dandy. She nodded. Then she breathed deeply and spoke, actually surprised that one of the two men hadn't taken the reigns from her by now. Maybe that just lent even more authority to her theory. "Chandra," she said, "his little girl is in that freezer in there."

# Eighteen

The sun was bright but not hot. It actually felt nice today. The snow was melting and the birds were chirping. Those birds that had not flown south for the winter. Shawn was watering the plants – those perennials she had somehow managed to keep alive for once. They hung from the balcony railing and brightened up the small space with their intoxicating colors and vibrant vitality. Shawn spent a lot more time out here than she had on her old balcony. That one had been much too small. But this one faced the west and had a nice view of Lake Arlington. Ever since she and Cory had moved in almost three months ago, she had taken in more sunsets across the lake than one woman deserved in a lifetime.

Her life had been a little emptier of the stresses as well. She was back to doing code full-time and loving it more than ever. There were more responsibilities in running the department, of course, but at least she still got to pour through code, acting as tier-two support when her two subordinates just couldn't figure something out. Sameer had promised her that in return for her loyalty and good faith, and of course keeping hidden that dirty little secret they all shared now, that a new project would soon be on the horizon. For now, it was all code, all the time. She did look forward to the next big thing, something he had not yet even hinted around about as far as what it involved, but his promise had been that it did not involve the dead, death or dying. Or the D Room. She had grown pretty tired of all the D words and was happy to be divorced of them. Another D word.

And it had not been that hard, in retrospect, for Shawn to accept his terms. There was, of course, a whole new can of worms being poured onto the floor when one talked about keeping a dead loved one in a freezer. But he had already served his time for her death. His hope, as he had shared that evening with Shawn, but in front of the entire group, was to perfect the science with which they had been experimenting. If he could get a string of successful resurrections, he would feel confident that he wouldn't do any further damage, and would also not ruin the one and final chance he might have to speak to his daughter. Crawling past the creep factor, Shawn could definitely see his reasoning and logic in it. He certainly wasn't keeping her body because he couldn't let go of her. In fact, with both Chandra and Shawn talking to him at the same time, they had forced his promise that as soon as he had gotten his time with her, he would give that girl her final rest. A proper burial or cremation. He had sworn it with his hand over his heart, that had been the intention the entire time. It had not taken much to convince Shawn and Chandra of this, even though Shawn felt like she was playing a role in abetting his further crime in maintaining possession of a cadaver. But in all truth, she had never seen the body, and neither had Chandra. They agreed there was enough plausible deniability there to overcome their concerns about letting him go on, and since his heart was in the right place, they let it go.

Jeremy had stepped forward that night as well, assuring he would be overseeing the final interview and that she would be treated with the utmost respect at its conclusion.

As she emptied the watering pot, she turned and set it on the shelf in the closet, then closed the door. Yes, this balcony even had its own closet! Imagine that! The entire place was a major upgrade. She and Cory had found the perfect place right on the edge of Dalworthington Gardens. It had two bedrooms, and they rented a garage beneath the apartment so they could keep their bikes out of the weather. The second bedroom served primarily as their shared office, which Shawn occupied for most of the week. Sameer no longer required her to come to work to do her job every day. One day a week he liked her to be there just to keep abreast of things. Not an unreasonable request from a manager. And she was happy to do so.

Jeremy had told her during her last office day, in fact, that the grand finale of Sameer's project had taken place. Monday, that had been. He said that over the weekend they had 'wrapped things up back there', pointing over his shoulder to the hidden complex of glass walls on the other side of the elevators. Shawn had not been back there since that night back in September when she had finally solved the puzzle. Jeremy's coded language was easy for her to decipher, but impossible to crack for the other woman who sat in the break room at the time.

Shawn had raised her eyebrows, trying to think of a coded way to ask if the other thing had been taken care of, reminding her of some mobster movie. '*So, did you take care a dat other ting?*' But the best she could come up with was, "And, uh, the cleanup?"

Jeremy had closed his eyes and nodded, shaking his head at the same time. That look said, '*Good lord, woman, you're bad at this. But yes.*' They both had a good grin at that.

Meanwhile, the third person in the break room went on flipping through her magazine, blissfully unaware they had just discussed the resurrection and reinterment of a little girl, all in just a few words. That third person was Shawn's newest support agent. And she was amazing.

Her name was Constance and she reminded Shawn so much of Lo it was not even funny. During the interview, Shawn had asked her some question or other – maybe something about punctuality – and the way Constance answered had sounded like a young Laura Carter was sitting in her office.

'I'm always on time. Five minutes early is almost late,' she had said. 'My daddy taught me right!'

Shawn's heart had skipped a beat. But she had lowered her gaze at the girl, taking in a deep breath, and stared at her for a moment before finally breaking into a smile. That was the moment Shawn had fallen in love with her. And had then taken her under her wing.

The secondary, and to Shawn, more important function of their second bedroom – the function *not* related to working from home – was that it now doubled as their music listening space. Lo's father had called Shawn out of the blue one day just a week or two after they had moved, and said he felt a strong calling to give Shawn her music collection. Shawn had frowned and smiled at the same time, going quiet on the phone, speechless.

"You there?" he had said.

"Oh yes, I'm here. Sorry. That just took me by surprise. Why would you want to do that? Those records are probably pretty valuable."

"I'm not concerned with their value, hon. I just know it's what she wanted," Lo's father said.

Shawn remembered having to stop and think about that sentence for a moment. He had not said the typical, *'what she* would have wanted' but rather *'what she wanted'*. This gave Shawn reason to believe he had some inside knowledge about his daughter's wishes. After mulling it over in her head, and his asking her again if she was there, she said, "I'm sorry. Yeah, I'm kinda speechless. How do you know what she wanted?"

"Well, much as it's not something anyone wants to admit, I did read her diary. And it's spelled out pretty explicitly in there."

"She kept a diary?" Shawn had asked, putting her hand over her heart, which had suddenly beat a little harder.

"Oh, yeah. You didn't know that?" Lo's father asked.

"Uh, no. I remember wishing she had so I could hold onto her a little longer. But no, I didn't know."

"Well, then you need to have that, too."

"Oh my God," Shawn had said, covering her mouth while the tears began their formation in her eyes. "Are you sure?"

"Yes, of course! We've already read it. If it seems special to you, then you're welcome to it," he had said. "I gotta tell you though, be prepared. There's a bunch of stuff in there about you, Shawn. That girl loved you like there was no tomorrow."

Shawn gasped – a combination of laughter and crying expelled all at once. And the tears were flowing. They were happy ones this time though. There were a lot more happy tears in her life these days. And many of them had come over the following few days after she had collected the records and stereo and turntable, and the diary. She had spent many hours just sitting on the floor after Cory hooked up the system for her, spinning the records she had bought at the flea market that day while she read through the pages of her best friend's most personal belonging ever.

She now kept it standing on her bookshelf right next to Miranda's. It was funny how life always seemed to come full circle.

Shawn leaned over the railing, letting the cool air nip at her cheeks. It was trying to warm up, but February days just weren't going to compete with the August ones she had lived through what seemed like lifetimes ago. How many lifetimes had come and gone between now and then? She had brought some of them back to have another go. Did those count too? A neighbor walked by walking his dog and looked up as he got close. Shawn smiled and waved. The man smiled and waved back. The dog even looked up and wagged its tail. *See that, Lo? Dogs can look up!*

Maybe her life had come full circle as well. All her mysteries solved, all her ghosts laid to rest. She had made peace with Lo's death. It had taken a long time and it was very painful, she wouldn't lie about that. But it had been a cathartic reckoning. The journal had helped ever so much. That girl had been so fun and so full of life that the *only* sad part of her death was the death itself. She had lived and laughed and loved – like a Hobby Lobby cliché board – so much more than most people ever did, that it was hard to feel sorry for her. Only the people left behind were left to suffer. But Laura Carter had made the most of her time here. She certainly wouldn't be mourning. About that *'it's not heaven'* comment, Shawn was never able to be clear. So maybe there was one mystery left unsolved. Because if anyone deserved to go to heaven, it had to be Lo.

Her bare feet were beginning to get cold. She took in another deep breath and looked out toward the lake. Some geese were coming in for a landing. She guessed they didn't fly south either. "Did you guys not get the memo? Even the monarchs go to Mexico!" she said.

The hardest part of the mystery to crack had not been that hard at all. Shawn had finally decided to use the internet, and the library, instead of just her massively powerful detective brain. And within minutes she had found everything she had been wondering about, all on the internet. What wasn't available for knowing online she found in the library's microfiche. And it was a heart-breaking story when she finally got to the bottom of it. There was still a lot of guesswork involved, but most of it had been confirmed.

Harrison Struck had been Miranda's biological brother. There had been three children. The third was Barogan. They had all been adopted out after a tragic accident where they lost both parents. And through some ridiculous oversight in the adoption process – or perhaps it was pretty standard and Shawn just wasn't familiar with the ins and outs – they had all three gone to separate families. The children were all very young at the time, all within a few years of each other. Miranda had been the oldest. And she had finally managed to find her brothers. She had gotten in touch with Harrison and actually reunited before his untimely death, shortly after that picture had been taken. This poor young woman had gone most of her life without her brother, and had finally found him. And then after they had gotten together he had died. Killed by some accident in the workplace.

Miranda had then gone to work trying to get Barogan, whom she – and apparently everyone – had called Linus, back to the States. She had taken care of all the legal fees and the visas and everything, apparently not entirely in accordance with his wishes. Reticent to return to the states, but at least interested enough to be back with his sister, he had gone through the process and made it back. Then Miranda had died, never to pick him up from the airport. And now he was stuck in the states. To go back to Scotland would have meant reversing and undoing the entire process, which was costly and time-consuming. The rest was history. Randi's assessment of her brother – according to one of her earlier diary entries – was that he was a speed demon. He proved that out on the motorcycle that night, taking the life of her friend, Heath and Linus all at once. *Full circle.*

The most comforting part of the tragic play that had become the poor girl's life, at least to Shawn, was that calling out Harrison's name during the interview. Shawn had realized in a flash of inspiration that Miranda wasn't looking for Harrison when she called his name. She had found him! At least one reunion had happened across the great chasm. And that brought her a little peace, when she took time to think about these things. Which was less and less frequent these days. Thank God for that. She was still getting over things, but those things only resurfaced every great once in a while. Shawn appreciated that slow pace rather than being bombarded with it all at once. She would make it out nice and easy, slowly healing from the inside. *Baby steps.*

As she turned to go back inside, pulling up on her pajama pants and arching her back, she looked toward the west again. The lake. That cold body of water also gave her peace. During the evenings when she would come out to have a drink, maybe do a little reading, she could always look through the bars and catch a glimpse of it. So calm. So serene. So beautiful. Her life was all of those three things now. At least to her. And perception was everything, wasn't it? She thought maybe her daddy had taught her that. *If you say you're happy, you're going to be happy.* Valuable advice from a man who had done it all.

She smiled at the thought as she stepped through the door onto the carpet, then turned to slide the door closed behind her. She never worried about locking this one. She was on the third floor here, and there was no way someone was coming up the side of that wall. Better neighborhood too. Safer. Just like her mom had always preached. Before she pulled her hand away from the vertical blinds to allow them to back-fill the space she had made to walk between them, she caught a glimpse of a monarch fluttering onto the balcony. Only here, there was no spiderweb to ensnare the butterfly. Here, there were flowers.

# Afterword

My friend Jessica and I were talking about *Midnight's Park* in the final days of May 2022. She was telling me what she thought had happened to Daniel Brandt, the lead character in the book, who just wanders off at the end. People ask me sometimes if I will ever bring him back in a later book. I always say no. I'm over him. Glad to be done writing him.

Well, Jessica wasn't having it. She said she thought Daniel had gone into the woods and hanged himself. I said, "Well, then that's probably what happened. You know him better than I do at this point." So that was settled. And then she said I needed to get Callie involved, have her grab the time machine and bring Daniel back to life.

Zing.

That was it. The idea of bringing someone back to life entered my mind, and it grabbed me hard. My characters have gone back in time. They've gone into space, aiming for Mars. They've gone to the deepest parts of the ocean. Down in missile silos, up on stages and about everywhere else I could think of. So this sounded new and fresh and exciting.

I started writing this book on May 31$^{st}$, and wrote every day, finishing on June 11$^{th}$. Forty-two straight days of writing and it was done. This was a personal achievement for me, since all of my other books were started and finished with years in between.

I always, always, always listen to music when I write. Usually it's rock songs. I wrote just about my entire second novel while listening to *Euphoria Mourning.* I discovered Kings of Leon while writing *Into the Darkness*. I'm usually blasting it and drumming on my keyboard during the moments I spend rereading a line I just wrote, or trying to come up with a word. I won't go through every piece of music I listened to while writing this book, but I will share two of them. The two that moved me perhaps the most.

I love the eerie place this plot took me. I never had trouble getting into character and writing about Shawn and her adventures. But when I knew she would be back in the lab, I was filled with a different kind of excitement. I listened to a lot of classical pieces and eerie movie scores while I wrote some of these parts. The movie *Arrival* is full of great stuff. *First Encounter* is one from that soundtrack that I heard frequently on this playlist. When you're dealing with something otherworldly – and I absolutely think of resurrection as that – this is an apt piece of music.

The other I repeated a lot, especially during the sad parts, was *Mercy* by Max Richter. Mari Samuelson accompanies his piano with the violin on that song. If it doesn't bring you to tears, I would submit that you're not paying attention.

It has always fascinated me how deeply music can draw on your emotions. It's a universal language. I don't have to tell you that *Mercy* is sad. If you listen to it, you will know. I don't have to tell you which songs to tap your foot to or which ones should make you want to dance. You know when you hear them. We all do. It's as understandable as a smile or a dog's tail wagging. It should therefore not surprise you that I use music to get the best of my emotions flowing while I'm writing.

I look forward to writing Shawn now, maybe even more than I did with Callie when I was still writing her. I have already begun my next adventure with her. And while it is a big one, I am excited to see if I can conquer it. She is a joy to write. I love her charming personality. Her always-happy demeanor and her ability to snap out of fear and depression and get her feet moving again. I envy that. I wish I could be more like her sometimes.

I hope you enjoyed this story. Feel free to drop me a line on my website. I would love to hear what you thought.

- brandon spacey
brandonspacey.com

Made in the USA
Middletown, DE
28 March 2023

27871454R00314